"THE BAJORANS ARE FURIOUS."

"But they can't think that the Cardassian government is behind this, can they?" Raffi said. "The Cardassians wouldn't risk a diplomatic incident over this guy, would they? He's yesterday's news. They can't think the Cardassians would *hide* him—"

"The Bajorans are increasingly indicating that they might come to this conclusion."

Raffi frowned down at the padd. Diplomacy. Always overcomplicated. But then, that was history all over. Complication upon complication, and the place where the Bajoran and Cardassian peoples intersected was surely one of the most tangled histories of them all. Raffi's single experience of the fallout from that long and tragic past had been enough to last her a lifetime; she was not keen to revisit it.

"I'm guessing Bajoran Intelligence is all over this?" she said.

Jean-Luc leaned over to open another file on the padd. "You're guessing right. Here's the latest from them. They think they've tracked some of his movements since he left Cardassia Prime."

Raffi read through the file. Near the end, she read that Bajoran Intelligence was certain that their target had boarded a transport en route to a Cardassian colony world. The name was one familiar to Raffi; one she had not thought of for many years. One she had gone to some trouble to forget. . . .

STAR TREK™
PICARD

SECOND SELF

Una McCormack

Based on *Star Trek: The Next Generation*
created by Gene Roddenberry
and
Star Trek: Picard
created by
Akiva Goldsman & Michael Chabon
&
Kirsten Beyer & Alex Kurtzman

GALLERY BOOKS
New York   London   Toronto   Sydney   New Delhi

G

Gallery Books
An Imprint of Simon & Schuster, Inc.
1230 Avenue of the Americas
New York, NY 10020

This book is a work of fiction. Any references to historical events, real people, or real places are used fictitiously. Other names, characters, places, and events are products of the author's imagination, and any resemblance to actual events or places or persons, living or dead, is entirely coincidental.

™ and © 2022 by CBS Studios Inc. All Rights Reserved.
STAR TREK and related marks and logos are trademarks of CBS Studios Inc.

This book is published by Gallery Books, a division of Simon & Schuster, Inc., under exclusive license from CBS Studios Inc.

All rights reserved, including the right to reproduce this book or portions thereof in any form whatsoever. For information, address Gallery Books Subsidiary Rights Department, 1230 Avenue of the Americas, New York, NY 10020.

First Gallery Books trade paperback edition September 2023

GALLERY BOOKS and colophon are registered trademarks of Simon & Schuster, Inc.

For information about special discounts for bulk purchases, please contact Simon & Schuster Special Sales at 1-866-506-1949 or business@simonandschuster.com.

The Simon & Schuster Speakers Bureau can bring authors to your live event. For more information or to book an event, contact the Simon & Schuster Speakers Bureau at 1-866-248-3049 or visit our website at www.simonspeakers.com.

Interior design by Kathryn A. Kenney-Peterson

Manufactured in the United States of America

10 9 8 7 6 5 4 3 2 1

Library of Congress Cataloging-in-Publication Data is available.

ISBN 978-1-9821-9482-6
ISBN 978-1-9821-9483-3 (pbk)
ISBN 978-1-9821-9484-0 (ebook)

For Matthew

"Be not afeard; the isle is full of noises,
Sounds and sweet airs, that give delight, and hurt not."

—William Shakespeare, *The Tempest*

HISTORIAN'S NOTE

This story takes place in 2399, after Jean-Luc Picard returns from the events on Coppelius (*Star Trek: Picard*—"Et in Arcadia Ego"), and just prior to his acceptance of the role of vice-chancellor at Starfleet Academy (*Star Trek: Picard*—"The Star Gazer").

PART 1

2399

AFTER COPPELIUS

1

Lieutenant Commander Raffaela Musiker was a whole new woman. Clean, poised, ready for action. Ready for something new—although the jury was out on what that something new might be. But history—whether public or private—sometimes has its own designs. Lays traps for the unwary. Guides you back to places you thought you'd long since left behind. Raffi Musiker didn't believe in fate, or destiny, but the upshot of this story is that they might well believe in you.

Raffi was in France. In Paris. She'd been here once before, a lifetime ago, when she had been a completely different woman. Young, and in love, and not yet a wife or a mother. She wasn't young now, nor was she a wife any longer, and she doubted the extent to which she had ever been a mother. But she was, at least, in love, and perhaps this was what allowed Paris to work its charms on her. Stepping out of the public transporter near the Gare du Nord, she clamped down her first impressions—of the pressing crowds, the noise, the crush—and allowed the city to spend the next couple of days ravishing her. Marveled at the light and the gardens. Felt the weight of history. Saw small trinkets she might get for a grandkid—if such a thing were ever to be allowed to enter this new life of hers—and instead picked up kitsch for Seven. A tiny Eiffel Tower. An "I ♥ Paris" T-shirt. Boxes of chocolate. She missed Seven, and wished she was here. At the Arc de Triomphe, she walked slowly around, counting off the twelve avenues that radiated outward, almost overcome by the choices that lay ahead. A whole new lease on life.

What do I do now? What do I do next? Where the hell do I go . . . ?

She chose coffee and patisserie, and, for the moment at least, less drama. The whole point of coming on this trip was to make a decision, wasn't it? About what to do next. About the person she was going to be, now that the old one didn't exist any longer.

On the morning of her third day in the city of light, Raffi picked up the flyer she was using for the rest of the trip and began her journey south and east toward La Barre. The summer had been hot and now, in September, the fields were looking yellow and tired. The harvest would soon begin. She arrived at the house midafternoon, stepping out of the cool scrubbed air of her all-new flyer to hit a wall of heat, the kind so heavy you might have thought someone was messing with the gravity. A woman was walking toward her: dark-haired and perhaps a little older than Raffi. Hard to guess, sometimes, with Romulans.

"Hey," said Raffi, uncertainly. They didn't know each other well—although they knew a great deal about each other. Raffi knew that Laris had once been Tal Shiar. With JL, she had helped Laris escape them and get to Earth. Raffi knew, too (and perhaps this could be seen in the lines and shadows that were settling on the other woman's face), that Laris was recently widowed.

"Hello," said Laris, folding her arms in front of her. "How was the trip?"

"Fine," said Raffi. "It's hotter than I expected. I thought Europe was meant to be *temperate*. Know what I mean?"

A small smile flickered over the other woman's face. "It'll rain tonight."

"You sure about that?"

"I'm sure. Let me take your bag."

Laris hoisted up the bag and led her inside.

"Where's JL?" said Raffi.

"The lord of the manor," said Laris, "is out with his dog. His—"

SECOND SELF 5

"—damn dog," said Raffi, with her.

"Don't get me wrong," said Laris. "I love the beast. But I might wish he was self-cleaning."

"Robotics," agreed Raffi. "Daystrom's missing a trick there."

Laris's smile almost became a laugh. Almost. A start. Something to build on.

They went into the kitchen—a cool stone room that managed to combine rustic simplicity with an air of quiet and sustained age—and Raffi took a seat, as directed, at the table. She watched Laris move around. There was a slight hesitation to everything she did, an air of distraction, perhaps, or the habits arising from the presence of another.

"Now where'd you put the damn tea strainer . . ." she muttered to herself. "Huh. I'd never have guessed."

Mint tea; refreshing in the heat. They sat at the kitchen table, trying to jump-start a conversation, until Raffi heard a clatter of claws on the flagstones outside the open door. The dog (Number One, if Raffi remembered correctly; oh, but how *droll* of you, JL) launched into the kitchen like a low-slung, short-haired, snub-nosed missile. Found his target, unerringly, and scrambled into Laris's lap.

"Great soft lump," she said lovingly, scratching between his ears. "Daft old thing." The creature's tongue lolled out and he looked up at her in adoration.

Footsteps on the path; a shadow in the doorway—and there was JL, stepping inside his family home, a whole new man these days. Raffi rose from her chair, and his face crinkled into a smile at the sight of her. *Great soft lump,* thought Raffi, moving over to greet him. *Daft old thing.*

"Raffi," he said warmly, drawing her into an embrace, which she clumsily returned. "It is so very good to have you here at last."

"Nice to get here at last."

"Laris," he said, eyeing the other woman anxiously. "All well?"

"All's well," she said, almost impatiently. "Don't *fuss.*"

6   UNA McCORMACK

There was a moment's awkward silence. Raffi put down her cup. "You know, JL," she said, "I've been here almost an hour and I haven't had a glass of wine."

Wine was brought, along with cheese and bread. By some steady and well-established process, this refreshment turned into a bigger but unfussy evening meal, and Raffi had the quiet but undeniable pleasure of watching JL sharply instructed on the correct assembly of a green salad. They moved from the kitchen to an outside terrace that gave a view out across JL's vineyards. His ancestral lands. Imagine living in a place with so much history, Raffi thought. History to which your own family was so deeply connected. There was plenty of wine now, although Raffi was careful to temper her intake. A new woman, remember. Clean, and dry enough. At the end of the meal came a crème brûlée that Raffi knew would live long in her memory. After this was finished, and contemplated, Laris stood up.

"Oh well," she said with a sigh. "Table won't clear itself."

"Need some help?" said Raffi, making to rise from her chair.

Laris, piling up plates, shook her head. "Number One'll keep me company. You stay and catch up with his lordship." And, with the dog trotting behind her, she went back into the kitchen. Raffi waited until she was out of earshot.

"How is she doing?" she said.

"Not well," admitted JL. "She and Zhaban were together a long time. Sacrificed their lives in order to be together."

Raffi, whose own losses had—to a great extent—been self-inflicted, pondered what this might be like, to have lived so closely to someone, for almost the whole of one's life, only to have that partnership suddenly and cruelly ended. "Jeez. There's no justice, sometimes, is there?"

"Not often," said JL. "But we try." He stretched in his seat. "I'm glad you found the time to come here, Raffi," he said. "But am I right in saying that something is preying on your mind?"

"I'm that easy to read?"

"Only to me."

"Huh. Well, you're kinda right. I'm trying to decide what to do next."

JL was picking at the bread. "I thought you were returning to Starfleet."

"Yes, that, but—it's a big outfit."

"It is."

"And, to my astonishment, the offers have been . . . Well, not rolling in, not that, exactly, but there've been more of them than I expected." Raffi held out her hands, as if weighing her options. "Daystrom asked me to consider a temporary transfer there. Join the Grand Tour, bringing the Good News about synthetics to all and sundry . . ." She trailed off. "I'm not sure."

"With the best will in the world, Raffi," said JL, "I'm not entirely sure that public relations could be considered your forte."

"You and me both," said Raffi. "Might be fun working with Agnes, though . . . Hey, don't give me that look! I *like* Agnes, god help me. But— no. Not me."

"You said 'offers,'" he prompted.

"Yeah."

"One of them is causing you . . . What is it? Concern? Hesitation?"

Raffi stared out. The fields were dark now, although she could see the lights in the houses of the nearby village. The heat was heavy. Weight of history. "Starfleet Intelligence has asked me to go back to my old job."

His eyebrows shot up. "Romulan Affairs?"

"Yep."

"You're considering it?"

"I don't know. That's the problem—I just don't know! You say I'm not cut out for public relations, and—yes, you're right. I know my strengths— and my weaknesses. I'm a *great* analyst. I size things up quickly, I make connections, I see what needs to be done, and I get it *done*. But . . ."

8　UNA McCORMACK

"But you're worried that going back into intelligence work will press the wrong buttons," said JL. "You're worried it makes you see things that might not be there. Makes you paranoid."

She leaned forward in her chair. These fears—these *truths*—were not easy to speak out loud, but how else would she be free of them? "Yes," she said quietly. "You know, what's unfair is that it didn't matter, in so many ways, that I was *right*. There *was* this big conspiracy. It still cost me my health. It cost me . . ." *Gabe. Jae. My little boy. My marriage. My old life.* "Well, it cost me."

"And you're worried what might happen if you drink from that well once again."

"You always put these things so prettily," she said.

"You know, Raffi, I spent a long time here—"

"Sulking," she said.

"Sulking, yes; but also writing. I learned how to turn a pretty phrase. All alone in the hills, with only my thoughts and my books for company. Prospero, on his island." JL smiled. "There are worse ways, I suppose, to spend one's later life than sitting in peace, reflecting upon one's past."

"What are you saying, JL? That I should go and write my *memoirs*? The world doesn't want to know the lousy details of *my* lousy past—"

"You know full well that I am saying nothing of the sort! But I agree that you are right to reflect on whether Starfleet Intelligence would be the best move for you." He cleared his throat. "I *had*, in fact, heard that the offer was out there . . ."

"Huh." She narrowed her eyes. "Not much gets past you, does it?"

"Not much. More positively, this means that I've also been thinking about what might suit you now."

"Thinking of little old me?" Raffi put her hand to her chest. "JL! I'm touched! No, truly!"

"Hmm. You know that I'm heading to the Academy."

"I heard," she said. "Vice-chancellor. I guess that the titles you've not held are few and far between. Might as well collect them all." Mischief bubbled up inside her. "Hey, is there a special hat? A really *good* hat?"

"It's a magnificent hat," he said, with measured dignity, "which—if I have been correctly informed—I shall be required to both don and doff periodically, and with great ceremony."

"There'll be some pretty decent dinners too."

"Banquets, I dare say," he agreed.

"Lots of people looking up at you in awe and admiration—"

"Sounds ideal for me, doesn't it?"

"Sounds *made* for you," said Raffi. "But enough about you. You said you'd been thinking about *me*."

"I have. I do. Why not come with me?"

"Excuse me?"

"Come with me," he said, again, and yet not, to her, more intelligibly.

"What?" she said. "To the *Academy*?"

"To the Academy."

"To . . . JL, that's a really *terrible* idea. I mean, *beyond* bad, even for you."

"Why, Raffi?" He seemed genuinely curious. "Why does it seem so?"

Raffi thought back to her own time at the Academy. She'd enjoyed it, she guessed, although the rules and regulations had been tiresome, and often circumvented. Story of her life. "Well, for one thing—what would I do at the Academy?"

"Teach, I should imagine," he said. "That being the purpose of the place."

"JL, *seriously*? Me? Shaping young minds? With my track record? The mother of the century?"

"Raffi, you were a good mother—"

"Oh no. No. Let's not rewrite history. I was a *terrible* mother. I was a *disastrous* mother."

"You were a good mother when you were there. You loved him. *Love* him—"

10   UNA McCORMACK

"Yeah, the problem was that I *wasn't* there. And even when I was there, my mind was elsewhere. I was too busy chasing conspiracy theories—"

"Theories which turned out to be true."

"And doing nothing approximating mothering, which begs the question why you think I would be any use as a *teacher* of young kids."

"Being a teacher is not the same as being a mother—"

"I mean, what exactly would I teach them? How to rub superior officers the wrong way? How to mouth off at exactly the wrong moment?"

"You could teach them endurance," he said quietly. "Honesty. Integrity—"

"You're drunk, JL. Get real."

"I'm serious," he said, and she was starting to think that he was. Misguided, perhaps, but serious. "Raffi, I believe you would find teaching at the Academy a truly satisfying and revelatory experience."

"Oh, I see what's happening here," she said. "You think this would put some demons to rest, huh? Am I right?"

"It might do that, but that's not the reason I'm making the suggestion. Quite the contrary. Raffi, have you considered that as you make your decision about what to do next, you would do better thinking less about setting your past straight, and more about the shape you would like your future to take?"

This, Raffi had to concede, was pretty good advice. But—the *Academy*? She shook her head. "I suppose there are worse ideas. Jaunting around with Jurati, for one . . ." She frowned. "Hey, isn't Elnor enrolling?"

"Elnor?" JL reached for his glass of wine.

No eye contact? A yellow alert sounded in Raffi's head. "Yeah, Elnor," she said. "Isn't he heading to the Academy next semester?"

"He's considering that option, yes."

That yellow alert rang more loudly. "JL, is *that* why you want me there?"

"What?" He looked up from his glass at her.

"Because you want someone to babysit Elnor?"

He shifted uncomfortably in his seat. "No," he said. "Anyway, he's not made a decision yet as to whether or not he's going—"

"But if he does, it would be helpful if I was there." Raffi shook her head. "While you're busy doffing your hat and eating your fancy dinners—"

"Raffi! It's not like that!"

"You know, I think the Academy could be a great move," she said. "For Elnor."

"I'm not so sure," said JL with a sigh. "Absolute candor does not win many friends."

"No, but he needs to find them."

"Friends?"

"Friends. People. Anyone he can call his own."

"You mean a crew?" said JL.

"That's a revealing insight into how your mind works, Admiral Picard. But I guess what I meant was—a family."

"Like a mother," said JL, his eyes twinkling at her over his glass.

"That boy," said Raffi firmly, "has surely had enough of older women ordering him around."

Laris came out, bringing coffee, and sat back down in her chair. As JL poured, she looked at Raffi. "Long face," said Laris. "I'm guessing he's asked you about the Academy."

"Yeah," said Raffi. "And I told him why it's a bad idea."

"Huh," said Laris. "You think it *is* a bad idea?"

"Yep," said Raffi. "Why—don't you?"

Laris shrugged. "If I've learned anything over the past year, it's that life can throw some unexpected curveballs. You never know where you're heading next. What you're about to become."

The word *widow* hung unhappily in the air. Raffi took the coffee cup and sipped the hot, bitter drink. Fortified, she said, "I'll think about it."

"Good," said JL. "Thank you."

"I'm not making any promises," she added. But if there was one thing Raffi knew from her long history with Jean-Luc Picard, it was that he had an annoying habit of getting his own way.

She was still irritated with him by the time she went to bed. Sometimes, in his desire to fix matters, JL forgot that people had desires of their own. He saw that Elnor was lonely, that Raffi was uncertain of her future, and in his mind bringing them together at the Academy (under his benevolent watch, of course) elegantly solved both problems. Whether either of them had any desire to be at the Academy (or, indeed, under his eye) was immaterial. Raffi sighed and turned over in her bed. She was hot, and restless. It was several hours before sleep came.

In the middle of the night, Raffi was woken by thunder. She got up and went over to the window. Lightning crackled on the hills ahead, great blue-white flashing lines, which, in this strange hour, seemed unearthly, more like the inscrutable signal of some mighty alien power than an entirely natural phenomenon. She watched the show, listening to the thunder draw nearer and nearer. It culminated in a great crash directly overhead, and then began its steady move away. Already the air felt fresher. She returned to her bed and let the steady fall of rain lull her back to sleep.

In the morning, the sun had returned but was much softer. The world outside was washed clean. The house was very quiet; her hosts, presumably, were still in bed, or maybe even out already. Raffi went down into the kitchen. Number One, head on paws, perked up at her approach, jumping up and trotting out after her into the cool morning. They walked companionably together for an hour or so, the dog wandering on ahead every so often to sniff out areas of interest, then returning to lead her down some favored path. Raffi thought about the conversation of the previous night. This clear new day, the Academy didn't seem such a ridiculous idea. This morning, everything felt possible. Maybe she did have something to teach. Maybe there was something—some expertise, some insight—that would benefit others at the start of their career. Right now, it was good simply to feel that there were options.

SECOND SELF   13

Back at the house, Laris was up. There was coffee ready, and the welcome smell of bacon cooking. Soon enough they were feasting, and talking about the storm, and how much better the heat was today, and Raffi thought that it was good to be alive—but didn't say so. After helping Laris to clear away, Raffi wandered through the house until she found the library. JL's whole oeuvre was on a shelf. "This should be good," Raffi muttered, choosing a history of the French Resistance during World War II. And it did turn out to be good: meticulously researched by JL and lucidly written. But of course JL would be an excellent historian. *Of course.*

Midmorning, the man himself appeared at last, a padd tucked under his arm. He took the seat next to her, throwing the padd, with some exasperation, onto the table, and picking up the book that she had been reading. He flicked through this, before putting it back down again next to his padd.

"It's good," she said. "You should think about taking up writing as a hobby."

"Thank you," he said absently.

So the smiles weren't going to be easily won today. She wondered why she continued to try to earn them, but tried nonetheless. "Hey," she said. "I remember that face. That face meant that people were making things difficult for you, and *that* meant that things were going to be made difficult for me."

"Well, I sincerely hope that I am *not* about to make my problems your problems . . ." He eyed her. "But perhaps you can help . . ."

Oh hell, thought Raffi. *I'm about to get suckered into something, aren't I?* She was right, although she didn't know at that moment the extent to which she was right. "What's going on?" she said, resigning herself to the immediate fate of providing a sounding board.

"Would you run away," he said, "if I said *diplomacy*?"

"No. I've walked far enough today. But diplomacy is definitely not my thing," she said. "Problem with the Romulans?"

"Not the Romulans this time. Something worse."

"Worse than Romulans?"

"Cardassians. Also—Bajorans."

14   UNA McCORMACK

"Ah," said Raffi. "I guess, in combination, that could be worse than Romulans." She clapped her hands together. "So. What's going on?"

"More fallout from the Occupation."

"Before my time," said Raffi. She had graduated from the Academy after the Cardassian Occupation of Bajor had ended, going straight to a desk job at Romulan Affairs. This had kept her away from the front during the Dominion War. Her experience of Cardassians was mostly limited to one admittedly intense encounter after that war had ended. Her experience with Bajorans was slim to none. But she knew that Bajor had been a special interest of JL's at some point or another. So many things had been a special interest of JL's, at some point or another.

"The Occupation of Bajor is increasingly before many people's time," said JL, his voice shifting into what Raffi thought of as lecture mode. Yeah, he was going to *love* the Academy. "But not quite consigned to history. Not yet. Not while some who were involved in those dreadful events are still alive. But this makes the situation complicated in other ways . . ."

"Come on," she said. "Let's hear all about it."

"Very well," he said with a smile. "How cognizant are you of current Bajoran-Cardassian relations?"

"I'm guessing they're somewhere between . . ." She waggled her hand. "Frosty and hostile?"

JL gave a low laugh. "Concise and precise. Yes."

"And I'm guessing it's something to do with the extraditions?"

"Ah," he said. "You *are* up to speed. I'm impressed."

"You don't get offers to rejoin Starfleet Intelligence if you're not up to speed. And you know what I learned over the years? Just because something wasn't in a box labeled 'Romulans' didn't mean that it couldn't blow up in Starfleet's face."

"No." He studied her thoughtfully. "People shouldn't underestimate you, Raffi."

"I've been saying that for years. So. Extraditions for crimes committed during the Occupation. I thought they'd been happening—or is the problem that they're stalled? Are the Cardassians refusing to hand someone over?"

"It's hard to tell." He sighed. "On the whole, you're right—the extraditions have been going slowly but smoothly. Considerably better than we might ever have expected. The new castellan is part Bajoran, you know. One of her grandmothers, it seems, had a liaison with a Cardassian officer. Consensual, I hasten to add."

"That will have helped smooth proceedings, I imagine."

"It has. And, to be fair to previous Cardassian leaders, the will to hand over the surviving perpetrators of the more egregious actions taken under the Occupation has been, on the whole, fairly consistent since the end of the Dominion War. I suppose making that a condition of continuing aid during the reconstruction didn't do any harm."

"That would focus the mind," Raffi agreed. The Cardassian Union had been all but annihilated by the end of the Dominion War, with over eight hundred million dead by the time the Dominion surrendered, and many more dying in the privation that followed. The numbers would have been vastly worse without Federation assistance during the aftermath. "What's the sticking point?"

"The Bajorans have requested the extradition of a specific individual."

"And the Cardassians are refusing?"

"Not quite. The Cardassian government claims that the individual concerned is no longer within their space. Indeed, he seems to have disappeared entirely."

"Huh," said Raffi.

Picard pushed his padd over to her, and Raffi read the file with interest—and increasing alarm. The individual concerned was high profile; had served in many roles for various Cardassian administrations both before and after the Dominion War; had even been ambassador to the Federation at one time. The details of his early years were very sketchy; so were the details of the last two or three years. For the previous nine months, there was nothing.

16   UNA McCORMACK

"I can see how this might cause difficulties," she said.

"The Bajorans are furious."

"But they can't think that the Cardassian government is behind this, can they?" she said. "The Cardassians wouldn't risk a diplomatic incident over this guy, would they? He's yesterday's news. They can't think the Cardassians would *hide* him—"

"The Bajorans are increasingly indicating that they might come to this conclusion."

Raffi frowned down at the padd. Diplomacy. Always overcomplicated. But then, that was history all over. Complication upon complication, and the place where the Bajoran and Cardassian peoples intersected was surely one of the most tangled histories of them all. Raffi's single experience of the fallout from that long and tragic past had been enough to last her a lifetime; she was not keen to revisit it.

"I'm guessing Bajoran Intelligence is all over this?" she said.

JL leaned over to open another file on the padd. "You're guessing right. Here's the latest from them. They think they've tracked some of his movements since he left Cardassia Prime."

Raffi read through the file. Near the end, she read that Bajoran Intelligence was certain that their target had boarded a transport en route to a Cardassian colony world. The name was one familiar to Raffi; one she had not thought of for many years. One she had gone to some trouble to forget. Ordeve. She felt suddenly sick, as if she had drawn unexpectedly close to a cliff edge, or a trap that was about to spring. JL was looking at her, very carefully.

You bastard.

Raffi cleared her throat. "I was stationed on Ordeve," she said. "At the end of the Dominion War."

"I know," said JL.

"You know," said Raffi. "Of course you damn well know. And you want me to go back there, don't you?"

SECOND SELF 17

"Raffi, I don't want you to do anything you don't want to."

"Oh, cut the crap, JL!" Raffi glared down at the file, made the text scroll until the information presented was nothing more than a blur. She tried to calm down. "I met him once, you know. Very briefly. When he was on Earth. But you know that too, don't you?"

"Yes, I did," he said. "You can assume that I've read your report from the time. Assume too that I've read the report from the inquiry afterward—"

"We were all exonerated," said Raffi.

"Quite right," he said. "But what those reports don't tell me is your impressions of the place, Raffi. I know—from what I've read—that Ordeve had some odd effects on people stationed there—"

"You know why?" said Raffi. "Because everyone there was doing a lot of drugs."

"Including you?"

"Less than you might imagine," she said.

"Was that all it was?"

"Yes," she said. "No . . . Look, the whole place was strange. There were dreams . . ."

"Dreams?"

"I said that people were doing a lot of drugs. Look, JL, I don't have happy memories of my time there." But who had happy memories of that time? What made her different from anyone else?

JL leaned back and folded his hands together. His professorial stance. "Tell me more about Ordeve."

"You said you've read the reports."

"Raffi."

She got up from her chair and walked across the room to the window. She stood, her back to him, hands folded behind her, staring at the garden beyond. Charming place. Did he water his own flowers?

"Ordeve was an extrasolar Bajoran colony," she said. "The Cardassians annexed it during the Occupation and settled there. The Romulans took the

18   UNA McCORMACK

place during the Dominion War, but it returned to Cardassian jurisdiction shortly afterward, and has remained in their hands ever since—"

"I know the history," he interrupted gently. "I was asking for your impressions. Why you think this particular man might be drawn to this particular place."

"I honestly have no idea why anyone would go there. It's the middle of nowhere. And you certainly wouldn't want to go *back* there."

"Because of the dreams?"

The dreams had certainly been one thing, but there was more to Ordeve than that. There were the deaths and the losses; the bloodshed and secrets . . .

"There was a reason that people were self-medicating," said Raffi. "It was like we all knew that we were in a place where bad things had happened, over and over. And there we were, sitting targets for the Romulans. All we wanted was to get out before the next round of killings began." She tried to collect herself. "The Romulans killed a lot of Cardassians after the ceasefire, you know. They were warming up to doing that on Ordeve."

"But they didn't," he said. "Those Cardassians must have been glad that Starfleet was there. That you were there."

"I guess."

"It must have been a terrifying experience, Raffi."

He wasn't wrong. But the events of that mission were not all that had frightened her during her time on Ordeve. Something about the place had been—there was no other word for it—uncanny. "JL," she said, "do you think that some places are cursed?"

"No," he said firmly. "No, I do not. I do not believe in the supernatural. I believe that the universe is ultimately explicable, but that we might not yet have found the language or the means by which it can be explained. But I am very interested that you describe the place in this way. What exactly do you mean?"

"I mean . . . that sometimes it seems there are places with a history of violence that runs so deep that it's like a wound that can never heal. That some trauma happened there, that keeps being repeated, over and over again. There are scars, that never go away . . ."

"Traumatic experiences are often relived. Flashbacks. The harm is kept in an eternal present, and never integrated—"

"Yes, that, but . . . I was fine before I went to Ordeve. It was the *place* that traumatized . . ." And had left her, wounded, in some way. Back near the start of her Starfleet career. Had anything gone right since?

"I see," said JL. He sat up straight, drawing a line beneath their conversation. "Thank you for telling me more, Raffi. I'm sorry to bring that time back."

She looked out over his land and wondered again what it would be like to be part of a history like this; to have a long connection to such a place. Raffi's own attempts to build foundations had come crashing down years ago, and it was only in the last few months that she had come to believe that she might, still, create something solid, something lasting, something that might become a home. But when you saw what JL had here, you wondered whether it was worth the effort.

"JL," she said, "is this why you invited me here?"

"What?" He sounded startled. "What do you mean?"

"Did you know about this, about Ordeve, before you invited me here?"

"Raffi, no, of course not—"

"Only sometimes I think that people"—*you*—"see me more as a resource than as . . ." As someone in her own right. As someone with hopes and fears, desires and dreams. Sometimes Raffi felt as if these things were not allowed for someone like her. "As me. As Raffi. As myself."

She still had her back to him. She heard the creak of the chair as he stood up, and soft footsteps on the carpet as he approached. He put his hand very gently on her shoulder.

"I swear to you," he said, "that I had no idea about this when I invited

20 UNA McCORMACK

you to visit. I wanted you to come—that's why I asked! This file arrived very early this morning. When I saw Ordeve mentioned, I remembered it from your file. I know you are pondering what you want to do next. That a return to Starfleet Intelligence was under consideration. I thought that perhaps a mission like this might provide, shall we say . . . a test-drive. A way for you to see if intelligence work is still to your taste—"

"To my *taste*?"

"Raffi," he said, "you must understand that *you* are in charge of your life now. Whatever happens next, the choices are for *you* to make. No—I did not invite you here to wine you and dine you and persuade you to take on a mission for me to Ordeve. But when I read the file, I thought it was something that you might like to consider—"

"You'd be glad if I took this mission, though?"

"I'd be glad that this mission was in the hands of someone like you."

"Nice save," she said. "The question is—do I really want to go back to that damn place?"

" 'The unexamined life,' " said JL portentously, " 'is not worth living.' "

"Where do you *get* this stuff? In a Christmas cracker?"

"I believe that's commonly attributed to Socrates."

"Yeah? And how did things turn out for him?"

He laughed and patted her arm. "You'll go, then?"

"You know I'll go. How do you turn down a request from Admiral Vice-Chancellor Whatever-You-Are-Now Jean-Luc fecking Picard?"

"You've been spending too much time with Laris."

"Laris has got the measure of you."

"She does indeed." JL gave a small, rather tight smile. "Thank you, Raffi, for agreeing even to consider this. Rest assured that you'll have everything you need at your disposal."

"Oh, I can't wait."

"And the offer to come to the Academy still stands."

"Oh *please*," she said, "hand me the cup of hemlock now."

Raffi took the dog for another walk. She was in the market for some unconditional love and Number One was happy to supply it. She stomped around the ancestral Picard lands, scowling at every damn ripening grape. She swore never to drink wine again, ever. She swore never to visit France again. As she trudged around, the dog running gamely alongside her, she realized that the most infuriating aspect of this whole damn thing was that JL was right. If she was going to return to Starfleet Intelligence, a mission like this would be a good way to find out whether she was still cut out for the work. Whether she wanted to drink from that well again.

"Damn you," she muttered. Number One gave her a quizzical look. Raffi crinkled her nose at him. "Not you," she said. "You're a sweetie. I'm talking about your damn master."

Was it her imagination, or did the dog nod back?

"I'm losing my fucking mind," said Raffi.

Later, at dinner, she was still angry, although JL tried to appear contrite. "Sensing a mood around the table tonight," said Laris as she poured the wine.

"JL has been JL," said Raffi, and offered nothing more.

"Ah," said Laris, with understanding. "That. Don't let him rope you into anything you don't want to do, Raffi. Though I'm one to talk."

Raffi snorted.

"Is this about that business with the Cardassian runaway?" Laris went on.

Raffi glanced at JL, who shrugged. "No secrets at this table," he said.

"Yes," said Raffi. "JL wants me to go and find him."

"And that's a problem how?" said Laris.

"Because the world where he's likely to be hiding, Ordeve, was the site of a deeply unpleasant experience I had during my early years in Starfleet."

"I didn't know that." Laris flicked a look at JL. "You didn't mention that."

"I understand," said JL humbly, "that I am asking a great deal."

Both women sighed and rolled their eyes.

"Read the damn room," said Raffi.

"Daft fecker," said Laris fondly. She pushed the cheese toward Raffi. "Try a bit of that camembert. And remember that you can always tell the admiral to get stuffed."

Raffi helped herself, and, as she did, she laughed—because she never could make JL understand her limits, and she suspected that she never would.

2

Returning home after La Barre took adjustment. Raffi had chosen her new apartment in Los Angeles because the area was vibrant, busy, bohemian. She was trying to reconnect to the human race and being around others was a start. There were cafés and galleries and theaters, and things to do and see whenever Seven consented to drop by, or when Raffi was needing company. But she hadn't yet got around to decorating, and the place seemed Spartan after the understated elegance of the Picard estate. Sure, it was better than the shack in the desert that had, until the previous year, been where she lived. (She didn't call that place home; home should not be associated with loneliness, pain, and regret.) There were some paintings that she hadn't yet put up on the walls, so she spent a morning hanging them, pondering the mission to Ordeve, and whether it was a good idea. Away from JL, it was easier to believe that you could indeed tell him to get stuffed. The trouble was that Raffi's curiosity had been piqued. She had unanswered questions about her time on that distant, troubled world. Perhaps this trip could bring some closure—some healing—to this particular wound.

When the paintings were up, Raffi stood and looked at them. They weren't portraits of illustrious ancestors, but they still looked pretty good. Her ex, Jae, had been a painter; still was, she imagined, though news was hard to come by and she resisted the urge to go looking. She had taken one or two of his pieces when they divorced, but got rid of them, a few years later, when she realized that contemplating them brought her nothing but heartache. These new paintings were nothing like Jae's work. Her ex took huge canvases and created vast explosions of sprawling color. These were small and intense. Three of them, in a line. Each depicted a circle—like a moon or planet—done in metallic gold or copper paint, and these had smaller, regular dots of paint enameled across them, like craters. Nothing like what Jae did or used to do. Had she unconsciously chosen ones unlike his work? That was an exhausting thought.

Raffi stopped and made a cup of tea and sat on her cushionless sofa staring at her new-hung art. She had seen them while walking around at a local art fair. Seven had pointed them out; they'd both liked them, so Raffi got them. Could she be more transparent? *Hey, Seven! I'm making the place nice for you!* That thought was painful in its own way. Why did it hurt, making the present better? Why did it hurt, creating a future? Growing pains, she hoped.

Raffi considered the past. Almost a quarter of a century since the mission to Ordeve. Her work at Romulan Affairs, and then what she thought of as her best years in Starfleet, serving on the *Verity* with Picard. Saving lives and making a difference, all the while trying to persuade herself that the damage being done to her marriage and her family would be fixable. And then the synth attack on Mars happened, and the *Verity*'s mission of relieving the Romulans—which depended on synth labor—was brought to an unceremonious end. JL threw the mother of all tantrums and stormed off. Doors slammed in Raffi's face. Her credibility, gone; her career, finished; her marriage, over; her baby boy . . .

Were the pictures straight? Sometimes you looked at something so hard that you couldn't tell any longer what was right and what was wrong. What was it JL had said? *The unexamined life is not worth living.* Sometimes Raffi felt that she had spent too much time looking back on the mistakes that she had made, regretting them, wishing that she could put things right. Was returning to Ordeve going to turn out to be yet another of those especially bad mistakes in which Raffi seemed to specialize?

SECOND SELF   25

The pictures were definitely straight, or close enough. She liked how the bold colors—black and gold and copper—stood out against the white walls. She liked how the circles intersected and interconnected. They were a start. They helped make the apartment look like a place where a real girl lived—even if she was heading off soon.

So, Raffi thought, *you are going.* No surprise there, really. JL knew her. The decision made, Raffi moved into action, heading over to her comm.

"JL," she said, when he appeared on screen, "is this secure?"

"Of course."

"Good. Then—I'm in."

"Raffi." He smiled. She was a sucker for that smile. *"You never fail me."*

"You're right," she said. "I never do."

"Should I put you in touch with my people at Starfleet Intelligence? At the Cardassian desk?"

"No, listen, I've been thinking about this. We need a more oblique approach."

"Oblique?"

"You want to keep this quiet? You don't want the Cardassians to find out that we're looking for their man?"

"Ideally not."

"In which case, I'm not sure that involving Cardassian Affairs is the best idea."

His eyes narrowed. *"I beg your pardon?"*

"We're allies now, right? With the Cardassian Union."

"Yes, thankfully."

"A hard-won alliance. Lots of work gone into that."

"Get to your point, Raffi."

"Don't be testy with someone doing you a big favor. When I was at Romulan Affairs, we had to walk a very fine line between building trust and knowing which cards to hold close to our chest. I built long-standing relationships with Romulan officers, some of them Tal Shiar. Having to keep secrets—having to *lie*—was the worst part of Intelligence. Not just because you felt duplicitous, but because of the consequences if you were caught. What I'm saying is—"

"You don't want to put any intelligence officers at the Cardassian desk into that position."

"You got it."

JL pondered this. *"Is there a danger,"* he said, *"in being caught in a lie to colleagues at Starfleet Intelligence?"*

"What lie? All I need is another reason to be out there."

"And is there one?"

"I'll find one."

She watched him weigh the options—the morality, perhaps—of this. Covert ops sometimes had to be more covert than was comfortable. If JL wanted results, he might have to suppress a few scruples. Wasn't that why he was asking her to take on this mission? Wasn't that the whole point of intelligence officers? To shield their superiors. To be the buffer between what you wanted done, and what you weren't prepared to do yourself.

"All right," he said at last. *"How do you wish to proceed?"*

"I need a route to Ordeve unconnected with the Cardassians. A back door."

"A back door?"

"Give me a day or two to poke around."

"A day or two. Very well. We'll speak then. Picard out."

She composed and sent a message to a former colleague at Romulan Affairs. She wasn't expecting to hear back today, so she went and washed up her cup. When she got back, there was a light already flashing on the comm.

"I've got an opening this afternoon. Come and see what we've done with the old place."

"All right," said Raffi to herself. "That's great. Let's get back out there." She looked at her pictures. "Talking to yourself. That's a bad sign. What you need is a robot dog."

The unexamined life, thought Raffi, standing at the security desk in the entrance hall of the small and unassuming office block at Starfleet Command that housed Romulan Affairs. She used to walk in and out of this place so freely. Then JL waltzed into her life, whisked her off on his grand mission, and when that blew up in her face, everything spiraled out of control. What if she'd simply stayed here? Been content with her desk job? Been present, for Jae, and for Gabe? The sense of a road not taken, a lost future that should have been hers, came to Raffi so powerfully that she was almost overwhelmed. There was no going back. There was no setting straight a crooked path. There was only living with the consequences and trying to stop your feet from faltering again.

A familiar figure came through security and into the hall: Commander James Northey, her one-time colleague at the Romulan desk. He lifted a hand in greeting. "Raaaaaafi Musiker," he said, "and to what do we humble padd pushers owe this honor?"

"I'm back in the area. Thought I might check in."

"Is that right? Well, come on. I'll get you a lousy coffee."

She followed him into the building and into the turbolift, which was smoother than she remembered. Northey smiled at her. She was starting to recall how much he irritated her. So cool; so dry; so English. He said, "A little bird told me that you're thinking of coming back here."

So that news was starting to go around, was it? Who had let that slip? Was somebody testing the waters? Trying to discover whether she might need other options? The Academy, for example? If Raffi thought too hard about that, she might get angry at the idea that someone was in her life trying to move her like a piece on a chessboard. So she didn't think more about that. For now.

"Everything's possible," she said. "In this, the best of all possible worlds."

The lift stopped, with a shudder.

28   UNA McCORMACK

"Hmm," said Northey, and led her out onto a rather faded corridor. This opened out, eventually, into a big open-plan office. A dozen or so junior analysts were there, doing their best to pretend that they weren't taking the chance to get a look at the famous (infamous?) Raffi Musiker. Northey sauntered past, making sure everyone got to goggle at her, and led her to one of the smaller meeting rooms. *Oh,* Raffi thought as she walked inside, *these rooms . . .* How she remembered these rooms. Crowded into them, sometimes until early in the morning, if there was a panic on, eating pizza and drinking coffee, trying to crack Romulan codes. They'd been in this room (or one very like it) eighteen years ago, when they'd finally realized the significance of the flurry of urgent messages that had been passing around the upper echelons of the Star Empire. They'd cross-referenced what they were reading with data from astronomers across the Federation, and suddenly understood what was going on. The Romulan sun was going supernova. They'd sat in this room and stared at each other, and someone (could have been Raffi herself, could've been someone else; they were that tightly knit as a team) said, "What the *hell* are we going to do?"

The Federation had never quite gotten the right answer to that question. They'd been living with the consequences ever since.

Raffi took a seat and saw that the same picture was still on the wall. A pastel image of a sunrise over some beach or other. Generic and bland. Was it meant to be motivational? She was never quite sure.

"Thought Starfleet might have redecorated by now," she said. "I know a good artist."

"We like the place as it is," said Northey. Two other people were entering now; people whom Raffi had known well, once upon a time. They'd gone to her wedding. She'd celebrated significant events in their lives too. Commander Vazreen Pella, a Betazoid whom Raffi had always liked. Raffi had gone to Vaz's mothering festival, even held the family chalice for parts of the ceremony. Commander Kebil Zi, a joined Trill. Raffi had taken part in Zi's *zhian'tara*, experienced the life of the second host. Zi wasn't meeting her eye, instead studiously reading from a padd in his hand. He pushed the door shut behind him and took his seat. The four of them, again, around this table, like the past twenty years hadn't happened. They'd joined Romulan Affairs at about the same time. Now they all outranked her. Those career breaks sure were costly.

"Hey," said Raffi. "It's good to see you."

Pella gave something close to a smile. "Strange to see you here again."

"Strange to be back. Hi, Kebil. Good to see you."

Zi grunted and kept his attention on the padd in his hand. Raffi looked at the other two. Pella looked back steadily. Northey leaned back in his seat. *Oh my,* she thought, *you guys really are still pissed at me.*

"Well," Northey said. "What can we do for you today? Is there another conspiracy theory for us to check out?"

Right, thought Raffi. *So that's how it's going to be.* She felt herself flush with embarrassment, thinking of the many calls put in to them over the years, begging them to check out the latest rumor that had come her way. They'd been kind, at first. Then firm. Then silent.

"In fairness to Raffi," said Pella, "her theory turned out to be true."

Raffi remembered why she'd liked Vazreen Pella. "Thank you."

"But I'd rather this was about something else," said Pella. "You mentioned Ordeve in your message."

"Yes," said Raffi. "I want to know more about what's happening there."

"Do you?" said Northey.

"Yes," said Raffi.

"Ordeve's a Cardassian world," he went on.

"Yes," agreed Raffi.

"So why come to us here at Romulan Affairs?"

Because I don't want your colleagues to find out that I'm trying to chase down a Cardassian war criminal. Because I'm trying to guard everyone's back . . .

"There's a Romulan refugee settlement there," Raffi said. "I'd like to know more—"

30   UNA McCORMACK

Zi threw the padd down onto the table. "Oh, come *on*!"

"You're going to have to be straighter than this if you want our help," said Pella.

"Okay," said Raffi. "Fair enough. First, I need to ask, what do you know about what's happening on Ordeve?"

"What do *you* know about what's happening on Ordeve?" said Northey. "More to the point, *how* do you know about what's happening on Ordeve?"

Raffi shrugged.

"We know *how*," said Zi. "Friends in high places. Admirals and incoming vice-chancellor friends in high places."

"I can help," said Raffi, leaning forward on the table. "Really. I can. And—more to the point—the admiral wants me to help. He's asked me to go. Do *you* want to tell him no?"

She watched them—her colleagues, once upon a time, in a different life; her friends, too, in that other life—glance at each other.

"There's a war criminal on the loose," said Raffi. "A dangerous man. The Bajorans want him; the Cardassians . . . they aren't exactly going out of their way to find him. And for the Federation he's an embarrassment they wish would disappear. Your colleagues over at Cardassian Affairs—they're in a bind. An important alliance with the Cardassians on one side; honoring commitments to the Bajorans on the other. It's a mess—for them. But for you?"

"You are very well informed," said Pella.

"I'd like to be better informed," said Raffi.

"I'm sure you would," said Northey.

"So, let's get this straight," said Zi. "After nearly twenty years, you walk back in here and ask us to help you lie to our colleagues at Cardassian Affairs and manufacture a reason for you to go and carry out some clandestine operation on behalf of your important and influential patron. Have I got everything straight?"

"You know that's not what I'm asking!" Raffi said. "Look, this can work for everyone. There's deniability for the people at the Cardassian desk, and if I'm successful, there's a reputational win for you guys—"

"And if you're not successful?" said Pella.

"I will be," said Raffi. "Anyway, if that happens—you can say what you like. You can say that you told me to fuck off, if you want. Which is more or less what you're doing, isn't it?"

Zi was shaking his head. "You've got some nerve—"

"Nerve?" she shot back. "Damn *right* I've got nerve! I'm going to find this guy, and I'm going to bring him to justice." Raffi reined herself back. "But I need a good reason to be out there. Is there something—*anything*—that I can use to justify a request to the Cardassian government to visit Ordeve? Something that won't make them suspicious?"

But Zi was standing up and gathering his padd. "I'm out."

"We're done," said Northey, pushing back his chair.

"What?" said Raffi. "You promised me coffee—"

"Why ask for coffee when you can be drinking Château Picard?" said Zi, heading for the door. *Why did I ever like you,* thought Raffi.

"I'll take Raffi back down," said Pella.

"Fine by me," said Northey. "Good luck with whatever you decide to do about Ordeve, Raffi. Most of all—good luck getting permission to visit. I hear from our friends—and they *are* our friends—over at the Cardassian desk that the new castellan is getting irritated at the way that Starfleet has been leaning on her over this extradition. She might not want you sniffing around the place."

Thanks for that vote of confidence, Raffi told Northey's departing back.

Pella said, "Come on, Raff. Show's over."

Pella led her back through the open-plan office toward the lift. Raffi, hearing the low whispering of the junior lieutenants as she passed by, was caught between anger at the treatment she had received, and deep regret for the decisions that had led her to this. These three people—they had been her *friends*. She had trusted them—and they had trusted her. Another part of her life, squandered, fallen into ruin and overgrown with weeds. In the turbolift, she leaned her head back against the wall.

"Damn it."

"I'm sorry that didn't go so well," said Pella.

"Are you, Vaz?" said Raffi.

"Yes," said Pella. "I never . . . I never *blamed* you, Raffi, for everything that happened. I know that the relief mission ending was a shock. I felt . . ."

Don't say sorry for me.

"I've only ever wanted you to find your way again," said Pella.

"That's what I'm trying to do," said Raffi. "Do you know that I've been invited to return to Romulan Affairs?"

"Yes," said Pella, and added nothing more.

"Hey," said Raffi. "Don't fall over yourself in excitement. Do the others know?"

"Yes," said Pella.

"And?"

"Well, I'd be glad to have you back," said Pella. "But that might not be the same for everyone. You know there *was* some reputational damage—"

"You said yourself that everything I claimed turned out to be true!"

"Yes, and maybe that's part of the problem. Have you thought about that? Thought about what it was like here? Romulan Affairs was the butt of every joke, for years. Good people, doing first-rate work, and everyone would finish up meetings saying, 'Have you run this past Raffi Musiker? She might have caught something you've missed.'"

"When you put it like that," said Raffi, "I can see how that might rankle."

"Anyway, this is what you'll be coming back to." Pella shook her head in exasperation. "You can't expect to walk back in after all these years, after everything that happened, and pick up where you left off! Particularly if it seems like important people are pulling strings for you—"

"That's not fair," said Raffi hotly.

"Almost certainly not," said Pella. "But that's what people are thinking."

SECOND SELF   33

She gave Raffi a sharp look. "And no, you don't need to be telepathic to know that." She leaned in. "Speaking confidentially, I think Kebil was probably angrier that you were the one recruited by Picard than at the shocking mess of things you made after the synth attack."

"I was right, Vaz—"

"Yes, Raffi, but *still* . . ."

Again, the memory of her desperation at that time made her burn with embarrassment. "Yeah," she said. "I know." She felt a smile twitch at her lips. "He didn't like that, hey?"

"You were the superstar, Raffi. Out of all of us. Kebil always resented that."

"I never knew."

"As long as you were part of the team, he could ignore that. He could feel like he was your equal. But then you got the call from the mighty admiral, and you left . . ."

"Yeah, well, look how that turned out," said Raffi.

"You made the right choice," said Pella. "We all would have jumped at the chance. You did great work, Raffi, for as long as you could. And it wasn't your fault the mission failed. I'm sorry you were another casualty."

That was good to hear. Kind. What a friend might say. They walked back through the entrance hall and Raffi checked herself out at the security desk. Pella followed her outside and they stood together in the bright sunshine.

"Anything you need," said Pella, "come straight to me. I'm not saying that people back there would set you up to fail, but they might not set you up to succeed."

"Copy that," said Raffi. "Were the internal politics always this bad? I don't remember them being this bad."

"Who knows?" said Pella. "I'm like the lobster in the pot. Maybe the water's been getting hotter all the time, and I've never noticed." She reached into her pocket and drew out an isolinear chip. "Apropos of nothing, you'll find this contains some interesting reading."

34 UNA McCORMACK

Raffi reached over to take the chip. "Yes?"

"The situation on Ordeve right now with the Romulan refugees is tricky. And you've got plenty of experience with Romulan refugees. Just read the files, Raff."

Raffi, staring at the crystal, said, "Vaz, are you *sure*?"

"Those guys upstairs," Pella replied. "Too emotional. But you're right. Someone needs to bring this man to justice. Cardassian Affairs can't intervene, and the Romulan desk can't justify intervening. So why not you?" Pella smiled. "Walking back inside that building was the easy part, Raffi. But you're going to need a big success on Ordeve, if you want to win back people's confidence. But you can at least consider me . . ."

"On my team?"

"Cheering you on from the sidelines," said Pella.

"Thank you, Vaz."

"It's okay. But Raffi—I want you to think carefully about this. Are you sure coming back here is what you want?"

"I don't know yet," Raffi admitted. "That's part of the point of doing this."

"You can't go back to how it was," Pella said. "None of us can. We can only . . ."

"Move on?"

"Move forward," said Pella. "You can't fix the past. Only learn to live with it."

That, thought Raffi, as she headed for the public transporters, would be better than nothing.

Vazreen's files were gold. Not for the first time, Raffi thought that it wasn't the friends in high places that mattered most. Friends in high places sometimes forgot to look down from their lofty heights. But people like Vaz Pella always came through. Her report on the Romulan refugee situation on Ordeve was precise, clear, and informative. The current governor of Ordeve—the exarch, to use the Cardassian term—had allowed a large number of Romulan settlers over the past decade. But over the last few months, fewer and fewer permits had been granted, and the exarch had indicated that she intended to stop the flow of settlers to Ordeve. Naturally, the Romulans were frustrated, because family members of people already living there were struggling to join them.

A matter requiring attention, Pella had written alongside this. *If only there was anybody available with expertise in the resettlement of Romulan refugees.*

Raffi, reading through the personnel files, saw that Vaz had highlighted one for her attention: the Romulan liaison to the Cardassian exarch, Nuvu Sokara. Raffi recognized his name immediately—in fact, it was a shock to see it, after all these years. Damn. How strange that he was back on Ordeve. Sokara had been on Earth throughout the Dominion War, a liaison between the Tal Shiar and Starfleet Intelligence. Raffi had gotten to know him during the course of the war. When she'd been assigned to Ordeve, she'd bumped into him in the capital, Merna. Their paths had then run alongside each other for a few short, intense weeks. After which—nothing. Until now.

Raffi studied his picture: he looked older (who didn't?), wearied no doubt by the struggles and privations of recent Romulan history. She had not liked him (was it possible to like a Tal Shiar agent?), but their working relationship during the Dominion War had been mutually beneficial. She hadn't trusted him (was it possible to trust Tal Shiar?), but she had respected him. He'd understood the gray area in which they operated, and how to make it work for both of them. He had come through for her on Ordeve. Now he was back there—a refugee, presumably, but one with some authority. How strange, though, that he should be on Ordeve. How strange that their paths would cross, once more, there, of all places. If you thought too hard about that, you might start to feel uneasy.

Securing a channel to speak to Sokara proved straightforward, testament to the length of time there had been Romulan settlements on Ordeve, and

36   UNA McCORMACK

hopefully indicative of the relative stability of the world in recent years. Raffi wondered, as she waited for him to appear on-screen, how different she might appear from the young lieutenant he had known all those years ago. She wondered how much she had changed.

When she saw him on-screen, her heart went out to him. These past years of chaos and turmoil had undoubtedly taken their toll. The austere, pristine, and seemingly unaging Tal Shiar agent that she remembered was now gray, tired, and wearing worn civilian clothes. But alive. How had Sokara escaped, Raffi wondered, when so many other Romulans had not? Membership in the Tal Shiar must have helped, easing his passage out of the danger zones when so many others were left behind. When they had been opposite numbers on Earth, he had been broad-minded and willing to work with her. And then, there was everything that he had done for her on Ordeve, a debt that she was not sure could ever be repaid. She was glad to see him and touched that he seemed glad to see her. His stern and weary face was lightened by a wan smile.

"Lieutenant Commander Musiker," he said. *"After all this time—what a surprise."*

"Pleasant, I hope."

"Entirely, let me assure you. I hope the passing years have treated you well."

Those years had been something of a mixed bag, but when Raffi compared her own recent history with what must have happened to him, she couldn't complain. She'd been lost, sure, but it turned out there had been places to come back to.

"They've not been bad," she said. "How about you?"

"Less than good," he admitted. *"But they could have been considerably worse. What can I do for you, Commander?"*

"It's more what I might be able to do for you," she said. "I took a break from Romulan Affairs for a while, but I've been back in touch with my old colleagues recently. They knew I was stationed on Ordeve once upon a time and drew my attention to what's happening there now."

"Yes?" He looked cagier now. *"What did they say?"*

"My information is fairly limited, but my impression from reading the files is that there's a continuing dispute between the Romulans and the Cardassians. I wondered if I might be able to help."

"Given your prior experience mediating between Romulans and Cardassians here?"

"Something like that," she said. "You never know when some pressure from Starfleet might come in handy."

"That was certainly what I learned all those years ago," he observed dryly. *"But I have to admit interest from a Starfleet officer would be very timely. The situation here is becoming acute."* He looked very weary now. *"I'd be glad to see you, Raffi. I'd be glad if someone helped."* He sighed: a man with limited resources that were surely close to being exhausted. Maybe helping him would make her less ambivalent. Maybe if her real mission did not work out (who even knew if her target was still on Ordeve; he could be long gone), she could do some good, for a man to whom she owed a great deal.

"I heard about your work with Picard on the Verity, *"* said Sokara.

"We tried," Raffi said. Which was true, although she was conscious—so very conscious—of how profoundly they had failed. "We'd barely started when the brass called off the mission."

The Romulan relief mission had depended critically—and unwisely, perhaps, in retrospect—on the use of synth labor for the rapid manufacture of the massive number of starships required to move thousands and thousands of Romulans. When the synths employed at the Utopia Planitia shipyards went rogue, killing everyone, it led to the subsequent ban on synthetic life. That ended the mission. It was, to Raffi, one of the Federation's gravest mistakes. Worse than that—one of the greatest betrayals of their ideals. Millions of Romulans left without assistance. A retreat from their oaths and obligations. A truly dark day for the United Federation of Planets.

"The movement of people out of Romulan space has continued apace." Sokara's clipped words concealed millions of devastating stories: homes aban-

38   UNA McCORMACK

doned, never to be recovered; people lost who could never be brought back. The Federation could have done more. They *should* have done more.

"You know," said Raffi, "I'm surprised any Romulan would choose to go into Cardassian territory." The Cardassian-Romulan front, during the Dominion War, had been a byword for brutality and excess. There was no love lost between these two species. "But I guess there isn't a choice when you're running for your life."

"Just so," said Sokara. *"But I must be fair to our hosts—they have been remarkably sympathetic to our plight. I think that after their own experiences, the Cardassians understand what it is like to be desperate. To be the beggars of the quadrant."*

Raffi could understand his reasoning. The Fire, they called it on Cardassia; the mass slaughter of the population and destruction of buildings and infrastructure that the retreating Jem'Hadar had inflicted across the entire Cardassian Union. Cardassia, bombed almost into extinction, had relied significantly on Federation aid during the postwar period. To their credit, they had rebuilt rapidly, and with considerably less of the nationalistic posturing that had been their pre-war trademark. Their population had grown, although it was nowhere near the pre-war levels, and to some extent you could even call them the success story of the quadrant. When the Federation withdrew from the Romulan refugee relief effort, successive Cardassian governments had enjoyed pointing out how much more they were doing for their Romulan neighbors. Taking the moral high ground over the Federation took some cheek, particularly when you had war criminals still at liberty, but nobody had ever said that the Cardassians lacked chutzpah.

"As far as I could tell from the reports, everything was going well on Ordeve," said Raffi, "until recently."

"The situation has been mutually beneficial," said Sokara. *"Many of the Cardassian colony worlds—like Ordeve—were almost emptied after the Jem'Hadar massacres. They needed people to rebuild. Romulan settlers have been extremely useful. That was the case here, for a long time."*

SECOND SELF   39

"Impressive," said Raffi. "Given the history."

"Indeed. But now we seem to have reached an impasse. A barrier to progress."

Faintly, as if from a great distance, Raffi heard a ringing in her ears, like a warning bell, an alarm. She shook her head. "Go on."

"We've been a model of successful settlement. We were made to feel very welcome. We helped rebuild the towns and villages. Brought in harvests. We have lived peacefully alongside our hosts for many years now."

This hadn't been the case on other worlds, Raffi knew, where the promises of good homes and real work had turned out to be nothing. The Romulans had been consigned to hopeless shanty towns. "What's gone wrong?"

"Success brings its own problems," said Sokara. *"As we put down roots, made lives here, more and more of us have been drawn to Ordeve. And now the Cardassians are refusing permission for us to expand."*

"You know," said Raffi, "Ordeve wasn't exactly the most overpopulated place, even before the Jem'Hadar were let loose. There's surely space—"

"There's land here that's been empty for decades. But the Cardassians intend to close Ordeve to new settlers . . ."

"Would it help," said Raffi, "if an independent observer came to Ordeve? Someone from Starfleet, there on the ground?"

He looked at her in amazement. *"You'd do that? You'd come back here?"*

The alarm went to red-alert klaxons. Raffi ignored it. "I'd do that. If you think it would help."

Sokara stared at her for a few moments, and then began to laugh, very quietly. *"Why not?"* he said. *"It worked well last time, didn't it? I'll put in a request to the exarch."*

"Let me see what I can do at this end," said Raffi.

"Thank you," he said. *"I . . . am very touched—very grateful—that you would consider returning here, on my account."* He gave a crooked smile. *"I still owe you that drink."*

"Why else have I tracked you down?" said Raffi. "But I think I'm the

40   UNA McCORMACK

one that owes you. Put in that request to the exarch's office. I'll get things moving here. And I hope to see you soon. On Ordeve."

Raffi cut the comm. She opened a new, secure channel and left a message. *"JL. We have our back door."*

"Not to take advantage of the man," Raffi said to JL, an hour later, "but the situation definitely works to our advantage. They've reached an impasse over new Romulan settlements on Ordeve. Sokara is happy for Starfleet to come and observe. But we'll need to get permission from the Cardassians to visit."

"I can understand the Cardassian perspective," said JL. Did he always have to be so damn evenhanded? *"Ordeve was almost taken from them by the Romulans at the end of the Dominion War. Perhaps they feel unwilling to hand the world to Romulan settlers—"*

"They're not being asked to give Ordeve over to Romulan jurisdiction."

"Perhaps they're concerned that it's only a matter of time," said JL.

"Things change," said Raffi.

JL eyed her thoughtfully. *"You're on the Romulan side in this dispute."*

"I know Sokara," she said. "I don't think he would ask for anything unreasonable."

"Things change," said JL. *"So do people. But perhaps we can do some good here, Raffi. Your prior experience with the place and Sokara surely puts you in an ideal position to act as mediator in this situation."*

Raffi couldn't help but laugh. "First you want me to be an Academy instructor, now you want me to be a mediator! Any other wildly inappropriate jobs you've got in mind?"

"Raffi," said JL, *"you're more than capable of handling this situation. Not least because it will most likely involve banging a few Romulan and Cardassian heads together."*

"Now, that I'll enjoy," she admitted.

SECOND SELF   41

"Besides," he said, *"this is only one part of your purpose on Ordeve. We must not forget the real mission."*

Track down the runaway—the war criminal—and bring him to justice.

"Do you think the Cardassians will suspect anything of a request to visit Ordeve?"

"There's only one way to find out," said JL. *"But given your prior experience on the world, and a request from Sokara for your personal involvement—I think this will make the request harder for the Cardassians to turn down. Particularly when it comes with my personal imprimatur."*

The confidence of the powerful. "Good to have friends in high places," said Raffi.

"So it seems."

3

Permission to enter Cardassian space and visit Ordeve proved surprisingly easy to secure. Raffi assumed that the name Admiral Jean-Luc Picard was the key that had unlocked that door, but JL was quick to point out that this had not been the case.

"The office of the castellan was not keen on Starfleet getting involved," he said. *"But the exarch of Ordeve heard that you were leading the mission and put in a personal request that you be allowed to come."*

"Sokara said he'd put in a good word for me," said Raffi.

"Not just that, Raffi. It seems the assistance you gave to the Cardassians all those years ago has not been forgotten."

That was gratifying, thought Raffi—and so was JL's mildly disconcerted expression. It felt good to be wanted on her own terms for once, and not simply because Admiral Jean-Luc Picard was pulling strings on her behalf.

"You must have made a good impression when you were out there."

"I guess I did. I do, sometimes."

"Exarch Shecol Khrill is very keen to meet you and wanted to pass on her gratitude that you were willing to offer your special understanding of the history of the world to assist in the resolution of this crisis."

"At least it won't be a wasted journey," said Raffi. "If I can't find our man."

"About that," said JL.

"Uh-huh?" Now that the trip was definitely happening, Raffi was al-

44 UNA McCORMACK

ready busy reading up on what needed to be done to make it a reality. "Have you seen the list of shots I need to go there?"

"Are they excessive?"

"Boucher's Ague? What the hell? I mean, is that even a *thing*? A thing that *humans* can contract?"

"Were you intending to be the test case?"

"What? Hell, no! Give me the shots. Give me *all* the shots. I'm not an idiot."

"Perhaps allow for a couple of days' bed rest after." He was smiling. *"They call it the three-day sweats."*

"You know what, JL? You're not grateful enough to me for taking this on."

"If you'll let me speak," he said, *"I've got some good news for you. The* Stargazer *has been tasked to take you to Ordeve."*

Raffi couldn't help herself; she smiled fully and frankly. That really was good news. Not only was the *U.S.S. Stargazer* a fine starship, but its captain was the one and only Cristóbal Rios. They trusted each other—and, more than that, they understood each other. Both had entered Starfleet as idealists; both had washed out, broken into pieces. Now they were putting themselves back together; Rios commanding a starship that should have been his years ago and Raffi testing the waters with intelligence work. If there was anyone she would want as backup on this mission, it would be Cris. She wished he had been there with her on Ordeve her first time around.

"I thought that might make you happy," said JL.

"It has," said Raffi. "More than you might guess. Does he know about the entire mission?"

"I'm going to leave that to your discretion."

"I want him completely in the loop," said Raffi, without hesitation.

"Whatever you need to get the job done," said JL. *"Good. I'm glad that you're pleased. I had to work hard to get the* Stargazer.*"*

"I'm delighted you did. Now, you can ask me the favor that you want. The next favor."

"I beg your pardon?"

"This is how these conversations with you were always structured, JL. Good news was always followed by bad news. Pleasant surprises followed by requests for a favor. Always. You never varied."

"Ah," said JL. He looked taken aback. *"I had no idea I was so transparent."*

"I never told you because it kept things simpler for me. What do you want? You *do* have a favor to ask, right? Another favor."

He had the grace to look sheepish. *"Yes, in fact, I do. I'd like you to take Elnor."*

"Excuse me?"

"Take Elnor. Please."

Raffi sighed deeply. "Oh, JL, no—"

"He might be useful—"

"Don't get me wrong! I *like* the kid, and he certainly comes in handy in a fight, but he has this *way* about him—"

"Absolute candor, yes, I know—"

"There's going to be delicate moments, diplomacy on the ground, angry Romulans, hostile Cardassians—" She could see JL was listening but not taking on board a single word she said; nodding his head while waiting for her to run out of steam so that he could make his final strike. "I mean, Sokara is former Tal Shiar. What's he going to think when I rock up with a member of the Qowat Milat?"

"He's lost, Raffi. He doesn't know what to do next."

There it was. That *thing* JL always did, which was to cut through every single damn rational argument that you were making with an appeal to the emotions that, if you refused, would only make you seem like some hard-hearted *monster*. Raffi was not—dammit, she was *not*—some hard-hearted monster. She was someone who had left more than her fair share of damage in her wake and was trying to make amends. Make something new, something better, of herself.

"I thought he was heading to the Academy," she said. "I thought that

46   UNA McCORMACK

was your plan for the three of us." Some kind of freakish family: wonder dad, disaster mom, and the weirdest kid in the quadrant.

"He's still wavering. This mission might help him decide."

"Or be yet another distraction."

JL smiled. *"Perhaps."*

"And what do I tell him, exactly? Do I tell him about the mission? The real mission, you know, the one about the Cardassian war criminal, the mission so secret that we've not even told our own people at Cardassian Affairs? Because the first thing Elnor is going to do is tell everyone we meet that we're there on a secret mission—"

"You'll know what's best when you see him," said JL with a smile. *"Perhaps this is exactly what he needs. He can learn discretion."*

That damn smile. He knew that she was going to say yes. Valiantly, Raffi tried to refuse—but what was the point? JL would regroup, marshal his forces, and come back—probably when she was halfway to Ordeve—with the absolutely irrefutable argument as to why he should send Elnor out to meet her. Best not to waste her energy and surrender to the inevitable.

"Damn! All right!"

JL's smile reached his eyes. *"Thank you, Raffi. I truly believe he'll be a great help."*

Picard cut the comm and disappeared from view.

"No, he won't," said Raffi.

The windows of the house in La Barre stood open to admit the fading light of evening. Picard, fresh from his call with Raffi, walked soft-footedly through his childhood home. At the door to the kitchen, he stood for a moment, looking inside. Laris was at the sink, washing wineglasses. He watched her for a while. She worked slowly, carefully, and methodically—base to stem to bowl—rinsing away the suds before setting the glass to drain and reaching for another. Three months since Zhaban had died, his heart giving out suddenly and catastrophically in the vineyard one blazing hot afternoon. After the initial shock and grief, Laris seemed, to Picard's eyes, to have gone numb. She had found many tasks like this to occupy her. Last week she had washed all the linen, including items that Picard did not believe had been used since his mother was alive. Before that, she had cleaned every single window. Tonight, it was the turn of the wineglasses. He wondered what she would find to do next, and what she would do when she came to the end of the tasks. Start over? Or move on?

She turned, suddenly, on full alert, relaxing only when she saw who was there. Did people like Laris ever put life as an operative behind them? Was that even possible?

"Oh," she said, her shoulders dropping, "it's you."

He crossed the kitchen to join her. He felt oddly apologetic. He was not the right man. "You don't have to do those by hand," he said. "They're quite robust—"

"I prefer it this way," she said. "It's meditative. But now you're here you can make yourself useful."

"Useful?"

"You can dry."

He took up the cloth that she indicated and, obediently, picked up the nearest glass. He followed her process—base to stem to bowl—carefully wiping away traces of water, setting each glass aside to be put away later. She was right. There was something contemplative about this, as there was about many small tasks. After his resignation from Starfleet, all those years ago, he had resented the quiet domesticity of this life. Perhaps he should have appreciated it more. You never knew when it might end.

"Did you speak to Raffi?" said Laris.

"I did."

"Did you tell her about Rios?"

"Yes."

"Was she pleased?"

48   UNA McCORMACK

"Very pleased."

"Good." Laris washed a couple more glasses before carrying on. He waited until she was ready to speak. "But not about Elnor."

"No-o," said Picard. "She was less happy about that. But she could have refused—"

"Oh, Jean-Luc," said Laris. "Why do you persist in this delusion that you give people a choice?"

"What do you mean, Laris?"

"As if anyone would ever say no to you."

He took the glass she was holding from her hand, dried it, and placed it with the rest. "I'd like to think that Raffi knows me well enough by now—"

"I feel bad," said Laris. She stopped what she was doing and stood with her hands in the cooling water. He put down his cloth and gently put his hand upon her shoulder.

"Bad? Why?"

"Well, she was hardly happy to go in the first place."

"No, not exactly—"

"I don't know the full story of what happened to her there all those years ago, but it plainly wasn't good. And now not only are we sending her back, but we're sending that boy along with her too." She tipped the bowl of suds out into the sink and they both stood watching the water swirl away. As the last of the water gurgled through the drain, she said, "Pass me that cloth, will you?"

He obeyed. She began to wipe down the sink.

"You didn't tell her everything, did you?" Laris said.

"No. But I've told her everything she needs to know. And—whatever you say—I've told her enough to be able to make the right decisions for herself."

Laris didn't reply. When the surfaces were satisfactory, she began to wring out the cloth—rather savagely, he thought.

"Laris," he said. When she didn't respond, he reached to still her hand.

"Laris. I have to ask. Are you quite sure about this? Are you sure that you still want to proceed?"

"How do we stop, now?" she said.

"There are many pieces in motion, but if you decide that this is not what you want, then I will find a way to stop them."

"The problem is—I don't know. If you'd asked me this morning, I would have said yes, absolutely, carry on. But now . . ."

"What's changed?" he said. "Is it Elnor?"

"Partly . . . But mostly—I feel as if we're using her. And Raffi doesn't deserve that . . ."

"I've been entirely clear with her what the mission is, and she decided it was something that she was willing to do. I believe that returning to Ordeve might put some of her ghosts to rest—but if you want me to stop her involvement in this whole affair, then I will do that—now. Raffi's knowledge of the place and the people will be invaluable, but there are others who could go."

She withdrew her hand from his and started to fold the cloth. She was less frenetic now, he thought. Good. "You have never told me," Picard said, in a neutral voice, "exactly what it was that he did to Zhaban."

"What is there to tell?" she said. "What do you think would happen between Tal Shiar and Obsidian Order?"

Picard didn't press. He turned his attention back to the glasses and began putting them away in the cupboard.

"I'll make some coffee," she said with a sigh. Five or ten minutes later, they reconvened at the kitchen table. She was sitting with her hands out, palms down, flat upon the table, staring at nothing. He poured coffee for them both. The scent or the movement stirred her; she wrapped her hands around her cup.

"Tell me," he urged her quietly, "what it is that you want."

"And you'll make it so?"

"If it's within my power, yes."

50   UNA McCORMACK

"I want him brought to justice, Jean-Luc. I want him punished."

He considered this. "You understand that while he might well be brought to justice for some crime, he will never be brought to justice for what he did to Zhaban?"

"I want him held to account for something!"

"You want revenge?"

"I want *closure*," said Laris. "I want to move on."

Picard picked up his cup. "Raffi will see it done."

Raffi always saw it done.

In the lounge, waiting for transporting, Elnor was sitting—tall and strange and striking—with a small bag between his feet and his staff strapped across his back. People were giving him a wide berth, but he was oblivious to this. He was staring down at his hands. He looked . . . *Oh sweetie,* thought Raffi, *you look so sad. You're not much more than a kid, are you?*

"Hey!" she said, waving as she made her way toward him, her tone full of false brightness. "Elnor!"

He looked up. He had this way of looking at you that made you feel like he'd stared through your head to the back of your skull. "Lieutenant Commander Musiker," he said, rising to his feet with the enviable speed and grace of the young, and giving her the open-book greeting of the Qowat Milat. "*Jolan tru.*"

"*Jolan tru,*" she said, returning the gesture. "How are you, honey?"

"I am unclear as to why I have been asked to join this mission," he said.

"I guess . . . that Picard thought you might find the experience interesting," she said.

"I see," he said. "You didn't ask for me to come?"

"I . . ." Was there any point lying to him? "No, I didn't. But you're here now, so welcome aboard."

"I didn't want to come either," he said.

SECOND SELF   51

"I see," she said, and then he looked so sad again—so tall, and so young, and so lost—that her heart went out to him. "Oh honey," she said, putting her hand upon his arm. "Did JL get to you too?"

"*Get* to me? I don't understand what you mean." He sounded frustrated. She guessed that this happened to him a lot these days. Not understanding what the people around him meant; not understanding what they wanted from him.

"I mean—what do you *want* to do, Elnor?"

But the question only served to make him even sadder. "I don't know," he said. "I don't know what I am supposed to do."

Damn, she thought. *All this plus a depressed Romulan. When this is done, I'm going to need a long holiday.* "Well," she said, "let's start by beaming up to the *Stargazer*, and see where that takes us, huh? Come on, Elnor. I'm sure we'll get along fine."

Captain Cristóbal Rios was there to meet them, looking spruce and handsome in his uniform and captain's pips.

"Hey!" Raffi embraced him. "Look at *you*! Don't you clean up well?"

They each pecked a kiss on the other's cheek. "Could say the same about you, Raffi. Right?"

She didn't miss the querying note. "Clean as a whistle," she said.

Rios looked over her shoulder to where Elnor was standing, a tall and particularly deadly third wheel. "Hey kiddo," he said. "Welcome aboard."

"*Jolan tru*, Captain Rios," said Elnor, opening his palms. "I like the transporter room of your ship."

"Thank you," said Rios. "I hope the rest of the ship lives up to your first impressions."

"So do I," said Elnor gravely.

Raffi winked at Rios, who was covering a smile. He led them off to their individual quarters. The grand tour, he promised, would come when they

52 UNA McCORMACK

were en route. Raffi cleaned up, unpacked, and checked her messages. An hour later, as planned, she and Cris reconvened in his ready room.

"Elnor not joining us?" she said.

"He'll be here in five minutes," said Rios. "I wanted to speak to you privately first."

"Sounds ominous."

"I hope not," said Rios. "But Picard hinted there was more to all this than the stated mission. Am I right?"

"You're right."

"And . . . do I get the full story?"

"You do."

"Good. My next question—what about the kid?"

"What about the kid?"

"Does *he* have the full story?"

"Not yet," said Raffi. "But he will."

Rios leaned back in his chair. He looked good behind that desk, Raffi thought. He looked at home. If Cris could find his place, after all that had happened to him, perhaps she could too. "Raffi," he said, "are you sure that's a good idea?"

"It's going to have to be," she said.

"I'm thinking," he said, "of Freecloud—"

"He did *great* on Freecloud!"

"Raffi . . ."

"Look, Cris, what am I supposed to do? I can't take the kid in blind. And he's not stupid. He knows when to keep quiet."

"I'm not sure that he does," said Rios, and then the chime on the door sounded and Elnor arrived. Raffi hoped that their welcome wasn't overly and suspiciously effusive. Easing out of her chair, she took up what had, once upon a time, been a familiar position—standing at the front of a room, delivering a briefing.

"All right," she said. "Our stated mission is to observe and, if necessary,

SECOND SELF 53

mediate between the Romulans and the Cardassians over the ongoing Romulan refugee crisis on Ordeve. I want to give you some background about the world. It's had a tangled history, and we need to keep all these nuances in mind while we're there. I think the Federation is the only local power not to stake a claim to the place, but even we have been drawn into its affairs over the years."

She called up a holo-chart of the Ordevian system and directed their attention to the fifth planet. "It's the only Class-M planet in the system," she said. "Settled originally by the Bajorans—we don't know the exact date, and the Bajorans don't either. There's a great deal about their earlier history that's lost to the mists of time." She stared at the image of Ordeve, a gold globe spinning beside her. "The Bajoran settlements weren't extensive and were primarily religious in nature. Monasteries, temples, and so on, although supported by small farming communities. I think the distance from Bajor itself meant that Ordeve drew people from contemplative orders. People who didn't mind the quiet. I'm guessing here."

She punched up some data, and the main dates of Ordevian history overlaid the holo-image of the planet.

"The Cardassians came to Ordeve in the 2330s. By 2340, there were no Bajorans left on the world. They moved on, the Cardassians claimed, but that's not completely true."

She saw that Rios was frowning; he got it. But Elnor said, "What do you mean?"

"I mean that at the very least, there were forced displacements. I'm also pretty sure there was at least one direct massacre. It's hard," she said, "after time passes, to prove anything. Isn't that incredible? Even now, with all the technology we have at our disposal, it's possible for a place to be remote enough that one group can, without impunity, murder members of another group. That seems to have been a pattern on Ordeve. That was the reason that I was ordered there after the Dominion War."

She pulled up some more key dates.

54   UNA McCORMACK

"Start of the Dominion War, 2373. The Romulan entry into the war, the following year. The Cardassian revolution, eight weeks before the war ended, in 2375. The Jem'Hadar massacre of the Cardassian people, generally known as the Fire, the last week of the war. The end of the Dominion War, 2375." She eyed her audience. "Cris, you must remember some of this. Elnor"—he was so *young*—"just try to remember the basics."

She brought up a second line of dates, that ran to the left-hand side of the ones already there. "If you picked out any Cardassian colony world, you'd find a very different story about what happened at the end of the Dominion War. A lot depended on how much damage the Jem'Hadar managed to do. Even more depended on whether they were on the Federation front, or the Romulan front. Ordeve was the latter. The Romulans arrived there a few months before the ceasefire. Starfleet sent in observers just after the Cardassians switched sides. When the war ended, the Romulans claimed the world. The Cardassians on Ordeve—there weren't many left by then, and most of them were civilians—believed that the Romulans intended to massacre them. They asked Starfleet to send in observers, peacekeepers, to make sure this didn't happen. That's why I was there. But we were spread pretty thin."

She took a breath. There was a trick to delivering briefings like this, where you'd been personally involved. Stick to the facts, and plow right on through.

"Tensions were high, particularly in this region." She focused the map on a specific area of Ordeve's main continent. "A Cardassian settlement, Ghenic, was coming under siege by Romulan forces. Starfleet intervention prevented a massacre, and the Romulans were ultimately persuaded by Starfleet to withdraw from Ordeve." She could see Rios, looking at her closely. He knew. He knew there was more to this. "After that, the world returned to Cardassian control, and has, more or less, thrived, although the population was reduced. After the Romulan star went supernova, they took in a large number of Romulan refugees. Scored a few points from the Federation. Despite the history of the world, the settlements have been successful. The problem is—the Romulans now want to increase their numbers on Ordeve. The Cardassians are flatly refusing permission. That's where we come in—Starfleet. I've been given this mission because I have experience on this world, and with one of the Romulans on the ground. This man."

She brought up a picture of Sokara.

"Nuvu Sokara. Ex–Tal Shiar, now a Romulan liaison to the Cardassian exarch on Ordeve. He's currently based in Ghenic, and we're going to meet him there. He was on Earth after the Romulans entered the Dominion War. We first met there, and we met again on Ordeve. We worked well together. I have his trust. I also have the trust of the Cardassians, from my previous work on their behalf."

"They're asking you to mediate, Raffi?" said Elnor.

"Stranger things have happened," Raffi replied.

"I suppose so," he said. "They could have asked *me* to mediate."

Raffi broke into a completely genuine smile. Bless the boy, he tried, didn't he? He really tried.

"At least they'd know they could believe everything you say, Elnor," said Rios, with great kindness. "That's not a small thing."

Elnor nodded. "Raffi," he said, "you said this was our *stated* mission. Does that mean that there is an *unstated* mission?"

Raffi glanced at Rios, who raised his eyebrows. *Your decision, Raff.* She swallowed. Was it wise, really, to apprise Elnor of the full situation? Would he remember that he could make a distinction between absolute candor and not saying absolutely everything that came into his head? Or would that strike him as sophistry; exactly the kind of deceit that the Qowat Milat abhorred?

The problem was that when you were offered absolute candor, it was hard not to give it in return. Truth begat truth; that was the Qowat Milat way, and it was damn effective. When it came down to it, Raffi couldn't bring herself to lie to Elnor. But she could, at least, hope that he would think before he spoke.

56   UNA McCORMACK

Filters, Elnor. Please, remember that you're allowed filters.

"I'm glad you noticed," Raffi said. "There *is* another reason that we're going to Ordeve. While we're there, that reason must remain between the three people in this room. Admiral Picard is in the loop, and a handful of people at Starfleet Intelligence. And that's how it has to stay."

Elnor screwed up his face. "Raffi," he said uncertainly, "I'm not comfortable with secrets."

"Elnor, honey, you're going to be fine—"

"Remember the advice we gave you last time," said Rios.

"The advice was not to talk," said Elnor.

"And it was *great* advice!" said Rios.

"Advice that remains completely moot," said Raffi, "if I never finish my briefing."

Both men looked at her contritely and—more importantly—shut up. Raffi turned back to the holo-display. The image of Sokara's face dissolved, and the face of their prey appeared. Romulan becoming Cardassian.

"Well, I guess you both know who this is, don't you?" said Raffi. She looked at her audience, who were shaking their heads. "You don't know who this is?"

Heads continued to shake.

"This is Elim Garak," she said.

"Nope," said Rios.

"Elim Garak. Cris, he was the Cardassian ambassador to the Federation for *years*!" She called up the relevant dates.

"Sure, okay, right," said Rios defensively. "You know, I think my parents were breaking up around then. Other things on my mind."

Raffi turned to Elnor, who said, "I was not yet born."

"Ancient history, Raff," said Rios.

"You be careful what you say, Captain," said Raffi sternly, but this had shaken her. Ancient history. Were they doing the right thing, tracking this man down? Should they simply leave this be? *The unexamined life* . . . But

SECOND SELF 57

that wasn't her decision. That was above her pay grade—and, ultimately, it was for the Bajorans to decide.

"Elim Garak's file, in the early years, is pretty sketchy. We know he was an Obsidian Order operative. We know he was the unacknowledged son of the head of the Obsidian Order, the late and almost entirely unlamented Enabran Tain." She looked at her audience. "You've heard of the Obsidian Order?"

Elnor put his hand up. "I have. They were like the Tal Shiar, only . . ."

"Cardassian," suggested Rios.

"That'll do," said Raffi. "We suspect he was high up in the Order, with all that entails. At some point, he was thrown out—why, exactly, we don't know, but people who have dealt with him say they're not surprised. He ended up in exile on Terok Nor, later Deep Space 9. He assisted Starfleet and the Federation with the war effort, code-breaking, and so on."

"He switched sides?" said Rios, leaning forward in his seat.

Ah, thought Raffi, *you're interested now.*

"How did that go down with the Cardassian government?"

"Better, when they switched sides," said Raffi. "Elim Garak was critical to the resistance movement on Cardassia Prime. This put him on the right side when the war ended. He was appointed Cardassian ambassador to the Federation, a position he held for fifteen years. Crucial to the postwar alliance and the Cardassian reconstruction. He retired from that post . . . maybe seven or eight years ago. He's been splitting his time between Paris and Ses'erakh—that's the Cardassian capital—ever since. Keeping a low profile. About three months ago, the Bajorans asked for his extradition based on evidence they'd gathered on the actions during the Bajoran Occupation. How the hell they put that case together after so long I don't know, but kudos to Bajoran Intelligence. Anyway, that was when it turned out nobody had seen him for over six months."

Raffi's audience was silent. They were looking at the image of the man in front of them: the sharp, intelligent eyes; the curve of the lips, that from one angle made his expression seem cruel and, from another, amused.

58 UNA McCORMACK

"The Bajorans want him. They're clear about that. The Cardassians— they seem to have washed their hands of him. And the Federation—Starfleet Intelligence . . . Well, they'd like to close the book on the whole business. People want him apprehended, but don't necessarily want to be the ones to do it. He's taken advantage of this. He's clever," said Raffi, "he's months ahead of us, and he is incredibly intelligent and dangerous."

"And you think you'll recognize him when you see him?" said Rios.

"He was pretty famous at one point, no matter what the two of you say," said Raffi.

"He'll have changed his appearance," said Rios. "That's easy to do—"

"I met him once," said Raffi. "When he was ambassador. He was very distinctive. Honestly, Cris—I think that's the least of my worries."

"Tal Shiar," said Elnor thoughtfully. "But Cardassian. Is he a liar?"

"I imagine so," said Raffi.

"And a murderer," said Elnor.

"A mass murderer," said Raffi. "If Bajoran Intelligence is correct."

"And we are to find him?" said Elnor. "And bring him back to make restitution for his actions?"

"Yes," said Raffi, wondering what that restitution might mean.

"And I am not to talk," said Elnor.

"Only when it's necessary," said Raffi. "But best if you observe."

"Observe," said Elnor. "Talk only when necessary. Make a liar face their truth. I understand."

Later, Raffi and Rios met for drinks in his quarters. Cris cracked open a bottle of pisco. "You know, Raffi," he said as he passed over her glass, "I thought you'd be more excited about getting back into the field."

"I thought so too," she said. "I guess . . . there's a couple of things going on. My former colleagues—they weren't so thrilled to see me."

"They're fools," said Rios.

SECOND SELF   59

Raffi smiled at him. Always good to have someone unequivocally on your side. "Anyway, this mission feels . . . make or break in some way. If it all works out, the path ahead becomes a lot clearer."

"You'd go back to Intelligence?" he said.

"I guess . . ." She sipped her drink. "Oh, this is good . . ."

"What's the alternative?" Rios asked.

"Not drinking?"

"Raffi . . ."

"JL thought I might join him at the Academy," said Raffi.

"Starfleet Academy?" said Rios. "You?"

"It's not that preposterous an idea, surely?"

Rios sipped and thought about that for a while.

"Take your time, Cris," said Raffi dryly.

"I think it might be good for you," he said. "Something completely different from anything you've done before. No need to look back. Just look forward. You said there were a couple of things going on?"

"This planet we're headed to," said Raffi, "I didn't have a great time there."

"I picked that up," said Rios. "There's what the report says, and what actually happened. Is there anything to worry about, Raffi? Any unfinished business?"

"No," she said. "I went out there, I tried to protect Cardassians, and I was able to do that. But it wasn't a happy time. It was a strange place . . ." She shook herself. "It was a long time ago. I'm different now." A new woman. Clean. "Have we heard any more from the Bajorans about our missing man?"

Rios shook his head. "Nothing new. The only trail leads to Ordeve."

"Or he's found a way off that we know nothing about. Or he was never there in the first place."

"I'll keep on top of this when the two of you are planetside. Watch your back."

"Hey," she said, "I've got Elnor for that."

60   UNA McCORMACK

"Ah yes," said Rios. "Everyone's favorite Romulan. Are you sure you're happy having him along?"

"What?"

"The kid. Are you okay with babysitting?"

Raffi shrugged. "JL insisted."

"Yeah," said Rios. "I'd kind of guessed that's what happened."

"He might come in useful."

"We've got the crew mission briefing tomorrow morning," said Rios. "I'm prepared to bet you a bottle of this fine pisco brandy that he blurts out the full story before it ends."

"You're on," said Raffi. She won. Elnor sat, hands folded, completely silent, and observed. It was more than a little unnerving. *Observe. Talk only when necessary. Make a liar face their truth.* It was clear that he had taken this mission to heart. Cris, handing her the bottle later, said, "You might succeed."

There was a great generational divide in Starfleet, between those who served in the Dominion War and those who did not. A green lieutenant at the time, Raffi had spent the war behind a desk at Romulan Affairs, preparing for what was to come; the inevitable scramble for territory and supremacy that followed the implosion of a great power. The collapse of the Cardassian Union was minor compared to what had happened to the Romulan Star Empire. The Cardassian worlds were still habitable. Still, the divide between those who had fought on the Cardassian line and those who had not was felt strongly by many in Starfleet. As the *Stargazer* approached the Cardassian border, it was plain that it was preying on the mind of the captain.

"For what it's worth, Cris," she said quietly into his ear, "I think it's better that neither of us have the baggage of that war. Think about who we'll be dealing with—Cardassians. Most of them won't have that baggage either. We can put all that behind us. Make the relationships we want to make."

"Unusually optimistic on your part," he said. "In my experience, history has a way of striking back when you're least expecting it."

Raffi, thinking about her time on Ordeve, could only hope that would not turn out to be true.

They were met at the border by three Cardassian ships. The captain of the lead ship, the *Corat Damar*, greeted them with considerable (and, one hoped, sincere) courtesy on behalf of Castellan Eleta Kalis, and indicated that they would be escorted through Cardassian space. Only fair. Federation-Cardassian relations were cordial; the long history of conflicts was behind them. The Cardassian Union was standing on its own feet, open and friendly. But many Bajorans still alive had survived the Occupation, and for them this was experience, not history, so there remained that unspoken sense that full reconciliation was not yet entirely possible. Perhaps this mission would help with that. Help bring some healing. Raffi hoped so.

Ordeve, as they made their approach, looked as golden as ever. Cris, standing beside her on the bridge, said, "Seems to be flourishing."

"Looks that way."

"You going to be okay, Raffi?"

"Let's find out," she said. Permissions to enter orbit were granted, security codes exchanged, and at last Raffi and Elnor were able to transport directly into the complex surrounding the exarch's residence in the capital, Merna.

The residence stood on one of the hills where the capital was built, giving a good view down into the small city. Raffi's memories of Merna were of a place devastated by four days of Jem'Hadar bombardment. The only buildings standing were Starfleet prefabs, thrown up to provide shelter. She could see evidence of one or two of these, still in use, apparently, as offices. She imagined this was the case across the Cardassian Union. But Merna was thoroughly Cardassian: straight lines and walkways, with the sudden upward sweeps of elegant curves. The buildings were burnished copper, with

62 UNA McCORMACK

the occasional splash of color—pink and blue and green—from the tinted windows. There was also—and this, surely, must be the main difference between temperate Ordeve and the punishing environment of Cardassia Prime—greenery, and even spring blossoms in the trees. The day was mild, perhaps a little too mild for Cardassian tastes. Raffi thought it was almost perfect.

"The exorch," said Elnor, his tongue tripping over the unfamiliar word. "Did I get that right?"

"Nearly," said Raffi. "It's exarch. The governor of Ordeve. Shecol Khrill. We want to keep on her good side." She looked at Elnor and sighed. Was bringing him a mistake?

Elnor's handsome face clouded. If he'd been only a few years younger, Raffi would have had no qualms about calling his expression a pout. "I'm not a child," he said. "People keep treating me like I'm a child. You can trust me, Raffi."

"I'm sorry," she said. "I'll remember that. Straighten your shoulders and put on your most daunting face. We have a Cardassian bureaucrat to impress."

Exarch Shecol Khrill turned out to be exactly the kind of official that Raffi had hoped would be holding the post: one without any personal history of the Occupation—or the Dominion War—one who owed a great deal to Starfleet's postwar efforts. Her office was busy, with an air of cheerful competence, padds and books scattered about. Raffi observed several volumes written in Federation Standard—and even what seemed to be a primer in one of the main Romulan languages. They were offered coffee, but Raffi instead elected to try a cup of *gelat*.

Khrill welcomed her guests warmly, calling them "our friends in the Federation," and promising to put whatever resources they needed at their disposal. But her affability and willingness to help hit a force field when the question of space for new Romulan settlements was broached.

"I want to be very clear about this from the outset," Khrill said, pouring the *gelat* from a copper urn into little cups. "There's no way that we can take in more Romulan refugees."

"I haven't had a chance to take a look around," said Raffi, taking her cup, "but my first impression is there's plenty of space even here in Merna. Surely there's room out in some of the more remote areas—"

"It's not simply a question of space," said Khrill. "It's a question of infrastructure. Ordeve is a remote world. We have limited resources. I know that you were involved in the relief effort yourself, Lieutenant Commander, when the Federation was concerned with such things."

Raffi took that one on the chin. She sipped the *gelat*, which was thick—like Turkish coffee—and bitter, with a faint taste of cinnamon. She could imagine acquiring quite a taste for it.

"Once the refugees are here," Khrill went on, "they need places to live. Homes, schools, hospitals. Work. We've reached our limit of what we can take on."

Raffi nodded her understanding. These were exactly the logistical questions that had constantly troubled the relief mission of the *Verity*. You couldn't simply move people from one place to another. You couldn't dump them planetside and leave them to their own devices. Starfleet's decision to end its relief mission meant that this had been the reality for those who had fled Romulan space. Elnor, beside her, was nodding. He had grown up in such a place.

Khrill said, "We will soon be in the position where the Romulan population outnumbers the Cardassian. That's a tricky proposition to sell both here and on Cardassia Prime."

But Raffi hadn't missed the exarch's remark; her slip: *a remote world*. She knew there *was* space, if they could work it out. She opened her mouth, but Khrill spoke again, and quickly, surely aware she had conceded a point that she had no intention of conceding.

"We cannot accept any more arrivals on Ordeve. There's no more that we can do. And, with respect, Commander—"

64   UNA McCORMACK

That was generally prelude to, at worst, an insult, so Raffi braced herself.

"With respect," said Khrill, "the Cardassian Union has already done more than enough for the refugees fleeing Romulan space. The Federation pressured us into taking large numbers. We were the only major power who continued to receive them. Where was the Klingon Empire? Where, indeed, was the United Federation of Planets?"

Given Raffi's position on the Federation's failure to live up to its ideals, this was a hard one to take. Suck it up and take it. Still, it was uncomfortable for a Cardassian to have the moral high ground.

Raffi gulped down the last of her *gelat*. "I don't disagree," she said. "I also don't make policy."

Khrill smiled. "There's a lot of goodwill toward Starfleet here on Ordeve as a result of their actions after the war. I know of your actions here. I am sure we can reach an understanding."

That was good to know, thought Raffi, since not all her superiors had been thrilled with what had happened here. She accepted a refill and sipped her drink.

"I gather you're going out to Ghenic," said Khrill. "Purely for old times' sake?"

Now they were on thin ice. "To be honest, ma'am," said Raffi, "I would gladly never visit that place again. But my friend Nuvu Sokara has asked me to come. See how they're getting along up there."

"Sokara has been an excellent advocate for the Romulan settlers," said Khrill. "Please convey my regards to him. Also convey my hope that we can find a mutually satisfactory solution."

"I'll do all of that. I hope I can help find that solution."

"In that case, you might want to consider the impact your friend will have." Khrill nodded toward Elnor, stiff and silent, holding his untouched drink out in front of him as if it might contain poison. "Armed Romulans cause some anxiety in that area, as I'm sure you understand. One more reason, Commander, why we are treading carefully, when it comes to receiving settlers, and having Cardassians on Ordeve outnumbered."

Given what had almost happened at Ghenic, Raffi could only be sympathetic. "I'll bear that in mind."

"Qowat Milat," Khrill said to Elnor.

"Excuse me?" said Elnor.

"You're Qowat Milat," said Khrill.

Elnor gave Raffi a worried look. She nodded.

"Yes," said Elnor, and nothing more. *Good,* thought Raffi. *He's learning.*

"You know about the Qowat Milat?" said Raffi.

"Everyone who has worked with Romulan refugees knows the Qowat Milat," said Khrill. "They are always present to assist. Refreshingly direct. They get things done."

That was how Raffi had gotten to know them, all those years ago. The *Verity* was transferring a group of refugees from Inxtis to the colony world of Vashti. A troublesome journey and the presence of the Qowat Milat had gone a long way to keeping things calm. That was when she and JL had met Elnor.

"I've never seen a young man among their number before," Khrill said.

"Elnor's special," said Raffi, with no trace of insincerity.

"He must be," said Khrill, with equal honesty. She gave Raffi an amused look. "Clever move," she said, "bringing Qowat Milat with you."

Is it? thought Raffi. "Thank you."

"I won't disbelieve a word you say. Because Elnor would surely correct you."

Elnor didn't flicker. "I would not be happy," he agreed solemnly, "if Commander Musiker told a lie." Raffi, parsing that, thought: *Wow, Elnor, that was positively ambiguous. Well done!*

"I'm glad to hear that," said Khrill. She turned back to Raffi. "My people will arrange your journey to Ghenic. But—and bearing in mind that I too do not lie—I must emphasize again that there is a limit to what we can do on Ordeve. We have reached that limit."

She offered her palm; Raffi pressed her own against it, Cardassian style, for a moment, and felt a pang of guilt about her duplicity. "I would not be happy either," Khrill said, speaking to Elnor but looking at Raffi, "if Commander Musiker told me a lie."

"I don't lie," said Raffi.

"Neither do I," said Khrill, "in exactly the same way."

4

Traveling up-country was like stepping back in time. Raffi had decided to make the journey by flyer. She wanted to see the land, she told Khrill; to herself she thought that a clear view, from overhead, might give her insight into the man she was hunting. What route would he have taken? Where might he hide?

In the flyer, she handed Elnor a padd opened to show a map of the local area. "Merna stands at the mouth of Parset," she said. "See here? It's the main river running through the main continent. We'll follow it north and west almost up into the mountains. But we'll stop when we get here."

She showed him a more detailed part of the map, an area where two rivers met.

"This is where the Parset is joined by the River Caanta," she said. "The Caanta comes down from the north through this narrow valley here. The mountains get high out there—it's very remote. I've never been out that far, and I don't think many people have."

"Even after centuries of settlement?" said Elnor.

"It's not easy to get to the Caanta valley, and it's even less easy to explore. The Bajorans didn't go that far, and if the Cardassians ever surveyed the valley when they took Ordeve, those maps have never been made available. The area we're visiting is here."

She pointed to a black square that marked a spot not far from the river confluence, but not at the confluence.

68   UNA McCORMACK

"This is Ghenic. The Cardassian military established a base here after they took Ordeve. It was attached to a scientific project—I think they were trying to use the waterfalls along the Parset to develop hydropower solutions. Either that or they were building bombs—I never did find out. But the engineers brought their families out—Ordeve's a long way from Prime. The project was as much a small town as a military base when I was there. When the Romulans arrived during the war, they were stationed here."

She pointed a few kilometers along the Parset.

"The Romulans have a handful of settlements along the Parset now," she said, showing a series of small black dots. "But Ghenic is the main one. The Cardassians didn't come back." Who would want to come back, after everything that had happened? Not Raffi.

"Raffi," said Elnor. "What's this?"

He was pointing at a small red-dotted circle at the point where the two rivers met.

"That was the Bajoran settlement. It was in ruins when I got here. You should explore it, if you get a chance. It's called Akantha. There was a temple there, once upon a time." She called up some files on the padd. "I've put everything you need on here. A history of the place, if you want more. My reports from the time, if you're desperate. But if I were you, I'd focus on the files from Bajoran Intelligence. I know we're going to be busy seeing what's happening with the refugees, but we can't forget why we're really here. I'd like you to know more about the man we're chasing." She lowered her voice. "He's smart, Elnor, and he's dangerous. I don't want you . . ." *Hurt.* "I don't want us going in unprepared."

Elnor bent his head dutifully over the padd. Raffi left him to his reading. She looked down at the land below. It had been summer, all those years ago, when she was on Ordeve, and the hillsides had been bright red with blood poppies. But it was spring now, and everywhere was green. The poppies were not yet in bloom. She had a strange sensation that time had been set into reverse.

Raffi stretched her back and neck and tried to pull herself back to the

SECOND SELF   69

here and now. The man she had been sent to find was dangerous. True, he'd been an ambassador, had played those smooth diplomatic games, but he was trained as an Obsidian Order operative. A skilled interrogator, which meant torturer. If he thought she was a threat, he would not hesitate to kill her. She brought out her own padd, read through his file again. So many gaps and silences; so many lacunae. A life led in shadow. There had been a rumor that the Obsidian Order had a base up there, once upon a time. What did Garak know about the area? About the Caanta valley? What had brought him here? Or was the whole thing a feint? Had he given Bajoran Intelligence the slip? Was he halfway across the quadrant, his face and identity changed, living comfortably in retirement on some paradise planet? Somehow, from his file, Raffi didn't think so. All her instincts told her that this was someone who would play the game until the last throw of the dice.

And that was what she had to go on: a hunch and a trail that was quickly going cold.

"Raffi," said Elnor quietly.

"Yeah, honey?"

"Did something bad happen to you here?"

Startled, she turned to him. "Whatever makes you say that?"

"You're preoccupied. Tense. When you talk about your time here, you only give briefings. Even when you're not giving briefings." He gave her a reproachful look. "You told me to observe. I've been observing."

"Oh, Elnor." *When did you get so wise?* "You're right," she said. "I had a bad time here. Look, you have to understand how brutal the fighting had been, between the Cardassians and the Romulans. I think the Federation only heard half of it. The Romulans were intent on killing every Cardassian at Ghenic. They were prepared to take out anyone who stood in their way, including Starfleet. And they got very close to succeeding."

He did not reply immediately. He went back to studying the map on the padd in his hand, with new attention. "This Tal Shiar officer we're meeting," he said, at last.

"I don't know if he's still Tal Shiar," she said.

"They don't stop being Tal Shiar," said Elnor firmly. "You said the Romulans here intended to massacre everyone. What was *his* part in that?"

"He helped," said Raffi.

"*Helped?*" said Elnor. "Helped who?"

"I imagine he carried out his duty," said Raffi. "But he also helped me. He didn't have to, but he did. I'm still alive as a result. A lot of people are still alive as a result."

"I don't understand," said Elnor unhappily.

"Life is complicated, kiddo. Sometimes, you have to play both sides."

"Why do people do this?" he said. "Why do people make things complicated? It might help me," he went on, "help our mission, I mean, if you were honest with me, Raffi. About your time here."

"Absolute candor, eh?" she said.

"It's usually for the best."

She tapped the padd he was holding. "The files are all there. Take a look at what I wrote back then. You'll get everything you need." Every last, damn heat-hazed minute of it.

He looked at her unhappily for a moment, and then returned to his reading. She closed her eyes. Fell to wondering: Did intelligence officers ever retire? Could they? Sometimes, the secrets and the lies seemed to ripple out forever, endless circles from which it was impossible to escape. Did Elim Garak feel the same way? Did he want to escape the past too? Did he think that was even possible? Old spies never die, she thought; they just get burned, over and over again.

A marked difference, Raffi thought, between the welcome she received from Nuvu Sokara, and the welcome (if you could call it such a thing) that she had received from her former colleagues at Romulan Affairs. Sad to think that those people, whose lives had been so closely interwoven with her own, were now so suspicious and mistrustful. Sokara did not embrace her, but she saw, in the brightness of his eyes, and the sincerity of his greeting, that this was someone who held her in regard. Good to be remembered as somebody competent, somebody worth knowing and worth working with. It felt like those dead years—those barren years—were being swept away. Perhaps Sokara felt the same way. Perhaps, seeing her again, the sadness of those past years of loss and dispossession was momentarily lessened, and he could recall the younger man he had been. Strange to find this same feeling in someone who had been—according to your government—your enemy, and not to find it with your own.

"*Jolan tru*, Raffaela Musiker," he said. "After all these years—to meet here, again, of all places! A different man might think that there was some design at work."

"*Jolan tru*, Nuvu Sokara," she said, with equal warmth. "I'm glad to see you safe and well. I hope that this time I can be the one that helps you, here."

"Well," he said, "let's see what can be done."

The plan was for Raffi and Elnor to see the Romulan settlements in the area. Sokara, as they got into his skimmer, eyed Elnor thoughtfully.

"Qowat Milat," he said.

"Yes," said Elnor, offering no more. He had taken the "shut up and watch" instruction to heart.

"Strange to see a male Qowat Milat," prompted Sokara.

"Yes, it must be," agreed Elnor. *The kid was turning positively laconic,* thought Raffi.

"Not the strangest thing I've seen," said Sokara. "I was Tal Shiar, once upon a time. I hope you won't hold that against me."

"That depends," said Elnor, "on what you do."

Laconic *and* unsettling. This could be a good look for Elnor, going forward.

"I can't say I haven't been warned," said Sokara.

"Shall we go?" said Raffi.

The skimmer set off. There were half a dozen settlements, Sokara explained, between their starting point—the old Romulan encampment—and Ghenic, where the old Cardassian town had been. His home was at Ghenic.

"The Romulans took it at last," remarked Raffi.

"The Cardassians didn't want it any longer," said Sokara. "I don't think any of them returned, you know, after . . ."

After running for their lives from advancing Romulan forces. After hiding themselves and their kids under the trees, in the hope of avoiding detection. After fleeing into unknown dangers rather than stay and face Romulan fire.

"I can understand that," said Raffi, and turned her attention to the present.

Raffi had seen a lot of Romulan refugee camps over the years, many of them desperate places, but the settlements and homes she saw along the Parset River were among the best she had encountered. Small populations; a few hundred here, a thousand there. The land was green and hospitable, and the towns well maintained. Nowhere did she see the hopelessness, the dead-endedness, that she had seen so many times, over and over, in camps where hundreds of thousands had been dumped, with the barest of necessities. Prefab houses and rationed replicators; enough to keep them alive, but nothing to give those lives meaning and purpose. Here, there was open space. Here, the homes were solid, had foundations, and did not look as if they hung on grimly, day by day. Here, the children were playing, not simply sitting and watching fearfully. Here, the adults smiled and could see some future ahead.

"I know how lucky we've been," said Sokara. "But the simple fact is that we need more room. People want to come here—"

"Khrill won't have it," said Raffi.

"But there's room, Raffi. There's room for all of us—"

"You know, the places you're showing us, they're working," said Raffi. "You might want to think carefully about expanding them. You could ruin what you have here—"

"I'm not talking about making these places bigger. I'm talking about new settlements."

Raffi frowned. "My understanding was that this part of the province had been designated yours, but not beyond. Wouldn't that mean expanding into Cardassian territory?" She shook her head. "Khrill is *never* going to accept that—"

"I'm not talking about moving onto Cardassian land. I'm talking about opening up new land."

It took her a minute before she realized what he was saying. "You mean going to the Caanta valley, don't you?"

"Yes," he said.

"Sokara," she said, "there was a ban on travel up there when I was here—"

"That ban is still in place," he said. "I want it revoked. Raffi, there's space up there! Space the Cardassians aren't using—won't ever use!"

"They'll never agree to it."

"But they might, if you asked them."

Raffi shook her head.

"The Caanta valley?" said Elnor. "That's the area beyond the river confluence, isn't it? Where you took cover . . ." He eyed Sokara. "In order to stop the massacre."

"Ah," said Sokara. "Absolute candor is at work here, I see."

"Always," said Elnor.

"Sokara," said Raffi, intervening before the endless battle between Tal Shiar and Qowat Milat could begin, "I have a question for you. Did you know back then about the travel ban?"

"Yes," he said.

"I see," said Raffi. "You know, if I thought that you, or anyone associated with you, was using me—using the refugee crisis—as a cloak for finding out what that ban was all about, I will be pretty annoyed—"

"I'm not offended by that, Raffi. I understand why you say it. There's no ulterior motive here. If the Tal Shiar want to find out what's in the Caanta

74   UNA McCORMACK

valley, they can do that for themselves. All I want is to help my people. And they need that land."

"The Tal Shiar," remarked Elnor, "do not follow the way of absolute candor." He looked at them both. "What? I'm only telling the truth—"

"I'm not lying," said Sokara.

"Khrill won't have it," said Raffi. "Do you realize how hard I had to work to persuade the Cardassians to go that way, back in the day? Some of them wanted to stay and face you rather than go into that valley—"

"I know there are superstitions attached to the area," said Sokara.

"They're not superstitions," said Raffi. "That place is *weird*." Her companions did not reply, and she realized how strange that must have sounded. "It's not a good place," she said. "Your people are better off here. Listen. I know they've lost their homes. I know how appalling these years have been. But what you've got here—what you've built—it's good. It's so much better than it could have been—"

"This is the truth," said Elnor. "I grew up on Vashti. There was nothing there. There was no hope."

"Raffi," said Sokara, "many of the people here are still separated from their loved ones. Parents, spouses, children, brothers and sisters—stuck in camps on other worlds, waiting for permission to come to Ordeve. But the exarch has severely restricted the numbers of Romulans who can come. She says there's no more room. But there *is* room. If we can go beyond the river and settle in the Caanta valley—"

"It's not going to happen," said Raffi. "I'm not convinced it should. We don't know what's out there."

"I know that your time there was . . ." Sokara rubbed his eyes. "I know that we caused terrible distress. I know that what we did—what we tried to do—all those years ago, was unconscionable. Raffi, please. The people here were not part of that. It's not their fault. They need help. They need *your* help."

Aw, hell, thought Raffi. Sokara knew exactly which buttons to press on a Starfleet officer. An appeal to her better nature. An appeal for aid.

"Okay, okay. What do you think I can do?"

The relief on Sokara's face was palpable. "We can go up there. You and I—"

"I'll be there too," said Elnor.

"Of course," said Sokara. "We go up into the valley and prove once and for all that there's nothing there. Just space. Show Khrill there's nothing to be afraid of, that she can lift the ban and let us settle there. That's all, Raffi. That's all I'm asking. Go across the river and look."

It was a bigger ask than perhaps he realized; or perhaps not.

"I'll come," she said reluctantly. "Elnor? Ready?"

"Now?" said Elnor.

"I take it you don't want us to transport there?" said Raffi to Sokara.

"No," he agreed.

"Why not?" said Elnor.

"The Cardassians would track transporter signals," said Raffi. "They'd know what we were doing and where we were going. No, we'll do this the old-fashioned way."

"What's that?" said Elnor.

"We'll walk, Elnor," she said. "We'll walk."

Rios, when she contacted him, was less than enthusiastic. *"How's this helping with the actual mission?"*

"It might. It might not. But I have a hunch—"

"Oh, if you've had a hunch, that's okay."

"This valley. It's a big unanswered question. What's out there. And there were rumors at the time that the Obsidian Order had a base there."

"That's less a hunch than a reasonable supposition," said Rios. *"Okay, let's get some answers. We'll run some scans. See what we can see from up here."*

"Huh," said Raffi, who had a feeling she knew already where that would lead. "Good luck with that."

"Rios out."

A couple of hours later, Cris was back. *"This is—"*

76   UNA McCORMACK

"Weird? Strange? Uncanny?"

"I was going to say odd, but whatever floats your boat, Raff."

"Couldn't find anything, huh?"

"Scans of the area revealed nothing. Which I thought was good—uninhabited area, nothing to fear—until the science team pointed out it meant absolutely nothing. No life signs of wildlife. I asked them to test for radiation levels to see if it had been a test site—again, nothing. Like there's a blanket over the area."

"Sounds familiar."

"And then we got some information from Bajoran Intelligence. They're sure there was a sighting of Garak in the area three weeks ago."

Again, that alarm. Faintly, the sound of a door creaking slowly shut.

"Raffi, are you sure about this?"

"I think it's unavoidable, Cris. Look, it won't be long. There and back in three Ordevian days." Sixty-six hours. Surely that was enough for Sokara. Would pay back her debt.

"Okay. Well, we'll keep trying to get past this blackout. I'll sleep easier knowing we can reach you. How's the kid doing?"

"Surprisingly well," she said.

"More power to him," Rios said. *"I'll be in touch, Raffi. Take care. Stargazer out."*

She slept uneasily that night. Dreams of lost children, separated from their parents, unable to find their way home. In the morning, she and Elnor went to see the ruins.

Elnor, standing at the place where two rivers met, looking at the rubble of a long-gone town, felt lost and sad. He had come on this trip to Ordeve because he knew that was what Admiral Picard wanted. He was going to the Academy because he knew that was what the admiral wanted. Elnor often did what others wanted. He was starting to believe he did so because it meant he did not have to think about what he wanted.

SECOND SELF   77

He looked back over his shoulder. Raffi was walking purposefully through the ruins. She seemed to know exactly what she was looking for. The commander always gave that impression. She stopped, suddenly, looking down at the ground. She knelt and began to clear away some brambles covering the spot.

Elnor dug the toe of his boot into the ground. Rich, black soil. If anyone had asked him—and people rarely did—he thought that the Romulan settlers should be allowed to go into the Caanta valley. This ban—it was ridiculous. Nobody knew for sure what was there. More secrets. Why not find out once and for all? Secrets led nowhere. Find out the truth, and then live with the truth.

"Hello!" a voice called out from behind.

Elnor turned to see a man, a Bajoran, heading his way. But hadn't the Bajorans left Ordeve years ago? Had some of them gotten left behind? The man, reaching Elnor, greeted him in a friendly manner. "Good morning! And what a splendid morning it is."

Elnor considered the spring day unfolding around him; the bright blue sky, the new green leaves, the gentle breeze. "Yes," he said. "It's beautiful."

"Well, don't sound too surprised!" said the man. "Ordeve's a very beautiful world. My name's Toze Falus, by the way."

"I'm Elnor. I'm . . ." Elnor struggled to think of something to say that was permitted. "I'm Romulan," he decided.

"I can see that!" said Toze. "Plenty of Romulans around here. Fewer Bajorans these days, of course."

"I was wondering," said Elnor, completely truthfully.

"Well," said Toze, "I'm an archaeologist."

"Oh," said Elnor. "So not local."

"No—"

"Because you all left."

Toze's face clouded, ever so slightly. "Not a happy history," he agreed. "But here. Have a look at what it was like here, once upon a time." He

78 UNA McCORMACK

reached into his pocket. Elnor's hand tightened on his staff. "You don't have to be afraid of me," said Toze. "Or this," he said, pulling out a small hand-held device. "It's a holo-projector. See? Let me turn it on."

Suddenly, Elnor was transported into the past. The old Bajoran town sprang up around him. Holo-images, so detailed and rich that he could almost be persuaded they were real. Where the blackened stones and rubble now stood, Elnor could see homes. Little low houses, with red-domed roofs and bright mosaics. The gardens around them, green and thriving. The streets . . .

"What is a town," said Toze, "without people?"

Suddenly the streets were full of life. Full of people, living their lives. Bajorans, who had settled here, and who had been forced to leave. Elnor's straightforward heart went out to them. He knew how that felt. He recalled—distantly—the beautiful world of Inxtis, where he had lived as a small boy. He remembered the grief of departure, and the slow sad realization that he could never go home.

"All conjecture, of course," said Toze. "We cannot know for sure. We cannot go back in time and be with them. But we can make good guesses. And . . . there was the temple."

Elnor looked along the street. There, at the far end, rising up before him, the highest building in the town, was the temple of Akantha. The dome was pale yellow and, with the sun behind it, seemed almost to be alight.

"This is incredible!" said Elnor.

"Isn't it?" said Toze. "A truly fine example of extrasolar religious architecture. The temple was a long way from Bajor but seems to have been of considerable significance in its day." He leaned toward Elnor, lowering his voice, as if to tell him a secret. "Speaking confidentially," he said, tapping his fingers to his lips, "I'm hoping to organize a dig here."

"Why confidential?" said Elnor, leaning toward him, all the better to hear.

Toze glanced back over his shoulder. "There's some textual evidence," he said, in a voice that made him sound like he was giving away state secrets,

SECOND SELF 79

"that we reached Ordeve by lightship much earlier than is generally believed. I think that a dig here, and perhaps at some other sites in the area, will help me find tangible proof of this hypothesis.

"But I know that others have been sniffing around Ordeve," he went on. "Deechi Lan at the University of Tamulna, for one." A fire was kindling in his eyes. "I swear," he muttered, "if Deechi Lan gets those permits before I do, I'll *kill*."

"The permits?" said Elnor. This conversation, twisting and turning every which way, was bewildering.

"Oh, the Cardassians are dragging their heels about permission to work in the area. You know what they're like. The *nerve*! It's not like Bajorans weren't living and working in Caanta for generations before they arrived. All I want to do is take a look—"

"We're traveling out to Caanta," said Elnor. "Later today."

"You got permission to go out there?"

"No . . . not really . . ."

Toze's eyes gleamed. "Aha! An illicit journey! Oh, how marvelous! May I come? Do say yes."

Elnor looked at the man in frank terror. Raffi was going to be very mad at him. "I don't know whether . . ." He looked back over his shoulder to where Raffi had stopped her impromptu weeding session, and was now standing again, looking down at the ground. "I mean . . ."

"Ah," said Toze, seeing Raffi. "A superior. Come on. Let's get her permission." He bounded toward Raffi. Elnor hurried behind.

"Hello!" Toze cried cheerfully, coming up on Raffi's right-hand side.

"Er . . . hello?" she said. "Elnor? Who is this?"

Elnor, who had the vaguest sense that they were interrupting something important, said, "I'm sorry to disturb you. This is Toze Falus."

"I'm a professor at the University of Ashalla," said Toze. "An archaeologist."

"Lieutenant Commander Raffi Musiker," said Raffi, "Starfleet. Can I help you, Professor Toze?"

80   UNA McCORMACK

"I understand from your young friend here," he said, leaning in, "that you're intending a trip into the Caanta valley . . ." He made it sound like they were intending to bury a few bodies at midnight.

Raffi gave Elnor a look best described as murderous. Elnor felt himself wither. "Do you indeed," Raffi said.

"Please don't be angry with Elnor," said Toze. "I did catch him unawares. And I understand the, er . . ." He ran the tip of his tongue across his lips. "The *sensitivities* involved in visiting the area. I've had a request for permission with the exarch's office for almost two years now."

"I'm sorry, it's out of the question," said Raffi, turning away. "Elnor, a word."

"Ah," said Toze. "I was afraid you might say that. This puts me in rather a difficult position . . ."

Slowly, Raffi turned to look at him. "Go on," she said, folding her arms.

"What I mean is . . . Oh dear, this is very awkward . . . But . . . My request to the exarch has involved many delicate negotiations. *Supremely* delicate negotiations. Should the exarch's office ever learn that I knew about your intended visit and did nothing to apprise them of the situation, then I'm afraid that my own visit there might be jeopardized and then, well . . ." He held out his hands. "Deechi Lan," he concluded, as if this explained everything.

"Deechi Lan?" said Raffi.

"He's at the University of Tamulna," said Elnor earnestly, in what he hoped would be a helpful contribution to the conversation.

"You," said Raffi. "Hush. I'll talk to *you* later." She turned back to Toze. "A competitor, eh?"

"Academia," said Toze. "Such a *bloodthirsty* profession."

"I'm thinking of heading in that direction myself," she said.

"Do," he replied. "You'll have a ball. So can I come?"

"I can't think of a way to say no," said Raffi.

Toze clapped his hands together. "*Marvelous!*" he said. "And, er—when shall we three meet again?"

"Dusk," said Raffi.

"Oh, dusk, of course!" said Toze. "How thrilling. Until dusk, then, Commander. I shall be here. Depend on it!" And he bounded off, back to wherever he had sprung from.

"What just happened?" said Elnor.

"What happened," said Raffi, "was that *you* didn't keep your mouth shut and *he* just blackmailed us to come along on our *extremely* secret trip across the river." She looked down again at the small slab of stone by her feet. "*Dammit!*" she said. Again, Elnor had the sense that he had interrupted something important. He opened his mouth to apologize, but Raffi was striding away, hitting her combadge as she did.

"*Stargazer*," she said. "Get me everything you can about Toze Falus, professor of archaeology at the University of Ashalla."

Elnor watched her go. Again, he felt that deep frustration at the concealments that went on around him, the purpose of which he could not see, and the mistakes into which this led him. That frustration turned rapidly into a deep well of sadness: that he would never fit into this world—this life—in which he found himself. Was he always going to be out of place? He looked down at the stone that had, until a few minutes ago, been the focus of Raffi's attention. There were a few words, in Cardassian letters, etched on it:

AVARAK OF VULCAN

2354–2376

FOR CARDASSIA

He turned to Raffi, to ask, but she was too far away.

Sokara, confronted with the news that someone was joining them on their journey into the Caanta valley, and hearing the circumstances, said, "This is what happens when you work with the Qowat Milat."

82   UNA McCORMACK

"I'm hoping," said Raffi, "that Toze's presence will come in useful. A cover story for why we decided to go against the ban and travel up there."

"Could work," said Sokara, a little doubtfully for Raffi's taste.

"His file checks out," said Raffi. "And if the Cardassians find out, they might be less likely to kick up a fuss if there's a Bajoran involved."

"Let's hope so," he said.

Toze was there, as promised, that evening, standing on the riverbank, and carrying a surprisingly small bag.

"I thought you'd come with more," said Raffi.

"Oh, you'd be amazed at our equipment these days," said Toze. "This little handheld device—why, Elnor can tell you, it conjures up all kinds of wonderful holos. I think it's best to travel as light as possible. Well," he said, looking at the three of them. "Shall we get started?"

He, Sokara, and Elnor got into the flyer. Raffi tapped her combadge. "Raffi to *Stargazer*," she said. "We're crossing the river. I reckon . . . another twenty minutes before we're in the blackout. Any luck with that?"

"Nothing yet. But we're working on it. Don't hang around, Raffi. Get in there and get out. Rios out."

Raffi cut the comm. "That's the plan," she muttered, and joined the others. They were soon in flight and crossing the river.

"This isn't how you got here, all those years ago, is it?" said Sokara.

"No," said Raffi.

"Took me a while to work out how you did it," he said. "No bridge. That's what gave me the clue, in the end."

Raffi smiled but said no more. She looked ahead, into the dark valley. Then the lights on the flyer's display began to flicker, and many of them went out. "Is there a problem?"

"No," said Sokara. "Not yet."

Raffi nodded. Machines broke down in the Caanta valley. Became unreliable. Didn't do what you told them, or what you wanted. Seemed to have a mind of their own.

"Entering the valley," she murmured. "Entering the blackout."

They sped on, into the night. Raffi took a deep breath, and thought, for a moment, that she could smell the scent of the blood poppies. But the poppies were not yet in bloom.

Cris Rios saw the moment when the flyer dropped off sensors, and a deep sense of foreboding settled on him. A lot could happen in sixty-six hours, and his hope was that his science team would find out what was causing this blackout and reestablish contact with Raffi. He was waiting for an update when a message came through from the exarch's office.

"A Bajoran ship has arrived in local space," explained Tanwar, his XO. "The Cardassians want to know why it's here and what we know about it."

"Have you told them we don't know anything about it?" said Rios.

"We have—but I get the impression they don't believe us."

"Anything to do with Raffi's archaeologist?"

"I doubt it," said Tanwar. "They don't look like academics, sir. They look serious."

Was this Bajoran Intelligence, dropping by to see how things were proceeding? What did they know about this mission? Did they know the real mission? "I think I should speak to Admiral Picard," said Rios. "Maybe he can shed some light on this." *And get them to back down.*

But Picard was none the wiser. *"Let me investigate,"* he said. *"In the meantime, continue trying to establish contact with Commander Musiker."*

"We're on it, sir," said Rios.

"Perhaps it was unwise to let her go into the blackout zone," said Picard.

I thought so. But instead, Rios said, "Raffi can take care of herself."

"She can indeed. I'll be back in touch shortly. Picard out."

Rios turned to his XO. "Tanwar, we should start thinking about arranging backup for Commander Musiker."

"I'd say that's a great idea, sir," replied Tanwar. "Only . . ."

84 UNA McCORMACK

"What is it?" said Rios. Again, that sense of dread, that feeling that something, somewhere, was about to go badly wrong.

"We were scanning the surface. Taking new readings from the blackout zone. And we detected something new. A force field has gone up, along the far side of the river. We can't follow her, sir, we can't get through."

Mierda, thought Rios. "Can we bring it down?"

"We're working on it, sir—but the codes are very old. Cardassian. But not military."

Rios knew what she was going to say next.

"We think they're Obsidian Order."

After about half an hour of increasingly rocky flight, Sokara admitted defeat and landed the flyer. "Not much use getting through the forest," he said, once they were down.

"Can we fix it?" said Elnor. Seeing Raffi and Sokara exchange a look, he said, "What? What is it?"

"This kind of thing used to happen a lot, Elnor," said Raffi. "Unreliable technology."

"I think you're overstating things, Commander," said Sokara.

"I think we should all stop being in denial about this place," said Raffi. "Strange things happen here."

"Absolute candor," said Elnor. "It's the best way. Does this mean we're going back?"

"But we've barely started!" said Toze.

"I'm not sure continuing is a good idea," said Raffi to Sokara. "Not with a civilian with us—"

"Oh, don't worry on my account," said Toze cheerfully. "I'm happiest outside. Digs, you know. I'm very good at camp cooking. Wait till you try my *hasperat*—"

"I think we should go back," said Raffi. "Sokara?"

SECOND SELF   85

"I agree," he said. "But I'm not sure we can." He handed her a padd. "It seems that a force field came up behind us, after we crossed the river."

"What?" She looked at the padd. He was right.

"No way back?" said Toze. "Then, really, what other choice is there? We go on."

"Not tonight," said Raffi. "We'll rest. See what the morning brings."

"Obsidian Order codes?" Picard was unsettled.

"Very old ones," confirmed Rios. "Should we assume our man has activated them?"

"It seems likely," said Picard. *"He was, as far as we know, the only surviving member of the Order."*

"Sir," said Rios, "I wasn't happy that Raffi was under a comms blackout. Raffi under a comms blackout and behind an Obsidian Order force field is beyond acceptable."

"What do you suggest?"

"We might have to bring the Cardassians on the ground into the loop."

"No," said Picard.

"I don't mind causing a diplomatic incident," said Rios.

"Well, I do," said Picard. *"Or, perhaps I should say, let's hold that in reserve. Bajoran Intelligence will have experience with codes like this. Let's see what they can do for us first."*

Sokara offered to take first watch. Toze went straight to sleep, but Raffi lay wakeful. She heard Elnor sigh, and, turning her head, she saw that his eyes were wide open and unblinking. Struggling to sleep, she ran through regulations and lists of dates and all kinds of tedious minutiae, but no use. She stretched and stood.

"I think I'll go for a walk. Clear my head."

86   UNA McCORMACK

Sokara nodded. He didn't need to say "Take care."

Raffi walked off under the trees, her light giving enough illumination so that she did not trip over any fallen branches. After only a little way, the trees thinned out to reveal a small glade. A tree trunk lay fallen on the ground, like a bench set out for a tired traveler. She sat, twisting the flashlight around in her hands. The light caught on the leaves of the nearby trees. Great spot for ghost stories.

There was a clump of blood poppy at the foot of a nearby tree, still in bud, the merest hint of the deep red petals visible. If they came this way in six or seven weeks, they would see the deep-red flowers in bloom. Eventually, the petals would fall away, revealing the treasure within. Raffi's colleagues, back in the day, had called the resultant product "sailors' delight." It had a pleasantly soporific effect on the human metabolism. The Cardassian nickname was "crimson shadow."

She folded her hand around the bud and closed her eyes. Memories of her previous visit to this world were returning thick and fast, and an increasingly all-pervading sense that something, somehow, was about to go horribly wrong. *This was the problem with fucking up your chemistry,* Raffi thought. The bad thoughts sprung up like wildflowers, and you couldn't tell which ones deserved attention and which were weeds, choking the life out of you. The blood poppies were gorgeous in bloom.

"Raffi?"

Raffi, startled, opened her eyes and looked back over her shoulder. She sighed. Elnor had followed her, like an overgrown puppy scrambling eagerly at her heels. *All I wanted was a moment to myself.* But no. As ever, Raffi was there to work on other people's problems.

"What's the matter, Elnor?"

"Nothing's the matter," he said. "I was worried about you. I wanted to make sure that you were okay."

Poor kid, Raffi thought. She had done him yet another injustice.

"May I sit with you?" said Elnor. "I can go back, if you want to be alone."

Raffi patted the bark at her side. "Make yourself comfortable," she said. "Though, I'm not in the mood for talking."

"That's fine," he said. "We can sit and watch the leaves. They're beautiful."

He was right; they were.

"Thank you for coming to find me, Elnor," Raffi said, after a while.

"You're welcome," he said. "I wanted to apologize for my misstep with Toze."

She shrugged, saying, "Let's hope that by the time we meet our man, Toze has had enough of sleeping outdoors and headed back to civilization."

"I hope so," he said. "Can I ask you something?"

"Go on."

"In the ruins, earlier. You were looking at a grave."

"Ah," she said. "You noticed that."

"You did tell me to observe."

"Yes, I did," she said. "I hope I don't come to regret that." He was looking down at the ground, unhappily, so she took pity on him. "His name was Avarak. He was my aide, when I was here before. He was killed."

"By the Romulans?"

"By the Cardassians, actually, so don't take that one onto yourself. Oh *hell*," she said, the words bursting out from her suddenly, "what a damn mess it all was! He was barely out of the Academy!" She had crushed the bud in her hand, it was staining her palm. "There's too much damn history in this place. I wish I'd never . . ."

"Was it very bad?"

"Oh, Elnor," she said. "It wasn't the worst thing that has ever happened to me." That was losing Gabe, over and over, with nobody to blame except herself. "But it wasn't good. There was an inquiry afterward. I wasn't reprimanded." Her reputation had preceded her for some time after, mind you, but Raffi's reputation was not Elnor's problem. That was her own problem, one that had been years in the making.

88   UNA McCORMACK

"Are you having bad dreams?" said Elnor suddenly.

"What?" Surprised, she turned to look at him.

"Bad dreams. Are you having them?"

The warning bells in Raffi's head now were very loud, like when a ship goes to red alert. She breathed deeply. The night was in fact very quiet and still. Elnor was unmoving, staring ahead, at nothing. Raffi reached out to rest her hand upon his. He did not react to this overture; neither to reject, nor to accept it.

"Elnor," she said gently. "How did you . . . Are *you*—"

Whatever answer he might have given her was delayed. There was a sharp crack, of a small branch or twig being broken underfoot, so loud as to surely be intentional. They both leaped to their feet, Raffi reaching for her phaser, Elnor for his staff.

A figure came out from the cover of the trees. A Bajoran man, elderly, in shabby clothes, and wearing a long earring. Raffi relaxed her grip slightly. Surely not a threat. More likely to be lost and looking for help. Elnor too was lowering his staff.

"I'm Lieutenant Commander Raffi Musiker," she said. "I'm Starfleet. We didn't think there was anyone this far out. Are you lost? Are you in need of any assistance?"

The man moved out of the darkness, surprisingly swift for his age. And perhaps it was this movement—its easy fluidity—or perhaps it was the more-than-slight flamboyance with which he brought out his own weapon—a snub-nosed disruptor—that gave him away. Most likely, it was his eyes, bright blue, and mocking. Raffi had met them once before, a long time ago, on Earth—fleetingly, but piercingly. Whatever the tell, she knew the danger at once.

"Don't move," she muttered to Elnor. "Don't move a muscle."

"I must apologize for this intrusion, Commander," the man said, "but I'm afraid I really can't allow you to go any farther."

"Ambassador Garak," said Raffi. "You're not at all how I remember you."

There was a pause, during which, Raffi presumed, a lie was formed and dismissed. The disruptor remained unwaveringly in place. The old Bajoran smiled.

"It's Garak," he said. "Plain, simple Garak."

PART 2

2376

AFTER
THE DOMINION WAR

5

During the very last days of the Dominion War, Lieutenant Raffaela Musiker—who had hitherto spent the war behind her desk at Romulan Affairs—accepted a coveted posting on the planet Ordeve, where the Romulan advance into Cardassian territory was proceeding apace, and where the handful of Starfleet personnel were becoming increasingly concerned about what might happen once the war was over.

Raffi's decision to take this posting was a no-brainer. The work that she had been doing was good—important—but, like many whose particular skills had kept them deskbound throughout the war—she felt guilt at having been out of harm's way. Guilt, and a little frustration. Still, she knew some people had misgivings. Her new boyfriend for one—a handsome young artist named Jae, whom she had been seeing for the last couple of months—could not understand why, just when their relationship seemed to be getting serious, Raffi would choose to leave for the front. (He would ask versions of this question many times over the years to come.) Raffi's colleagues at Romulan Affairs—her friends, whom she had known since the Academy—were taking this temporary abandonment in good spirits, although there was some envy that she was the one going. Raffi suspected that at least one of them had applied too, although none of them had said so.

"You'll be back," said James Northey.

"Won't be as much fun there," said Kebil Zi.

"We'll miss you," said Vazreen Pella.

94   UNA McCORMACK

"You three." Raffi was sorting through the files and messages on her computer. She was hoping to hear from Jae, but he had a major show next week. Raffi was missing the opening; another reason to feel guilty. "You're like the Furies."

"What are they?" said Pella.

"Ancient goddesses of vengeance," said Northey.

"Nice," said Kebil, with a shudder.

"Also known as the kindly ones," Northey added.

"Humans," said Pella, "have a strange sense of humor."

"Yeah, well, this whole war has been a riot, hasn't it?" said Raffi. She was about to sign off from her computer for the last time when a message arrived. Not from Jae: it had an official Romulan heading. She was about to pass the problem on to one of these three reprobates, when she saw the sender. Subcommander Nuvu Sokara, a liaison officer at the Romulan embassy, had been surprisingly amicable since the Romulan Star Empire joined the war against the Dominion, particularly since he was surely Tal Shiar. Sokara was sending his thanks for some recent information she had relayed from Bajoran Intelligence and wishing her the best with her forthcoming posting. He noted that he would shortly be leaving Earth for what he called his "next adventure." Raffi fired off a response, noting that she still owed him a drink. *I won't forget,* he shot back. *Good luck, Lieutenant, until we meet again.*

Her work here was done. She snapped off the computer and let the team take her to a local bar for a long and very cheerful farewell. Jae turned up, forgiving her absence, making their goodbye very sweet. Raffi set off to her new post, only slightly worse for wear. In lunar orbit, at Sharman Station, she sat in one of the observation lounges, sipping a strong coffee to help with the hangover and plowing through the latest reports from Ordeve. A Vulcan ensign approached her.

"Lieutenant Musiker?"

"That's me. Who's asking?"

The young man gave a formal bow. He was tall, achingly young, and im-

SECOND SELF 95

maculately presented, not a hair out of place. Raffi felt almost embarrassed at her own slightly slipshod appearance. She tugged her jacket straight.

"I am Ensign Avarak," he said. "I have been assigned as your aide for our forthcoming mission." He observed her coffee cup and the stack of padds. "Am I disturbing you?"

"What? Oh, no, kiddo, no! Glad to meet you. Pull up a seat."

Avarak looked around, noted that the chairs were all fastened to the floor, and took the one opposite her.

"Have you heard the latest?" said Raffi.

"The latest?"

"From the war?"

"Like us all, I have been monitoring the situation closely for months," said Avarak.

Raffi smiled. Other people, she knew, found this kind of precision irritating, but (and maybe this was her imagination) Raffi always got the feeling that Vulcans were teasing humans. "The Cardassian leader, Damar, has gone AWOL with a bunch of ships," she said. "Sounds like the Cardassian military are about to rebel against the Dominion."

One arched eyebrow lifted. "That would certainly have a significant impact on the course of the war," Avarak said. "Will this affect our mission in any way?"

"Well, I hope the Cardassians are starting to grasp that siding with the Dominion to wage war on the entire Alpha Quadrant hasn't exactly endeared them to the rest of us," said Raffi. "But I doubt that switching sides this late is going to win them friends among the Romulans."

Avarak, who was nodding, plainly needed no explanation, Raffi was pleased to see. The Romulan-Cardassian front had been brutal, pitiless. This was one of the reasons they were being sent out to Ordeve. As the Romulans took control of the planet, their Starfleet colleagues on the ground were becoming increasingly concerned about what this might mean for the Cardassian civilians there. Raffi was being sent to talk the Romulans down—

or indicate that Starfleet was keeping a close watch on the proceedings. They sat for a while discussing their mission. Raffi began to talk about how she thought the war was going to end, but Avarak clearly did not see the purpose of such speculation. At last, they got their summons. The *U.S.S. Gráinne* was ready for them to board.

Raffi watched the endgame of the Dominion War on the *Gráinne*, en route to Ordeve, sitting in the mess with a dozen or so of the crew. She saw the speech that Damar gave, telling the people of Cardassia to resist, and was surprised to find a tear come to her eye. Dammit, he sounded like Spartacus. Seemed to go the same way too, too quickly—the next news was that the Dominion had wiped out all his ships, and Damar had been killed. But then there were sightings of him—all around Prime, all around the Union. And then—could you believe this? The Cardassian people started to rise up. Who had predicted that? No one at Romulan Affairs, although her friends back there were reporting that their colleagues at the Cardassian desk were looking very smug these days. Perhaps Starfleet had a hand in getting the rebellion going, but no one was talking.

What happened next nobody predicted, although perhaps, in retrospect and knowing their enemy, they should have. The Dominion, responding to the attacks on their bases, destroyed a major Cardassian city. Bombed it from the air. Two million people, gone in a matter of seconds. The Cardassian people kept on fighting, and the Dominion responded, in force. Raffi, sitting in the mess of the *Gráinne*, watched the reports coming through. She would remember for the rest of her life the moment when one of the lieutenants said, "What are the Dominion trying to do?" Avarak offered, "The logical deduction is that they have decided to exterminate the Cardassian people."

Her blood ran cold. He was right, wasn't he? The Jem'Hadar, stationed in every single part of the Union, had decided that the Cardassians were now surplus to their requirements.

"Jeez," she breathed. "This is *appalling* . . ."

"Or karma," said one of the lieutenants. "Payback for the Occupation."

That, Raffi was glad to see, earned significant pushback. The lieutenant kept his opinions to himself after that. But they all stayed glued to the Federation News Service and watched the catastrophe unfold. After a couple of hours, it became clear that the scale of the devastation was almost too much to comprehend. Whole cities were being turned to dust. Millions upon millions dying. Most of those present gave up. Some went on duty. Some went to bed. But a few dedicated, hardcore news junkies remained sitting in the mess, watching as the fire raged through the Cardassian Union. None of them had ever seen anything like this and hoped they never would again. It was some years before the Romulan star went supernova.

Occasionally someone spoke. "This is from Cardassia IV." Or, "Look, the university in Culat is on fire." Or, "How is anyone going to survive this?" Or, "Does anyone want some more coffee?"

Raffi accepted the offer of coffee but otherwise remained quiet, watching the Dominion War end. Watching the real-time collapse of the once-great Cardassian empire. Many of her friends from the Academy had been serving on the front lines for the last year or so. Sometimes they sent her messages telling her that she was well out of it. Raffi knew that she should not wish herself into combat, but a small part of her felt that she had been cheated of a once-in-a-lifetime opportunity to prove herself.

"Holy shit," said a young ensign to her left as a huge and elegant building exploded on the screen in front of them. "Do you know what that place is?"

"No," muttered a couple of people.

"That's the Detapa Council building!"

There was a silence, during which it became abundantly clear that not everyone understood the significance of this.

"The equivalent," explained Avarak, "would be the destruction of the Federation Council tower."

There was another short pause, and then: "Holy shit . . ." someone agreed, in something close to appropriate awe.

Raffi rubbed her eyes. There were studies that proved that watching continuous footage of unfolding news was bad for you. Those constant endorphin hits and then the immediate crash, and the hunger for the next hit. Wasn't healthy, sitting here watching this apocalypse when there was nothing she could do, but, like the rest of them, she couldn't tear herself away. More coffee came. More news came. More and more Cardassians died. Raffi watched on, like an addict chasing the next fix. But she was asleep when the war ended, slumped in her chair, waking only because the young ensign was shaking her.

"Hey, wake up. They've surrendered."

"What?"

"The Dominion. They've surrendered. The war's over."

Raffi sat up straight and stared at the screen. Everyone still in the mess looked at one another, uncertain as to what this meant or whether a celebration was appropriate, given the smoking ruins and the soaring death rate. Somebody gave a nervous cough.

"Hurray, I guess," said the young ensign. A shipwide message came through from the captain, announcing the news, and instructing the senior staff to the observation lounge.

"On to the next war," said the ensign. She stood and stretched. Her joints cracked, and she went on her way out of the mess. Altogether, Raffi thought, it was something of an anticlimax. Nothing had changed, and nothing ever could or would. But as she went to wash her face and make herself presentable for the meeting, she made herself a promise: no Cardassian still left alive on Ordeve was going to die on her watch. It was no small undertaking; if she had known a little more about the situation on the ground, Raffi might have hesitated in making such a promise. Perhaps, if she had, at this point in her life, known more about the Qowat Milat, she might have held back. Promises are prisons, after all, and the breaking of a promise can poison. She would often think about this, later in life, when she was forced out of Starfleet, with very few friends who would accept her call. She would often wonder where and when and how everything started to go wrong.

Nineteen hours later, the *Gráinne* arrived at Ordeve. Raffi had gotten some sleep, and, with Avarak at her side taking careful notes, spoken at length with her colleagues back at Starfleet Intelligence. Their chief topic was the ongoing state of the delicate Romulan-Federation alliance, whether it would survive the war, and how to avoid giving the Romulans excuses to escalate hostilities and end the alliance. Ordeve—which seemed very remote and unimportant—could provide exactly the kind of flashpoint that would give the Romulans that excuse. And the political status of the planet was confused. The Romulans had more or less taken Ordeve in the last few weeks, but the Cardassians had switched sides and joined the battle against the Dominion, which meant they had a continuing claim. But were there any Cardassians, either on Ordeve or Prime, to take charge? Was there a government right now on Cardassia Prime? Damar had died in the final battle to get through to the Founder's bunker. Was there anyone left alive from his rebellion to take up the mantle of leadership?

As a result of all this confusion, transporting down to Ordeve took longer than anticipated. The Romulans, for whatever reason, decided to change their minds about their previous agreement to let further Starfleet observers visit the surface. Several hours of fraught negotiations followed. Pleas were made. Threats were issued. Concessions were offered.

"Might as well chuck dice," said Raffi. "The problem is that this mostly has nothing to do with us. There'll be a minor official somewhere—probably not even on Ordeve—trying to get some advantage or save face, and we're the hill they've chosen to die on. Something will shift. Or it won't. In which case we can all go home."

100   UNA McCORMACK

Her prediction proved true, as suddenly the ban on their going down was lifted, and Raffi and Avarak found themselves scrambling to the *Gráinne*'s transporter to head to the surface while they had the okay.

Raffi's first impression of Ordeve was of summer heat and the faint smell of rotting, overlaid with the sharp tang of skimmers overhead and the odor of alien bodies. The spaceport, which stood close to the capital, Merna, was Cardassian built: that odd combination of graceful architectural curves and steely functionality. However, there were no Cardassians to be seen, only armed Romulans, checking every ship coming in and out. Raffi, looking around for Starfleet uniforms, finally saw a grubby-looking lieutenant commander hurrying toward them. She was Lafleur, an engineering officer who was part of the small Starfleet team here.

"Welcome to Ordeve," said Lafleur. "We're very glad to have you here." She looked them over. "Just the two of you?"

"Were you expecting more?" said Raffi. "We're only here to observe."

"Huh," said Lafleur, leading them away. "How long is the *Gráinne* hanging around?"

The *Gráinne* was due to leave orbit the next morning. "What's been happening?" Raffi asked quietly.

Lafleur briefed her quickly, and without affect. "It's been brutal. The people here in the capital were holed up in the spaceport when the Cardassians switched sides. There was . . ." She sucked in a deep breath. "As far as we can make out, there was a massacre. Jem'Hadar killing Cardassian troops. Our orders were not to intervene. And the Romulans certainly weren't going to help. Left them to finish off each other. After a while, everything went quiet. Then we got the news that the Dominion had surrendered. About an hour after that, the Vorta came out, with the remaining Jem'Hadar." Lafleur shook her head. "That Vorta is lucky not to have been killed on the spot. Smirking at the Tal Shiar."

Yeah, thought Raffi; lucky to be alive. "Where's the Vorta now?"

SECOND SELF 101

Lafleur pointed toward the far side of the port. "She and the Jem'Hadar are under lock and key in one of the hangars over there. I'll be honest—if the *Gráinne* doesn't take them, I'm not sure they'll survive this."

"It's one of the terms of the surrender," said Raffi. "What about the Cardassians?"

"What about them?" said Lafleur.

"Are there any left?"

Lafleur sighed. "A few. The ones here at the spaceport are currently under Starfleet protection and awaiting evacuation. I don't know where they're planning to go . . ."

"Prime's certainly not fit to receive them," said Raffi. "But perhaps they'd rather be home." Or what was left of it. "Tell me more about where we're heading. Ghenic, right?"

"A former Cardassian base. Upcountry. The Jem'Hadar haven't been out there, and it's remained under direct Cardassian control. The Romulans were closing in when the Cardassians switched sides, and when the surrender came, they stopped their advance. We've got a handful of our people out there, but it's only a matter of time before the Romulans move in. If there was a significant Starfleet presence, we might be able to stop them. We asked for backup." She eyed Raffi and Avarak. "I'm guessing you're it."

Raffi gave a wry smile. "Afraid so. What you see is what you get." She nodded toward Avarak. "He's great, mind you. Are we heading out to Ghenic now?"

"Yes," said Lafleur. "By flyer. The transporters have been fritzing. Better not risk it."

"Indeed," said Avarak.

"Everything's been fritzing," said Lafleur as they headed toward the flyer. "Transporter, long-range comms, replicators. Whatever the Romulans are doing, it's working too well."

102   UNA McCORMACK

They had just reached their flyer when Raffi saw him: a familiar Romulan face in the crush.

"Sokara?"

The Romulan turned. Raffi saw the surprise on his face, quickly masked by a wry smile. He collected himself and walked over to her.

"Lieutenant Musiker," he said. "I didn't know this was where you were being sent."

"Same back atcha," said Raffi.

They stood for a moment, each conscious of the rapidly altering situation. Allies only a few days ago, holding each other in professional respect. Now, neither was quite sure what they should be to each other, how exactly they should act toward each other.

Sokara made the first move. "I'd offer to buy you that drink," he said. "But I've an onward journey."

"Me too," said Raffi.

"I'd imagine so," said Sokara. His upper lip curled into a half smile. They were surely heading in the same direction—out to Ghenic, where the action was. Her suspicions were more or less confirmed when he said, "Perhaps I'll get the chance to make good on my promise sooner than we might think."

"I hope so," said Raffi, and watched him go. He'd been an honest broker throughout the war. She hated that she might have to start thinking of him as her enemy.

"Who was that?" said Lafleur.

"Tal Shiar," said Raffi.

Lafleur gave her a narrow look. "Brotherhood of spooks, eh?"

"Something like that," said Raffi, and got into the seat next to Lafleur. Avarak sat in the back. The flyer lifted, and, for a moment, Raffi was able to see the whole spaceport from above; the blackened ground, the people scurrying around like insects, the scars and the damage from years of struggle. Then they were on their way, out into green and open countryside, leaving the machinery of war behind them, the whole business like a dream from which they were awakening—or perhaps a mass delusion.

Ghenic was a four-hour flight from the spaceport. It stood near the confluence of two rivers: one that cut a broad swath back down to the coast, and the other that started in the mountains beyond Ghenic and ran through a deep-cut and mist-shrouded valley before meeting the bigger river. They made their descent through the mist of an early summer morning. Raffi looked out to see hazy mountains; along the riverbank, heaps of big stones looked as if they had been thrown down from the mountains by giants.

"Is that the old Bajoran town?" she said.

"Yes," said Lafleur. "The Cardassians built their base a couple of kilometers away and the place fell into disrepair. Standard operating procedure for the Cardassians in many places. Move in, starve the nearby settlements of resources. Eventually the local Bajoran population would be forced to move away. The Cardassians would claim that the Bajorans had left by choice, that they were moving into land that was no longer wanted."

"I thought the Occupation was more brutal than that," said Raffi.

"Yes," agreed Lafleur. "It was." She glanced down at the old stones below. "That town was called Akantha. There was a Bajoran settlement there for hundreds of years. All gone, by the time the Occupation ended."

"So Ordeve became Cardassian by default," said Avarak. "And now the Romulans are claiming it by right of conquest."

"I'm not going to pretend to be an expert on the extraplanetary claims," said Lafleur. "All I can say is that there are almost a hundred terrified Cardassians currently living at Ghenic, a company of Romulans stationed four kilometers away, and a handful of Starfleet officers are all that stands between them."

"I'm amazed we're being allowed to fly into Ghenic," said Raffi.

"So am I," said Lafleur. "For the moment, our Romulan allies are still

104   UNA McCORMACK

allowing Starfleet traffic in and out of the area, but we're not sure how long that will last."

Great, thought Raffi. *We're arriving just in time for a siege.* She looked upriver. "What's on the other riverbank?"

"Don't know," said Lafleur. "Never been that way."

Raffi got a good look at the compound from the air. A handful of Cardassian military block buildings, and a single Federation-style building, hastily replicated and thrown up. There were two long blocks that Lafleur said had been given over to the civilians from the engineering project when they arrived at Ghenic.

"But there's not enough room," she said. "A hundred civilians, in a space that should house forty at the most. At least it's summer. Half of them have been sleeping outside. We've been replicating tents for them."

The flyer landed in the main square of the compound. Raffi—stepping out—got her first glimpse of a sight that would become all too familiar later in her career. The misery and hopelessness of a refugee camp. The arrival of their flyer did little to stir the torpor of the adults sitting there, although a few of the children came running forward. Avarak dug into his pockets and began, gravely, handing out small gifts. Vulcan sweets.

"Kids . . ." muttered Raffi. "Damn. I wasn't expecting kids . . ."

"The Cardassian commander here, Gul Assott, brought everyone over from the engineering project six weeks ago," Lafleur said. "These people had been there awhile. Brought their families with them. They've survived the Jem'Hadar, but . . ."

Imagine surviving the past few years, even making it through the Jem'Hadar massacre, only for the Tal Shiar to gun you down. "This is a hot mess, isn't it?"

"It's a nightmare," said Lafleur. "Look, let me take you to meet Com-

SECOND SELF **105**

mander Byrne. She's the ranking Starfleet officer here. She'll fill you in on the details."

The three of them walked through the compound, the children chasing after them, until it became clear that Avarak's pockets were now empty.

"Good thinking," said Raffi quietly, filing that one away. She would use that tactic again and again, years from now, with Romulan kids, and think of Avarak every time. JL would remark on it, one time, saying that he was impressed.

"We are here to help these people," said Avarak. "Consoling their children assists in promoting a general air of well-being. Adults rest better when their children are calm, and children are calmer when their adults are rested. It is all quite logical."

"You keep on using that kind of logic," said Raffi, "and we might get through this."

The heat was rising. As they walked through the compound toward the Federation building, Raffi was conscious of how few people were moving about—military mostly—while the civilians sat and watched the new arrivals with anxious eyes. Just sitting there, waiting—for what? For the world to end? The world had already ended. Cardassia was burning. For the Romulans to make their move? Would it feel like mercy? Raffi shook herself. That was morbid. That wasn't going to help. Avarak said, in a quiet voice, "With your permission, Lieutenant, I would like to explore the compound and, perhaps, make the acquaintance of some of the residents here."

Raffi sent him on his way. They would fill each other in later. She followed Lafleur past a blocky building in front of which two flags were standing limp in the heat. One showed the banner of the Ninth Division of the Fifth Order. The other was the black-and-gold flag of the Cardassian Liberation Front. As they passed the door to this building, Lafleur hesitated, and sighed, and said, "For what it's worth, I suppose you'd better meet Tradall."

They went into the building. An air scrubber was working away with a

106   UNA McCORMACK

high-pitched whine. There was nobody here. Lafleur tapped on the second door along and, after a moment, the door slid open. There were two Cardassians in the room: a young man sitting behind a desk who looked up with glassy eyes and, standing behind him, a much older man, a noncom garresh.

"More Starfleet," he said. "But not enough, I bet."

"There's me," said Raffi. "I'm extraordinary—but wait till you meet my aide."

"There's *two* of you?" The garresh began to laugh. He turned to the young man. "See what I mean? Starfleet. They make promises that they never keep—"

"This is Lieutenant Raffaela Musiker," said Lafleur to the young man. "Raffi—this is Glinn Tradall. He's in command at Ghenic."

Tradall stood up, sending the padds on his desk flying. When he reached across to press palms with Raffi, she saw that his hands were shaking. "Are there really only two of you?"

"I'm afraid so," said Raffi. "But I have experience dealing with Romulans."

"Your allies," said the noncom.

"That's right," said Raffi. "There's a new Romulan officer. I've worked with him extensively over the last few months. I take that as a hopeful sign."

"I'll take anything," said Tradall. He sat down again, heavily. "Have you spoken to Byrne yet?"

"She's next," said Lafleur.

"Thank you for stopping by here first," said Tradall. "That was courteous."

"Oh yes," said the garresh. "Plenty of courtesy. Just nothing in the way of actual aid."

"There's a lot going on out there," said Raffi. "A lot of people trying to help on Cardassia Prime. We're here."

"If you're expecting gratitude, Starfleet," said the garresh, "you won't get it from me."

They left. "Jeez," muttered Raffi. "That poor glinn . . ."

"He's no Gul Assott, that's for sure," said Lafleur.

SECOND SELF 107

"That noncom looked like the real power behind the throne," said Raffi.

"Zhol," said Lafleur. "He can't decide who he hates more—the Romulans or Starfleet."

"We're not the ones trying to kill him," said Raffi.

"Not right now, no," said Lafleur, and, seeing Raffi's puzzled look, said, "Zhol is a veteran of the Federation-Cardassian wars."

Raffi pushed out a breath. The long, tangled, bitter history of these quadrants. How were they ever expected to make peace? How were all these years of combat and mutual recrimination and dislike ever going to be put aside?

"All we have to do here," said Lafleur, as if following the track of Raffi's thoughts, "is remain neutral. Those are our orders."

Neutrality, thought Raffi, *is not always possible.*

Lafleur took her off to the Federation building, to meet Commander Byrne. Her office was dark. When Raffi walked in, Byrne looked past her into the corridor. "They've sent *one* of you?" she said in horror.

"Two," said Raffi, holding up two fingers. V for Victory. "But I sent him for a breath of air."

"Two of you," said Byrne. "How long is the *Gráinne* intending to stay?"

"I think the intention was to drop us off and pick up the Vorta," Raffi began. "This system is under Romulan jurisdiction—"

"If they could find an excuse to remain for a couple of weeks, it might make all the difference." Byrne gestured to Raffi to sit down. "Are you up to speed on the situation here?"

"I've got the general idea," said Raffi, taking a seat. "About a hundred Cardassian civilians, eighteen Cardassian military, four Starfleet—six now— and a company of Romulans waiting to move in when we leave to finish the job the Jem'Hadar started. But we're not leaving, are we?"

Byrne rubbed tired eyes. "I don't know. For the moment, my orders are to wait and see."

"Those are not particularly helpful orders," said Raffi.

108   UNA McCORMACK

"You're telling me," Byrne muttered. Reaching for the computer on her desk, she brought up a holo-map of the area. Raffi, who was becoming increasingly familiar with the main landmarks, picked out the big river Parset, the confluence with the other river, a red mark where the Bajoran town had been, and Ghenic, a little distant from the river.

"If the Romulans arrive—" Raffi said.

"*When* the Romulans arrive," said Lafleur.

"Yeah, exactly . . . *When* the Romulans arrive," said Raffi, "are we supposed to stand by and let them take the Cardassians away?"

Byrne and Lafleur looked at each other. "Your guess is as good as mine," Byrne said. "But Starfleet Command has been very clear. In the ongoing dispute between the Romulans and the Cardassians over possession of Ordeve, the Federation must remain neutral."

"There is an alliance at stake," said Lafleur, her voice now so dry that Raffi could almost feel her eyeballs shriveling.

"That alliance," said Raffi, "isn't worth anything now that the war's over."

"Is that the official position of Starfleet Intelligence?" asked Byrne.

"That's the official position of Lieutenant Raffaela Musiker, who—when it comes to Romulans—is generally the best-informed person in the room," said Raffi. "Anyone at Starfleet Command or the Federation Council who believes that the Romulans will continue to honor that agreement now that the Dominion is beaten is deluding themselves. Anyone believing that is almost certainly not on the front line. So," she went on, examining the map of the area that Byrne had brought up, "say we decide to evacuate. Where would we go?" She peered at the map. "What's the name of that other river?"

"That's the Caanta," said Lafleur. "It comes down from the mountains. The high ones that we saw in the distance."

"Uh-huh? And what's in the valley up there?"

"I don't know," said Lafleur. "I've never been across the river."

"It's pretty remote," said Byrne. "The Cardassians don't go there."

"Could we hide there?" said Raffi. "Until we got support?"

"We could try," said Byrne. Lafleur shrugged.

Raffi frowned. The fatalism in this room was depressing. These people had been here a long time. Perhaps they'd gotten locked into a certain way of thinking. They were no longer able to see a way through. But Raffi was damned if a massacre was going to happen on her watch.

"On the assumption that hypothetical support might at some point arrive," said Byrne bitterly, "we might be able at least to hide safely for a while."

"Big assumption," said Lafleur.

"Perhaps," said Raffi. "I'm just making Plan B."

"This isn't Plan A?" said Byrne.

"No," said Raffi. "Plan A is meeting the Romulans in the area."

"You want to meet the *Romulans*?" said Byrne.

"Yes," said Raffi. "I want to talk to them. You know—ally to ally. Pal to pal."

"Do you think I haven't tried that already?" Byrne said. Her irritation was beginning to show. "I've had call after call with their commanding officer about evacuating at least the civilians to Merna—"

"I think there's been some personnel changes over there," said Raffi. "So, first of all, I'd like to have a meeting with the Romulans. I'd like to say 'hi.' At the very least it'll let them know that Starfleet Intelligence is watching this place closely."

Byrne shrugged. "All right. I'll ask for the meeting. We *are* still allies."

"And once you've carried out Plan A?" asked Lafleur. "Do we then move to Plan B?"

"We do not wait for Plan A to succeed," said Raffi. "We start to prepare Plan B. I want to know how we get everyone currently living here at Ghenic away from this place, how quickly, and where we can take them."

The two other women looked at each other. Lafleur was shaking her head. "Damn," said Byrne, sighing deeply. "I wish Assott had made it. You know, Lieutenant, he was on his way to the Romulan base when they got him. He wanted to negotiate with them too."

"There's a difference," said Raffi, "between assassinating a Cardassian gul and assassinating a Starfleet officer. The Romulans may be duplicitous, but they aren't stupid. They're not going to give Starfleet the pretext to send a couple of starships over here to join the *Gráinne*. We'll be fine."

She spoke with perhaps more confidence than she felt. But they wouldn't, would they? They wouldn't be so reckless, surely?

Byrne waved her hand and the holo-map disappeared. The tint in the windows behind her desk began to dissolve until at last Raffi was able to look through the transparent aluminum. The haze of the early morning had lifted, and the vast mountains in the Caanta valley were at last visible. They were bright red.

Raffi stared. "What the *hell* has happened out there?"

Byrne looked back over her shoulder. "Ah," she said. "The blood poppies."

Raffi blinked. Everything became clear. There had not been some terrible massacre. The sides of the mountains were covered in bright red flowers.

"Beautiful, aren't they?" said Byrne.

"They're certainly striking," said Raffi.

"Wait till you see the side effects," said Lafleur.

6

"The Cardassians here call it crimson shadow," said Avarak later, sitting across from Raffi in the small office that had been assigned to her. "It is produced from the sap of *Papaver ordeviensis*, which you may observe flowering in abundance throughout this entire region. The substance may be injected by means of a hypospray. It may also be smoked, although my understanding is that the effects are reduced that way."

"And what are the effects?" said Raffi.

"I have not myself tried—"

"The Cardassians," said Raffi, "what do they want from it?"

"Want from it?"

"People don't put this stuff into themselves without a good reason. What does it do?"

"I see," said Avarak. "I believe that relief is the first immediate effect, followed quickly by a growing sense of detachment from one's immediate environment, both of which contribute to an overall sense of well-being."

"Well, that makes sense," said Raffi. "Who wouldn't want to detach themself from the destruction of their civilization. What's the payback?"

Avarak looked puzzled.

"There's always a price," said Raffi. "It's never all sunshine and smiles."

"From what I have learned from the medical files," said Avarak, "continued use can lead to anxiety, depression, and, in some cases, delusions."

"Hallucinations?" said Raffi.

UNA McCORMACK

"Not that I have seen reported," said Avarak. "But one might consider such a distinct possibility."

"Great," said Raffi.

"The use of crimson shadow is extensive throughout the adult population here," said Avarak. "Particularly among the military—the junior officers and the younger foot soldiers."

"And their commander," said Raffi.

"Ah," said Avarak.

"What about the civilians?" said Raffi.

"There is less use than among the military," he said, "but my understanding is that consumption has risen steadily in the past few weeks. I must admit that I do not understand the logic behind such behavior," he said thoughtfully. He had an interesting way of speaking, Raffi thought. Often with Vulcans, you got the feeling that they considered the more irrational behavior of other species to be tiresome and childish. But with Avarak, his confusion seemed to lead to a kind of humility, that while he would not choose such behavior, there were clearly reasons why others might, which was his part to comprehend. The gap in understanding was his responsibility to overcome. "To seek relief in a substance that is known to leave one in a depressed state. This puzzles me."

"People need solace, Avarak," said Raffi. "They need relief. Sometimes the horrors in your head are too much. Their *world* is ending . . ."

"The Vulcan insistence upon logic was a response to such cataclysmic events," Avarak said. "Our rituals and meditative practices arose in direct response to the terrors of our violent past and offer a similar release. But I would suggest that such practices lead to more positive outcomes—both personal and cultural—than the ingestion of substances such as these." He held his hands together, palm to palm, pressing the tips of his fingers against his lips. "I do not believe that this opinion arises from a sense of cultural superiority on my part. Nevertheless, I must consider this further."

"You said almost all the Cardassian adults here are using the stuff," said Raffi. "What about our people?"

"I beg your pardon, Lieutenant?"

"Who among the Starfleet personnel here is using the stuff? Byrne? Lafleur?"

Avarak lifted one of those perfect eyebrows. "That would be a direct violation—"

"Yeah, yeah, I know the regs. We have four people stuck here with an impossible mission and no meaningful support. How many of them?"

"I . . . do not have that information," said Avarak.

"Care to guess?"

Avarak pondered this question for a moment. "Not Commander Byrne," he decided.

"Yeah," said Raffi, "that was my guess too."

"Lafleur," offered Avarak, "told me that they have a different name for it."

"Which is?" said Raffi.

"Sailors' delight." Avarak shook his head. "I do not know the meaning of this."

"I do," said Raffi. "It's an old rhyme. 'Red at night, sailors' delight. Red in the morning, sailors' warning.'"

Avarak pondered this. "I believe this refers to sunrise and sunset," he said.

"Very good, Ensign," said Raffi. Sailors' delight. But how delightful, exactly? Raffi had many questions. Lafleur, it seemed, might know the answers. Who else?

"Let's keep an eye on this, Avarak," she said. "There's enough stress around here without adding hallucinations to the mix."

As predicted, the meeting with the Romulans took several days to arrange. First, Tradall—or, rather, Zhol—would not allow it. Only when Byrne

114　UNA McCORMACK

threatened to pack up and leave immediately did Tradall say that he couldn't exactly stop them. Raffi had the distinct impression that Zhol was ready to help them onto the flyers.

Contact was made with Iloba, the Romulan commander in the area, and the principle of a meeting agreed. Then came the wrangle over location. The Romulans said that they would come to Ghenic. But if there was one thing that all parties at Ghenic were agreed upon—whether Starfleet or Cardassian, officer or noncom—it was that no way were they allowing the Romulans to come and get a good look inside the base. The Romulans, however, played the same card.

"*You cannot expect us,*" said Iloba, "*to welcome members of the Cardassian military to our base. May I remind you that it is barely a month since we were at war—*"

"I'm not expecting you to welcome members of the Cardassian military to your base," said Byrne firmly. Raffi applauded her direct and obdurate tone. In her experience, Romulans were particularly ill equipped to deal with that combination of bluntness and obstinacy. "I'm hoping that you will be prepared to meet the new Starfleet officer who has recently arrived in the area. In the spirit of our continuing alliance."

Iloba did not laugh out loud at the mention of the alliance, Raffi noted. She would like to consider this a positive sign that there was at least the show of ongoing friendship. But so much of dealing with the Romulans was working through layers upon layers of secrecy and deception. Sometimes, Raffi knew, they didn't know themselves what agenda was being served.

"Besides," added Byrne, with some asperity, "it's not been safe, in recent days, for Cardassian officers to move around the countryside."

Iloba's expression was unreadable. "*I was saddened to hear about Gul Assott.*"

Unlikely, thought Raffi, given that Iloba had almost certainly ordered the killing.

SECOND SELF **115**

"We were all sad," said Byrne. "Assott believed we could find a peaceful solution to this situation."

Raffi did catch something then in Iloba's eyes; she feared it was: *We don't.*

"You can come," said Iloba. *"You and your new officer. I'll instruct my assistant to find a suitable time and day."*

"Your attention to this matter is appreciated," said Byrne, just getting her last words out before Iloba cut the comm. She eyed Raffi, who had been sitting out of view on the edge of her desk throughout. "Well, you've got your meeting."

"Not yet," said Raffi. "There'll be a string of cancellations and postponements first."

Twice, she and Byrne were in flight when Iloba's office contacted them to say that the commander was no longer able to speak to them that morning.

"Told you," Raffi said, on the second occasion, turning the flyer back toward Ghenic, monitoring the Romulan flyers that tracked them all the way to the edge of what remained, nominally, Cardassian territory.

"I didn't disagree," said Byrne. "But I'm wondering how long you're holding out hope that this meeting will ever happen."

"It will," said Raffi. "They're just trying to make us jumpy."

"They're succeeding," said Byrne.

"First rule of dealing with Romulans," said Raffi. "Don't let them mess with your mind."

"That ship," said Byrne with a sigh, "has long since sailed."

On the third attempt, they were able to land at the Romulan base. Perhaps it was a coincidence, Raffi thought, that they were arriving on the very same day and at the very same time that ground cannon were being unloaded. She was surprised by the lack of nuance in the display. Romulans were usually more subtle. Or maybe the show of brute force was intended as an insult: *This is how we rate your intelligence, Starfleet. We assume you would miss anything less obvious.* The problem with dealing with Romulans, Raffi thought, as she had so often thought during her short career, was

116   UNA McCORMACK

that their paranoia was infectious. You began to second-guess everything in front of you.

There was nothing subtle about the half-hour wait to see Iloba.

"My time is less valuable, I suppose," said Byrne, pacing the small room to which they had been ushered.

"That's what he'd like you to think," said Raffi, relaxed in her chair, legs out and crossed at the ankles, working through number puzzles on her padd. "My suggestion? Sit down and try your best to *look* laid back."

Byrne snorted, but she took her seat and, eventually, brought out her own padd. Soon her face took on a less worried expression. Perhaps she did number puzzles too, thought Raffi. Perhaps she was working through Vulcan verb conjugations. Whatever did the trick. Raffi tried not to judge people by the medicine they took.

Eventually, a young officer arrived to take them to Iloba, leading them through a series of corridors by a route that—predictably—frequently backtracked upon itself. Raffi was sure that they came down one corridor in both directions twice. She wouldn't have been surprised to discover that Iloba's office was directly adjacent to their waiting room, and possibly accessible by means of a hidden door. She wouldn't have been surprised to be led back to the room where they'd started to find that it had been redressed in the interim, but, on this occasion, they were brought somewhere else. A small room made smaller by a folding screen, and seemingly without natural light. They took their seats, and their guide left them, the door closing with an audible *clunk*, like an old-time prison cell.

"Fuck's sake," muttered Raffi. "Where's the oubliette?"

The folding screen retracted slightly. A tall uniformed Romulan wearing a commander's insignia came out. Iloba, presumably, although he did not condescend to introduce himself. Sokara, as expected, was behind him. Raffi felt a brief upsurge of optimism, which she swiftly tempered. During his time on Earth, Sokara's purposes had been best served by assisting Raffi. She had no reason to believe that such was the case on Ordeve—quite the contrary, in fact—and no reason to assume that he had ever felt any kind of personal loyalty or affection toward her. To think that way would be to make a big mistake. But perhaps something could be salvaged from this mess. The commander took the remaining seat. Sokara remained standing, by the folding screen. His eyes flicked up, briefly.

"Hi," Raffi said, with a small wave. "Good to see you."

Sokara tilted his head, almost imperceptibly, but made no other movement.

"You know our liaison officer?" said Iloba.

"You know I do," said Raffi.

Iloba smiled, and then turned to address Byrne. "Allow me to be direct."

"Oh, this should be good," murmured Raffi.

"As pleasant as it must be for our liaison officers to renew their acquaintanceship," said Iloba, "I find it disappointing to see so many new Starfleet people in the area."

"And I'm overwhelmed by the sheer number of reinforcements sent to me," said Byrne, refusing the trap Iloba had set to be led into specifying how many. Raffi approved.

"One would hope not," said Iloba. "But we have been very clear that we are expecting a peaceful transition of the Ghenic base to our control within the week. Why are there any new Starfleet personnel here at all?"

"Perhaps they wanted a change of scenery," said Byrne. "New faces."

"This is a very serious situation, Commander," said Iloba. "I wonder if such flippancy is appropriate."

"I'm completely sure that it's not," said Byrne. "Which is why you may be sure that I, too, am very serious. There are over a hundred Cardassians still at Ghenic. The majority are civilians. We're concerned about them."

"Concerned?"

There was no simple way, Raffi thought, whether obliquely or not, to accuse one's allies of intending a massacre.

"Yes," said Byrne calmly. "Concerned."

118   UNA McCORMACK

"I understand," said Iloba, "that the base has room for fifty civilians at most."

"You're well informed," said Byrne.

"I am," said Iloba. "Conditions must be getting uncomfortable there, in this heat. Even for Cardassians. Do you require our assistance?"

"Only to allow us to take these people to Merna, and then, if necessary, offworld," said Byrne.

Iloba shifted in his seat. "The postwar agreement between our governments puts this world under Romulan jurisdiction. We have no need for you to carry out such an evacuation."

"I guess we could tie up teams of diplomats with the right expertise for years," said Byrne. "But we don't have years, do we?"

"If you and your officers are not happy here," said Iloba, "you're free to leave."

"Agreed. If I can take the Cardassians with me."

Iloba smiled. "This world, *and* its inhabitants, fall under Romulan jurisdiction."

Raffi thought, *He's looking forward to next week. He's looking forward to getting stuck in* . . . Well, he could get fucked. Raffi was not leaving this place. She would do whatever it took. She glanced at Sokara, who was looking at his commanding officer's back.

"I think," said Iloba, "that our next step should be to agree to a timetable for the removal of however many Starfleet personnel remain at Ghenic from the area. We can most certainly ensure safe passage back to Merna. Perhaps the *Gráinne* can return to collect you. You should probably take advantage of that offer, Commander," he added. "Ranking officers have not had much luck in this area in recent weeks."

And there was the threat, laid out plain. If Starfleet officers remained at Ghenic, Iloba would consider them fair game.

"I'm curious," said Raffi. "Are your superiors prepared to risk the peace for the sake of a hundred Cardassians?"

Iloba laughed. "The question, Lieutenant Musiker, is surely—do you think your superiors are willing to risk the alliance for the sake of a hundred Cardassians? I'm sure of my orders. Are you so sure of yours?"

They left shortly afterward. Raffi had not been able to catch Sokara's eye again. He had appeared entirely impassive throughout—textbook Tal Shiar—but was it her imagination that he wasn't happy? Still, she couldn't risk making her decisions based on suppositions.

"I hope that was worth it for me to be so comprehensively insulted," said Byrne, on the way back to Ghenic.

Raffi didn't answer.

"Tell me about the Tal Shiar agent," said Byrne.

"His name is Nuvu Sokara," said Raffi. "He was my opposite number at Federation Affairs throughout the last six months of the war. By the end, we were dealing with each other almost daily."

"Huh," said Byrne.

"What?"

"Strange to think of them having 'Federation Affairs,' isn't it? But it makes sense when you say it. You two got on?"

"He played fair. Not usual in a Tal Shiar agent. We were both agreed that the war needed to be won as quickly as possible."

"You think he'll help?"

"I am under no such illusions," said Raffi.

They flew on, through hostile territory, the river Parset running swiftly beneath them. As they drew nearer to Ghenic, Raffi looked north and east, and saw the high mountains of the Caanta valley rising in the distance, red flowers in bloom across them.

"And are you happy now?" said Byrne.

"Happy?" said Raffi. "Of course not. But I'm absolutely clear what we need to do."

"Plan B?" said Byrne.

"Plan B," agreed Raffi. "And a very good plan B. Or there won't be a Cardassian alive in Ghenic by the end of next week."

120   UNA McCORMACK

"I told you there was no point," said Zhol later, when Raffi and Byrne went to brief the Cardassians about the meeting. He was pacing up and down Tradall's little office, his hand not far from the disruptor at his side. "They're murderers, every single last one of them. It's a whole fucking society of psychopaths. I hope they all burn." He turned to Tradall, who was sitting hunched in the commanding officer's seat, face hidden behind one hand. "I'm going out again tonight with three of the men. We'll pick off as many as we can—"

"You can't kill them all that way," said Raffi. "There are too many of them."

"What else do you suggest, Lieutenant? They're not going anywhere."

"I've no problem with you and your officers playing cat and mouse with the Romulans," said Raffi. "Do whatever the hell you want on that score. But it's not a viable plan for helping the civilians, and you might want to consider whether it's likely to lead to reprisals."

"The civilians know their duty," said Zhol. "They're true Cardassians. They know that victory for Cardassia requires sacrifice."

"Current estimates put the number of Cardassian dead at eight hundred million," said Raffi. "Do you seriously want to add to that tally?"

She heard Tradall give a soft gasp. *He's weeping . . .* Zhol muttered something under his breath that plainly wasn't complimentary.

"Tradall," said Raffi. "I want to go and look at the old Bajoran town. There might be something there—hidden rooms, cellars, *anything*—that we can use to hide people. Some of the children at least."

"For what purpose?" said Zhol.

"To buy us some time," said Byrne.

"Why? Is Starfleet coming?" Zhol gave a bitter laugh. "Of course they're not. So it's a waste of time." He leaned on the desk, looming over Tradall. "I'm going out again. You stay—you'd be no use anyway. Just remember— Starfleet aren't coming to help us. It's down to us to kill whoever we can."

SECOND SELF **121**

Tradall moved his hand. Yes, he had been crying. "You mean save whoever you can, don't you?"

Zhol snorted and left the room. Tradall looked at Raffi and Byrne. "Why aren't your people coming? You had a *ship* here at Ordeve. You took the damn Vorta!"

"We're here," said Raffi firmly.

"All six of you," said Tradall.

"It's a start," said Raffi. "Do I have your permission to visit the ruins?"

Tradall, reaching to open a drawer, took out a hypo. "Do whatever you want."

Outside his office, Raffi said to Byrne, "You heard what he just said, didn't you?"

" 'Do whatever you want,' " said Byrne.

"Yeah," said Raffi. "How *widely* do you think we should interpret that? Because, you know what? I've found it's often better to ask forgiveness than permission."

A small smile ghosted across Byrne's face. *That,* thought Raffi, *is a start.*

"I've found," said Byrne, "that deniability can come in handy. So have a pleasant afternoon, Lieutenant. Whatever you happen to end up doing."

Raffi left a message for Avarak, telling him where she was going. She requisitioned a small Starfleet skimmer, hoping that this would safeguard her. She followed the course of the Parset down through empty and untended fields where the skeletons of old structures—barns, perhaps—were crumbling into the grass. She brought the skimmer down near the point where the two rivers met, and walked along the riverbank, searching the broken building stones for something that might help. The town was long gone, only the vaguest sense of the streets and houses that had once been here. All that was left were the tumbledown and weathered stones, weeds and long grasses, and the occasional clump of blood poppy. The river ran past, becoming swift and

122 UNA McCORMACK

powerful where the Parset and the Caanta met. There was no bridge. She stood on the bank and looked over to the mountains, high and red, before continuing her search of the ruined town.

After an hour or two, Raffi came to a halt amid a pile of rubble that had clearly been a building of some prominence. She sat down on a big stone, about the size of a home replicator, and covered in faint markings. It looked like it had been painted, once upon a time. There was nowhere to hide here, she thought. The town was flattened, as if by a cataclysmic event. Dead end.

Raffi reached down and plucked one of the poppies. She wondered how Jae's show was going. Something from a different world, a different time. She began to pick off petals, one by one. *He loves me; he loves me not. He loves me; he loves me not . . .*

Someone behind her spoke her name. "Raffi."

She turned and saw Sokara. "Damn," she said. "Hello."

"I thought I might find you here," he said. He walked over and sat down on the stone next to her. She plucked off the last petal and threw the pod into the long grass. *He loves me not.*

"Should I ask how you got your flyer past our security?" she said.

"You can ask," he said with a smile.

"I'll work it out later," she said.

"I would not use those scrambling codes again."

They sat together for a while in silence—almost peaceably, Raffi thought—watching the river run past. "I still owe you a drink," said Sokara.

"The mess at Ghenic has *kanar*," said Raffi. "But I don't like *kanar*."

"Nor do I," he said.

"I'm not sure even the Cardassians do," she said. "Why don't we see where we stand in a few weeks' time? All debts might be voided by then."

"Or further increased?"

Raffi turned to look at him. "I sincerely hope not."

Sokara sighed and looked around the ruins. "What have these old stones told you?"

SECOND SELF 123

"That this has not been a happy world for many years."

"No," he agreed. "But the war is over now, at least. Perhaps better times are coming for worlds like this."

Quietly, she said, "These people here—the Cardassians, I mean—some of them are kids. So much has happened to them already. The war's over, and yet those kids are still waking up in fear for their lives. If you could see them—"

"What do you think that we are going to do to these children?"

"Sokara," she said, "you tell me."

"This world is under Romulan jurisdiction," he replied. "The treaty between our governments makes it very clear that there should be no intervention by Starfleet personnel—"

"And that," said Raffi, "*that*, there, is my chief difficulty. You—even you—fall back on these platitudes! You stop talking to me like a *person* and you start sounding like a *rulebook*, and the only reason that people start talking like rulebooks is that they're trying to protect their goddamn asses!"

"I see," he said. "Do you want to know what *my* chief difficulty is in this situation?"

"Go on," she said.

"Our base assumption—when dealing with Starfleet, or with the Federation—is that at some point, they will act in contradiction to their stated principles."

She looked him straight in the eye. "Are you calling me a hypocrite?"

"Quite the contrary," he said. "This is what I mean by my difficulty. If anyone else were here, I could work on the assumption that Starfleet would withdraw before the end of the week. Oh, there would be much hand-wringing, and many sternly worded communiques, but they'd be gone." He rubbed his tired eyes. "My *difficulty*, Lieutenant, is that I don't see *you* doing that."

"I'm trying to tell whether that is a compliment or complaint," said Raffi.

124 UNA McCORMACK

"Take it whichever way you prefer," he replied. "Either way, it means that you're unpredictable. I don't know what you're going to do next."

"Good," she said. No need for him to know that she also didn't have a clue.

He pondered the stones. "Do you know what happened here?"

"The Bajorans had a town here, didn't they?"

"There was a temple," said Sokara. "I understand it was quite a revered place."

"I didn't know you were interested in Bajoran history."

"I'm interested in all kinds of things. For example—I'm extremely interested to know what the Cardassians told you about what happened at Akantha."

"They haven't told me anything."

"No? Nothing secondhand? Not even the story about the Bajorans drifting away when the Cardassians settled? About them not wanting to live side by side, but leaving to take their chance elsewhere?"

Raffi looked around. "It's as likely a story as anything else."

"*Really*, Lieutenant?" The scorn in his voice was palpable. "This is what we mean about Starfleet, about your ability not to see what is plain to everyone else. You can sit here, looking directly at these stones, and pretend not to understand exactly what happened—"

"I'm not *pretending* anything—!"

"And I had you marked down as one of the few honest Starfleet officers—"

"All right," she said impatiently. "You've made your point! I'm a damn hypocrite like the rest of Starfleet. What did happen?"

Sokara opened his hands and gestured around. "You can see. If you look closely enough. If you open your eyes."

Raffi looked around. Perhaps the sunlight shifted. Or perhaps it was simply that, at his instigation, she was seeing properly at last. She saw the stones as if for the first time. Saw how black so many of them were.

"There was a fire . . ."

"They burned this place down," said Sokara. "Your Cardassian friends. They marched in, and arrested everyone, and they burned the town and the temple to the ground. Some of the adults survived. But there's a question mark over the children. Two dozen of them disappeared. Nobody knows what happened to them." He pushed the toe of his boot into the ground, dislodging some earth and a few poppies. "And nobody's come digging. Yet."

"How do you know this?"

"The Bajorans have excellent documentation. The handful that survived reached refugee camps and were interviewed there. Their accounts are accessible to anyone that bothers to look." He looked around. "I took the time to find out everything I could about Ordeve before I came here. The Bajorans shared the information quite willingly."

Raffi hadn't even thought to ask. She swallowed the sour taste in her mouth. "The people here. The Cardassians, I mean. They weren't involved—"

"Are you sure? And if not—how do you know they haven't done similar, or worse? Those Cardassian soldiers you're standing beside—do you think some of them were on Bajor during the Occupation?"

Raffi thought, suddenly, of Zhol. He was old enough. Tradall most likely not, but Zhol, certainly. What about the other? What about Gul Assott, so beloved and mourned? What had he been ordered to do during the Occupation?

Sokara was looking at the hills in the distance. "I bet that I could open the files of half a dozen of the officers at Ghenic and find lists of supposed atrocities about which the Bajorans would like to question them," said Sokara. "And not just on Bajor. Against Romulans, in this war. Against Starfleet, during the wars you fought against them. We don't have to go back far. What have they done in recent months—"

"All right, I get it. And perhaps you're right—"

"You know I'm right. So, the question I would ask you, Lieutenant, is—are you really willing to die for these people?"

126   UNA McCORMACK

"Nobody," said Raffi firmly, "has to die."

"*Everybody* has to die."

"Not like this." She gestured around. "Not again."

He brushed his hands against his uniform. "Are you sure?"

"I'm going to make damn sure."

"Thank you," he said, and stood up. "All I wanted to learn today was your intentions." He sighed. "I knew them already."

And then he was gone, walking back down the hill, leaving Raffi with the distinct impression that she had given away considerably more than she even knew. She thought, *I could send a message back to Ghenic and tell them to watch out for a cloaked Romulan flyer, heading back from here to their base. They could bring him down, and this would all become so much less complicated.*

But she couldn't do that. Hell, they were supposed to be allies, weren't they? Instead, she stood, looking steadfastly down at the ground so that she did not have to see the evidence around her, walked to her flyer, and went back.

Back at Ghenic, Raffi strode into Tradall's office. He was alone—Zhol out taking pointless potshots at Romulans, presumably. He jumped when she entered (Dammit, had he been sleeping with his head on the desk?) and sat up straight.

"I've had an interesting day," she said.

"Yes?" asked Tradall. "Are your superiors sending support? Or do you mean there's more bad news?"

"I went down to the old town."

Tradall looked at her uncomprehendingly.

"The ruins," she said. Did he even remember their conversation? "The Bajoran ruins. To see if there was anything to help us—"

"The Bajorans left Ordeve years ago—"

"So I was led to believe," she replied. "But not without some encouragement."

Tradall propped his head up in his hands. "Do you want me to apologize personally for the Occupation, Lieutenant? I wasn't there, but I will apologize, if it will get us some help to get out of here."

"It's not me that's owed the apology, is it?" said Raffi bitterly. "But I'd like some honesty, if that's possible. Before I put myself in the firing line." She considered that. "Further into the firing line."

"I'll tell you whatever I know," Tradall said. "But I don't know much."

"Yes," she said. "There's been a lot of willful ignorance around here, hasn't there? A lot of letting things pass, letting things slide. My understanding was that the Bajorans packed up and left. Once the Cardassians arrived, the people living here just left. That alone constitutes a crime against a sentient people, but it's not the whole story, is it?"

"Lieutenant, it was a long time ago."

"Living memory for some. The Bajorans didn't just leave, did they?"

She saw him try to decide what he could safely say; what might incriminate him should anyone be listening. That must have been trained into him when he was young. He was going to have to give up on that, she thought, if there was any chance that Cardassia was going to survive and rebuild. "I don't know much," he said, at last.

"Oh, come *on*!" Raffi said. "I was there an hour ago! The place was burned down!"

"All right! I'll take your word for it! I've never been to look!"

"No, who would want to come face-to-face with history like that?"

"I wasn't even born!" he said. "It was ages ago! Decades!"

"Uh-huh? Carry on."

"I think there was a temple here," he said. "That weird religion they have—"

"They worship the Prophets," said Raffi. "An alien species that has intervened on behalf of the Bajoran people on numerous occasions across their history. So. A temple?"

"A temple, a shrine, I don't know what they call these places. Yes, I think it was burned down—"

"Really *nice* use of the passive there," said Raffi. "These things don't burn themselves down, you know."

"Maybe it was the candles," he said.

"Oh, *please*!" she snapped back.

"All right!" He put his hand to his head. "Yes, I think that whoever was stationed here at the time ordered the place burned down. I don't know why. Maybe there was Resistance activity in the area. The locals were sent to resettlement camps, I think."

"And the children?"

Tradall blinked at her. "What children?"

"There were two dozen children here. They were unaccounted for."

"Who have you been talking to?" said Tradall, suspicion entering his voice.

"I'm with Starfleet Intelligence, sonny," said Raffi. "You know what an intelligence agency does? Like the Obsidian Order, right?"

He shuddered. Even years after its demise, the Order still cast a long shadow. "I don't know anything about any children," he said, putting his hands up, like a shield.

"All right," said Raffi. "I believe you. Next question. Is there anybody stationed here now, or living here now, that might be implicated in what happened back then?"

"I don't know that either," he said.

"You haven't asked a lot of questions about this place, have you?" she said.

He gave her a withering look. Of course not. Why would he? Why would he potentially incriminate himself in that way? "Can I ask *you* a question, Lieutenant?"

SECOND SELF   129

"Shoot," she said dryly.

"If there was someone here who was involved, would that be sufficient reason for the rest of us to be murdered by the Romulans?"

"Federation law doesn't work like that," she said.

"No?"

"No."

"Do you know what Starfleet's reputation is," said Tradall, "among the Cardassian military?"

"No," Raffi replied.

"We think you're all hypocrites."

It was the second time in one day that Raffi had heard that said. Truly this mission was turning out to be full of revelations. "Maybe," she said. "But at least Earth isn't on fire."

He was already reaching for his hypo. She strode out of the office block into the night. Outside, a sweet scent pervaded the air, compounding the sense of claustrophobia. The sense that there was no escape.

We have to get these people away. But where? How?

Where could they go to? The base here would soon be under attack; the ruins of the old town offered nothing in the way of cover. Their defense lay in the hands of a bitter old soldier fighting past wars, a broken young man who could barely sit up straight, and six Starfleet officers in varying states of despair.

Do we leave? Do we try to get news out about what's happening here?

Who would come? A war had just ended—a great and terrible war that had brought an empire to its knees. Thousands and thousands must still be dying in the aftermath: lack of food, the threat of disease, a million small grudges being settled. People were trying to help, but they were exhausted, stretched thin, close to reaching their limit. A treacherous thought came to mind:

Is this the hill I want to die on?

The night was still and hot. From the civilian area, Raffi heard a child

130 UNA McCORMACK

wailing. In the distance—well beyond the compound—she heard the faint crackle of what she thought might be disruptor fire. Zhol was on the hunt. There was a light on in the Starfleet building, and she went to look.

Lafleur was there, with the two other Starfleet personnel, two ensigns: Kovar from New Berlin, and Turan from Kashgar. There were two Cardassian gils there as well, both young men (all the women seemed to be over on the civilian side). The five of them were sitting around a table playing cards.

"Blind Moon's Draw," said Lafleur. "Do you know it?"

"No," said Raffi, taking a seat. Both the gils looked pleased at that news.

"You'll work it out," said Turan.

"Before I'm bankrupted, or after?" asked Raffi.

"I've always found," said Kovar, "that the more I lose, the quicker I learn the rules."

One of the Cardassians dealt. Three cards to each of them. Raffi looked down at what she'd gotten. She didn't even know the suits. She didn't even know if a Cardassian deck of cards had suits. One of the cards had a stylized figure that from the insignia might be a legate. Another card showed four red trefoils; another showed three black discs. "How much of this is skill, exactly?" asked Raffi. "And how much is chance?"

Lafleur pulled out a hypo. "Ain't that the billion-latinum question." She offered the hypo to Raffi. "Take the edge off?"

And Raffi thought, *Why the hell not?*

7

That night, Raffi dreamed vividly. In her dream, she was walking through the ruins of Akantha. It was night, and winter. The air was bitter cold.

Why am I here?

She reached the riverbank and stood watching the water swirl past, as the two rivers joined and rushed on toward the coast. On the other side of the bank, the Caanta valley was completely dark, but, as Raffi watched, she thought she saw a pale white light, from deep within the trees, getting brighter. Suddenly, there was a flash—and the other side of the river was illuminated: the tall and ancient trees, the red flowers, and three dark figures standing there. She felt certain—that way that you do feel certain, in dreams—that she knew these people, but she could not bring their names to mind. They were beckoning to her.

Come! Come!

"Where?" said Raffi. "Where do you want me to come?"

Here! Here!

"I can't," she said. "There's no way over. I can't fly—they'll detect us. And there's no bridge . . ."

Come! Come quickly! Come soon!

The light went out. Raffi woke in her own bed, still dressed in her uniform, and not entirely sure how she'd gotten there. In her hand was a hypo. Her mouth was dry, and she had a low throbbing pain at the base of her skull. She rolled out of bed, ignored the mirror, and drank a liter of water.

132   UNA McCORMACK

The cards had not smiled on her, she thought, although she recalled a general air of goodwill between Starfleet and Cardassian officers that might, under other circumstances, have been heartening. After that, a blur, although some vague memory of her dream was coming back, the river rushing past, some figures in the distance. She tried to push the dream aside. She didn't want to dream of Akantha. Whatever had happened there, she didn't want those horrors in her head.

She sat on her bunk, fresh glass of water in hand, fingers pressed against her temple, looking down at the hypo. A mistake, one she wouldn't make again. This kind of stuff—it always clouded your thinking, in the end. Like right now, there was something she was trying to remember, something she'd noticed, and she couldn't bring it back to mind.

The door chimed.

"Damn," Raffi muttered. She shoved the hypo under her pillow, and said, "Come in!"

Avarak entered, looking fresh and youthful. Was it possible to hate someone so intrinsically decent? "Am I disturbing you, Lieutenant?"

"No, no. Something you need?"

"I was hoping to hear about your impressions of the ruined town," he said, taking a seat. "Did you find anything of interest?"

Raffi shook her head carefully. "Nuh-uh. There's nowhere to hide. The Cardassians leveled the whole place, years ago. Not that it's done them any good in the long run."

Avarak folded his hands in front of him. "That is most disappointing. I confess I am struggling to find a way through our dilemma."

"You and me both, kid," murmured Raffi. Fragments of the dream were still pushing through. The river. The figures. *Come . . . Come . . .* Easy to say that. Less easy to do.

"Perhaps," said Avarak, "you might describe what you saw?"

"Big stones. Rubble. Quite a big river. Another smaller one. Also— Sokara."

"Sokara?" Avarak's eyebrows shot up. "That is not entirely good news for our air security."

"He wanted to talk. I got the impression he was trying to get us to leave . . ."

"We are not leaving, are we, Lieutenant?"

"No," she said. "Absolutely not."

"I am relieved to hear you say that," he said. "Since I would, in all conscience, have to remain."

"You're a good officer, Avarak."

"I try to act according to logic," he replied. "There is no logic to murder."

"No," she said, and sighed. "You know, the town was heartbreaking. Must have been a decent-sized place, once. The temple looks like it was pretty substantial. And for some reason the Cardassians decided it had to go."

He was nodding. "I have visited ruins on Vulcan," he said. "And while it is not logical, one cannot help but try to imagine what the lives of the inhabitants must have been like. Farmers, I imagine."

"I guess."

"Making their living from the river traffic. One often sees towns like this, stretched across rivers."

"Huh," said Raffi. She was thinking of the figures in her dream, beckoning her across. *How do we get there? There is no bridge.* "There's no bridge," she said.

"No?"

"No. So how did people get across the river?"

"Do you believe this is significant, Lieutenant? Or, at least, relevant to our immediate problem?"

"I mean, you could build a ferry, couldn't you? But I didn't see any structures like that . . . I know that the Bajorans were technologically advanced—of course they were, to get here in the first place—but there's not always a flyer to hand. So how did they get across the river?"

"A bridge would be unlikely to survive the Cardassian destruction of the town, not least because it would block any escape route. We can easily determine whether or not there are ruins by a simple geophysical analysis—"

"What's that?" said Raffi.

"A survey of subsurface features that can, for example, reveal traces of structures that no longer exist. An old archaeologist's method."

"Yeah? Well, I'll be sure to mention it, next time I meet an old archaeologist." She stood up and drained the last of the water in her glass. "Get Lafleur. We're going back. I want to take a closer look at the riverbank. Carry out this analysis."

Come, said the figures in her dream. *Come . . .*

"Lieutenant, we do not have a great deal of time—"

"I know. So we'd better hurry up."

He went to fetch Lafleur. Raffi showered—very quickly—and joined them outside.

Lafleur looked sleepy. "What's this about a bridge?" she said.

"There isn't one," said Raffi. "There should be one."

"Um, Raffi." Lafleur glanced over at Avarak, and lowered her voice. "I know last night was the first time you tried that stuff. It can be a bit weird? Give you strange dreams?"

"This isn't to do with dreams. Are you coming?"

Lafleur, shaking her head, nevertheless got into the skimmer, and soon they were over the old town. "Look down," she said. "No bridge. I don't see any sign of landing sites, either. For ferries—"

"Those structures may have been wooden," said Avarak. His tricorder was out, and the survey was underway. "And long gone. But I detect no traces."

"They were building in stone," said Raffi. "Are you getting anything, Avarak? Anything to suggest there was a river crossing?"

"No," he replied. "It is most odd. There are some anomalous readings north of the temple."

"Anomalous?" asked Raffi.

SECOND SELF   135

"Where the soil has been disturbed. I would conjecture that a substantial area there was dug up at some point."

Raffi swallowed. Were they about to solve the mystery of the missing children?

"Land near the temple," she told Lafleur.

"Raffi, are you sure about this?" said Lafleur. So she had the same thought.

"Yes," said Raffi. "Let's go and look, at least."

Lafleur brought the skimmer down near the stones where Raffi had met Sokara the day before. "Okay," Raffi said. "I don't know what we're going to find here. It might be . . . It might be evidence of a terrible crime. I hope it's not. I hope we're going to find something to help us—"

Lafleur said, "So you don't really know what we're looking for?"

"No."

"But we'll know it when we see it."

"Yes," said Raffi. "I think we will."

Avarak found the path, after a short search, leading north from the temple along the riverbank. It was overgrown, weeds and grasses and poppies bursting through the cobblestones, but still recognizable. They followed this old way out from the temple and were soon under cover of the trees. The path went on. The river was still audible, to the right.

"Where is this going?" said Lafleur.

"I don't know yet," Raffi admitted.

"Okay," said Lafleur. "Well, it's not like we have anything else to worry about."

The path became increasingly broken, the roots of old trees forcing their way through, and, at last, faded to nothing, the bracken and branches far outnumbering the last stones. They were standing in a small clearing. The air was very still. The poppies were everywhere. Raffi closed her eyes, breathed their scent, and tried to capture some of the dream again. *Come . . . Come . . .*

"Lieutenant," said Avarak. "Look at this."

136   UNA McCORMACK

Raffi opened her eyes and went to join him. He had found some more stones, bigger this time, but no more than a meter wide and high, and he was pulling away the bracken. "Stand back," Raffi said. She put her phaser on low, and the others followed suit, removing the coverage. There was a big stone slab underneath. A tombstone? Oubliette?

"Okay," said Raffi. "This might be distressing. If you don't want to look, step back."

"We're in this with you," said Lafleur.

Lafleur and Raffi took one end and Avarak the other. They struggled in the heat to shift the stone. *Don't let there be skeletons,* thought Raffi. At last, sweating and breathless, they moved it, revealing stone steps leading down.

Lafleur gave a nervous laugh. "No *way.*"

"Shall we take a look and see what's down there?" said Raffi.

"You first," said Lafleur.

"Why me?" said Raffi.

"Your damn idea," said Lafleur.

True enough. They took out their flashlights, and went slowly down the steps—Raffi, Lafleur, and then Avarak. At the bottom of the steps, a tunnel was revealed, high enough for even Avarak to stand upright, and wide enough for two of them to go together. Raffi, waving the flashlight against the walls, saw the same yellow stone that comprised the ruins of Akantha. Here and there were the faint remains of paintings. Figures, and, every so often, a circle with rays emerging, like a sun, or a flashing light. "The Bajorans built this," she said, almost in awe. They had traveled through space long before humans. Their civilization was old, and, in this dark tunnel, one could almost believe that it was god-touched.

"Lieutenant," said Avarak, kneeling, "look. This is interesting."

Raffi saw a small metal box, about the size of a desk companel. "What is it?" she said. "Lafleur?"

Lafleur, the engineer among them, bent to take a closer look. "It's Cardassian in design . . . Does that mean they know about this place?"

"Not necessarily," said Raffi. "The Bajoran Resistance made use of Cardassian technology. They might have brought it here. What does it do? Any idea?"

"I think . . ." said Lafleur. "I think it's a holo-filter. Avarak, go back up again . . ."

He went up and outside. Lafleur operated the device and called up. "Anything?" There was no reply, so she powered it down again. Avarak reappeared.

"Your conjecture was correct. The opening disappeared, and I could only see foliage. Did you speak?"

"Yes," said Lafleur.

"I heard nothing."

"Holo-filter," said Lafleur. "And sound dampener. We can conceal the entrance."

"That might come in useful," said Raffi. "Shall we go on?"

They walked on carefully. There was a faint but steady sound of dripping water.

"We have to determine whether these tunnels are structurally sound," said Avarak, walking behind. "If we intend to bring the civilians this way."

Raffi turned to smile at him.

"That is your intention, is it not?" he said.

"Yeah," she said. "That's my intention."

Their conversation altered after that. From then on, as they walked, they were in practical mode. The commander took readings, looking for weak spots. Avarak and Raffi discussed logistics—how to get the people here, how to get them through safely, what supplies would be required, what they would do on the other side.

"Do we wait for the long-range comms to start working and call for reinforcements?" said Raffi. "Or try to get people through to Merna? I don't even know if there's a way, or if we're heading into a dead end."

"Let's get folks across the river first," said Lafleur. "We don't even know where this leads yet."

138   UNA McCORMACK

They walked for twenty minutes before they found the next set of steps, leading up to another slab.

"Let's hope there's nothing heavy on top," muttered Raffi, and pushed. The stone moved away easily. She climbed out onto a grassy area. The forest loomed ahead. When she turned to look back, she saw the river, running swiftly past, and the broken town and—beyond—the faint gray hint of the base at Ghenic. She had a flash of recognition. She was standing, she thought, more or less in the same place as the figures in her dream.

"Well," she said. "Here we are. Let's take a quick look around—make sure this area, at least, is safe. But we need to get back." She turned to her two colleagues. "We've not got a lot of time to mount this operation," said Raffi, feeling at last a glimmer of hope, and seeing it reflected in Lafleur's face, "but I think we can do this. I really think we can!"

Lafleur took a deep breath. "I think you might be right."

"This is why we were sent here, after all," said Avarak.

Yes, thought Raffi. *This is what Starfleet does.*

Byrne stood in her office looking over at the Caanta valley as Raffi briefed her.

"Lafleur and Turan are down there right now, taking a closer look at the structure. Seeing whether it's sound enough to get everyone through," Raffi reported. "The last thing we need is a cave-in. Of course, we're very short on time, but once we're sure the tunnels are safe, we'll get Tradall and Zhol on the case. We'll need their help to move people—so let's hope that the civilians are willing to obey the military without complaint." She paused for breath. "You don't seem too excited about this plan."

"We have been instructed," said Byrne thoughtfully, still staring out at the mountains, "to observe, not to intervene."

"And when do we stop observing?" said Raffi. "When the Romulans line up the Cardassian soldiers and shoot them one by one in the head? When they do that to the civilian adults? To the children? Or when everyone's dead and the Romulans decide they may as well start shooting the witnesses—"

"Lieutenant, these are our orders—"

"Commander," said Raffi, "those orders can get fucked."

Wearily, Byrne took her seat. This fatalism here; this sense that there was nothing they could do. Raffi understood—she'd felt the same last night. She'd given up, hadn't she, gone and played cards and taken some of that stuff. *Sailors' warning.* But she'd been wrong. There was a way. Starfleet always found a way.

"You know what they think of us," she said to Byrne. "The Cardassians. The Romulans. Both of them. They think we're hypocrites. Well," she amended, "they think *Starfleet* are hypocrites. But I'm not, and I don't think you are either."

Byrne sat staring at her hands.

"Commander?" said Raffi, after a moment or two passed. "Emily, please."

"I don't think that you're a hypocrite, Raffi," Byrne said.

What about their superior officers? Was Byrne willing to face the consequences?

"I'm glad you're here, you know," said Byrne. "I'd lost my nerve." She looked up and smiled, and Raffi thought, suddenly, that they might just get away with this. "So," said Byrne, "fuck orders. What does this mean, exactly?"

Raffi, pulling up the map of the area, began to show Byrne what would be involved in moving the civilians across the river.

"Once they're there," said Byrne, "what do we do? How do we protect them? How long do we wait?"

"As long as it takes," said Raffi. "Maybe this will persuade—" *Or shame . . .* "—our superiors to send us a little backup."

Byrne contemplated the map. "Not quite the peaceful handover to the Romulans that they're imagining will happen," she said. "You realize that if this goes wrong, we might well be hung out to dry by Starfleet Command. If it means saving the alliance."

"What would that mean? A reprimand? Demotion? Discharge?" Raffi shrugged. "You know what? All sounds a small price to pay to save those civilians. I'll pay the price."

"Then I will too," said Byrne. "But we still have to sell it to the Cardassians. Zhol, for one, isn't keen on abandoning Ghenic to the Romulans."

"Zhol isn't in command," said Raffi. She stood and walked toward the door. "And if we can't persuade Tradall to go against him, then we'll take the civilians at least. The military can stay here and get on with whatever heroic last stand they want to make."

"Good luck persuading Cardassians into civilian disobedience," said Byrne.

Raffi stopped with her hand just above the door panel. "What do you mean?"

"Historically, they've been an extremely biddable people. The Obsidian Order was a very effective organization."

"The Order's defunct."

"The military isn't," said Byrne. "Zhol, for one. Very much alive and kicking."

"The Cardassian military walked their people into their near extinction," said Raffi. "There was a civilian uprising on Prime only a few weeks ago—"

"Against the Dominion," said Byrne.

"The Cardassian military itself mutinied," Raffi said.

"Again, against the Dominion—"

"But the *principle* is the same. And if they've done it once, they'll do it again—"

Byrne held up her hands. "All right," she said. "We'll see. But start with Tradall. The last thing we want here is the Cardassian military turning on their own people. That would not be an acceptable solution, for anyone."

No, thought Raffi; their superiors would not be happy. And the Romu-

SECOND SELF 141

lans, surely, would be angry at losing their chance to kill a few spoonheads. "All right. I'll talk to Tradall."

"Please," said Byrne, "tread carefully. I know your expertise is with the Romulans. But Cardassians are trickier than they look."

This time, Zhol was very much in the room, looming tall and bulky over the proceedings. He reminded Raffi of the ruined stones by the river confluence; an unfortunate effect for Zhol, since it only hardened Raffi's resolve.

"We're not leaving the base," he said. "We're not giving Ghenic to the Romulans."

"You won't be giving it to them," said Raffi. "They'll be *taking* it from you, in a matter of days. That's going to happen, no matter what you say, so the decision you have to make," and here she made sure that she was addressing Tradall, "as the senior officer here, is whether or not that's going to happen over the bodies of a hundred civilians."

"Starfleet could help us protect this base from those *skrit*," said Zhol. "If you wanted."

Raffi ignored him. "You need to make a decision soon, Tradall," she said. "We still have time to save lives—"

"We're not leaving Ghenic," said Zhol. "If we die, our blood is on your hands. *Starfleet's* hands—"

"We've drawn up plans for the evacuation. There's a route through the old Bajoran town across the river and into the Caanta valley—"

"No!" said Zhol, and he was, if anything, even more bullish. "Not that way!"

"We can defend that position. We can . . ." Raffi didn't want to say, *shame our superiors into sending help*, so tried, "We can get there, maybe find a way back around to Merna—"

"Not that way!" said Zhol.

Tradall let out a quiet, desperate moan. "Stop, please, both of you!" he said, covering his face. His hands were trembling again.

142   UNA McCORMACK

"What is it?" said Raffi gently. "What's the problem?"

"We are not going that way," said Zhol.

"I'm not asking you!" shot back Raffi.

"We have standing orders," said Tradall. "From Gul Assott. Not to enter the Caanta valley."

"Why?" said Raffi.

"I've no idea," said Tradall.

"Zhol?" she said, looking at him.

"I never asked. Why would I ask? Gul Assott's orders were perfectly clear."

"A little more asking a little earlier might have saved us from this predicament," Raffi said, but Zhol looked at her uncomprehendingly. She turned back to Tradall. "You might have to decide," she said, "between those orders, and the lives of everyone here."

"No," said Zhol. "We have our *orders*!"

"Let *him* decide," said Raffi.

Tradall's whole body was shaking now. Raffi averted her eyes. After a moment or two, the young man collected himself. "The word was . . . The *word* was . . ." His voice dropped to a whisper. "That there was an Obsidian Order facility up there."

There was a silence. "Well, what difference does that make?" said Raffi. "The Order's defunct—"

"So they say," whispered Tradall. "But even if it is . . . These *places* that they had . . . I don't want to know. I don't want to see."

Ghoulish images came to Raffi's mind. What the hell could be up there? Weapons research? Interrogation chambers? A secret unit of crack agents, hiding out in the mountains until their moment came? Raffi shook herself. The Obsidian Order was finished; had ended years back in an ignominious blaze when its former head, Enabran Tain, marshaled them to make an ill-advised assault on the Founders' homeworld. The Order had gone down in flames.

SECOND SELF 143

"Guess what?" Raffi said. "I don't give a damn about the Obsidian Order."

So much for Cardassians not having religion. It was as if she'd blasphemed. Zhol's eyes flashed, and Tradall looked about ready to faint. Raffi pressed on with her assault.

"These are fantasies. You're scaring yourselves with make-believe. The reality is that the Romulans are here, on your doorstep, warming up to killing you all. That's your real problem, not some imaginary threat from a defunct set of gangsters."

But Cardassians, it transpired, were, as Byrne had warned her, even trickier than they looked. Tradall was looking at Zhol, who was shaking his head.

"No," said Tradall, "not that way."

The following morning, they received reports that a further three dozen Romulan troops had arrived in the area. "It won't be long now," said Byrne. "We're going to have to make a decision soon."

"I've made my decision," said Raffi. "I'm not leaving these people to be murdered."

"The last thing we need is to get into a shooting battle with the Cardassians," said Byrne. "Not least because we're outnumbered."

Fair point. Raffi's mind raced, hunting around for options. She didn't want to die here, stupidly, pointlessly. Was it worth trying to speak again to Tradall, this time making sure that Zhol was not present? Could she persuade him to change his mind?

Midmorning, Avarak came to find her.

"Ensign, what do you need?"

"This is more to do with what *you* might need," he said quietly, and he looked back over his shoulder. He seemed . . . could a Vulcan be ruffled? "I wonder, Lieutenant, if you might come with me."

144   UNA McCORMACK

"Sure," she said, joining him in the corridor, securing the door behind her. "Where are we going?"

He shook his head and gestured to her to follow. They went through the compound toward the civilian section. Whatever happened here over the coming weeks, thought Raffi, these people couldn't stay much longer in conditions as cramped as this. Too many of them, in too small a space. If someone got sick . . . She couldn't hardly bear to think about it. That this should be happening, to citizens of what had been, until only a few short months ago, an advanced galactic power . . .

A handful of children came running out to greet Avarak. They seemed to know him very well. As he went past, he dug into his pockets. He brought out snacks and handed them over, like a somber Santa dispensing gifts. This boy was wise beyond his years. When he was done, he led Raffi on to a small building where two Cardassian women were waiting. The older of the women stepped forward. She looked tired and unkempt.

"Lieutenant Musiker," she said. "I'm Professor Ijin Mesat. This is my friend and colleague, Doctor Eksa Prok. We are—were—both engineers at the hydroelectric project farther along the Parset."

"Good to meet you," said Raffi. She glanced at Avarak. "There's a reason, isn't there, why you've brought me here? Away from the military buildings?"

"Yes," said Mesat quietly. "We understand from Avarak that you wish to evacuate the civilian population. Do you think that will save us?"

"I don't know," said Raffi honestly. "But I think it's a better option than sitting here and waiting for the Romulans to arrive."

Both women, shuddering, nodded their agreement.

"Commander Byrne is willing to help," said Raffi. "But . . ."

"But Zhol won't allow it, and Tradall is only half conscious," said Prok bluntly.

"That's about the size of it," said Raffi.

The two women gave each other careful looks. "Then," said Mesat, "on behalf of the civilian population here at Ghenic, I would like to make a formal appeal to Starfleet for your help in removing us to safety."

Oh, thought Raffi. *They've only gone and done it.*

Both women were staring at her now, and Raffi's heart went out to them. Trying to look dignified, but both were clearly desperate. What had their lives been like, only a few months ago? Both professionals, well regarded, working on a highly technical project for an advanced civilization. Now they were refugees, their homes in ruins, begging a Starfleet officer for help. How quickly events moved. How thin the line was between prosperity and poverty.

Avarak said, "I have explained to both the professor and the doctor that our orders are to observe and not to intervene. And that our treaty obligations toward the Romulans significantly complicate our position here."

"I doubt that's much consolation," said Raffi.

"Indeed not," said Avarak. "And, therefore, I have under my own volition been investigating Federation law as it pertains to the protection and preservation of sentient life. And while the Cardassian military in the area might not request our assistance, a direct appeal for aid from recognized civilian representatives cannot be ignored."

"And do you two have the status of recognized civilian representatives?" said Raffi. "I'm assuming you do?"

"I believe," said Avarak, "that determining the legitimacy of any local Cardassian democratic structure to be fraught with difficulty at the moment."

"Well," said Prok bitterly. "Prime *is* on fire."

"We took a vote last night," said Mesat.

"You took a *what*?" said Raffi.

"A vote," said Mesat. Her voice was shaky. "All the civilians here. A new experience for us. But the outcome was quite clear. The majority voted to make a direct appeal to Starfleet. The overwhelming majority."

"And the rest?" said Raffi, to be certain. "Did they say no?"

"They abstained," said Prok. "Some habits are hard to break."

"So that you fully understand what is at risk here," said Avarak, "this vote was dangerous for those who participated. Ghenic was under martial law when the Dominion surrendered. Gathering in such a fashion was technically illegal. And making such an approach to a foreign power might be considered treason."

"I think," said Raffi, "that we can sort out these niceties when we've got these people and their kids to safety. But I'm not going to breathe a word of this to Tradall. Or Zhol, more importantly."

Both women looked much happier.

"One last question," said Raffi. "I have a plan to get us out of here, but I need to know that you're going to be happy with where we're heading. We're going across the river, and into the Caanta valley."

Prok started. She said, "Wasn't that where—" She cut herself off.

"Go on," said Raffi.

"Yes," said Mesat. "Carry on, Eksa."

"I don't know anything," Prok said. "Not really. Only that the Caanta valley was rumored to be under Obsidian Order control. I know Assott wouldn't talk about the place. I asked once whether we should cross the river, conduct a survey, and he refused permission . . ." She shook her head. "That's all I know."

"If that's the way we have to go," said Mesat.

"Then that's the way we're going," finished Prok. "The Obsidian Order can go hang."

If anything was needed to demonstrate beyond doubt that the old Cardassia was dead, thought Raffi, this was surely it. Would Prok have dared to say that out loud only a few short years ago? Mesat put her hand upon her friend's shoulder. "Well said."

"All right," said Raffi. "Then we're underway." She pressed palms with both women, and then walked back with Avarak across the compound to the Starfleet building. "Well done," she said to him.

SECOND SELF 147

Avarak bowed his head in grave acknowledgment. "The preservation of life is vital," he said. "And inaction—*observation*—is not always sufficient. One must do, as well as be."

"Is that from Surak?" said Raffi.

"That," said Avarak, "is from Avarak."

"Well, you tell him from me that he's my hero."

"I most assuredly shall," Avarak replied.

After that, their plans were set quickly in motion. Zhol's guerrilla battle against the Romulans had accelerated over the past couple of days with him taking out key people farther along the river to pick off whoever they could find, and Raffi's intention was to move the civilians, under cover of darkness, as soon as Zhol was away from the compound. She was pretty sure that Zhol would open fire upon any civilian trying to leave; she was less sure about Tradall, but her instincts told her that this was the kind of direct order that he would dodge. They had to cover the two miles down to the river, get through the tunnels, and out into the cover of the forest before dawn.

Raffi tried to get a few hours' sleep. But she tossed and turned in bed, occasionally dozing, mostly lying in that halfway state between oblivion and wakefulness, where the mind does not rest and the thoughts and images that are created are magnified in meaning and intensity. Another dream came with the same kind of quality as the one she had on the night she tried sailors' delight. This time, she was walking under a dark and shifting canopy, which was revealed to be the leaves of trees, huge and ancient trees. She was walking through the woods—but this time she was on the other side of the river, in the Caanta valley. What would they find here? Had the Order been here? What had they done? What other crimes had been committed in this place?

After a while, Raffi became aware of the rushing of water—the river, she guessed—and, faintly, the whisper of the wind throughout the rippling

148   UNA McCORMACK

forest. There were no other sounds; no small forest creatures; no birds; no people. The path opened, and Raffi entered a clearing.

Three dark figures were standing beneath the trees. There was white light, of uncertain origin, behind them. She could not see their faces, but she was sure again, somehow, that she knew them—or would, one day, know them—very well. They raised their hands—in greeting, she thought, so she did the same. "We're coming," she said. "I'm going to bring them. Bring them all. Save them all. We'll come over to the valley. We'll find a way through. Get down to Merna, somehow."

Suddenly, their demeanor changed. Their hands lifted, not in greeting, not in welcome—this was a warning, hands up, palms out, pushing back, as if to say, *Stop! Stop! No farther!*

"But you told me to come," Raffi said.

The movement of their hands became more urgent, pushing her away. *Stop! Stop!*

"I have to come! They'll die if I don't! There's no other way."

You must not come any farther.

The wind was picking up. Overhead, the trees began to shake and rock. There was a sudden rattling sound, like weapons fire. Raffi woke, sweating and frightened, and gasping for air. Her hand touched something small and hard. The hypo. Sailors' warning.

And someone was tapping at the door.

"Lieutenant," said Avarak. "It's time to go."

PART 3

2340

DURING
THE OCCUPATION

8

Mas Gherrod arrived at Ghenic on the back of a military truck. They had set out before sunrise, and the last red rays of Ordeve's sun were dipping behind the hills when the truck pulled up at the gates of the compound.

Gherrod yawned and stretched. The truck, presumably having passed whatever security checks were in place, bumped on into the compound. One of the packing cases in between which he was wedged shuddered, and he laid a restraining hand upon it. He had spent the first part of the journey picking the locks on the cases and looking for anything that might come in useful. Thus he equipped himself with eight ration bars, a small disruptor, a tiny multifunctional screwdriver, two miniature surveillance devices, a couple of reusable hyposprays, a variety of other small components, and a new pair of boots, which, although by no means stylish, would last him through the next few months.

Then there was nothing else to do but sit and wait. He could make no real plans until he arrived and got the lay of the land. He had read the files, looked at maps, understood his purpose—but all of this was background. Context was everything. He took out a pack of cards and practiced with them. When the road got too bumpy, he put the cards away and ate some dried *leya*, slowly, eking them out. He tried to keep awake by reciting all 111 of Akleen's *Precepts of a Dutiful Citizen* but nodded off somewhere between 76 (*"Obey the father of the house; obey the fathers of the Union"*) and 84 (*"A child is both treasure and tool; guard them and guide them"*). He always

152   UNA McCORMACK

struggled to get through the ones about the family. Context, of course, was everything, and on that score Gherrod was lacking.

When he woke, it was dark outside. Soon the truck slowed down and came to a halt. He peered through the slats and saw the flare of light from a watchtower, heard the bark of a duty officer ordering them to pass. At last, the truck halted, and the back opened. The driver, a stocky garresh old enough to be his father (if Gherrod had such a thing), jerked his thumb. "Out," he said. "Start making yourself useful."

Gherrod jumped down, landing on the ground with a squelch, immediately glad of the boots. He started to unload the cases onto a nearby hover-trolley. A bored gil read out the contents of each one, ticking them off his manifest as Gherrod hauled them over. When that was done, the gil came over to Gherrod and gestured at his arm. Gherrod held it out so that the gil could check the identity chip in his wrist, feigning indifference as his record came up.

OFFENDER: GHERROD, MAS

OFFENSE AGAINST THE STATE: VAGRANCY, IDLENESS, MULTIPLE
    DERELICTIONS OF DUTY (MINOR)

DISPENSER: ILIANA MA'TAN, JUNIOR ARCHON (THIRD CLASS),
    MERNA/DARAM DISTRICT JURIDICAL SERVICE

DEGREE OF GUILT: MIDTERCILE, UPPER RANGE

PENALTY: MANDATORY LABOR

TARIFF: SIX MONTHS

The gil flicked the garresh a weary look: *How do we get stuck with these floor sweepings?* "All right, on your way." His interest in Gherrod finished, he turned back to the hover-trolley, setting it in motion, and following it off into the darkness.

Gherrod looked around. The garresh, seeing this, pointed farther into the gloom and said, "Civilian quarters that way. Get yourself a bed." He

SECOND SELF 153

nodded toward a low but brightly lit building closer to hand, on the left. "That's the mess, when you're done. Report to the central office at oh-seven-hundred tomorrow."

Gherrod, who had the layout of the compound committed to memory, nevertheless said, "Thanks," to the other man's back, picked up his bag, and slung it over his shoulder.

"Thank you, *sir*," the garresh called back over his shoulder, heading in the direction of the mess. "Don't make life harder for yourself than it has to be, son."

"Yes, sir. Thank you, sir."

Gherrod watched him go. He sucked in the cold night air, and blew it out again, the steam of his breath curling in front of him. Miserable, hopeless planet. He walked off to find the cover of the barracks.

The compound delivered no particular surprises. The military built them quickly, according to a standard layout, scaling up as necessary. Ghenic currently housed sixty-six members of the Ninth Division of the Fifth Order, tasked to provide military support for the scientists and engineers at the research base farther along the valley, and to protect the river crossing by the old Bajoran town of Akantha. There were about thirty-three civilians too, supplying administrative and other support functions. Gherrod was there to do whatever anyone told him. The only people lower than him were the Bajorans, and they didn't count.

Gherrod made his way through the chilly night, finding the civilian accommodation behind the soldiers' barracks. The big dormitories were sparse and cold, but considerably better than the pen in Merna where he'd been held before his sentencing. There were beds for nine in each dormitory and a shared washing area. Privacy would be a problem, but there were always hidden spots to be found when necessary. There were a couple of people in there already, sleeping or resting, so he moved around quietly until he found an empty cot. He locked his bag in the container underneath. He got a shower—that, at least, was blessedly hot—and went in search of something to eat.

154   UNA McCORMACK

Outside, it had started sleeting. Gherrod hurried into the mess, which was noisy and busy and full of warm bodies. He inched his way through. He was down to his last ten *lek*s, and unlikely to be paid for at least a nine-day, so he took a half portion of *taleva* and a flatbread and found a place at a table on the edge of the room. The *taleva* wasn't bad, for military food, although Gherrod would have used slightly less salt and slightly more *ayit*. He ate slowly, trying to persuade his growling stomach that there was more. He was good at persuading himself that things were better than they were. When he was done with his supper, he sat back in his seat to watch the room. There was a sweet scent in the air that he couldn't place. Reaching into his pocket, he took out his pack of cards and began to shuffle them, with quick, clever hands.

It was like lighting a lamp and watching the stone-wings come fluttering. Three junior officers—two glinns and a gil—hoping, no doubt, to make some easy money from this scruffy, shabby new service drone. One of them asked him what he was drinking and bought him some cheap *kanar* with a rough and chemical taste.

Gherrod held up the cards. "Well, gentlemen—what's it to be? Blind Moon's Draw?" His voice came out clipped and sharp, pure East Torr.

"Why not?" said one of the glinns, Antek, a tall and heavyset young man who looked like he'd stepped out of a recruiting holo and wasn't remotely Gherrod's type.

Gherrod dealt, and they played. Within two rounds they'd realized that he wasn't the easy prey they were hoping for, but he was so easygoing, and so obviously not a physical match for any of them, that they didn't feel threatened. Everyone relaxed. The other glinn, Khenet, bought some bowls of *canka* nuts for the table to share, and another round of drinks. Partway through the next round, someone brought out a couple of hyposprays. When they used them, the sweet odor became very strong. Antek pushed one toward him. "Try it."

"What is it?" said Gherrod, handling the hypospray suspiciously.

"The locals call it Prophet's kiss. We call it crimson shadow. Try it. It doesn't bite."

Gherrod could recognize an order when he heard one, so he put the thing against his wrist. No pain, just a little pressure. He quickly felt calm, at ease. The room and the people in the room blurred ever so slightly around the edges, but not so that he was impaired. Best of all, nothing hurt, and he could believe that nothing would ever hurt ever again. By the end of the night, they were all best friends. Gherrod was warm and relaxed and didn't feel hungry anymore. He knew everyone's names and roles, and now he had a fairly good idea of their strengths and their weaknesses. He knew that Glinn Antek didn't like to lose. He knew that Gil Fusot was missing his sweetheart. He knew that Glinn Khenet, the aide to the base commander, was smarter than the rest of them put together. A few of the foot soldiers had been admitted to the circle, and he knew a great deal about them too. He learned how the crimson shadow came into the compound, who sold it, and for what kind of price. He let Antek win more than he deserved, but still came away with enough to eat decently until payday. And when he stood up to go to bed, swaying slightly as you might from too much liquor on a nearly empty stomach, he caught the eye of Glinn Khenet, gave him his best blue-eyed smile—and Khenet smiled back. Yes, he thought, this one. This is the one.

Gherrod, who was used to early starts, was awake before most of the others in his dormitory. They nodded brusque but not unfriendly greetings to the newcomer and went off to their various tasks. Gherrod had another hot and almost leisurely shower (if there was one thing to appreciate about being away from Prime, it was the abundance of water), and presented himself as instructed at the central office at oh-seven-hundred. To his relief, he was sent off to the kitchens. Yes, he would be on his feet all day, and probably yelled at by some petty tyrant, but it would be warm, there

156 UNA McCORMACK

would be no shortage of food, and maybe he could sneak some flavor into the *taleva*.

The days passed. Gherrod chopped vegetables, washed dishes, and scrubbed surfaces, and did that for eight days in a row with the ninth off. The head cook, Logar Prill, was bad-tempered but took pride in his work. As long as you made him look good, you could more or less help yourself to what was there, and Gherrod was fast enough on his feet to avoid getting hit when Prill started throwing things. Every evening, he went to the mess and played cards and took a little crimson shadow. Only a little; hardly anything you'd notice and just to keep the chill from the bones. He won some; he lost some. Nothing that would stand out. The officers thought his patter was funny and treated him like a clever pet. One time, Khenet, who had lost heavily to Glinn Tretor, handed over the *lek*s and said, sadly, "'Like *ithian* leaves they fell, and they did not return.'"

"Is that from one of your books?" said Antek.

"Yes," said Khenet, and the other officers groaned and rolled their eyes.

"*The House Between the Ithian Trees*," murmured Gherrod, for Khenet's ears only. "Eleta Preloc."

"That's right," said Khenet. Several times that evening, after that, Gherrod caught Khenet looking at him. Khenet, he noticed, drank moderately and did not use.

One afternoon, taking his break, Gherrod sat on the steps outside the kitchen eating hot *canka* nuts, wishing he was warmer. The day was damp. The sky was wet and watery; the sun weak as a Bajoran.

"Gherrod."

Gherrod looked up, shielding his eyes against the white light. Glinn Khenet was standing there, in uniform. Gherrod scrambled to his feet. Service grades stood up when an officer was around. Being penned for vagrancy was one thing; being flagged as potentially dissident was something else. Who wanted a visit from the Order? "Yes, sir?"

"Are you meant to be sitting outside eating *canka* nuts?"

SECOND SELF 157

"It's my designated break, sir."

"Oh, you get those, do you?"

"Mm. Fifteen metrics sitting out here with a bag of nuts and I'm a new man. Fired up and ready to serve."

Khenet suppressed a laugh, just. "Oh, well, we all have our duties to perform. Our respective tasks in life."

"And mine"—Gherrod mimed using a knife—"is chopping *parlik* roots for Cardassia."

Khenet laughed properly this time. He nodded at the bag of nuts. "Don't waste those," he said, and Gherrod, noting and appreciating the consideration, carried on eating.

"So," Khenet went on, watching him, "what brought you here?"

"I, er, made some bad decisions, sir."

"What kind of bad decisions?"

Gherrod, finishing the last nut, screwed up the bag. "I didn't do my chores."

"Oh, I see." Khenet, leaning his shoulder against the wall, relaxed. "Well, you seem to be making up for it."

"I want to get home as quick as I can, sir." He looked around. "This place is a dump."

"Yes, it is. And where's home?"

"Prime."

"You're from Prime?" said Khenet. He sounded surprised, impressed. *Yes,* thought Gherrod, *I might be trash, but I'm not provincial trash.*

"The capital. East Torr." He always said East Torr, which he knew so well you might even think of it as home. He always seemed to drift back there, in the end. As good a place as any. "What about you, sir? If you don't mind me asking?"

"Kelvas V."

Provincial world. Farming, mostly. Very dull. Gherrod had passed that way, once. "That's meant to be nice, sir."

158   UNA McCORMACK

"Yes, it is."

"Not nice enough to stay there though, sir?"

Khenet eyed him thoughtfully. "Tell me about the capital."

Suddenly, the kitchen door opened, and Prill shouted out, "Gherrod, you lazy *skrit*! Get your arse back in here or I'll have you mucking out the shithouse with the Bajorans!"

Gherrod mimed using the knife again. "Duty calls."

Khenet said, "Sorry if I've got you in trouble—"

"Don't worry, I'm always in trouble. Buy me a drink later, and I'll tell you about the time I saw Eleta Preloc in Tarlak."

After his shift, Gherrod lingered outside the mess rather than going in. Khenet, coming past with his brother officers, saw him and went over to speak to him, sending the others on ahead. "Not going in?"

"Been stuck inside all day. I'd rather get some fresh air."

"Even when it's this cold?" said Khenet.

"Mm." The door to the mess swung open to the uproarious sound of drunken soldiery. A blast of sweaty air rushed out too, sweetened by crimson shadow. Gherrod sighed. "Did you want to play cards again tonight?"

"You know," said Khenet, watching a couple of foot soldiers stagger past, "I can take it or leave it."

"Me too."

"Let me go and buy a bottle of *kanar*," said Khenet. "That'll keep us warm."

Gherrod, freezing inside his too thin jacket but glad of the new boots, kicked his heels until Khenet returned with a bottle. Seeing Gherrod shivering, Khenet frowned and said, "Aren't you cold in that?"

Gherrod shrugged. "It's all right. Where are we off to, then?"

"Let's go around to the back of the kitchen," said Khenet.

"What? I've spent all day over there—"

"Yes, but the back wall stays warm from the cookers."

"Oh. Good idea."

They walked along side by side, not talking. Khenet was right—the wall was warm, and there were a couple of stools stacked up together. They grabbed these and sat down. Gherrod leaned against the wall and felt a little welcome warmth seep into his bones. Khenet cracked open the bottle, took a swig, then passed it to Gherrod. A hit of *kanar* took away more of the chill, but, still, he took out a hypospray.

"That stuff," said Khenet, in a disapproving voice, as Gherrod pushed up his sleeve and pressed the hypo against the veins of his wrist. Just a little to take the edge off.

"What about it?"

"Not good for you. Gives you nightmares."

"Yeah, well, keeps out the cold." His breath curled in wisps in the air. "Shitty little planet."

"Not so bad in spring," said Khenet. "Even pretty, in places." He sighed deeply. Melancholy suited his handsome face, made him look like the poet Lukhan in the portrait during his exile. *Yearning for Home*. Was that Khenet's problem? Was he missing home? Was that the key to unlocking him?

"But you'd rather be somewhere else?" said Gherrod. His voice, if anyone attentive had been listening, sounded subtly different. More city heights; less Torr. More interrogative; less servile. But Khenet, although kind and well-meaning in his own way, was not really paying attention. Not to the kitchen drone.

"Well, who wants to be stuck out here?" Khenet said. "The locals are all mad. At least it's quiet. No Resistance activity in years."

"You were telling me about Kelvas V."

"Farming world. Boring. That's why I signed up. *You* were telling me about the capital."

"Big. Busy. Not enough work. My fault, somehow." Gherrod twisted the hypo around in his fingers. He'd used the last and there wouldn't be more until tomorrow. "That's why I'm here. Didn't you want to hear about me seeing Preloc that time?"

160   UNA McCORMACK

"Actually, what I want to know is—when did *you* read Preloc?"

Gherrod stiffened. His voice came out pure Torr. "I'm not stupid."

"I didn't mean that—"

"Do you think because I'm stuck washing dishes that I'm stupid?"

"I'm really sorry, I didn't mean anything like that—"

"I can read, you know! I've had a run of bad luck, that's all."

"It came out wrong—I'm sorry, I didn't mean anything by it. There's no reason you wouldn't have read Preloc—"

Gherrod started ticking them off angrily on his fingers. "I've read her enigma tales, I've read the pastorals, I've read her iterative verse *and* her recursive verse, and I've definitely read *Meditations on a* fucking *Crimson Shadow*, all right?"

"All right, I'm sorry!"

They sat side by side, both angry and embarrassed. After a moment or two, Gherrod reached out to tap Khenet gently on the arm. When Khenet was looking straight at him again, he gave a crooked smile—his absolutely winning crooked smile—and said, "I read them in the pen last year."

They both burst out laughing. Khenet looked nicely scandalized. That was the thing about these provincial boys. It didn't take much to shock them.

"What had you been *doing*?"

"Best not to dwell on such minutiae."

"More bad decisions?"

"I make a lot of those." Gherrod pushed over the bottle of *kanar*. "Friends again?"

Khenet took the bottle back and drank. "Friends."

Gherrod rubbed his hands together; his fingers were frozen stiff. "Sorry, sir," he said, "but I think we'll have to walk around for a while." Pride pushed him to say, "Can't stand the smell of the kitchen."

He watched Khenet take in his shivering body, his ashy face, his cold hands. Saw the young man's compassion. Almost felt sorry for him. What good was pity, for any of them? Khenet said, "Hey, listen, I've got a good idea. We'll go into the office."

"Is that okay? Thought I wasn't allowed?"

"I'll say I forgot some files," said Khenet. "Or needed you to carry my bag. We'll think of something."

"All right," said Gherrod. "Beats sitting out here." He followed Khenet around to the administrative block. "Never been in here before," he whispered as Khenet put his palm on the entrance panel. The lights were dimmed but Khenet led the way confidently down the corridor and into his office. Gherrod took the lay of the land; mapped reality against the plans he'd studied in the files. Not a big space. Computer on the desk. A couple of chairs. There was a door in the wall that led to the adjacent room.

"That's where the old man lives," Khenet said.

"Yeah? What's he like, the commander?" said Gherrod.

"Old Entrek? He's all right. He's fine, actually. Fair." Khenet shrugged. "I've served under worse. Let me turn the heating up."

"Huh." Gherrod perched on the desk and, while Khenet was busy fiddling with the heater, placed a couple of surveillance devices (their ranges significantly boosted) under his desk. "So," he said. "Preloc. I was working as a gardener in one of the big state parks in Tarlak—"

"A *gardener*, Mas?"

"Those stone gardens don't weed themselves. Anyway, one day this woman walks past carrying a big display of *perek*. I thought it was going to be for one of the legates, but no—she went to one of the little slabs and laid it there. I read the name on the slab—Tret Preloc. A son, I think. Then I recognized her from her state lecture."

"I love her books," said Khenet quietly. "She's incredible. What was she like?"

"Don't hate me, but she was dowdy. No sense of style." Gherrod sniffed.

162   UNA McCORMACK

"Then I thought—imagine having a mind so rich—so self-reliant—that you don't worry about how you look. How you present yourself to the world. Because everything you need"—he tapped his temple—"is up here."

Khenet was smiling at him, his head tilted, his eyes warm. "Gardening, cooking, literature, aesthetics. Is there anything you don't know about?"

"The military," said Gherrod. "Problems with authority. That's official, by the way. My last state-appointed conservator had it entered specially on my record."

Outside, they heard voices. People leaving the mess for the night.

"I'd better start heading back," said Gherrod. "Curfew, yes? For our own safety, of course."

"Yes, of course," said Khenet politely, a little distantly. They went back out into the cold night and meandered around the compound, finishing up the *kanar*, and walked toward the civilian accommodation block. Gherrod saw the place through Khenet's eyes. You might think twice about putting Bajorans here. You'd still do it, though.

"This is my stop," said Gherrod. "I'd invite you in for *gelat*, but there isn't any."

Khenet eyed the building as if he'd never been this way before. "Mas," he said, "you need to get yourself a coat before winter really sets in."

"I know."

"Do you need, well, money?"

"It'll be all right."

"Because I can help—"

"I'll work something out."

"All right. Well, goodnight then, Mas."

"'Night, sir."

He didn't tell Khenet what he was doing for money, which was a little sideline selling hypospray refills to his fellow drones in the dormitory. Cheap stuff, nasty, but the days were getting cold. Khenet would have had to report him if he knew, with a *this is for your own good* or *this hurts me more than it*

SECOND SELF 163

hurts you expression. Worse, he might try to talk him out of it. Try to save him from himself.

After that night, they met two or three times a week, in Khenet's office, if they could, which was useful, but it hadn't yet offered the opportunity to get inside Entrek's office. Frustrating. Khenet always brought a bottle, and Gherrod usually filched something from the kitchen. He brought crimson shadow too, despite the disapproval. Khenet talked about his home (which he obviously missed), his job with Entrek (more routine than he would like), and his ambitions (to get out after twenty years and travel). Gherrod filed that one away: desire to travel was a common early warning sign of dissident tendencies. In turn, Gherrod told tall tales about his past that stayed just the right side of shocking and made Khenet gasp and laugh. They never talked directly about books, but they did bat quotations at each other. Some nights they couldn't go to the office and had to walk around outside. One night, after the weather took a definite shift for the worst, there was snow on the ground. As they walked around, Khenet said, "Mas, have you still not got a coat?"

"They're not cheap, you know—"

"Is that all that's stopping you?"

"Sir," said Gherrod, teeth chattering, "it's a pretty big barrier to entry."

"What are they paying you?"

Gherrod gave a hollow laugh. "Let's say I'm glad I'm working with food."

Khenet gave Gherrod the bottle and sent him off to bed. The next time they met, Khenet was carrying a large parcel. "Don't ask," he said, shoving it into Gherrod's hands. "Just put it on."

Gherrod untied the parcel and took out a greatcoat. Third-, maybe fourth-hand, rubbed thin around the elbows and not quite black any longer in places, but thick, heavy. Warm. Gherrod put it on. It was slightly too large. "I must look appalling," he complained. "Like a vagrant."

"You *were* a vagrant," said Khenet. "And you're welcome."

It made all the difference. Between the coat and the bottles of *kanar*

164 UNA McCORMACK

(and the shadow), they were pretty cheerful. They began to meet more nights than not. One morning their days off coincided, and Gherrod hung around the door to the mess, wondering if Khenet would come past. He did, midmorning, and, seeing Gherrod, barked at him, "You! I want a word with you."

Had he found the surveillance devices? That could cause problems. Gherrod slouched after him, surly but obedient, and found to his surprise that Khenet was leading him off the base. "He's with me," Khenet said to the foot soldiers on guard, and they went out of the compound. They walked along the road awhile, and then turned down a lane leading to the river. Khenet relaxed and became himself again.

"Sorry about that," he said. "It's just . . ."

"Yeah?" said Gherrod.

Khenet was looking shifty. "It's all right us going about after dark. In private. But . . ."

But Khenet, an officer, shouldn't be seen hanging around with a service grade. Might affect his promotion opportunities. This was a new low. Being patronized by a provincial boy who quoted Preloc in a Kelvasian accent. He didn't even alter his voice to get the rhymes right in "Concentric Circles." Three hundred lines, half of them mispronounced.

"It's not personal, Mas—"

"It's okay," he said with a shrug. "Just how it is, isn't it?"

"Do you want to see the town?"

"The what?"

"The town. The Bajoran town."

Not really, thought Gherrod, with some irritation, since it was not anywhere near Entrek's office, and he was getting anxious about how long it was taking to get inside. "All right," he said. He reached into the deep pocket of his big coat and pulled out his hypo.

"Do you have to?" said Khenet.

"I don't have to," said Gherrod. "But I want to."

SECOND SELF   165

Khenet sighed but didn't say anything more. Gherrod soon felt warmer, relaxed, and while he longed to be back on Prime, back in Torr, sitting in the market sipping *gelat*, trekking through the mud didn't feel so bad. Miserable country, though. The trees were bare, black lines, and the ground mulched with dead leaves. At last, they drew closer to the town, passing by a number of run-down wooden barns.

"What's in those?" he said.

Khenet shrugged. "Don't know. Never looked. Empty, I think."

Gherrod sniffed the air: musty, damp, and, underneath, something metallic and burning. Was anyone still farming around here, or had they all drifted over to the mining operation back near Merna? Did he even care? He trudged on beside Khenet. Soon they reached the old Bajoran town of Akantha.

The place was pitiful, dying a slow death. Some of the buildings were already ruined; the rest were falling down. People sat in doorways, watching listlessly as they picked their way along the wet and filthy main street. Those locals who were moving around scurried past them eyes averted and heads down. At last, they came to the river, brown and slow moving. A few boats were moored there, but they too were abandoned and decaying. Everything was rotten.

"Hey," said Gherrod. "Thanks for bringing me here. It's great."

Khenet laughed. "Yes, on reflection, perhaps we should have waited for the spring."

"At least I've got some exercise."

"Do you want to see the temple?"

Why would he want to see some ramshackle site dedicated to the ludicrous gods of a superstitious people? "Okay."

Khenet pointed to a path that led along the river. They walked beside the river for a little while, until they reached a building bigger than the rest, built from the same crumbling yellow stone, with a big pink dome. The building had a red door, the paint peeling to show the grain of wood beneath. On

166   UNA McCORMACK

either side of the door were two small trees, evergreens, an unexpected and surprisingly pleasant flash of color.

"The temple of Akantha," said Khenet. He sounded pretty pleased with it—or with himself. "What do you think?"

Gherrod considered this. "I think it's falling down."

"Yes, a shame they don't take care of their heritage," said Khenet.

"Better for them if it's gone," said Gherrod.

"What do you mean?"

"Well, it's not doing them any good, is it? All this stuff about Prophets. Who runs Bajor now? Best thing we ever did, getting rid of religion." Gherrod reached down to pick up a stone. He was aiming it at one of the evergreens, but Khenet stopped his hand.

"Don't," he said. "We're not thugs."

"All right," said Gherrod. He put the stone in his pocket. "Don't care either way."

"I thought you'd be more interested," said Khenet. "You seemed to be interested in . . . Well, art, and architecture, and history."

"I guess. Bit cold, that's all." And the hit was wearing off and he didn't have more with him and he was nowhere near Entrek's office.

"Shall we go inside, then?"

"Okay."

Inside, the temple was warm and dimly lit. Gherrod's eyes began to sting. Looking ahead, across a big low room, he saw rows and rows of lit candles. A few wooden chairs were set out in front of these, in lines.

"Look," said Khenet, walking forward. "Look at those paintings!"

There were figures painted on the walls, but they were so faded and stylized that Gherrod could not really decipher them. What was interesting him more was that the building gave the impression of being much smaller inside than suggested by its exterior. On each of the side walls, there were three doors, painted red again and peeling, the planks of wood plain underneath. There must be small rooms lining the interior walls of the temple.

Curious, he went over to one of the doors. He tried the handle, but it was locked.

"How do you like our temple?"

Gherrod swung around. An elderly Bajoran man, white haired, in robes, wearing an earring and holding a candle, was walking toward them. Khenet favored him with a smile. "I think it's charming!"

"Thank you," said the vedek. "You're interested in the paintings?"

"Yes, they're splendid. Very nicely done for rustic art."

"They're about seven hundred years old," said the vedek, which gave Gherrod a moment's pause. It was not quite a hundred and fifty years since Cardassia achieved spaceflight, and the Bajorans settled other worlds half a millennium before that. But what had they done in this time? Nothing. Brought their backward superstitions to the stars. Stagnated. Cardassia was in the ascendance now. The Bajorans didn't know how lucky they were.

"Remarkable!" said Khenet, in that bright tone of voice, like he was talking to a child.

"What are these doors for?" said Gherrod.

The vedek turned to look at him. His eyes were weary but penetrating and, for one scary moment, Gherrod thought that he had seen through the mask. Then the vedek tapped the palm of his hand with the candle. "Prayer cells," he said. "The monks at Akantha were celebrated for their piety and attracted a wealthy clientele that was willing to pay for private audiences with such holy men." His mouth twitched. "I shouldn't think the monks let their devoutness obscure their business acumen."

Khenet gave a knowing laugh. For some reason, Gherrod liked him less here. "At heart," Khenet said, "religion is the source of great corruption."

"Do you think so?" said the vedek, tilting his head. Gherrod whistled under his breath. If this had been one of the other officers—Antek, say—this old man would now be nursing a broken nose for such impudence. But Khenet was better than the rest—or fancied himself that way, at any rate.

"Do you not?" said Khenet.

168   UNA McCORMACK

"On its own, belief causes little in the way of harm," said the vedek. "Context is everything." He walked over to the nearest row of candles. Gherrod followed slowly. "Power is the chief source of corruption," said the vedek. "Power, and the desire for control." He turned to Gherrod. "What do you think?"

Gherrod shrugged. "Don't ask me," he said. "I wash pots for a living."

"Somebody always does," said the vedek. He offered Gherrod the candle. "Light it," he instructed.

"I don't think that would be right. I don't believe—"

"No," said the vedek. "Light it anyway."

Well, why not? Wouldn't cost him anything. Gherrod put the wick to the nearest flame, and, when the candle was lit, set it in place.

"There," said the vedek. "I'll keep you in my thoughts."

"Just don't say a prayer for me," said Gherrod.

Once again, the vedek gave him that penetrating look. "No, I won't do that."

Behind them, Khenet was getting restless. "Come on, Mas," he said. "It's time we got back to the base."

"Yeah," said Gherrod. "I mean, yes, sir."

Outside, Khenet said, "You were a hit."

"Huh." Gherrod shook his head. He felt oddly unsettled by the whole experience. "Stupid place," he said. "Stupid superstitions." He took the stone out of his pocket and, this time, threw it before Khenet could stop him. It knocked over one of the little green trees. Perfect aim. "Stupid," he said, again.

They didn't talk much on the walk home. Back at the compound, Khenet said, "Well, see you, Mas," and walked off. Something had gone wrong. What had gone wrong? Gherrod swallowed. He still had to get inside Entrek's office and he didn't want to have to resort to burglarizing the place. Too many risks involved, and Mas Gherrod was in enough trouble already without that on his record. Khenet was still his best way in. So he swallowed his pride and chased after him.

SECOND SELF 169

"Sir," he said.

"What is it?" said Khenet.

"I'm sorry it seemed I didn't like the temple." *Humble yourself before your superiors*, Mas thought. That usually worked. "It was good. I learned a lot. Thanks, sir."

Khenet looked at him thoughtfully, and then gave a rueful smile. He patted him on the shoulder, like you might pet a favorite riding-pup. "Oh, forget about it, Mas," he said. "Let's have a drink later, hey? But do leave that awful stuff behind, yes?"

"Yeah," said Gherrod. "All right."

They went back to their evening meetings, but they weren't the same. The differences between them that they had been ignoring for the sake of comradeship—Khenet's higher status, conferred by birth and position; Gherrod's manifestly sharper intelligence—had been shown for what they were, and they couldn't go back. Khenet talked over him, didn't make eye contact so much, and there were no further invitations to join him in his office. And this was becoming a serious concern: the surveillance devices that Gherrod had so far managed to plant were a washout. Entrek seemed to do nothing in his office but play card games. Not even good ones. He liked the one where you laid out the cards facedown in a circle and had to find all of one suit. Kids' stuff. What Gherrod needed were visuals—and he wasn't going to get them without placing something inside the room. The days were ticking past, and they would be asking questions back on Prime.

The idea had been to get as close to this young man as possible—turn him in some way. Get him using crimson shadow, maybe—seduce him, if necessary—then turn the tables. Exert pressure. Twist Khenet to his purposes. Find something by which he could control him. Then the information would flow, straight from Entrek's desk to Gherrod and from Gherrod back to his superior, whose all-seeing eye had fallen on Gul Entrek, and who

170   UNA McCORMACK

suspected him of crimes to which Gherrod was not privy. Gherrod did not need to know. He only needed to obey. But something had gone wrong. Khenet was pulling back. Ever since they went down to that wretched temple. Bajorans. They were always a problem. Someone ought to deal with that.

One night, Gherrod hung around the mess, waiting for Khenet to appear. He did, at last, and, when he saw Gherrod, he nodded but made to move past him.

"Hey," said Gherrod. "I mean, good evening, sir."

"Hello, Mas. How are you?"

"I'm okay. I was wondering . . ."

"Yes?"

Gherrod found himself in the unusual position of being stuck for words. There wasn't, really, a way for someone like him to say to an officer, *Do you want to spend some time together?*

"Er . . . Nothing, really. Saw you coming and thought I'd tell you how good the coat is. Lifesaver." He gave a nervous laugh. Hopeless. This was turning into a disaster.

"Well, I'm glad to hear that, Mas. Look, I'm supposed to be meeting some of the other officers tonight and I'm quite late. Was that everything?"

"Oh," said Mas. "Yeah. I guess so . . ."

"Then I'll get on," said Khenet with a brisk nod. He was about to walk past, when Gherrod, rather desperately, put his hand on Khenet's arm, and said, "Sir!"

They looked at each other, lonely young man to lonely young man. Gherrod could have sworn that Khenet was starting to soften. But then the door to the mess opened. Bright lights and noise and the sweet scent poured out, and so did Gul Antek. He took one look at the scene in front of him, walked across, pulled Gherrod away from Khenet, and punched him hard in the stomach. "Take your filthy fucking hands off him, you *skrit*!"

Gherrod plummeted to the ground. Dimly, he heard Khenet say, "Antek, what in the name of Tret Akleen do you think you're—"

SECOND SELF   171

But Antek was already putting the boot in. "I've been watching you," he said to Gherrod. "With your mouth and your cards and your cheap shadow. Sidling up to officers. You little bastard—"

Gherrod hated being called that. Really hated it. Between gasps he spat out, "Fuck you!"

"You piece of shit," said Antek, and bent down to pick him up so he could carry on punching him. Khenet, meanwhile, was trying to pull him back.

"Stop it," he said. "Leave him alone!"

"He needs to learn," said Antek. "Learn who he is in the order of things—"

"I'm warning you, Antek," said Khenet. "Don't touch him again."

"I'll do what I like," said Antek. Punched him back down to the ground.

Gherrod, who had his hands up now to cover his head, didn't see what happened next. But he heard it. A disruptor being drawn, a shot being fired and then Antek was shouting in pain. What a time to play the hero. Gherrod kept his arms wrapped around himself, and the next thing he knew, he was being dragged away. Not long after that he was lying on the floor of one of the compound's tiny pens, curled over on himself, his ribs aching, longing for a hit, scared almost out of his wits at how this situation had spiraled out of control. His mind was racing, but always circled back to the same terrifying thought. That some children were born to be tools, not treasures, and that useless tools were cast away like trash.

Tain is going to kill me.

Gherrod spent three nights and two days in that little room, wondering what was happening, trying to work out what had gone so badly wrong and what could be salvaged. Not much, he feared, and even more he was afraid of what the outcome of this was going to be. How had he been so stupid as to put his hand on Khenet's arm? You didn't do that as a civilian, and cer-

172   UNA McCORMACK

tainly not one this far down the ladder. Not to a superior, and certainly not to an officer. Obstructing a military man was assault, and in some circumstances might even be classed as sedition. Officers were an instrument of the state. People of consequence had been ruined for less.

In the dead hours, he tormented himself with what was coming: the appearance in front of the local archon; the reading of the verdict (unlawful handling of a military officer); the consideration of his record; the careful assessment and gradation of his guilt; the sentence. Two years at a labor camp? Three? Would Tain come to help? He doubted it. He'd been given his chance to make something of himself and he'd messed it up. All that was left was poverty and crime, bad jobs and prison sentences. Wasn't that always the way, though, with people like him? You gave them a chance, but there was something wrong with them. Would Mila come? Would Tain allow that?

On the morning of the third day, the door opened, and Mas was bundled out and brought before Gul Entrek. He stood, eyes down, head hanging like a kicked hound. He had wanted to get into the commander's office, he thought, but not this way.

"Well," said Entrek with a weary sigh. "What a mess. What a stinking mess."

Gherrod risked a quick look at his target. First time he'd gotten this close, and he shouldn't waste the opportunity. He should always do his chores. Entrek was in his middle years, in decent shape, but had a tired air about him. Defeated. His desk, now he was able to take a look at it, was a mess. What could Tain possibly want with a man like this? Was he really some kind of threat? Gherrod reined that treacherous thought back immediately. Not his business. His business was to monitor this man as closely as possible and report back on what he observed. Nothing more; nothing less. The Order knew its own mind. He was merely the instrument in its hand—and that was enough. More than enough. That knowledge would sustain him for a large part of his life, even during the leanest years. These, right now, were not—incredibly—the leanest years.

"If I had my way, you'd be heading to a labor camp right now," said Entrek. "But Glinn Khenet pleaded for you. Said this wasn't your fault and a misunderstanding all around. And the good news for you, Gherrod, is that I like Khenet. He's a fine young man and an excellent officer. Cardassia is not served by losing men like him. If I prosecute you, Khenet's name will be dragged through the dirt. Questions, as to why he shot a fellow officer, on behalf of you. You, of all people. For pity's sake!" Entrek shook his head. "That will do him no good. So, here's what will happen. You will go back to work today, half pay, and you will work harder than you have ever worked, and you will do that for the next four months, and then you will leave here and get back to whatever passes for the pathetic life that you were leading before you ever darkened my door, and after that I will never hear from you again. Do you understand?"

"Yes, sir."

"Do you have any questions?"

"Well . . . yes, sir."

Entrek sighed. "What is it?"

"What about Glinn Khenet, sir? What's going to happen to him?"

There was a pause. "I'm glad you asked. Khenet is being transferred to Ashalla. Gul Feris wants him on his staff."

"Thank you, sir." No point asking about Antek. He'd probably gotten a pay raise.

Entrek sat back in his chair. Gherrod risked another quick look. Entrek, catching his eye, said softly, "I know your kind, Gherrod. Clever, but undisciplined. Think you're better than you are. Never accept responsibility. Never knuckle down to work and duty. You're trash, you know, and you always will be. And I don't care whether or not you spend your life going from pen to pen, from gutter to gutter, filling your veins with some junk or other, but this time you nearly took a good young man down with you."

And the simple fact was that some young men were worth saving on their own account, and others weren't.

174   UNA McCORMACK

"Yes, sir," said Gherrod.

"Get out of here. Tell Prill he's to come and see me. I want him on your case. And one last thing, Gherrod—"

Gherrod, who had by now shuffled over to the door, stopped and looked back.

"I'd watch out for the other junior officers if I were you," said Entrek. "Don't let them find you in a quiet corner one night. They liked Khenet. They don't like you."

And Entrek wasn't going to stand in their way. Gherrod muttered another "thank you, sir" and slunk off. On the step outside the officers' block, he ran into the garresh who had driven him over to this benighted place. The older man looked at him with something close to pity. "Sort yourself out, son," he said. "Before it's too late."

Gherrod mumbled his thanks—but inside he was burning. These people. These *mediocrities*. What did they know about him, really? The path he was on had been chosen for him by powers far greater than any gruff but kindly garresh, any gentle and cultured glinn, any weary, beaten-down gul. They served Cardassia, but he served Cardassia too, and the work he did— the work he might yet do—would outclass them all. Besides, he'd gotten that surveillance device into Entrek's room at last. So that was a start. The start of something new, something better. Had to be.

Two days later, sitting outside in the cold, taking his break, he heard footsteps and looked up to see Khenet. He stood up. You stood up when an officer was around.

"Hello, Mas."

"Hello. Sir."

"I'm leaving today. I didn't want to go without saying goodbye."

"Oh," said Gherrod. "Right."

"I'm sorry for everything that happened."

"Not your fault, sir."

"I feel like it was—"

SECOND SELF 175

"It wasn't," said Gherrod, in a rare moment of complete honesty. "I should . . . I should give you back your coat."

Khenet smiled. A generous smile. Kind. He was a good man, really. Didn't know much about how things were, but good as he could be in a world like this.

"That was a gift, Mas," Khenet said. "What does Preloc say about gifts? " 'Your birth is your family's gift. Your schooling your teacher's gift. Your duty is Cardassia's gift. Your spouse is life's gift. Your children are the future's gift.' "

Preloc's *Summer by the Lake*. Khenet, he saw, was waiting for the last line. He owed him that. " 'And the gifts of friendship enrich us all.' "

"That's right," said Khenet. "A gift of friendship. Good luck, Mas," he said, and went on his way. Gherrod never saw him again. He looked him up, years later, when he was sitting in splendid isolation on a cold, bright space station, with nothing to do, and wondering where the lives he had touched over the years had led. Only ten years' service, in the end. Not enough to get the travel permits he'd longed for. Went back to Kelvas V and entered the family business. Joined with a local woman and had seven children. That was before the Fire, of course. He didn't check afterward. There was nobody left, afterward, and there was already too much guilt to bear.

After Khenet's departure, Gherrod did what Entrek said and kept his head down. Slunk between the kitchen and the dormitory. Work and sleep. Tried not to be alone. Not that it would make any difference. Everyone knew what had happened, right down to the other civilians in his dormitory, who were keeping their distance. He hadn't made friends there, other than to sell a little shadow. He'd expended his energies on cultivating Khenet. That had been a mistake. He wouldn't make that mistake again, if he got another chance. What did Preloc say, in *The Dark Fields of Home*?

Plant your garden wisely; do not trust a single seed.

The first beating, when it came, was finely judged and very thorough. These boys were professionals. The days were getting shorter. It was dark when he went to work, and dark when he ended, and his hours were completely regular. He tried altering routes, but the compound wasn't that big. Antek and three gils grabbed him on the path by the side of the accommodation block. Dragged him off to some lightless corner. Kicked him around. Called him a few names. *Stinking skrit. Little bastard.*

When they were done, Gherrod lay in the mud for a while, then hauled himself up and checked himself over, piece by piece. Nothing broken, he thought, but he was going to ache again for days. He dragged himself back to the dormitory, slinking past the others to the washroom, and looked at himself in the mirror. His nose had made it through intact, but the area around one eye was swelling. He went to bed and took out the hypo. Old friend; reliable friend. He'd been lucky tonight, he knew. The problem was, he didn't think this was going to satisfy them. They'd tried their luck and got away with it. They'd tasted blood. They'd be back for more.

The next few days were another low point. He worked through the pain and Prill's abuse. He hid as best he could. In the evenings, he worked on the remote boosters that would extend the range of his surveillance devices. Each evening, sitting outside behind the farthest accommodation block, cold fingers working cleverly, patiently, until he was able to monitor the whole set of offices. Faithfully, diligently, he recorded everything he saw and heard—although he was baffled. There was, as far as he could tell, nothing of note. But then, he was only one small part of a large machine. The Order had its own purposes. One did not question; one simply obeyed. For Tain, or rather for Cardassia, which were as close to being the same thing in his mind that he was barely able to distinguish the difference.

He felt better for this progress, nonetheless, and perhaps that made him lower his guard. Anyway, the next attack didn't come in some dark quiet corner. It came in broad daylight, in the middle of the compound, with at least a dozen other people walking by. A couple of gils were walking past. Suddenly, one of them dived in close, and punched him hard, in the gut. He went down, doubled over, retching and coughing. He heard their laughter. He heard the same old insults, thrown back casually as they went on their way. He saw others walking past. Across the way stood Entrek, who took in what was happening and looked away. When Gherrod got his breath back, he staggered over into the dormitory, where a couple of the others took one look at him and turned their backs. He fell onto the bed. Fumbled around for the hypo. Tried to take the pain away.

The next morning was his day off. He woke early, well before dawn, still sore. The walls seemed closer than usual. He had to get away. He didn't have permission to leave the base, but he didn't care. He slid out of bed—everyone else was still sleeping—and was through the back fence within fifteen metrics. When he reached the Bajoran town, he walked down to the river. A boat had arrived—a major event by the standards of daily life in the town—bringing in boxes of food and other supplies. He watched as it was unloaded and then as it started on its slow journey back downstream. Then he went to the temple. The little green tree was upright again, and the door was open. He went inside.

The air was full of a sweet clean scent that was completely unlike crimson shadow. Had there been a ceremony? Gherrod knew only a little about their superstitions and had no framework by which to make a guess. He should learn about that, he supposed. They were Cardassian subjects after all, and information was his business. Better to know, than to be caught unawares. He sat down on one of the wooden chairs and put his head in his hands. He breathed in, hating the smell. He hated this whole world. He longed to be back home, on Prime, walking through East Torr. The smell of familiar spices, the oil and the tar from the river, the dry heat, something other than this wet and rotting place.

178   UNA McCORMACK

A hand upon his arm. Pale and alien. Gherrod looked up. It was the old vedek. He said, "You're in pain."

Pain. They should do something about that. Find a way to stop it. Make it go away.

"What?"

"I'm sorry to see you like this." The vedek sat down beside him. He folded his hands upon his chest and stretched out his legs. Completely at home. *What are we doing here?* Gherrod thought seditiously. *Why did we ever take these worlds?*

"You're alone this time," said the old man.

"Yes."

"Well," said the vedek, "temples are places of sanctuary and contemplation. You're welcome to sit here for a while and see what a little quiet can do for you."

Again, he gave Gherrod that intense and rather unforgiving gaze. Why did he think he could do that? He must know, surely, that even a service grade like Gherrod only needed to say that one of the Bajorans had stepped out of line, and there'd be reprisals. Gherrod stared at the candlelight. He'd heard pity in the vedek's voice. Pity.

Suddenly, Gherrod saw himself through this man's eyes. Shabby, underfed, beaten down. But that was not who he was. Not really. He was someone else, really. He wasn't sure, right now, who that person was, but it wasn't this. This was a part he was playing for a while. A mask he was wearing. "A vedek is an unusually high rank for a temple this small and remote," he said, a little Order steel creeping into his voice. His right, as a Cardassian, to be acknowledged the superior here.

"Oh, well, Akantha has its charms. There was a big monastery here once, a few centuries ago. This temple was part of the monastery, a very holy place. It's all that remains, of both city and monastery. And my rank remains. There's always been a vedek at Akantha." He smiled. "You haven't told me your name."

SECOND SELF   179

"Mas Gherrod."

"Mas Gherrod. I am Saba Taan. You're not, I think, a religious man."

"No, I'm not."

"Faith can be a great support, you know," said the vedek. "We all need something, especially in trying times." Again, that pity. Pitied by a Bajoran. "What supports you, Mas Gherrod?"

"I have things I believe in," he said. Why so defensively?

"That's a start," said Saba. "There *is* an order to things. What, for example, do you think, has brought you to Akantha?"

"There was no plan. I made some bad choices."

"I see. A lucky man."

"Lucky?" A little bitterness slipped through.

"Not everyone gets the chance to step aside from the path of his life and have time to reflect."

Just in time, before nodding, Gherrod caught the ghost of a smile pass across Saba's face. He burst out laughing. The vedek was actually teasing him. "My own personalized homily!"

"With my blessing," said the vedek dryly.

"I'll try to take it to heart." Gherrod took a deep breath. "I should go. Thank you for your time, *Da'eel. Vatay-ja.*"

A look of deep sadness crossed the vedek's face. What had he said? That was the right honorific, wasn't it? The right phrase? He didn't think he had offended. So what had he done? Was it simply that this Cardassian had taken the time to learn such things? But information was his business. He was showing this old man that he knew his business. As he tried to rationalize this, Saba leaned over and placed his hand upon Gherrod's face. His touch was very gentle, almost tender. "*Ja-rataja,* Mas Gherrod." Ever so slightly, his thumb stroked the ridges on his cheek. "Oh, I do forgive you, you know."

"Forgive me?"

"For everything you are about to do." Saba drew back his hand. "Mas Gherrod. May the Prophets guard and guide you on your path."

180 UNA McCORMACK

"Do you know," observed Gherrod, "I don't think you've mentioned the Prophets before."

"No," said Saba. "I haven't."

Gherrod, who was a little shaken by this exchange, and whose cruel streak was, by this point in his life, starting to win out, said, "It's nonsense, you know. Superstition. Lies."

Saba gave a low laugh. "Lies often conceal a deeper truth."

"That's sophistry."

"Tell me," said the vedek, "is the path you're on now making you happy?"

Happy? What did that have to do with anything? It was his task, his role, his function. It was what Tain required—what Cardassia required. He was nothing, had nothing, came from nothing. And yet the Order had found a place for him. A family. And family was all. What did happiness have to do with any of that?

Beside him, the old man sighed. "I do wonder," he said, "what would happen if you came to see me again. I could tell you everything about those paintings, you know. I think you'd be interested."

"I think I would," said Gherrod, and stood. "Perhaps I will come again," he said, but even as he said it, he knew it was a lie. He schooled his face into a bland smile that one day he would use so often it would fit like a second skin. "Thank you for your time, vedek," he said brightly, tilting his head. "Most helpful. Very kind."

The old vedek closed his eyes. "Goodbye, Mas Gherrod. Be seeing you."

That night, tired and afraid and deep in the embrace of the crimson shadow, Mas Gherrod dreamed. He was walking through the temple once again. A bright light flashed, and he saw three figures, walking slowly around him. One of them was Vedek Saba. He was telling him, again, that he was forgiven—for everything he was about to do. The other figure, he did not know. A young human, of all things, a Starfleet officer, very beautiful, and

SECOND SELF   181

he was telling him that he was forgiven—for whatever it was that he had done. The third figure, he knew all too well. Tain, brutal and jovial as ever, telling him that he could not forgive what he had done, but he could try to forget.

Gherrod woke, sweating, and with full understanding. He knew, now, without doubt, the truth about Akantha. He understood, now, everything that he had seen. The prayer chambers. The empty barns. The desolation. The world had tilted. The everyday and commonplace had taken on a new, more sinister, complexion.

How could I have been so blind? So completely, utterly stupid?

He sat for a while, his hands on his knees, calming himself, thinking through what had to happen next. He got up, and dressed, and slipped through the base, and down toward the town. On the outskirts, he broke into a run, stumbling slightly, only stopping when he came to the temple. The door was locked, but that was no challenge. He was inside in a matter of moments. The candles were out, he noticed. No, you wouldn't want naked flames burning unattended around here. He took out his flashlight, its bluish, artificial light alien in this ancient, sacred place, and made his way toward one of the red doors.

He scrabbled with the catch, some of the stone crumbling in his hand. When it finally came loose, he opened the little door. He shone the flashlight inside, revealing to him a miniature armory. All the necessary materials to make explosives. Grenades. In the name of Tret Akleen, ground cannon! He pulled out some of the hand weapons. Ancient phasers. Plasma rifles. Many different makes and worlds. There were even some Cardassian disruptors. Chamber after chamber revealed the same story. He walked out of the temple and looked around the town. The temple contained a large cache, but there were about fifty buildings in the town, not to mention the barns on the outskirts . . . No wonder the fields looked so poor. Akantha had not been a farming community for many years, but not for the reason they thought. It was a storage and supply center for the Resistance.

182   UNA McCORMACK

Gherrod put together the likely pieces of the operation. The weapons arrived farther up along the Parset river, no doubt. Brought here from around the quadrant. Little ships, slipping past their sensors. Cargo transported onto the planet's surface from orbit, or perhaps they even landed there to unload. Carried downriver, to Akantha, that neglected and forgotten town, where they were dispersed through Ordeve and then, via as-yet-unknown routes, into the Bajoran system. The remoteness of the town meant that the few troops stationed here were looking mainly at the engineering project. Not to mention their inexperience, or, in Entrek's case, their apathy. How long had this been going on? Two years? Five? Little Resistance activity here, Khenet had said. He really had known nothing. They all knew nothing.

Silently, Gherrod left the temple, closing the door behind him. He slipped back through the darkness to the base. This time, he went in through the main entrance. As he made his way through the compound, his whole bearing altered. Gone were the slumped shoulders, the downcast eyes, the hangdog expression. He moved with confidence and surety. His back was straight. His eyes, blue and bright, were unblinking. He would perform this transformation many times across the years to come, until the whole change—there and back—could take place in the blink of an eye. This was his true purpose. This was what he had been trained to do—and if, at the back of his mind, he thought that now he might be able to redeem himself in Tain's eyes for the disaster his original mission had become, then who would blame him?

Gherrod marched straight into the main office block, down the corridor, and into Entrek's office. Entrek was in there, drinking *kanar* with a couple of the junior officers, Antek included. When Antek saw the kitchen boy stride into his commander's office, ill-fitting threadbare coat trailing behind him, his eyes flashed in fury. "Gherrod! You little shit! Do I have to kill you to make you understand what you are?"

Elim Garak reached across the desk and hit the console. "Clearance

SECOND SELF   183

code verification nine two one eight"—his eye fell on Entrek as he gave the last word—"*black*."

There was a pause, and then a *beep*.

"*Clearance code verified.*"

"You?" whispered Antek. "*You're* with the Order?"

Garak turned his eye on him. "We are everywhere, soldier. You would do well to remember that in future."

Entrek was collecting himself. "Sir," he said, standing and saluting a man young enough to be his son, "we are here to serve."

"I'm glad to hear that," said Garak, moving to take his place behind Entrek's desk. His desk now. "Because we have work to do." He pointed at Antek and didn't give him a second look. "You, get me some armor."

The first order was to contact the capital and request reinforcements, but the base comms were down, and the officers responsible couldn't say why, and couldn't say when they'd be back, and looked terrified at having to deliver this news to the Order. That, at least, should spur them to find a solution in record time. Or Garak would want to know why.

"Sabotage," said Garak. "The Bajorans know what we've discovered. We need to move quickly." Equipped now with armor and a disruptor, and with Antek scrambling like a hound at his heels, trying to win his favor, Garak assembled the junior officers and the foot soldiers and gave them their orders. Most of them looked terrified. He realized, as he spoke, that more than half of them had never taken part in a real military operation before. Serving meant sitting around in a remote backwater on a colonized world, waiting for your tour to end. It didn't mean firing weapons and shooting people. Entrek, to give him his due, knew his business. He slipped seamlessly into the role of second-in-command.

Within the hour, the operation was underway. The company moved into Akantha. Within the next hour, two-thirds of the buildings had re-

184 UNA McCORMACK

vealed weapons' caches, and Garak had fifty hostages at his disposal. Two Cardassian foot soldiers and eleven Bajorans were dead. Five of those Bajorans had been killed in scuffles, the other six Garak had ordered shot, one by one, until the rest surrendered. A dozen or so were still loose, by their best estimate, so Garak ordered his captives marched down to one of the barns and locked inside.

"I want this whole area searched," he said. "I want every single Bajoran still alive in the area brought here. And—when you find him—I want to speak to the vedek."

Yes, he thought, he particularly wanted to see Saba Taan again. Speak to that old man, who must have known, both times, exactly what his temple contained, who had tricked him—a member of the Order! Saba Taan had lied to him, and he would pay the price for that.

All night, Garak watched the officers fall over themselves to obey his every order. He watched them snap out salutes to him. He watched how they could not meet his eye, from the sheer terror of what his reprisal might be. He thought: *This is how it feels to be powerful. In control. This is how they all must feel, all day and every day.* He would come to crave this feeling.

After a couple of hours, Entrek came unwillingly to speak to this cold and brutal young man, his superior. "Gherrod, sir," he said, "there's still no sign of the vedek."

"No," said Garak. "There wouldn't be. What about the rest?"

"We think we have the whole adult population—"

"Adult population?"

"We can't find any of the children, sir," said Entrek unhappily.

"The *children*?" Garak stared around the town. How had they missed them? Where had they gone? What was going on here?

"What are your orders, sir?" said Entrek.

"Set charges on the buildings," said Garak. "I want the town leveled and burned. And I want Saba Taan and the children found."

The junior officers standing by looked at him, and then at Entrek.

SECOND SELF **185**

"Sir?" said Tretor uncertainly, to Entrek. Why was he looking at him? Garak was in command now. Garak was their superior.

"Start with the temple," Garak said.

"Gherrod . . ." said Entrek. "Sir—"

"Why are you all still standing here, looking at me?" said Garak. "You have your orders."

"Sir," said Entrek, "we still haven't been able to reach Merna. We don't know whether there are more of them out there, and we're very exposed—"

"Oh *please*!" spat Garak. "This town—through your dereliction of duty, Entrek—has become a major supply point for the Bajoran Resistance. Another few months, and they might have been able to take Merna. Take back Ordeve. Your watch"—he eyed them all—"all of you. They'll have taken heart from this. Confidence. I want that heart ripped out. I want this town destroyed. I want that *temple* destroyed."

"Is this why you came here?" said Entrek. "Did you know this was going on?"

"The Order's business is its own," said Garak. "You have your instructions."

From the barn where the Bajorans were being held, a song began. All those voices, coming together, united in their hatred. *All of them,* thought Garak distantly. *We may end up killing all of them . . .* He looked at Entrek and the others. He was aware that his situation was perilous. That these officers—who already had no liking for him—could simply shoot him now and be done with him.

"Listen," he said, pointing his disruptor toward the barn. "That's your enemy. Burn the town. Put anyone you find—child or adult—in the barn with the rest. But when you have Saba Taan, bring him straight to me."

"Sir," said Antek, saluting. "We'll get it done."

"Yes," said Garak. "Yes, you will."

They went off, issuing orders to the foot soldiers to lay charges. The temple went first. Garak stood for a while and watched the fire take hold.

186   UNA McCORMACK

Watching it, he understood properly why he was here. Why he existed. The relief was overwhelming, the clarity, too, and so much better than anything that any drug had offered. All the pain and fear and isolation—it had *purpose*. The Order had purpose and passed that on to him. He was a weapon, finely tuned, brought out and used at need. At Cardassia's need. He could see now why he had been born; why he had been allowed to live. And as the fires spread, and the buildings crumbled, he promised himself: *You will never be vulnerable again. You will survive this, and everything else that comes your way. You will build a Cardassia so strong that whatever happens, you will be safe, and you will* thrive.

A few hours before dawn, Garak, Entrek, and two other officers gathered back at the base to assess their current situation. The comms specialists had still not been able to reach Merna. Garak was wondering what threat might stimulate them to better service, but, "I'll handle this," said Entrek, and went to speak to them. Garak sat in Entrek's chair, looking around the office, while Antek and Tretor sat with their eyes averted, waiting to be required. When Entrek came back in, he said, "Within the hour. They're sure of that."

"They'd better," said Garak, brushing ash from his shoulder.

The Bajorans were contained—just about. There were barely enough men from the garrison to guard the barn. Whenever the singing got too loud, they were reminded of the fate of their town and their temple, and that this barn too could be set on fire. That damped them down for a while. Long enough, Garak hoped, for contact to be reestablished with the capital.

"Of course," he said to the others, "we have no good intelligence on how the Resistance is operating in the rest of the area. Let's hope they're not currently planning a counterattack."

Antek shifted nervously. "You're scaring the life out of me."

"Good," said Garak. He looked at his disruptor, which he had been gripping now for hours. He put it down on Entrek's desk and flexed the muscles in his hand. He supposed this meant he was feeling more secure now. He rubbed his face. He didn't feel more secure. He felt like there was something he had missed. The children. The vedek. Was there anything else?

The others were moving on from operational issues to dissecting the day's events. The two glinns had never experienced anything like this. *A rude awakening,* Garak thought, looking around the office. Entrek had a picture on his desk. A woman. Two boys; a girl. Garak stared at them. They looked like a nice family. Family was all. He felt a jab of pain behind his left eye. He wanted some sleep. But still, that sense of something missed. He picked up his disruptor and waved it up at the shelves by the door.

"Entrek," he said, "what's that?"

He was pointing at a black box, about the height and width of four padds.

"I've no idea," said Entrek. "I've never seen it before."

Garak put down the disruptor and went over to the shelf. He lifted the box down and set it, very carefully, upon the desk. He opened the lid, already certain of what he would find. The wiring would have been done months ago, throughout the whole base. Bajorans came in and out, cleaning. That should not have been allowed. All that was needed was for someone, realizing what was happening in the town, to hit a switch somewhere. He should have had the compound swept, of course. But you couldn't think of everything, and he was the only one here thinking of anything at all.

Garak checked the timer. "Gentlemen," he said, "I don't mean to alarm you, but in about eight and a half metrics, this base is going to be blown to smithereens. Might I suggest we evacuate?"

They didn't move.

"I assure you I'm not joking," he added.

"Can't . . . can't you defuse it or something?" Antek said.

How they had come to rely on him. "I could, if I had about thirty metrics. But I don't."

He was impressed at the way Entrek moved into action. He hit the

188   UNA McCORMACK

alarm on the desk. "The civilians," he said. "I'll get them. You"—he looked at his glinns—"get out." He eyed Garak. "And you. You'll need to make your report, I suppose."

None of them needed any more persuasion. They sprinted out of the building and through the compound. They ran past the perimeter fence, and into the open fields. Behind, Garak heard screams, cries—the civilians, roused from their beds, being herded out as quickly as they could.

The base blew exactly on time. Garak flung himself to the ground, covering his head with his arms. He felt someone crash down next to him. A few pieces of debris, flung up and out by the force of the blast, clattered down on top of them. Everything went quiet. A cool rain had started to fall, but otherwise everything was still. Beneath him, the grass was springy and sharp, and a little damp. Garak looked up. Behind him, the buildings of the base were on fire. Beside him lay Antek, gasping for air. Under his breath he was whispering, "*I hate this planet.*"

Garak stood up and pulled Antek to his feet. "Get a grip, soldier," he said. "Look after those civilians." He made his way back down to the river, where the guards outside the barn were looking very twitchy. Inside, there was shouting and cheering—the Bajorans knew exactly what had just happened. It was tempting to open the doors and start shooting. So very tempting. *We may end up killing all of them.*

After that, time seemed to crawl. The taunting of the Bajorans turned into chanting. Bloodthirsty patriots caged fifteen yards away had a demoralizing effect on the men. To keep them occupied—and warm—Garak sent them off in pairs, checking that the barn was secure all the way around, patrolling the area. The more frightened he sent back down to the ruins of the base to help Antek with the civilians. He himself kept moving, trying to speak to everyone as often as he could. Eventually, he couldn't listen to the chanting any longer. Making the excuse that he wanted to check on the civilians, he left the men with strict instructions as to what they should do if there was an emergency. Start shooting. Kill the Bajorans. Yes, all of them, if necessary.

He walked quickly back to the wreck of the base. He did not want to use his flashlight: he had no idea whether anyone was lurking around, and, besides, the dark was a relief. The stink was hideous. The night air hung thick and heavy from the burning of both town and base. He found Antek, who had done a better job than expected. The fire was out. The civilians were huddled together. They'd pulled out some emergency lights and resources from the wreckage. Entrek was dead, killed getting the civilians out. Perhaps that was better for him all around. Garak left them to get on with it and turned his face back to the river. He wasn't sure the officers there could do what was necessary, but he could. He knew now exactly what he could do, if necessary. For Cardassia.

Walking back through the darkness, he realized someone was moving a few yards ahead. He quickened his step. He drew his disruptor.

"Stop," he ordered.

The figure turned. He held up his flashlight.

A Bajoran girl, no more than thirteen. "Don't shoot me! Please! Don't shoot me!" she begged, wide-eyed with fear.

Garak licked dry lips. He felt so very tempted. "Why not?"

"I only did what I was told!"

"Only following orders? Who isn't?"

She looked at him blankly. She had no idea what he was talking about.

"You can go," he rasped at her. "But tell Saba Taan that I know what's happening here. Have you got that? The Order knows about the Resistance. You tell him that."

She nodded, completely terrified.

"Now get out of here before I do something unkind."

She ran. He knew that he would recognize her if he ever saw her again. Utterly drained, he fell, staring up at a dark sky full of strange stars. If the Prophets were guiding and guarding his path, he wanted nothing of it.

As dawn stole over the empty fields, the comms came back up and they were able to reach the capital. Reinforcements from Merna were transported

190   UNA McCORMACK

over immediately. They found the garrison camped outside a barn, and the civilians together near the smoking ruin of the base. They were greeted with relief by the officer in command, a young Obsidian Order agent with a bright-blue thousand-yard stare who was gripping a disruptor like his life depended on it.

"The Order," said Gul Merok disparagingly to his second-in-command, as they surveyed the chaos. "Always has to be a bloody melodrama."

They never found Saba Taan, or the children. They were gone, long gone, up along the Parset river, Garak assumed; offworld, no doubt, via the same route that the weapons came in. He spent the next two months on Ordeve, establishing the Order's investigation, conducting interrogations, overseeing the sentences, and rolling back the Resistance operations along the Parset river. It was the cusp of spring when he left the area. He didn't see the blood poppies in full bloom. In Merna, he received a data rod containing a new identity, credit to the value of ninety *lek*s, and a one-way ticket on a civilian freighter back to Cardassia Prime. And that was the end of Mas Gherrod.

Avek Rignor arrived in Ses'erakh to the suffocating heat of midsummer with enough *lek*s to rent a room at the end of the tramline in East Torr. It was tiny and airless, and he was kept awake by the pounding of the industrial replicators across the highway. During the day he would catch the tram down to Torr Central and sit by the river in the shade of the covered market watching the people and drinking *gelat*. He would tell himself how beautiful his home was, how vibrant; how much he loved the street music and the busy walkways and the spicy food and the pink sunsets. How, if all else failed, he could always come back here and start again, among the people and the places that he loved. Sometimes he would think about the crimson shadow, and the sweet relief it brought, but since this was no longer available to him, he forced himself to put that out of his mind.

SECOND SELF   191

After a couple of weeks, the *lek*s ran out. There had been no contact from his superior. The work record on this new identity was patchy—an occupational hazard for an operative—but there was always somewhere that needed a pot washer, and thus he sweated through the rest of the summer, tired and bored, waiting to hear what his next assignment would be, sealing away thoughts of fire and mass murder. To amuse himself, he started to inhabit the part of Rignor more thoroughly. Spun a few stories about his childhood. Decided his tastes in food and music. Dressed for the part. Blurred the lines between memory and lie. Slept with an earnest and beautiful young medical student. Broke it off after a month. Locked this secret, like the rest, deep within, a seed lying dormant underground.

Autumn was well underway before anyone made contact. He had begun to worry that he was out for some reason—but realized later that this break from operations had been intended partly as a holiday after the intensity of the cleanup on Ordeve, and partly as punishment for the whole Khenet affair. He went, as instructed, up to the house. Mila opened the door and, without even a flicker of acknowledgment, took him through to the study. She introduced him as *Mr. Rignor* and closed the door behind him.

Enabran Tain, the head of the Obsidian Order, was sitting at his big wooden desk, studying something on a shielded computer. Spread out around him were padds, real books, and parchments (he collected First Republic parchments, very fine). Not for the first time, Garak envied Tain this room, this desk, this space to sit and read and think. He stood by the door, hands tucked behind his back, feeling grubby and out of place. He had cleaned and pressed his jacket as best he could, but he was regretting now not investing some time in making a smarter one.

At length, Tain looked up. "Ah, Garak!" he said cheerfully. "There you are!" He stood up, and ambled over to an ornate wooden cabinet in which glasses and bottles were kept. "*Kanar*?" said Tain, taking out one of the bottles. "No," he decided, almost immediately, "there's probably been enough in the way of indulgence over the last few months, wouldn't you

192 UNA McCORMACK

say? I'll ask Mila to bring you some tea." Tain put through the order, and, after a few minutes, Mila arrived with a tray and a bland expression. Garak was at last instructed to sit down, and watched Mila pour him a cup of redleaf tea.

"Thank you," he murmured. His voice, in this room, always sounded like someone with years of education behind him. Perhaps there had been. Perhaps that was yet to come.

"Pleasure, Mr. Rignor," she said. She was doing North Torr.

"A shame about Entrek," said Tain, as Mila was leaving. He was drinking *kanar*.

"He allowed the Bajoran Resistance to smuggle arms through the Parset valley under his watch," said Garak. "He's lucky he got an honorable death."

Tain was chuckling. "No pity in you, is there?"

"Pity," said Garak, "was not in the job description."

"No," said Tain. "It wasn't." He eyed his protégé thoughtfully. "Tell me, do you consider your mission to Ordeve to have been a success?"

"We broke a major Resistance gun-running operation," said Garak.

"Hmm, yes," said Tain, and Garak—on yellow alert whenever he entered this room—moved closer to red.

"Pacified the local population," Garak said. The fiercer the act, he had found in the past, the more Tain seemed satisfied.

"Yes . . ." said Tain noncommittally.

"Extracted a significant amount of information," Garak offered, slightly desperately.

"I suppose so," said Tain. "Still, you missed that bomb. Rather a lot of damage to the base. Expensive. A little less show next time, hmm? And it's disappointing that so many of the locals got away."

"Got away?"

"The vedek," said Tain. "For one."

"He was an old man," said Garak. "There was no real threat there—"

"And, of course, there were the children."

Garak, who had not mentioned to anyone the girl he let go, resisted the urge to swallow. "Most of them were quite young."

"Yes," said Tain, and leaned back in his chair. "The trouble with Bajoran children, I've found, is that they grow into Bajoran adults. And Bajoran children forced to escape their burning homes tend to grow into Bajoran adults who hold grudges."

There was a silence. Garak looked down at the steam rising from his teacup. "I can go back," he said. "It's been a few months, but the trail won't be completely cold."

"No," said Tain. "A waste of time. Entrek was my real interest, and that business is finished. Still, it's very odd," he said. "And knowing your sentimental streak."

His words hung between them, like the stink of something rotten.

"Tain," said Garak. "Are you suggesting that I let those children go?"

"Did you?" said Tain affably.

"No!"

"Good."

"That would never happen!"

"Never?" said Tain.

"Well," said Garak, "not unless it served Cardassia."

"Quite," said Tain, lifting his glass. "No, one shouldn't go back. Onward! I have a new job for you, Garak. I think you'll find it interesting."

Garak—who had been starting to think that there was nothing more for him, and that kitchen work was going to be the end of it—straightened in his seat. "Yes?"

"Mila has the files. But I'd like you to have a medical check first," said Tain. "We have a new device available which I think you'll find useful."

"A medical check?" The walls inched inward. "I'm quite well, I assure you. Never better—"

"It's a very small procedure. You'll hardly feel a thing." Tain refilled his glass. "Your choice, of course."

194   UNA McCORMACK

"I'm sure it's for the best," said Garak. Tain smiled and drank to his good health. By the end of the following day, the implant was installed. There was some discomfort with the first incision, but after that, nothing more. Garak quit the kitchen job over the comm. He was already on his way to the spaceport, where a berth was booked for him under yet another name on a freighter heading toward Ab-Tzenketh. After that came the next job, and the next, and the next. And so it went on, down the road that would lead in time to Romulus, to exile, to the war, and the Fire—and whatever lay beyond.

PART 4

2376

AFTER
THE DOMINION WAR

9

A hot summer's night. The heavy scent of poppies in the air. Not much noise, for so many people, and the worst of it, thought Raffi, was the quietness of the kids. Long gone past fear into stunned and wide-eyed watchfulness. Clutching the hand of the nearest adult, or of an older child, keeping quiet and doing what they were told.

When everyone was out of the accommodation block, there was a head count. Everyone present and correct. They were in little groups of ten, families as far as possible, but with a senior Cardassian woman overseeing each group. Raffi and Byrne were up front, Lafleur and Turan at the rear, and Avarak and Kovar with the groups in the middle. Limited to what they could carry. A few small replicators, and as much other equipment as the adults could strap on their backs. They had no idea how long they were going to be out there.

At last, the flow of people began, heading from the civilian area toward the eastern exit of the compound. The gate was manned by two young Cardassian foot soldiers, and it was closed. They came forward, disruptors out, lifting them slightly. Raffi said, "It's okay. You can let us through."

"We're not supposed to let anyone through," said the slightly senior of these two boys. His name was stamped on the front of his armor: *Tohk*. "Zhol's orders."

"Zhol isn't in command here," said Raffi.

"Neither are you," said the slightly younger one, who looked like he didn't much care for Starfleet. His name was Ghorik. Tohk was already busy requesting backup, and, within a few minutes, another couple of armed foot soldiers arrived. Behind, some of the civilians were getting anxious. Raffi saw Avarak among them, exuding calm, and she raised her voice, speaking clearly and firmly. "Remember, people, we're keeping things quiet," she said. "These guys are making sure we're all right, that's all. We'll soon be on our way—"

"No, you won't," said Ghorik. He swung his disruptor around. The people closest by shrunk back in fear, and the ripples were quickly felt throughout the crowd. Some of the kids began to cry.

"Gil Tohk," Raffi said. "Let's keep things calm. Nobody wants anybody to get hurt."

"They've got to go back to their billets," said Ghorik. "They're going to get us all killed—"

One of the little ones began to wail, a thin and desperate noise that sounded like it might never stop. Raffi watched fingers get twitchier on disruptors. But then the crush of people fell back, and a figure came through. Half dressed and stumbling slightly; you'd think he was a vagrant. But it was Tradall. Up close, he looked worse than ever. Bloodshot eyes; trembling hands. That giveaway sweet scent that followed him around. "What's . . ." His voice was cracked and hoarse; he coughed. "What's going on here?"

"Starfleet," said Ghorik. "Interfering."

"These people want to leave," said Raffi.

"They *can't*," said Ghorik.

Tradall looked around. "What do you expect me to do?"

"Order them back to their beds," said Tohk.

"Let us go, Tradall," said Raffi. "We've got time to get them all to cover, but not if we delay much longer."

"You're not going anywhere," said Ghorik.

"We're not staying here to die!" someone cried out from the crowd, and this was picked up and passed around. Raffi lifted her hands: *Calm, calm;*

SECOND SELF   199

stay calm . . . She saw Avarak, and Kovar, and several of the Cardassian adults, doing the same farther down the line.

"What I mean," said Tradall, and he was saying each word very carefully. "What I *mean*, soldier, is . . . Do you expect me to force them to stay?"

Raffi felt a cautious hope rise up.

"Because I'm not going to force them to stay," Tradall said, still with the over-precise diction of a man not entirely in command of himself. "And the last I checked, you take your orders from me. I'm the senior officer here. Not you, not Zhol, certainly not Starfleet. So put that disruptor down, and if you don't want to help these people leave, stand back and let Starfleet get on with it. Because somebody has to."

The young man's voice got steadier throughout this speech, and Raffi could see the effect on the foot soldiers present. Something deeply ingrained in the Cardassian military was coming into play. They could no more disobey Tradall than betray the Union.

"Nobody else here is going to die," Tradall finished. "You got that?" he called across the crowd. "Has everyone got that?" He turned to Raffi. "That help?"

"Yes," she said. "Thank you."

Tohk lifted the barriers out of the compound, and the flow of people began to pass through into the darkness beyond. Some of the other soldiers who had gathered around to watch were starting to help. Raffi turned to Tradall. "What are you going to do when Zhol gets back?"

"I'll deal with Zhol," said Tradall. "Probably should have done ages ago." He looked around blankly. "I don't feel so good." He propped himself up against the wall of the hut. "You'd better go now," he mumbled. "Before they decide they don't have to do anything I say." He laughed. "Who would blame them?"

"You should come with us," said Raffi. "Bring those soldiers who want to come along with you—"

"No." Tradall shook his head. "Zhol will come after you."

200 UNA McCORMACK

"You think so?"

"He won't like this."

"People will *die*," said Raffi. "He can't want that."

"He's past caring," muttered Tradall. "All that matters to him now is holding things together until the end. This . . ." He nodded at the people hurrying past. "This looks like things falling apart." He pushed himself up, wavering on his feet. "I'll keep him busy, Lieutenant. Get these people as far as you can, quick as you can. Got to make sure someone makes it." Tears were running down the gray ridges of his face. "Because there's nobody left back home." He thumped his fist into his leg, using the shock of the physical pain to make him focus. "When I'm done with Zhol, we'll give you cover when the Romulans get here."

Raffi's heart was filled with pity for this young man and what was happening to him. The drug, the end of his world, how hard he was trying to pull himself back from the brink while it still mattered. She reached out and squeezed his arm. "Don't stay here too long," she said. "The Romulans will butcher you."

"Mercy killing," he mumbled.

"No," she said fiercely. "Dead is never better than alive. Don't stay too long. Get out when you can."

"I'll try," he said. "Got to survive Zhol first."

The last people were coming through. Time for Raffi to go.

"Goodbye, Starfleet," said Tradall. "Good luck."

They reached the Bajoran town in the dead of night, moving quickly past the stones and the ruins of the temple toward the entrance to the tunnel. Lafleur, coming up from the back, deactivated the holo-filter. The first group, led by Kovar, entered the tunnel. Two Cardassian foot soldiers had caught up with them, sent by Tradall to help expedite their passage, and they stood on either side of the tunnel mouth, disruptors in hand, alert.

SECOND SELF 201

The first three groups had gone down the steps and into the tunnel when Raffi heard a disturbance from farther down the line. She turned to Byrne, who was standing by, and said, "I'll go and see what's happening." Discreetly, she nodded at the foot soldiers. "Keep an eye on them," she murmured. "They're looking twitchy to me."

Raffi hurried down the line, where a Cardassian girl—not a little one, but not yet an adult—was sitting on the ground, her arms around her knees, weeping and shaking. "I won't go down there!" she said. "I won't!" Mesat was kneeling beside her, stroking her hair, trying to quiet her, but the girl's voice was getting louder. "I don't want to be buried alive! The Order buries people alive!"

Mesat, seeing Raffi, came to explain. "Her father was taken by the Order when she was a small child," she said in a quiet voice. "Never came back. We all know . . ." Mesat closed her eyes for a moment, as if to deal with some great pain. "We all know the kinds of things that the Order did to people, Lieutenant. And it seems that word has got around that the Order were in the Caanta valley."

"I dreamed about him," said the girl. "I dreamed about *Edde*. There was a bright light. He was warning me. I don't want the Order to take me!"

One of the foot soldiers had come to see what was happening. "She needs to shut up," he said to Raffi, as if the child's distress was somehow her responsibility. "She's going to give us all away."

The girl, seeing the soldier looming over her, started to shake. "Oh, please, don't let them take me away—"

"Hush, Gheta!" Mesat was saying. "It's all right! Everything will be all right."

"Shut her up!" said the foot soldier, lifting the disruptor. Raffi, her hand on her phaser, said, "You have a job to do. Back up the line."

"My orders are to keep these people safe as they get through the tunnel," he said. "She's putting them in danger."

"I swear to you," said Raffi, "if you don't put that disruptor away, you won't see daylight."

202 UNA McCORMACK

"Lieutenant," said a quiet voice. "I believe I may be of assistance."

Raffi turned to see Avarak, standing beside her. "What? Did you pack some sedatives?"

"Not drugs," he said. He knelt down beside the girl and put his hand against her face. "Gheta," he said. "We have met. We have talked."

The girl's sobbing began to steady. She looked up into his eyes.

"You can trust me," said Avarak. Ever so gently, he began to increase the pressure of his hand. "My mind to your mind," he said. "My thoughts to your thoughts."

The soldier moved forward. "What are you doing to her?"

"*Shut up!*" hissed Mesat, and the young man, startled by such a vicious outburst from a civilian, pulled back. As they watched, Avarak rubbed his fingers in a slow circular motion around Gheta's temple. Her breathing steadied. Her eyelids began to droop. After a minute or two, she was asleep, leaning against Mesat. Avarak released his hold and stood. He turned to the soldier. "She'll sleep for an hour or two," he said. "Perhaps you might carry her through the tunnel in the meantime?"

The young soldier, gaping, quickly holstered his disruptor and picked up the girl. "Yes, yes, of course."

"Great job, Avarak," Raffi said quietly, watching them go.

"Gheta and I had already had several conversations about her experiences," Avarak said. "But—if I may issue a warning, Lieutenant, you may find that resistance to entering the Caanta valley is more widespread than you realize. Fear of the Obsidian Order runs very deep—and is by no means irrational."

"I'll bear that in mind," said Raffi. She hurried back to the tunnel mouth, where Byrne was waiting.

"What was that?" said Byrne.

"One of the girls got spooked," said Raffi. "Didn't want to enter the tunnel."

"Some people don't like underground spaces," said Byrne.

"It's more than that," said Raffi, lowering her voice. "The rumor that this area was under Obsidian Order control has been going around."

"Ah," said Byrne.

"Also," said Raffi carefully, "she has been having bad dreams."

"Bad dreams?" said Byrne. "Well, no wonder. She's a traumatized child being chased by a company of Romulans intent on murdering her. Bad dreams are going to be the least of it for years to come—"

"Commander," said Raffi, "have you had any dreams while you've been here at Ghenic?"

"Excuse me?"

"The last few nights, in particular."

"Why?" said Byrne. "Have you?"

"Yes," said Raffi.

Byrne didn't reply straightaway. She watched the next group of people go through. "Lieutenant Musiker," she said, "have you tried sailors' delight since arriving at Ghenic?"

There was a pause. "Once," said Raffi.

"And was that when you dreamed?"

"Yes, but—"

"Then there's your explanation. Listen," said Byrne, "I know that almost everyone here is taking that stuff. I know that Lafleur and Kovar in particular are using it. But we know very little about its effects on human metabolism and . . . Really, Raffi, for *fuck's* sake!"

"It was a bad mistake," Raffi admitted. "I won't do it again. But, Commander, the dreams I've had, one said to cross the river, the other said to stay back."

"Dreams don't contain some kind of fucking message, Raffi!"

"But other people are getting them. That kid, Gheta, she had the same kind of dream—a warning from someone about the Caanta valley."

"Raffi! We have a hundred Cardassian civilians whose lives depend on us. Are you seriously suggesting we stop this evacuation because you've dabbled in local delicacies and a distressed kid has had a nightmare?"

"No," said Raffi. "I'm just saying . . . We don't know what's over there."

"Trees, mountains."

"Assott left standing orders not to enter the Caanta valley. You seemed to think Assott was a thoughtful man. Level-headed."

Byrne didn't answer right away. Raffi, looking at her, suddenly understood. "You've been having these dreams too, haven't you?"

Byrne, reluctantly, nodded.

"And you haven't touched the stuff, have you?"

"I know the regs, Lieutenant," said Byrne sharply.

Raffi looked into the darkness where the river and the Caanta valley lay. "Damn . . ."

"Dark figures," said Byrne. "I can't hear them, but I know what they're telling me. *Stop. Don't come any farther.*" She shook her head. "What are we supposed to do? Dreams can't foretell the future! But I know . . . I know . . . that we're entering an area about which we have very limited information. That might well have been under Obsidian Order control."

"The Order's defunct," said Raffi. "Has been for years."

But what if some of the projects were not. Perhaps this had been a test site for some experimental weapon. That was well within their modus operandi. There were parts of Bajor where nothing would grow for centuries. There might be a good reason for putting a ban on entering the valley.

Byrne took a deep breath. "You know what I think?"

'Go on."

"I think the ban is because of the massacre at Akantha. I think maybe there's some evidence out there. A mass grave, perhaps. The Order forbade entry to the valley and since then all these stories have sprung up. We're all stressed, and we're all having the same kind of dream. Look, it's as rational an explanation as any."

SECOND SELF   205

"So we go on," said Raffi.

"Yes," said Byrne. "We committed to this course of action. We're going to see it through and we're going to present a united front."

"Absolutely," said Raffi.

"But"—Byrne looked fearfully across the dark river—"I'm afraid of what's over there. And I think that's a rational fear."

"Oh, I'm all for rational fears," said Raffi. "Rational fears stop us from doing stupid things. But you're right. We have to get these people away. We know what's behind us. We'll deal with what's ahead when we get there."

About half an hour before dawn, most of the Cardassian civilians had entered the tunnel and were, Raffi hoped, under the cover of the forest on the other side. Comm silence meant she was relying on word-of-mouth messages being passed back, but she knew that Byrne and Kovar were through, organizing people on the other side, while Lafleur and Turan were down in the tunnel monitoring its structural integrity. Raffi and Avarak remained on the near side, keeping folks calm until their turn came, ensuring that the shuffling queue did not become a dangerous press or push of people, quickly assuaging any fears that were expressed.

The two last groups were getting ready to head into the tunnel when Raffi heard the sound of craft flying overhead. Not the Romulans, surely, not already. Not when they were so close . . . She turned to one of the young Cardassian foot soldiers, Entheny, who had proven to be solid and dependable during the course of the night. "See if you can hurry things along," she told him. "Try to get the rest into the cover of the tunnel, at least. Tell Lafleur she might need to conceal the entrance."

He went off. Raffi turned to Avarak, who was taking sensor readings. "It is a Cardassian skimmer," he said. "Although of course one cannot infer from that information alone whether or not it is crewed by Cardassians."

The last of the civilians had just reached the bottom of the steps when the skimmer began its descent, throwing up dirt and rubble all around. La-fleur activated the holo-filter, and Raffi and Avarak went to meet the skimmer. It had barely touched the ground when Zhol emerged, armed and angry, dragging Tradall out behind him. Raffi looked at him in fury. Had he given them away? His eyes were averted; when he drew closer, Raffi could see dark bruises across his face. Maybe he hadn't surrendered them so easily after all.

Zhol marched right up to her. "Where are they?"

"Who?" said Raffi.

"Where have you *taken* them?" he yelled. "You Starfleet *skrit*—"

"I've sent them where you should have sent them, days back. To safety."

His disruptor came up. "You've overstepped the mark."

"I've done your damn job for you!" Raffi shot back.

"We're not allowed into the Caanta valley!"

"Who says that's where they went?" said Raffi.

"Don't fucking lie to me, Starfleet—!"

"Either way, you might be under orders, but I'm not—and none of those people are either."

I should be de-escalating this, thought Raffi. But the truth was that she was angry—with Zhol, for his lack of care for these civilians; with Tradall, for his vacillation; even, a little, with Byrne, for waiting too long and trusting that Starfleet Command—so far away—would somehow resolve this for her. Raffi stood her ground—and kept in Zhol's face.

"What are you going to do, huh? Drag them all back to face the Romulans? You'll have to find them first—"

She saw his grip tighten around his weapon. She thought: *Shit, should've kept my mouth shut.* Then, unexpectedly, *insanely*, she saw Tradall lunge forward, trying to grab the weapon in his hand. Zhol swiped the younger man with the back of his hand, sending him flying. "Should have put you out of your misery months ago," he said, targeting the disruptor on Tradall and raising it to fire.

And then . . .

Oh, sweet mother of mercy, no—

Avarak was there, moving—swiftly and with great surety of purpose—to put himself between Zhol and Tradall.

Zhol fired.

And Avarak went down, half his chest gone. There was an awful, cruel moment of quiet and then, with a scream like something from a nightmare, Tradall launched himself at Zhol. He tore the disruptor from the older man's hands, and he shot—again and again and again—directly into Zhol's face.

After that came silence.

"Oh no," whispered Raffi. "Oh no, no . . ." She moved toward Avarak, her hands reaching out, shaking. Tradall grabbed her arm.

"Move," he said. "Get out of here."

"Is he . . . ?"

"Of course he is."

"I can't leave him," said Raffi. "I can't leave his *body*."

"I'll see to that. They're on their way, Lieutenant. The Romulans. Ghenic will be theirs by the morning. Get everyone safe."

Not everyone, thought Raffi. Even now, she couldn't move; Tradall had to push her into action. He seemed different, somehow, as if he was at last in control of himself. As if he was suddenly, indisputably, in command here. A little late in the day. She tried to shake his hand off her arm, but he was guiding her back through the ruins toward the river.

"Lafleur," said Raffi into her combadge. "You can come out."

The holo-filter came down. Entheny's head popped up, and then Lafleur's behind him. "Raffi, what's going on?"

"Get your damn hand off me, Tradall!" said Raffi.

Tradall released his hold on her arm. "Entheny," he said. "I'm going to need you now." He placed his palm gently against Raffi's back and pushed her forward. "Lieutenant," he said, "it's time to go. We'll go back to Ghenic, hold out there as long as we can. Buy you some time to get on your way.

If you see me again, it means the Romulans are coming." He took a deep breath. "I'm sorry," he said. "He was . . . he was just a very good officer."

"We're not even at war," whispered Raffi. "This is peace?"

"Raffi," said Lafleur, more urgently, "what's happened?"

Raffi shook her head. She climbed down the steps and entered the tunnel. Behind her, the holo-filter came up once more, hiding them away.

10

In later years, Raffi would try not to think about the underground journey that followed. Sometimes, though, memories would surface—as memories are wont to do—and fragments of that awful night would return. The overpowering heat of the enclosed space, exacerbated by the number of people that had passed through and were still passing through. The dim light from Starfleet- and Cardassian-issue flashlights, showing, here and there, the strange and ancient figures on the walls. Sometimes, one of the Cardassians ahead would look back, and she would see their alien features—gray and ridged—thrown into sharp relief, etched with fear and exhaustion. Raffi found herself thinking about the kids from Akantha, the Bajorans, wondering whether they too had come this way all those years ago; wondering whether they had survived the days that followed. Just behind her walked Lafleur, whom she had rapidly briefed, and who cried for a while, very quietly, and then stopped.

At the far end of the tunnel, on the other side, Raffi and Lafleur waited until all the Cardassians were out before coming themselves up the steps. They stood for a moment, trying to regain their composure, as the night dissipated around them. At last Raffi said, "We should make sure we're under cover before it's full light."

They hurried on, after the last of the civilians, finding the encampment about half a kilometer away. Most people were lying down, exhausted from the night's events. Lafleur went to find her ensigns. Byrne, seeing Raffi, came toward her.

"Where's Avarak?" she said.

"He's dead," said Raffi. "Zhol shot him."

"Zhol?" Byrne looked back to the other bank. "Is he coming?"

"No," said Raffi. "Tradall killed him. Tradall's gone back to delay the Romulan approach. Damn! It was all so fast! Avarak jumped between Zhol and Tradall." Raffi could feel the tears welling up; forced herself to stop. People were already looking her way. They couldn't see the Starfleet officers losing it. "There was nothing I could do."

"Raffi, I'm so sorry," said Byrne. "He was . . ."

"I know . . . I wish I could've *buried* him."

"We'll go back, after," said Byrne.

"His first mission," said Raffi. "His first damn mission. We're not even at war." They had been sent to help keep the peace. He had been sent here to *protect* these damn people, and Zhol had blasted a hole into him. Raffi rubbed her face. "I'll be okay . . ." she said. "I'll be okay."

"We'll put a marker there, Raffi," said Byrne. "I promise."

Some consolation. "Let's get through the next few days first," Raffi said. "How are things going here?"

"A few panicky moments," said Byrne, "but everyone's calm now. One of the Cardassian doctors, Ihslek, has been administering a few sedatives." She lowered her voice. "Not everyone is happy about sleeping."

Because of the dreams. Raffi shivered, despite the heat, wondering what dark figures would wander through her sleep.

"How are the long-range comms?" she said.

"Nothing yet. Kovar is working on trying to boost them."

"There'll be flyovers, once the Romulans take Ghenic. We need to make sure that we're blocking any life signs, so they can't find us." Were her words slurring? Raffi wasn't sure.

"Mesat has some people working on that. Also—there seems to be a force field up ahead."

"We need to get that down. Get farther into the valley."

SECOND SELF   211

"Prok is working on that." Byrne's hand was on her arm. "Raffi. You need to get some sleep. Don't . . ." She took a breath. "Don't take sailors' delight. Ask for Ihslek, if you need help sleeping."

"All right," said Raffi faintly.

"We'll come back, Raffi," said Byrne. "We won't let him be forgotten. I promise."

Raffi found a quiet place under the trees, laid out a bedroll, and fell into an exhausted sleep. She woke, midmorning, to the quiet rustle of leaves, and the careful, stilted conversation of tired and scared people. Cardassian faces, all around her, and Raffi wondered what dumb piece of luck had brought her to this world, to die on account of strangers whose history she hardly knew and understood even less. Sokara's words came back to her. *Are you really willing to die for these people?* Avarak had been willing. He believed that life was precious and should be defended. He had come here to protect Cardassian life, and he had done so, without discrimination.

Raffi felt tears forming in her eyes. She got up, quickly, and went in search of her colleagues. There had been no crises in the last few hours, she was glad to hear. People were calm—although very frightened—and anxious to know what was going to happen next. Raffi and Byrne convened a short walk away from the encampment and hastily sketched plans.

"We should get some distance between us and the river," said Raffi.

"Farther into the valley?" said Byrne.

"I guess . . ." Raffi said. "We can follow the course of the river. Keep under the cover of the trees, as much as we can."

"There's still this force field ahead," said Byrne.

"What do we know about that?" said Raffi.

"It seems to be Cardassian, but not any codes that Mesat and her people recognize, nor any of the military." Byrne sighed. "Which seems to add weight to the idea that the Obsidian Order was here."

212 UNA McCORMACK

"We need to get past," said Raffi. "Get as far as we can into the valley. Work on boosting the long-range scans and hope we can get a message through to Merna. We can't stay here. If the Romulans cross the river, they'll find us in no time."

"I'll try to sell it to the Cardassians," Byrne said. "But ignoring Obsidian Order dictates does not come easily. Mesat and Prok will help."

They did help, and by midafternoon the whole group was making its way slowly but steadily through the forest farther into the valley. The Caanta river was on their right-hand side, bearing farther right; sometimes visible, sometimes a faint rush behind the trees. Raffi moved up and down the line as much as she could. After a couple of hours, even the older children were too tired to press on, and the adults, too, were exhausted. They hadn't come far, not quite three kilometers, but it was clear they weren't going to manage much more that day.

Byrne ordered a stop. The fine weather and the forest cover meant they were already sheltered, and the summer heat was enough even by Cardassian standards. Supplies would not be an issue as long as the field replicators kept working, although they were concerned about whether the small power surges would be detectable. Lafleur set Turan to work on this, drawing support from a couple of junior Cardassian civilian technicians recommended by Prok. The rations that they generated were certainly palatable for the Starfleet personnel; a few of the Cardassians looked less than happy at what was on offer, but nobody had the energy reserves to complain about the hospitality. The camp settled wearily.

Raffi sat, tired but twitchy, watchful and unable to rest. A few feet away, a couple of the younger Cardassians were passing around hypos. One of them saw her looking their way.

"You want some?"

Damn, though, she was tempted. A few seconds, and all the knots in her back and her shoulders would dissolve, and her worries would smooth away, and her grief would seem more manageable, and maybe she would

SECOND SELF 213

even sleep and wake in the morning refreshed. But she shook her head. Because it didn't work that way. It never worked that way. The benefits were always temporary, and the crash afterward, when it came, seemed heavier and harder every time. Instead, she lay on her side, and closed her eyes, and tried to ignore their soft conversation—even laughter, dammit—and the sweet scent in the air. They were asleep long before she was. She heard their breathing settle, while she was still staring into darkness.

In the end, she did sleep, and she dreamed again, more clearly than ever before. The forest was clear to her now, perhaps because she had seen the place, and unmistakably this part of the world, beyond the river crossing and leading up into the Caanta valley. Everything around her seemed mono-chrome, black and white and gray, except for the poppies, which were blood red. She waited for the figures to appear, and, when they came, they were clearer to her as well; three of them, again, although even with their faces visible she was still unable to identify them. She had never met these people, and yet she was sure that she knew them. They stood in a row, their hands held up, beseeching her:

Stop. No farther . . .

She tried to speak, but her mouth was dry. She willed them to under-stand her.

Who are you? What's the matter?

At first, looking closer, she thought that one of them was Avarak, with his high cheekbones and arched eyebrows, but no—this young man, al-though about the same age, moved like a killer, and carried a long staff. She might have thought he was Romulan, but there was something about his manner—looking at her so directly—that did not seem right for a member of that most secretive of cultures. There was another young man too, his short, dark hair cropped close to his head, and Raffi was even surer that this was someone she knew, but the name seemed to slip away from her grasp be-fore she could hold it to her. The last figure was a woman, with long, blonde hair, and a strange dark mark above her left eye, like an implant or a tattoo.

214   UNA McCORMACK

Raffi did not know her, could not place her, could not begin to guess who this was—and yet knew that she was, somehow, critical to her.

No farther, they all told her. *Go back . . .*

Why? She willed them to explain. *We can't go back! We have to go on—or we'll die.*

But they became more urgent: *No farther! No farther!*

Raffi woke without answers. When she drifted back to sleep, she dreamed once again of the trees, but the figures did not come. Perhaps they thought they had delivered their message clearly enough; perhaps the threat no longer existed. The next couple of days were a slow stumble deeper into a dense alien forest. The heavy perfume of the poppies was everywhere, and at night Raffi was caught between bone-deep weariness and the fear of what dreams might find her. On the afternoon of the third day after they escaped through the tunnel (the third day since Avarak had been killed), Tradall caught up with them. He, and the two foot soldiers with him, were the only survivors of the soldiers who had remained at Ghenic.

"It's in Romulan hands now," Tradall said. "We held them back as long as we could." They had brought as much equipment as they could carry: another couple of field replicators, and some other kit that the engineers fell upon. They tried, over the course of the next day or two, to boost their comms signals to reach as far as Merna, but no use. They were far out, and, by necessity, getting farther and farther out each day. Whatever Romulan blackout had been troubling their comms at Ghenic was now reaching this far. It was only a matter of time before they crossed the river. That afternoon, the first of the flyovers came.

Everyone hunkered down on the ground, beneath the trees. Kept as silent as a hundred scared civilians and their children could manage. Covered themselves with foliage or blankets. Of course, if the sensor jammers weren't blocking their life signs, Raffi thought, what use would leaves and blankets be? But the flyers went past overhead, and they heard them heading back toward Ghenic. After that, Raffi wanted to press on as quickly as possible,

SECOND SELF   215

get as far into the valley as possible, but significant resistance was building. The dreams were becoming more vivid and more urgent, and their message was remarkably consistent.

Stop. No farther. Go back.

Byrne convened her key staff, and Tradall, to discuss what to do next.

"I want to talk about the dreams," Byrne said bluntly. "I'm tempted to blame them on a less-than-winning combination of recreational drug use and war trauma, but the simple fact is that people that I know have not been using this stuff are having dreams. Me, for one."

"I've not used it since we crossed the river," Lafleur said. "And I'm dreaming too."

"I won't pretend," said Tradall, "that I haven't used the shadow a little." *More than a little,* thought Raffi, and he went on, "Okay, a lot. But I haven't, since . . ." He gestured back toward the river. "Since then. And the dreams are as bad as ever . . ."

"Avarak seemed to think that Cardassian biochemistry was unusually receptive to the hallucinatory properties of crimson shadow," said Raffi. "I don't know. It's not like we can conduct a full study. And, before you ask, Commander, I haven't tried the stuff since that one time, and—when I sleep—yes, I dream."

"You'll sleep tonight and properly," said Byrne. "That's an order. But what are we supposed to make of this? I know we're tired, and under terrible stress, and frankly I'm not keen on suggesting that there is some *meaning* to these dreams, but it does seem unlikely that this many people are having similar dreams—"

"I know a little about crowd psychology," said Lafleur doubtfully, "but I'm certainly not a psychologist. But cases of shared delusions do exist." She looked at Byrne. "I'm not saying you're deluded, sir."

"Thank you," said Byrne.

"I guess to some extent it doesn't matter what the cause is," said Raffi. "Whether we're simply a bunch of people under stress, some of whom have

216   UNA McCORMACK

been experimenting with the local flora, or whether there's something behind all this. We might never know. What really matters is how much this influences our decision about what to do next. And I do think that—dreams notwithstanding—we would be safer going farther into the valley."

Tradall was shaking his head. "I wish we'd gone anywhere else but here," he said. "I wish we'd never risked this. The Order did some *terrible* things. I don't want to see any of that firsthand."

"We don't know it's the Order behind this," said Byrne.

"But, as Raffi, says—that belief might be enough," said Lafleur. "You know, Mesat was telling me that some of the Cardassians are saying they would rather go back and take their chances with the Romulans than go farther into the valley."

"That's crazy," said Raffi. "The Romulans are a clear threat. We know what they'll do when they lay their hands on these people. And a few nights under the trees, having some bad dreams? That's enough to make people want to go back and face them? We've not even gotten very far. If we're located, the trees won't be any protection from aerial assault. We should be pressing on as quickly as we can, finding some real cover, trying to reach our people in Merna."

Byrne was nodding. "I know, Raffi. I know what you're saying is right. Let me sound out Mesat and Prok. See what they advise, based on the mood among the civilians."

Caution was their chief advice, and perhaps a day where they did not try to travel. Raffi chafed against the delay, the kilometers lost, the unknown advances that the Romulans were making while they did not move. But she had to admit that everyone around her seemed happier as a result and that the mood in the camp seemed less febrile. She was able to persuade people to be cautious, however: no breaking cover during the daylight hours; no heading down to the river. She was glad she had insisted on these precautions when, midafternoon, they heard the unmistakable sound of a flyer, in the near distance.

SECOND SELF   217

Byrne ordered every piece of equipment powered down, and there was silence beneath the trees. At last, the buzz and whir of the flyer faded, and eventually was gone.

"Starfleet?" asked Tradall hopefully.

"No," said Raffi, who would recognize a Romulan flyer anywhere. Then, "Shit!" said Lafleur. "The jammers are down!"

There was a dash and rush, and the engineers and technicians hurried to get everything back up and running. No more than eight minutes, but terrifying while they were unprotected. "All we need," said Byrne, "is for the machines to start fritzing."

Raffi got out her tricorder to check whether it was still functioning. A small light was flashing, alerting her to a message, sent on a secure channel. Not from Merna; no, this was a channel she had used repeatedly throughout the Dominion War, to communicate privately with her opposite number in the Tal Shiar. She would leave the office, and head to a favorite café, quiet, and off the beaten track, where they could talk in private. Exchange news; pass on items of interest; small matters that perhaps they did not want to bring to the attention of their immediate colleagues or direct superiors. Raffi quelled the light but read the message. Coordinates, nothing more, but she knew what this meant.

Sokara wanted to meet. He wanted to speak to her.

Without other people to encumber her progress, Raffi was able to hike back to the river in a matter of hours. She waited until evening before entering the tunnel, coming out into the ruined town under the cover of darkness, lifting the holo-filter behind her. The faintest line of the larger Ordeve moon was now visible in the sky. The other, smaller, moon would not make an appearance for another night or two. She wondered where Avarak was buried, but she did not have time to search, and she would not have known where to begin. Instead, she moved silently, quickly, past the burned and tumbled

218   UNA McCORMACK

stones, until she found the site of her previous meeting with Sokara. He was there already, still and dark, like a statue. When he moved, raising his hand in greeting, Raffi was reminded, piercingly, of the shadow figures from her dreams.

Stop. Come no farther.

"Raffi," he said. "I didn't know whether you'd get the message or if you'd come. Thank you for making the journey."

"What do you want?" she said, barely able to keep the anger from her voice.

He registered her tone of voice—he could hardly miss it—and said, "What's happened?"

"What's *happened*? Really? Are you *joking*?"

"The situation in which we find ourselves is no joking matter," he replied.

"Avarak is dead," said Raffi. "You met him, back in Merna."

"The Vulcan?"

"He had a name. Avarak. An ensign on his first mission. Now he's dead."

"Who killed him?" said Sokara and, when she didn't reply, he gave a wry smile. "A Cardassian, I imagine. They're not good people, Raffi. There's a sickness in their culture. They've rotted, from within. I'm sorry he has been collateral damage—"

"Avarak would not have been here without the threat posed by the Romulans."

"You can't blame this on me," he said.

"Not you, no," she said. "But the people with you? Iloba? Yes, I can, and I will. And if this leaves you feeling uncomfortable, or angry, then ask yourself *why*, exactly."

"I'm not angry," he said. "I'm sorry that you've lost someone who mattered to you. But these things happen in war—"

"We're not *at* war," said Raffi. "This is *peace*."

A chilly silence fell.

"Why are you here?" Raffi asked at last. "Are you going to try to persuade me to surrender?"

"I doubt the effort would be worth my while," he said. "But you do know that you can't hold out for much longer, don't you? That forest can't provide cover indefinitely. And I'm not sure that you'll persuade everyone to go that way. I know that many of our people aren't keen." He shot her a sharp look.

"No?"

"There are many rumors about that valley," said Sokara.

"Oh yeah?" said Raffi. "What have you heard?"

"That it was a test site for biogenic weapons. Overseen by the Obsidian Order. That the land is poisoned and it kills." His voice went very quiet. "Don't go into the Caanta valley, Raffi. Please." There was an urgency to his tone that was unlike him, and Raffi wondered, for a moment, whether he, too, was experiencing the dreams that they all were. No, nonsense. No chance. She was tired, and frightened, and starting to see ghosts.

"That's great advice," Raffi said. "So where do you think we should go?"

"I think," said Sokara, "that I can help with that." He reached into his pocket, and then held out his hand. "Here," he said. "Take this."

"What is it?"

"Take it."

Raffi took what turned out to be a data crystal. "Sokara—?"

"That contains information about our troops in the area. Codes for our secure channels. You should be able to monitor aerial traffic, for one thing, and that alone should help you prevent us from locating you. You'll also find some files on there, when this is over, which you may find of use."

"What are they?"

"Wait and see. They're time coded."

"Sokara, is this for *real*?"

He shrugged.

"But *why*?"

220   UNA McCORMACK

"I know you've been having trouble with long-range comms," he went on. "I know you've been struggling to reach Merna."

"You're very well informed."

"We have been having the same trouble, in recent days."

Raffi frowned. "We thought it was you, blocking signals."

He shook his head. "No. It's very strange. We're quite isolated. This gives certain people—Iloba, for example—an unpleasant belief that they are free to do as they wish. We've not been working as hard as we might to restore long-range comms, as a result. But I have. I should be able to contact Merna within the next day or two. And when I do, I'll alert your people there that Ghenic has been taken, and that you have moved on. I'll suggest that a Starfleet investigation of the situation unfolding at Ghenic should be considered a matter of some urgency." He looked at her steadily. "All that you and your people—and your charges—have to do now is hold out. Try not to get found."

But this was *hope*. Not to mention treason. They wouldn't shoot him quickly for this. They'd make the punishment take a very long time.

"Why are you giving me this? Why are you *doing* this?"

"I'm sure you'd like to know," he said.

"Dammit, yes, I would."

"What do they say about Romulans?" he said. "Never ask a straight question."

"How do you expect me to *believe* you?"

"I've told you everything you need to know," he said. "The choice is yours." He eyed her thoughtfully. "I don't suppose you know what's in the Caanta valley, do you?"

"No," she said.

"A shame," he said. "That might have been useful. Perhaps . . . I should let you find out, rather than any Romulans."

"Is *that* why you're helping?"

"If it will make you act on this information, then, by all means, believe that's why. Or else . . ." He shrugged. "Remember that the Tal Shiar move in mysterious ways."

"Oh, give me a *break*!" Raffi said, but she knew she wasn't likely to get a better answer from him. Whatever complicated agenda he was serving—some scheme of some shady official back home, she imagined—she was going to have to hope that their interests continued to be aligned until everyone was safely out of this hellhole. Everyone except Avarak.

"If you could destroy that rod when you've removed the relevant information, I would be grateful," he said. "It's identifiably Romulan." He pushed himself up. His mood shifted slightly; he seemed more awkward. "There is . . . There's a fresh grave," he said. "In the ruins of the temple. I think perhaps that might be where you'll find your friend. Good luck, Raffi. Be seeing you."

She watched him disappear into the darkness. She waited awhile, and then went to look. Her flashlight gave enough illumination to show that what he said was true: the ground there had been dug and then covered over. Someone had even taken the time to place a small flat stone on top, as a marker, onto which some Cardassian words had been etched:

AVARAK OF VULCAN

2354–2376

FOR CARDASSIA

The last line startled her at first; but, sitting back on her heels and staring at the words for a little while, she began to find meaning and even some consolation in them. She picked a few flowers and laid them on top of the stone. *Papaver ordeviensis*; blood poppies. Then she took out her tricorder and recorded a holo-image, for his family, when—if—she got out. She turned off the flashlight and made her way back silently to the tunnel. Her hand was wrapped tightly around the rod. She pondered its contents. Tried to decide whether or not she could trust Sokara. Tried to determine whether or not this was all too good to be true. She stopped and ran her tricorder over the rod. No sign of any tracking device.

Near the entrance of the tunnel, she looked back, but she could see no sign of Sokara, only the old stones, looming in the night. If he was waiting to see her route back, she could not see him. She lifted the holo-filter, entered into the tunnel, and put the filter in place behind her. She could be leading them straight into the hiding place. Sokara could be bluffing, double bluffing, bluffing in triplicate. This was the problem, dealing with Romulans. Their paranoia was infectious, like a plague. She walked along the tunnel, her flashlight catching on the carvings, cursing whatever bad luck had brought her to this forsaken place, cursing that she had to rely on the kindness of strangers.

Damn Romulan secrecy. Damn Romulans.

11

"Well, this is absolutely and definitely not a trap," said Byrne, when Raffi showed her the isolinear rod. "Do you really trust this guy?"

"He's a Tal Shiar officer working for a government that's historically hostile to us, currently stationed at a base commanded by someone who intends to overrun our position within the next few days and murder all of us."

"So definitely not a trap," Byrne deadpanned. "But what's your reading of this?"

"We worked together for almost the whole of the Dominion War," said Raffi. "He was always trustworthy. But I have to be honest with you. I can think of no reason—absolutely no reason—why he would pass us the intelligence we need to get through this. Which is chiefly what makes me think that this information is solid."

"Perhaps he doesn't want to see a massacre either," said Lafleur.

"What does it say about us," said Byrne, "if we're not able to recognize an honorable gesture when we see one?"

"I'd say it means we've just come out of a brutal war," said Raffi. "And that our allies haven't always been the most trustworthy people. Commander," she went on, "I think we should take this on face value. The fact is, we're hardly in the most defensible of positions. We've got decent cover under the trees, but we're using a lot of resources hiding our life signs and other signals, and I don't know how long we can do that."

Which would mean that they could be located, if there were more fly-

224 UNA McCORMACK

overs, and, while the ability to monitor aerial traffic might help them, moving this many people was not a small task. Even worse, not being able to hide power signals meant the field replicators would become useless. Which would soon mean over a hundred hungry people. Maybe they could feed a handful of them from what they could find in the forest, but not everyone . . .

"There's one other thing using this information allows us to do," added Raffi. "We won't have to move farther up into the valley. We can hunker down here."

"Good," said Byrne. "Focus our attention on trying to contact Merna."

"Sokara told me that he was intending to alert our people there," said Raffi, and watched as a faint ray of hope appeared on Byrne's face.

"Do you think that's true?" said Byrne. "Wouldn't that be—"

"Treason, yes," said Raffi.

The three of them fell silent, caught between wanting to believe that they'd been given exactly what they needed to survive and the dread that trusting a Tal Shiar officer was going to lead exactly where they feared.

"All right," said Byrne. "We'll take what we've been given." She seemed relieved to see the other two nodding their agreement. "But let's not tell our Cardassian friends the source of this information, eh? Let them think that our ability to break Romulan codes is far better than they ever realized."

That seemed wise, and if Tradall had questions about where this new intelligence came from, he was clearly prepared to delay asking until everyone was safe. The relief that there would be no further advance up into the valley was palpable, and people brought new energy to their tasks. A team headed by Lafleur and Prok was working on maximizing their ability to mask their power sources, and with the better protection they were able to run the field replicators more often. The weather held out and could even be described as pleasant. There was a danger, Raffi thought, that they might become complacent about their position, but the flyovers continued—and so did the dreams.

Byrne came to find Raffi, sitting down beside her, startling Raffi with her taut expression. "What's happened?"

"I dreamed last night," said Byrne.

"All right," said Raffi cautiously. "Was it okay?"

"I dreamed of my husband."

Raffi sat back, slowly, and gave the other woman space to speak. This situation had made them close colleagues, but they had not exactly had a chance to become friends.

"We always joked we were soul mates," Byrne said. "From when we met at the Academy. Our eyes met across a *Kobayashi Maru* simulation . . ." She laughed. "We married right after graduation. Spent a lot of time apart. Different ships. Promised we'd get an assignment together after the war. He was serving on the *Cairo* . . ."

The *Cairo* had been ambushed and destroyed by the Dominion last year. No survivors.

"I'm so *sorry* . . ."

"Yeah, ain't that a bitch, eh?" said Byrne. "And there he was, last night, like he'd never been away, and . . ."

"Did he tell you anything?" said Raffi.

"Oh, Raffi," said Byrne. "You know what I think. These dreams don't mean anything . . . We're under intense emotional stress. Of course I'm going to dream of my dead husband . . . But since you ask . . ." Byrne's face went very still, but her eyes were huge and shining. Raffi understood, suddenly, what she was seeing. A deep, enduring, trustful love.

"There was a bright light behind him. He seemed to emerge from it. Walked toward me. Our fingers touched." She held out her hand, palm up. "And I was consoled." Raffi clasped her hand. "We've done the right thing," said Byrne. "I'm sure of it."

Two more days, hiding beneath the trees. Two more days, trying to boost the long-range comms. Two more days, monitoring Romulan transmissions, trying to establish when the flyovers would happen, hiding when they did,

226   UNA McCORMACK

hoping that they would remain concealed. More dreams, although people were reporting the same as Byrne. That they were consolatory. That—in staying where they were—they had done the right thing.

On the third day after Byrne came to tell Raffi about her dream, they learned that more flyovers were planned for that afternoon. They heard the machines, faintly at first, in the distance, but drawing ever closer. They were about half a kilometer away, Raffi guessed, when the signal jammers went down. Every single device in operation—not to mention every live body—was broadcasting their position.

"Off!" yelled Raffi. "Turn everything off!"

There was a mad flurry of activity as people dashed to obey the order. Handheld devices, tricorders, replicators, disruptor and phaser charging stations. Damn, thought Raffi, even out here, trying to keep their usage to a minimum, there was so *much*. So much to miss; so much to forget. Within a couple of minutes, a terrible silence hung over the camp, as Cardassians and Starfleet alike stared around, wondering whether they had turned off everything, wondering whether there was anything still running that could give them away. Raffi saw Mesat and Prok and Turan and Lafleur trying frantically to work out what had gone wrong. Overhead, she heard the flyers bank, and turn, and start to head back toward their position.

"Hey," she said, hunkering down beside them, "any chance of a miracle?"

"I'm an atheist," said Turan.

"I'm a humanist," said Lafleur.

"If you want a miracle," said Prok, "you should probably ask a Bajoran."

But all the Bajorans in the area were long gone, or long dead. Raffi looked up at the trees. *Oh well,* she thought, *it's been a good run.* She wondered how long the Romulans would take over the whole business. She didn't want to see the kids get hurt. Neither did she want to leave them to their fate.

The flyers were very close now; the upper branches of the trees moving rapidly from their passing. The silence all around—from so many people, from so many *children*—was awful. Raffi would dream about this, in later

SECOND SELF   227

days, and these visions would always be accompanied by the scent of flowers in bloom. *Papaver ordeviensis*. Sailors' delight. Crimson shadow. She put her head into her hands. Was this what Sokara had intended all along? She was the one that had persuaded Byrne to bring them here; the one that had persuaded them Sokara's information could be trusted. And now they were going to die.

I've fucked up again. I've got everything wrong, again.

And then:

"What?" muttered Lafleur.

"What just happened?" whispered Turan.

Raffi looked up. The lights on the jammers were green.

"What does that mean?" she said.

"Lieutenant," said Prok, "I believe that this is that miracle you requested."

Overhead, the flyers banked, and turned again. Ten minutes later, there was silence in the forest of the Caanta valley. Somehow, inexplicably, they had survived.

"I . . . don't know what happened," admitted Lafleur later. "There was no power. Really, nothing, those things were not working. And then . . . There seemed to be a kind of surge and the jammers came back on."

"Oh good," said Byrne, "more unexplained phenomena. I'm going to enjoy putting that into the report."

"I guess we could always show a little gratitude to our hardworking people," said Lafleur.

"Don't thank us," said Kovar. "It definitely wasn't us. Not that I'm complaining. But I don't know what happened, and it was nothing that we did."

"Raffi," said Byrne. "Any thoughts?"

"I've no idea," said Raffi after a while. "I thought we were done for." The expressions on her colleagues' faces were enough to tell her that they

228   UNA McCORMACK

had been thinking pretty much the same thing. "I don't understand what happened."

"Perhaps your Tal Shiar friend."

"He's not a friend."

"Your Tal Shiar *acquaintance*," said Byrne. "Perhaps he was able to exert some influence."

"That's the only explanation I can think of," said Raffi unhappily.

"Well timed if so," said Lafleur.

"*Deus ex machina*," agreed Turan. "What?" he said, when his colleagues stared at him. "I've read things."

"'There are more things,'" said Raffi, "'in heaven and earth . . . than are dreamt of in your philosophy.'"

"That's good, Raffi," said Kovar.

"That wasn't me," said Raffi. "But I understand the sentiment at last."

It seemed unwise to remain exactly where they had been camped, so they moved cautiously a kilometer into the forest, but no farther. Another two days passed, without any flyovers. And then came the sound that they had all been dreading—people coming toward them through the trees. They got the children to the back, armed as many of the civilians as they could, and put them in front of the children, and the Starfleet officers and remaining Cardassian military took position up front.

The trees parted, and Raffi saw an away team—red and yellow shirts—heading toward them. "Damn!" she cried out. "Where the *hell* have you all been?"

"Nice to see you too," said the commander heading the team. "What has been going on out here?"

Raffi and Byrne went forward to speak to them. Never had Raffi been so glad to see people in Starfleet uniforms. Despite her opening words, she felt a deep and passionate gratitude for these colleagues—strangers—who

SECOND SELF 229

were here, with their training, and their professionalism, and their great calm and energy. They looked fit, and rested, and competent, damn them. She surrendered herself willingly to their care. She could only imagine how the Cardassians felt.

They were quickly brought up to speed by Commander Furukawa. They were from Merna, where, earlier in the week, they had received a coded message advising them that Ghenic had fallen to the Romulans, and that the Starfleet personnel and Cardassian civilians were in immediate danger and in need of assistance. So Sokara *had* come through.

"Then we had a hell of a time locating you," said Furukawa.

"Signal jammers," explained Raffi.

"Yeah, well, your engineers are too damn good. The message suggested you were most likely in the Caanta valley, but we didn't have the resources to come and look."

"What changed?" said Byrne.

"The *Gráinne* arrived early this morning, Merna local time," said Furukawa. "That focused the attention of the Romulans. I understand there's been a change of commanding officer. Iloba's been recalled. The new guy is—"

"Let me guess," said Raffi. "Nuvu Sokara."

"Yeah, good guess," said Furukawa. "How did you know?"

"We go back," said Raffi. Had that been the plan, then? To remove Iloba? Raffi sighed. Who knew what the deeper schemes were? At least they had worked to their advantage.

"He's pulled the troops back from Ghenic and upriver. The base is open for our use now, I guess, although technically it's still Cardassian."

"I think Glinn Tradall will welcome your assistance," said Byrne.

"I thought Gul Assott was in command here?" said Furukawa.

"We've lost a lot of people in the last few weeks," said Byrne quietly.

"Well, I'm glad we're here now." Furukawa looked around. "Look, I hate to be the one to bring bad news, but you guys might be facing some trouble over all this."

"Trouble?" said Raffi.

"The Romulans aren't pleased about your intervention."

"They were going to kill everyone here!" said Raffi.

"They're claiming there's been a misunderstanding," said Furukawa. "That there were divisions among the Cardassian military at Ghenic—a mutiny, in effect—and that one faction was holding the Starfleet officers present hostage. They claim they were trying to take Ghenic to help." He eyed them. "I'm guessing that wasn't the case."

"There *was* some disagreement among the Cardassians," said Byrne. "But not by the end. We're not really going to get stitched up for saving all these lives, are we?"

Furukawa shrugged. "Who knows what the *hell* is happening these days."

After that, Raffi saw little more of Ordeve. She and the rest of the team from Ghenic were transported back to Merna, leaving the evacuation of the civilians to the away team. They were being brought to Merna, where the rest of the surviving Cardassians were waiting to hear whether they were to be taken back to Prime or could remain on Ordeve. She found messages waiting for her too, backed up since she had been out of range. One was from Jae. Dated about a fortnight ago. Telling her that the opening of the show had gone well. Like a message from another world. There was a follow-up, too, about a week later, asking whether she'd gotten his letter. Saying he was starting to worry about her. She replied straightaway.

I'll be home soon.

Though when, exactly, that would be, she wasn't sure. Byrne came to find her one evening, saying, "There's going to be an inquiry."

"Huh," said Raffi, "are we going to get keelhauled?"

"I don't know," said Byrne. "But a Starfleet officer died."

"I know," said Raffi. "I know."

"I don't regret what we did," said Byrne. "We saved a lot of lives."

"Yeah," said Raffi. Later that night, she drew out the data rod that Sokara had given her. Time coded, he'd said. When she checked what was there, she found a whole new set of files. Communications between Iloba in Ghenic, and his commanding officer in Merna, and their commanding officer, back on Romulus. All the proof Raffi needed to show that the Romulans had intended to kill everyone at Ghenic—their Starfleet allies included.

Six months later, it was spring, and Raffi—stiff and upright in her dress uniform—was sitting in front of a board of inquiry into the events surrounding the evacuation of the Cardassian population in Ghenic. There were some questions to be answered, or so Raffi was given to understand, about whether the officers on the ground had exceeded their authority and disobeyed orders to remain neutral.

Raffi watched the whole proceedings with as much detachment as she could muster. Of course they had exceeded their authority. Of course they had disobeyed the orders to remain neutral. There was absolutely no question about that, and she would have been the first to say so—if her legal representative hadn't issued a stern warning that she was to keep her mouth shut as far as possible. What was fascinating was watching the captains and admirals in charge of the inquiry bending over backward to exonerate everyone stationed at Ghenic. Because what else, really, were they supposed to do, and remain Starfleet? There were some halfhearted suggestions about reprimands, but nobody on the panel could quite bring themselves to commit to this. The fact was a hundred Cardassian civilians were alive who would not otherwise have survived, because of the actions taken by Byrne, Raffi, and their Starfleet colleagues.

"You caused a lot of trouble, Lieutenant," one of the admirals said to Raffi as they stood side by side waiting for the turbolift. "Try not to make a habit of it." It was good advice—although Raffi couldn't, in later years, say that she had followed it.

232   UNA McCORMACK

The inquiry closed with an official statement to the effect that the officers, while deviating from orders, had acted appropriately given their knowledge of the situation on the ground. The subtext was clear: best to exonerate everyone and move on. But there was—as predicted—an uproar from the Romulans. This was a *cover-up*, their ambassador to the Federation fulminated; an abnegation of commitments made under a *treaty* and heads should *roll* . . . Whereupon Starfleet (courtesy of Raffi) were able to show their treasure trove of incriminating communiques between the Romulan officers concerned. Raffi left the fallout from this in the capable hands of the diplomats, but she was not surprised to hear, a few weeks later, that the Romulans had agreed to drop their territorial claim to Ordeve and were intending to withdraw all troops by the end of the Ordevian year, leaving the world in the hands of the Cardassians. Those that were still alive.

And that, as far as Raffi was concerned, was surely that—apart from an achingly painful conversation with Avarak's parents, neither of whom showed any outward expression of emotion, but nevertheless seemed to be aging palpably in front of her eyes.

"He joined Starfleet," said Selkiak, his father, "because he reasoned that it was the place where his actions were most likely to have the greatest beneficial effect upon the greatest possible number of people."

"He was right," said Raffi. "There are many, many people alive now because of your son's presence on Ordeve. The choices that he made directly preserved lives."

She watched them turn to look at each other. Their forefingers overlapped.

"I wanted to ask . . ." Raffi went on; this was a difficult subject, a delicate one. "We can arrange for him to be brought home. If you would prefer—"

"No," said T'Kyl, his mother. "The body is not him. Let that rest."

Raffi would think of them often over the years, particularly after she had squandered her relationship with her own son. Gabe thought her theories were nothing more than a paranoid fantasy; even when she had been proven

SECOND SELF   233

right, he could not forgive her. Sometimes, when the sadness over her loss became too much (a double loss, once her grandchild was born), Raffi would find herself remembering Selkiak and T'Kyl, and their son. At least, Raffi would try to remember, she inhabited a universe where Gabe lived, and prospered. Where his life had not ended, young, and all the things he might have thought and said and done were never to be. At least, Raffi thought, sometimes, sitting in her shack in the desert, blowing out her brains with snakeleaf, there was still a chance that something might be salvaged from her ruins.

There was one brief coda to Raffi's first visit to Ordeve, its importance only apparent many years later. After the inquiry closed, everyone was sent on their way to continue much as they had done before, or else to pick up the pieces left by the terrible war that had recently concluded. The smoldering Cardassian Union tried to rebuild; the Klingon Empire toasted its triumphs; and the alliance between the Federation and the Romulans acquired a slight frost. Raffi returned to her desk at Romulan Affairs, where her colleagues welcomed her back warmly, and congratulated her on her consummate work at taking that alliance to the brink of extinction without actually ending it. Raffi sank back behind her desk with considerable relief, although the boredom that had originally propelled her to request active duty quickly set in once again, and soon another request was in the works. Jae proved her chief source of entertainment now. Raffi suspected he might be "the one" (although it turned out that not even Jae and their son were enough to keep her on Earth).

During this period Raffi received an invitation to attend a reception to honor the Starfleet officers at Ghenic. She called Jae straightaway.

"It's in Paris," she said.

"Paris?"

"Invitation says bring a guest. Wanna be my guest?"

234   UNA McCORMACK

"Can't resist an offer like that, Raffi," he said, with that gorgeous smile that in later years she would no longer be able to summon, that would turn into sadness, and sorrow, and resignation, and—in the end, and most heartbreakingly—indifference. *"Let's go to the ball."*

They visited Paris together, and while it was autumn, not spring (perhaps she should have read the signs much earlier), everything was otherwise perfect. They were young and in love. Raffi had lately escaped death, and they had a tendency—she and Jae—to push each other into taking risks. They were both stoned, maybe, when they arrived at the reception. At first everything seemed hilarious—the grandeur of the building, the formality of the welcome. Byrne sized up the state of them both immediately, her eyebrows lifting as she watched Jae pile food upon his plate.

"Raffi," said Jae. "What the hell *is* all this? You never told me this part of the job. Why would you hide that this was part of the job? I totally approve of your job."

Dimly, Raffi began to sense that perhaps their behavior was a little out of line, so she pulled Jae to one corner, where he continued to eat, but at least wasn't talking so much, and she could catch her breath and watch the proceedings. Not long after this, it became clear that their host intended to address the gathering. Conversation died down, until there was complete quiet. The Cardassian ambassador to the United Federation of Planets stepped forward, but Raffi, from her corner of the room, could not see him clearly. She was standing at the wrong angle, and in the wrong place, with too many people in the way. His voice was clear, however, and he spoke eloquently and with what seemed to be complete honesty about his gratitude to all present for their assistance on Ordeve. Then he asked a representative of the Cardassian military to speak. He gestured across the room, and a young man in uniform came to stand beside him.

It was Tradall. Raffi hadn't seen him since leaving Ghenic. He looked much better—he wasn't shaking, for one thing—and he seemed fitter too. He spoke, rather haltingly, about his gratefulness to be here this evening,

SECOND SELF   235

thanking their old friends and new allies in the Federation, and then he recounted his memories of the events. When he said Avarak's name out loud, his voice cracked.

"I'd be dead," he said, "if not for him. If not for what he did. What he chose to do, on behalf of a *Cardassian*." He took a moment to collect himself. "I'm not sure what I did to deserve that. My life for his life. I think about that every day . . ."

As Raffi listened to him speak, the crash came, and suddenly nothing that was going on around her felt funny at all. Jae was now an irritation. The reception room seemed hot and crowded. Tradall was recounting the last few hours, before Starfleet arrived, their terror when they realized that their jammers were no longer working; the moment when the power surged, and the jammers came online once again. Raffi looked around at her colleagues and saw on their faces that complex mixture of gratitude and fear at the strange events of that day. The gratitude that they had made it through; the fear—still unspoken, even to each other—that something inexplicable had happened in the forest of the Caanta valley. That some *power* had acted to save them . . . Lafleur had her hands pressed together, tapping the tips of her forefingers against her mouth. Byrne was shielding her eyes. All of them knew something had happened; none of them could say what, or even admit that this had been the case.

Tradall finished speaking, and the ambassador took the floor again. And then Raffi had what she could later only call an "experience." The room around her, and the people, seemed to fade away. She was in a nowhere-place, neither here nor there, but it reminded her of the ruined town, with its burned stones and buried bones. Three figures emerged from the light: the same three she had dreamed about, relentlessly, on Ordeve—familiar, but not yet known.

We're not finished, said the woman with the implant.

We've not even begun, said the young man with close-cropped hair.

We are in between, said the Romulan with the staff.

236   UNA McCORMACK

"Raffi," whispered Jae. "Are you okay?"

"Mm," she said, and wiped the sweat from her forehead. She gritted her teeth until the ambassador finished and the applause was done. When the conversations started up again, she said, "I'm gonna get some air."

"Want me to come with?" said Jae.

"Nuh-huh." Raffi nodded at the canapes. "Mind the shop."

She stumbled through the room toward some huge glass doors that led out onto a terrace. Behind her, she heard Byrne say, "Is she all right?" Jae replied, "Sure, yeah, no worries."

Outside, it was still quiet, the guests having come indoors to listen to the speeches. There were lanterns in the garden, so she wandered onto the grass, and stood in their half-light, sucking in breaths of air. The night was chilly; yes, this was definitely the fall. The trees were dark shapes, but where the lamplight hit the leaves, she could see their variegated colors, half green, half yellow. She stood under the nearest tree, pulling a leaf from its branch and studying its intricacies. Did this help? A little. Something upon which to focus.

"Lieutenant Musiker?"

She looked up. There was a Cardassian a meter away. She hadn't heard him approach; he must be light on his feet. The way he was standing, with the room behind him, she couldn't see his features very well. She reached to move the lantern hanging on the tree until she was better able to see him. The insanely well-cut suit. The precise flamboyance of his movements. The distinct contours of his face. The bright blue eyes.

"I wanted to thank you in particular," said Elim Garak, "for everything that you did on behalf of our people on Ordeve."

"You're welcome," said Raffi.

"Also, to express to you my deep regrets for the death of your colleague."

She did not repeat herself since that would have been a lie. He was not welcome. Avarak should not have died. And, to give the man his credit, he heard her silence, and understood its meaning. He nodded slowly.

"For what it's worth, Lieutenant, you have friends within Cardassia." He pressed his hand against his chest, and then held up his palm, that very Cardassian gesture of courtesy and respect. "Within its government."

He tilted his head, turned, and walked back briskly indoors. Raffi stayed outside, staring down at the fading leaf she was still holding, the lantern swaying above. Friends within Cardassia. She swore to herself she would never set foot on Ordeve again. She swore that she would never willingly go into Cardassian space again. But promises, as Raffi Musiker would learn later in life, can, like marriages, turn out to be prisons.

PART 5

2399

AFTER COPPELIUS

12

"Oh!" said Elnor. "You're the wanted war criminal!"

"For the record, Elnor," said Raffi, through gritted teeth, "it's best to withhold critical information until you're ready to reveal it."

"I agree," said Garak. "But thank you anyway. It saves me having to force that information from you."

Raffi raised her palms, outward, a gesture of appeasement. She saw Garak spot the stain from the blood poppy on her palm; wished she hadn't picked the damn thing. He'd use that, somehow. "You know," said Raffi, "I'm not here to arrest you."

"You're not?" said Elnor, bewildered.

Garak laughed.

"All I want right now," said Raffi, "is to find out what's going on in the Caanta valley. Perhaps we can pool resources?"

"My dear commander," said Garak, "I'm old now, but I'm not senile. I know full well that Starfleet, in their beneficence, have decided I can no longer be left to my quiet retirement, and that there is more to be gained from placating their Bajoran friends than currying favor with the current castellan—"

"That's not how it is," said Elnor.

"Excuse me?" said Garak.

"The current Cardassian administration thinks you're an embarrass-ment," said Elnor. "A relic from a former age. They'd be happy if you dis-

242   UNA McCORMACK

appeared. Same with the Federation. That's what I got from the files." Elnor looked uncertainly at Raffi. "Have I said too much again?"

"I think that this time you've hit the mark," said Raffi. "It's not nice to realize that you've become disposable, is it?" She had some sympathy with that, but not much.

"That remains to be seen," said Garak. "But at least we all now know that we're not simply here on a walking tour."

"If I wanted to arrest you," said Raffi, "I could contact my ship right now—"

"Oh *please*," said Garak. "You'll have to do better than that. There's a comms blackout across the whole Caanta valley, never mind the force field that's just gone up behind you. You'll find, too, that there's another up ahead. All behind security encryptions using Obsidian Order codes . . ." His eyes sparkled dangerously, ever so Cardassian behind the Bajoran mask. "Now, who in the area might be able to help with that?"

"Like I said—do you want to pool resources?" said Raffi.

Garak looked at them in turn. "Much as it intrigues me as to why a washed-up Starfleet intelligence analyst is bumbling around a Cardassian forest with a juvenile Qowat Milat, I believe this is a mystery I am happy to leave unsolved." He raised his disruptor. "I think this conversation is over."

Raffi tensed. Did she have time to grab for a weapon? She could feel Elnor coiling like a spring beside her, ready to move. Garak would get one shot off, Raffi reckoned, before Elnor covered the ground between them.

But Garak didn't get the chance. From the trees, a dark figure came crashing out, slamming into Garak, and sending him flying. It was Toze, of all people, looking absolutely baffled at what was going on. Elnor didn't waste any time. Younger than Garak, much quicker, he soon had the other man disarmed, and facing his own disruptor.

"Toze!" said Raffi. "What the hell are you doing here?"

"I woke up," said Toze, his eyes wide. "I . . . I . . . I . . . I went to get a breath of fresh air and I tripped and . . . and . . . What is going *on* here?" he said. "Why are you pointing a disruptor at an elderly vedek?"

"A *vedek*?" said Raffi.

Toze touched his ear. "The earring. This man is a vedek."

Now, Raffi thought, she had heard everything.

"My name is Vedek Saba Taan," said Garak smoothly. His voice was completely different: gentler, more temperate, the voice of a kinder man. "And please—don't blame the commander. I startled her, and that's why she's pointing her weapon at me." He smiled at Toze. "I know this valley well," he said. "I can help you." He turned to Raffi. "If you'd like."

Sokara came out of the trees.

"Prophets," said Garak. "Four of you!"

"Raffi," said Sokara. "What's going on? Who's this?"

"An old Bajoran monk," said Garak. "On pilgrimage to a lost temple. There is one, you know," he said, "farther in the valley. Or so the stories say . . ."

"Really?" breathed Toze.

"Oh yes," said Garak. "And I think I know the way . . ."

"We're going back," said Raffi firmly. "Back to the river. We'll get past that barrier."

"But the codes," said Toze. "Obsidian Order codes—"

"I'm sure we'll think of something," said Raffi. "You know, the Bajoran Resistance knew a great deal more about the Order than they might have liked."

"Yes, I heard that was the case," said Garak. "Although, speaking as one who remembers those days, I suspect that it may have been somewhat overstated."

"I'm sure I'll find something in the databanks I can use," said Raffi.

"I'm sure you will," said Garak. "But . . . are you quite sure you wouldn't like to see what's up in the valley?"

"No," said Raffi. "Anyway, you said there was another force field up ahead."

244   UNA McCORMACK

"There is," said Garak. "But did you know that when those barriers went up, a beacon activated, beyond the second one?"

"What?" said Sokara.

"I don't believe you," said Raffi.

"Commander!" said Toze, his voice shocked. "Forgive her impertinence, *Da'eel*," he said to Garak. An honorific. *Holy man*. Raffi thought she might throw up.

"Of course!" said Garak graciously. "By all means check, Commander. I'm not lying."

Raffi pulled out her tricorder. He was right. A second barrier, farther up the valley, and beyond that, a faint beacon, transmitting coordinates.

"Perhaps," said Garak, "there might be something there to help us?"

Or an Obsidian Order trap, Raffi thought.

"I've come a long way for this pilgrimage," Garak said piously. "Guided by the Prophets. Is nobody else curious to know what's happening in this valley? I know I am."

"We shouldn't interfere with his journey," said Toze. "I'll help, *Da'eel*."

"Thank you, my child," said Garak gravely.

Dawn light was stealing through the forest. "Whichever way we're going," said Sokara, "we should start soon. I'd like to press on, Raffi. We said three days—I don't want to waste that time."

"I intend to go on," said Garak. "Unless anyone objects?"

"I'll go with you, *Da'eel*," said Toze. "Another temple . . . I never thought . . ."

Sokara was already heading back to their camp. Raffi, taking out her tricorder, saw that the displays were going wild.

"Odd, isn't it?" said Garak. "Happens all the time here." He frowned, and, for a moment, Raffi almost believed that he couldn't quite understand these strange effects either. Then he walked on, catching up with Toze. Elnor, walking behind with Raffi, whispered, "I don't understand. Why are we keeping this secret? Why don't you arrest him?"

SECOND SELF 245

"Because I can't crack these codes," said Raffi, "and he might be able to. Hell, he might be the one responsible for the barriers in the first place. But most of all—Toze is a civilian. I don't want him caught in the crossfire. The less he knows, the less inclined Garak will be to kill him."

"And what about Sokara?"

Raffi put the tricorder away. "I'm not sure what he'd say now."

"Perhaps we should have told him the truth from the start," said Elnor.

"Well, that's the situation we're in, so we have to live with it. Let's use Garak for now to find out what's going on and deal with the rest later. Preferably when we've managed to reach the *Stargazer*." She saw his uneasy expression. "It's not *lying*, Elnor—"

"I know. It's withholding critical information until we're ready to reveal it."

Raffi patted his shoulder. "You're getting there."

"I hope not," he replied.

"Sir," said Tanwar. "We have Romulan ships incoming."

"Romulan?" Rios got out of his seat and came to join her. "How many?"

"Two . . . No, three. Scout ships." She was frowning. "Who knows what's coming behind them . . ."

"Have they hailed us?" he said. "Have they hailed the authorities on Ordeve?"

"Nothing." She shook her head at the sensor readings. "Sir, I think these might be Tal Shiar ships."

"Oh *great*." Rios went back to his seat. "Get me the exarch's office. See if they know anything about them."

Khrill herself came on the line, and she was none the wiser. *"I was about to contact you, Captain Rios,"* she said. *"Starfleet, the Bajorans, now the Tal Shiar, we assume—all this focus turned toward our world is very surprising."* She gave him a penetrating look. *"I don't suppose you can shed any light on this?"*

246   UNA McCORMACK

In the back of his mind, Rios heard Admiral Picard insisting on the continued secrecy of the mission. "No idea. Perhaps they heard of our interest
in the refugee settlements?"

"Perhaps," said Khrill.

"There's only one way to find out," said Rios. "We ask them."

"If you get a straight answer from the Tal Shiar, Captain," she said, *"you're
cleverer than I am. Khrill out."*

Rios pushed out a breath. "Tanwar," he said. "Whatever you're doing to
reestablish contact with Commander Musiker, speed it up."

Throughout the day's walk, Raffi alternated between trying to get through
the blackout and keeping a close eye on Garak. He seemed, in the main,
content to walk beside Toze, spinning the archaeologist a tale about how he
always promised himself a visit to the ruins of Akantha. During the afternoon, however, he insinuated himself beside Elnor. Raffi, looking up, heard
him say, "Only the truth. What a remarkable way to lead one's life . . . Do
tell me more . . ."

Raffi moved quickly to intervene, sending Elnor to walk up front with
Sokara.

"I don't want you talking to Elnor," she said.

"But Commander!" Garak said with a smile. "Absolute candor, no less! I
am sure there is a great deal that I could learn from that young man."

"Leave him alone," said Raffi.

"Or else what? You'll hit me? You'll break every bone in my body? I'll
enjoy detailing that to my legal team."

"Well, at least you're seeing where this ends," she said.

"Where does this end, Commander?"

"With you standing trial for your crimes."

Garak laughed softly. "Oh, we're a very long way from that," he said. "A
very long way."

SECOND SELF   247

In the early evening, they stopped and made camp. The beacon was still active. They shared out rations, and sat eating, but not talking. Nobody seemed to want to try to go to sleep. At length, Toze broke the silence.

"I understand from Elnor that this is not your first visit to Ordeve," he said to Raffi.

"No," said Raffi.

"When were you here?"

Raffi and Sokara exchanged looks. "A long time ago," she said. "Just after the Dominion War."

"An unhappy time for many people," said Garak.

"Well, that's war, isn't it?" said Raffi. "Particularly when people choose the wrong side. I feel sorry for the civilians. Caught up in decisions made by people who think they know best—"

"Yes, one weeps for the civilians," said Garak, without any apparent falsity. "One might understand how people—caught in the middle of horrors—would look for solace in all kinds of places. Prayer. Meditation. Substances." Garak's gaze drifted down to Raffi's palm. She had washed her hands clean much earlier, but the memory—the *feeling*—of the stain was still there. She clenched her hand into a fist.

"You sound like you know what you're talking about," she said.

"Old habits die hard," he said with a smile.

"Tell me, Vedek Saba," said Raffi, "have your habits stood you in good stead over the years?"

"Oh, the jury's still out on that," he replied. "But I'd like to hear more about your time here."

I'm sure you would, thought Raffi.

"I know I still have a few questions," said Sokara. "Raffi and I were both here at the end of the war," he explained, "at Ghenic."

Garak's eyes lit up. "Were you *really*? How fascinating . . . Of course, the Romulans and the Federation were allies, weren't they? I often thought, over the years, how *timely* the Romulan entrance was into the Dominion

248   UNA McCORMACK

War. How the Federation would most likely have been overwhelmed without their aid. I'm sure there must be a story there . . ." He clasped his hands together, the very model of a holy man. "May the Prophets be praised," he said, with great sincerity, "for their intervention."

"I doubt it had anything to do with the Prophets," said Sokara with a frown. "The wormhole aliens, I mean. But there were many unexplained phenomena during those days. Wouldn't you agree, Raffi?"

"Yes," she said. "Not all of which can be put down to Cardassians using too much crimson shadow."

"Crimson shadow?" said Elnor.

"The local drug of choice," said Raffi. "And before anyone says it—yes, some of the Starfleet officers here used it too. It didn't have as much effect on us as on the Cardassians, mind you. But our homeworld wasn't in flames." She looked straight into Garak's eyes. "I guess we all know that the Cardassians were nearly massacred here on Ordeve. I was one of the Starfleet officers that tried to protect them. We came out here—across the river. We didn't think we were going to survive. We escaped here, into the Caanta valley. Managed to evade capture by blocking our life signs, our power signatures, and so on. We'd been out several days when our jammers went down. We thought we were all dead. And then there was a massive power surge. Everything came back up. And that's why we all lived."

"So that's what happened," said Sokara. "I've wondered for years."

"Sheer, dumb luck," said Raffi bitterly.

"I wonder," said Toze. "This was a holy place, once upon a time."

"Do you have *any* idea what happened?" said Garak. He seemed genuinely fascinated.

Raffi shook her head. "Never did find out."

"So strange . . ." he murmured. "But then, I suppose, there are more things in heaven and earth, than are dreamt of in our philosophy . . ." He saw Raffi's expression and sniffed. "I never really liked Hamlet. A childish idiot."

"I can see how Iago might appeal," said Raffi.

SECOND SELF   249

"These days," said Garak, "I feel a certain sympathy with Lear. But strange things do happen. We must be grateful to the Prophets," he said, with great devoutness, "who are surely walking beside us. We must be grateful for our survival."

"Yes," said Toze, smiling. "We walk with the Prophets."

Raffi, barely able to keep herself from giving Garak's performance the slow handclap that it deserved, looked instead down at her palm. She would give anything right now for that sweet taste. Suddenly, Elnor said, "Is anyone else having strange dreams?"

Nobody replied, but the space around them was now crackling with tension. "I am," said Raffi. "The same when I was last here. Bad dreams." She nodded at Sokara. "How about you?"

He dug the toe of his boot into the soil. "I'm not sleeping as well as usual."

"Let's say I wouldn't mind being in my own bed again," admitted Toze.

"What about all those years ago, Sokara?" said Raffi, curious, now, as to how it had been for him. "Did you have bad dreams then?"

"It was a stressful time," he said, avoiding her eye. "I'm not sure anyone slept particularly well. On either side."

"When I said strange dreams," said Elnor, "I didn't mean *bad* dreams. Just . . . strange. What, are you all having nightmares or something?"

"You aren't, honey?" said Raffi.

"Not nightmares," he said. "Figures, speaking to me. They're . . . comforting. They're bathed in light, and I can't quite see who they are, but they seem to know me. They seem to want me to know that everything will be fine. They feel like . . . They feel like Zani, or how it felt when Jean-Luc read to me. They're not *bad*. Just strange. I'm sorry that you're all having nightmares," he concluded. "I wouldn't wish that on anyone."

Garak was chuckling. "Elnor," he said, "you've missed your calling. Starfleet Intelligence should recruit you as an interrogator. I've never seen so much information so freely given."

250 UNA McCORMACK

"What about you, *Da'eel*?" said Toze. "Are your dreams troubled?"

"Oh, I'm an old man," said Garak. "I sleep when I can, and I sleep well. Speaking of which . . ." He moved a little distant, stretched out, and closed his eyes. *Liar,* thought Raffi, watching him go—and saw the same on Elnor's face. The young man opened his mouth to say something and closed it again. He sighed and settled down himself.

You're learning, thought Raffi. Toze, too, soon went to lie down, but Sokara stayed, sitting opposite from Raffi. They waited until everyone was asleep before speaking to each other, in quiet voices.

"Were the dreams very bad?" said Raffi. "Last time?"

"There was just one," he admitted, "but it was terrible. I've never told anyone about this."

"You don't have to tell me now," she said, "if you don't want to."

"Perhaps it would be better if I did. It was the night before I came to meet you at the ruins . . ." He stopped to take a deep breath. Whatever he'd seen, it had clearly shaken him. "I saw Romulus on fire. Burning . . ."

"Oh, Sokara, *no*—"

"I thought at the time that it was because of all the images coming from Cardassia Prime, you know? That I'd transposed them into my dreams . . . Strange to think that this was prophetic in some way . . ." He shook his head. "So, I saw that . . . and then there were three figures—"

"Three?" said Raffi.

"All of them wanting to warn me. Telling me that we should withdraw, or else we'd die. When I woke, I tried to tell myself that it was nothing, that I shouldn't pay attention, but it was like I could hear an alarm ringing in my head. I knew I couldn't stop the advance that was underway—what, exactly, would I have said to Iloba?—so I did the only thing I could. I contacted you."

"I'm grateful you did," said Raffi.

"What were your dreams like, Raffi?"

"Same sort of thing. Three figures. First, they told me to cross the river, and then, later, to go no farther. And now, this time, the same three figures telling me to go on. When I was here, before, I didn't know who they were. This time around, I think I do." She did not elaborate, and Sokara—who knew the importance of secrets—did not ask. Watching his face, tired and anxious, Raffi wondered whether she should explain to him what was happening. Who exactly Garak was, and why she had come out again to Ordeve. But she hesitated, caught between wanting to trust a friend, and her instinct to preserve the confidentiality of the mission.

Eventually, Sokara said, "I think I'll try to get some sleep now, Raffi. Wake me in an hour. You should do the same."

The moment had passed. Soon enough Raffi was left alone to the stars and her secrets.

In the middle of the night, Garak made his move. Raffi was on her feet and in pursuit within seconds, but Toze got to Garak first. He brought the other man down heavily to the ground, knocking the breath out of him, hit him—hard—for good measure, and, while Garak was still gasping for air, brought out restraints and cuffed him. Garak lay on his side, coughing, his hands bound.

"Very impressive," said Raffi. "For an archaeologist."

"You'd be amazed," said Toze, "at what you can learn on digs."

Sokara, who was right behind Raffi (had any of them been even trying to sleep?), said, "Do you want to tell us who you are, Toze?"

"I've told you," Toze said. "I have a professional interest in the history of this place."

"Yeah," said Raffi. "I think we know your profession. We're all in the same business, aren't we? Tell me, are you with the *Koma Tath*?"

"Well done, Commander," said Toze.

"Oh," breathed Garak, pulling himself up to a seated position. "How unfortunate. For me, I mean. Though perhaps for you too."

"It's definitely unfortunate for you," said Toze. "I like my work."

252   UNA McCORMACK

"So did I," said Garak.

"What's the *Koma Tath*?" said Elnor, who had belatedly joined them, and was rubbing his eyes. The only one of them who had been sleeping, apparently. Oh, to be young again, thought Raffi, and blameless.

"A special branch of Bajoran Intelligence," said Raffi. "Their main task is tracking down and assassinating Cardassians who committed crimes during the Occupation."

"What?" said Sokara, staring at Garak.

"Not always assassinating them," said Toze. "Bringing them to trial is acceptable. It depends how much they struggle."

Garak held up his bound hands. "I'm not struggling," he said. "Yet."

"And I'm not killing you," said Toze. "Yet."

"Let's not talk about killing anyone, okay?" said Raffi. "You're on Cardassian territory, Toze. Ordeve is under their jurisdiction. That means arrest, it means extradition—"

"If you think I haven't killed Cardassians on their own ground before, you do not understand the *Koma Tath*," replied Toze.

"It's certainly what I would do," put in Garak. "Tidier, that way."

"Yes, you'd prefer that, wouldn't you?" Toze looked at Garak with loathing. "But you? I particularly want to see you brought to trial. Everything by the book. Everything in the public eye."

"Oh, I can't wait," said Garak. "I do hope you'll let me change first. I have a number of very good suits that will be perfect for the occasion."

"Oh, you'll look different, I promise you," said Toze. "You'll be yourself, for one thing." Some of his anger bubbled over. "Changing your face to look Bajoran? You're *sick*—"

"I must confess I do feel somewhat queasy whenever I catch a glimpse of myself—"

"Okay," interrupted Raffi, "stop this—"

"Might I ask the charge?" said Garak, ignoring her advice. "I'm prepared to admit that once upon a time I worked for the Office of Public Records, but in a very minor capacity. I've been a gardener—"

"When you were an undercover operative on Romulus," said Toze.

"And a tailor," said Garak.

"After you were sent into exile by your father," said Toze.

"Oh, you *have* done your research," said Garak. "You recall, then, what happens next? I put myself entirely at the disposal of Starfleet Intelligence. I provide information and, ah, other support that proves critical to winning the Dominion War. I assist in instigating the resistance on Cardassia Prime. I serve as an advisor under successive postwar administrations, most notably as ambassador to the Federation—"

"Oh yes," said Toze. "You've done a great job putting a shine to your name. Not to mention covering your tracks."

"And now I am retired. I live very quietly at home in Ses'erakh and Paris, reading, writing, and gardening. Sometimes I embroider—"

"You're a former member of the Obsidian Order," said Toze.

"Raffi," murmured Sokara. "Did you know about this?"

In the gap before she replied, Garak slid in. "Caught in a lie, Commander?" he said, his lip curling. "I've never denied my association with the Obsidian Order." He stopped himself. "In fact, I have *often* denied that association, but not in recent years. Does anyone even *care* these days?"

"You joined the Order around the age of seventeen. I wonder if you ever stopped. It's not easy tracking down information about you, Garak," said Toze. "You've destroyed most of it, and the Fire took the rest." He gave Garak a cold smile. "Took so much with it, didn't it, the Fire? But you've been a special study of mine."

"How flattering," said Garak, sounding bored.

"I've been investigating you for years. Monitoring you. Following you long before you took that face. Tracking you here, all the way to Ordeve. Why here, I wondered. This place, of all places."

254   UNA McCORMACK

"It's rather pleasant in the spring, don't you think?" said Garak. "I should have retired here."

"One of the benefits of working for Bajoran Intelligence," said Toze, "is that our records are not only extensive—they're extant. We know that the order to burn down the temple at Akantha was given by a young Obsidian Order agent. We know that he was undercover using the name Mas Gherrod—"

"Which, I must point out, is not my name—"

"We know that he matches your age, and your description."

"Gray skin, spoon on head, devastatingly handsome. You realize that might be many *thousands* of people," said Garak. "And it was all *so* long ago. You'll need more than that if you're planning to persuade the castellan to extradite me, or the Federation to receive me. And I have been *such* a good ally, you know, over the years—"

"You'd love to know what else I know, wouldn't you?" said Toze. "You'll find out, in time. I assume you came here to destroy whatever evidence might remain—"

"Now I see we're moving to conjecture—"

"An old Bajoran, making a pilgrimage to a place he once knew. Nobody would ask questions. Everyone would treat you with respect. Help you on your way. It hasn't worked." Toze turned to Raffi. "Thank you for your assistance, Commander. If you're willing to help in getting this man back to Merna, I believe you can consider your mission to Ordeve fulfilled."

"Mission?" said Sokara, frowning. "Raffi, what is going on here?"

Elnor said, "Saba Taan isn't Saba Taan. He isn't Bajoran, either. He's a Cardassian called Elim Garak. He was a—"

"I know who Elim Garak is," said Sokara sharply. "I didn't know he was on Ordeve."

Raffi, conscious of Sokara's eyes on her, swallowed and addressed Toze. "The *Stargazer* is on hand, if you need support."

"There are Bajoran ships en route," said Toze. "We'll be able to transport him back to Ashalla."

"You've not got permission to extradite me yet," said Garak. "Or you didn't, last I checked."

"It's only a matter of time," said Toze.

"So many things are," said Garak. "But a war criminal in the dock is worth two in the forest. Good luck getting that force field down without my help."

"The *Koma Tath* is pretty good," said Toze, "at cracking Cardassian codes."

"Raffi," said Elnor urgently, "have I said something wrong? I thought this meant everyone knew about the real mission." He stopped, looking at Sokara. "Raffi, I'm confused. I don't know what to say and not to say—"

"*Real* mission?" said Sokara. "Raffi?"

"Oh dear," murmured Garak. "Commander, have you strayed from the path of absolute candor? Corrupting a young Qowat Milat!" He tutted. "And you considering a move to the Academy! Are you sure it's the right place for you?"

"All right," said Raffi roughly. "Toze, he's your prisoner. Get him over there and keep an eye on him. We've still got a couple of hours before daylight. We should get some rest, and then decide whether we're going on or trying to get back."

Toze stood up and hauled Garak to his feet. "Elim Garak," he said. "I am arresting you under section 6.2 of the Historical War Crimes Act. This law is recognized as a result of treaties between the Cardassian Union and the United Federation of Planets. You have the right to legal representation. You have the right to remain silent."

For a moment, everything was still in the dark night of the Ordevian forest, as if even Garak felt that history had caught up with him and could not find words. He quickly rallied. "Such *drama*," he said. "It's like the good old days. I feel positively invigorated."

Toze pulled him back to their camp and shoved him to the ground. Garak sat with his back against a tree, his cuffed hands in front of him, looking around with bright alertness. He definitely wasn't going to sleep.

256   UNA McCORMACK

"Sokara," said Raffi, lowering her voice. She was bitterly regretting not bringing him into the loop. "Please, let me explain—"

"Elim Garak," Sokara said. "He's the reason you came to Ordeve."

"Yes," she said. "I was asked to find him and bring him back."

"But you needed a cover story. The refugees—"

"I needed a cover story, that's true," she agreed. "But I wanted to help too—"

"You used us," he said. "Romulans are suffering, and you used us—you used *me*—to find this man."

"I think accusing me of keeping secrets is a little rich coming from a Tal Shiar agent," she shot back. "What did you expect me to do? Wear a sign?"

"You told the boy," Sokara said, walking away. "That more or less amounts to the same thing."

Elnor was still standing there, looking bewildered. "Have I done something wrong?"

"Oh, honey," said Raffi, patting his arm, and watching Sokara leave. "You might be the only one here acting in good faith."

13

Nobody went back to sleep. They sat around the camp heater, not speaking, not looking at each other—except for Garak, who seemed to be studying each of them in turn, a small smile dancing on his lips. Raffi, who had read his files (she wondered what Bajoran Intelligence had on this man that they hadn't shared), knew that this was exactly the kind of setup that suited his *modus operandi*. He might be bound and tied, and in the custody of the *Koma Tath*, but he was still able to exert control over them. He was the one most likely to be able to remove the force fields—and he would keep this *kotra* piece held back until he could play it at the best moment.

Toze sat with a phaser in his hand and a padd on his knee, half working on it, half watching Garak. The rush of exhilaration that coursed through him after making his arrest had, to Raffi's eyes, completely gone, and the reality of his situation—stuck in a forest with a dangerous prisoner who knew more than he was letting on, and far from backup—was starting to sink in. Was he trying to get past those Obsidian Order codes? Could he do that?

Sokara was sitting with his back against a tree, but he was motionless, staring out into the forest. Elnor sat for a while looking around, as if trying to work out what exactly was going on, but eventually sighed, and dropped his head, sitting like that, almost bonelessly, as the night wore on. Eventually, dawn light began to trickle through the leaves overhead.

"Okay," said Raffi. "I guess we're all awake. We need to make some de-

258   UNA McCORMACK

cisions. Do we go on, see whether we can push beyond the next force field, or do we go back, and try to get down to Ghenic? I say we go back."

Elnor, in a quiet voice, said, "I agree with you, Raffi."

"I don't agree," said Sokara, so quickly Raffi suspected that whatever she had said, he would have chosen the alternative. "I don't care why anyone else is here. I want to know what's going on in this valley, and I want to make sure that my people can come here. If it means walking into an Obsidian Order trap . . ." He looked at Garak. "The Tal Shiar outlasted the Obsidian Order by decades. I'm not afraid of the traps laid by the dead."

Garak snorted. "I'm almost impressed. No, wait. I'm not impressed at all."

"Toze," said Raffi. "I'm guessing you want to go back. Get on your way as quickly as possible?"

Toze didn't answer. He was staring at the padd in his hand.

"Toze?" said Raffi. "Something the matter?"

"The force field is down," he said.

So he'd done it. "Then we're going back," said Raffi. "Sokara, we'll return— I promise. I won't leave Ordeve until this is settled—"

"No, no," said Toze quickly. "Not the one we came through. The one ahead."

"What?" said Garak. "I mean, are you sure?" But the mask had slipped, however briefly. This was not something he'd anticipated.

"I'm sure," said Toze. "Whatever lies ahead—we can go and see."

"Oh," said Garak, covering his slip with false levity. "Then by all means I vote that we go on. I understand that this might not be a popular position but I would *much* rather walk into an Obsidian Order trap than a Bajoran prison."

"You don't get to vote," said Raffi. "Toze? How did you bring it down? Can you do that to the other barrier?"

"I didn't do it," said Toze. "So, no."

There was a silence.

SECOND SELF 259

"It just came down," he added. "If that helps."

"Oh," said Garak, delighted, "by *all* means we must investigate!"

"I agree," said Sokara.

"I don't," said Raffi. "Toze?"

"What do you think might be there, *Koma Tath*?" said Garak softly. "What proofs or evidence might you find? The answer to what really happened at Akantha, perhaps?"

"He's baiting you, Toze," said Raffi. "Ignore him."

"You won't get back across the river without my help," said Garak, to Toze. "And I want to know what's up there. Shall we make a little detour, you and I? Obsidian Order and *Koma Tath*, working together at last. Or shall we go back and sit by the river, while you bang your head against those encryption codes, and I lie back in peace and watch the poppies grow?"

"We'll go on," said Toze.

Garak smiled, like a shark.

"This is a terrible idea," said Raffi, in no uncertain terms. "Toze, there'll be people trying to reach us. They'll be trying to bring that barrier down—"

"They won't be able to," said Garak. "Believe me."

"You've got your man," said Raffi. "But you have to keep him—"

"Are you afraid, Raffi?" said Sokara. "Of what you might see up there? Everyone was always afraid, weren't they? Of what was in the Caanta valley."

"I was more afraid of what was chasing me," said Raffi. "A bunch of bloodthirsty Romulans, set on murdering me and my colleagues—"

Garak was laughing, ever so softly. "Oh, I am *enjoying* this—"

"Enjoy it while you can," spat back Toze. "Because all you've got ahead of you now is that Bajoran prison—"

Sokara stood up. "I'm going on," he said. "You can come with me, or you can stay. But I want to know what's up there."

Garak stood up. "I'm ready to move on. *Koma Tath*? Shall we go?"

Toze got to his feet. He put away the padd and held up the phaser.

260   UNA McCORMACK

"You first, *skrit*," he said. Whatever the word meant—and it was Cardassian, clearly—it reached its target. Garak blinked, and swallowed, and something hardened behind his eyes.

"Such discourtesy these days," he said, "among the young."

"We are what you made us," said Toze. "Get moving."

Garak walked on. Toze followed, phaser ready, and Sokara fell in step behind. He looked back over his shoulder. "Joining us, Starfleet?"

Captain Cristóbal Rios was sitting at his ready room desk when he accepted an urgent message from Exarch Khrill.

"Captain Rios," she said. *"I have some concerning news. We've been trying to reach your officer on the ground, to advise her of the Romulan ships in orbit, but it seems that she, her Qowat Milat, and the Romulan liaison, Nuvu Sokara, have gone missing."*

Rios ran his hand through his hair.

"Also missing is a Bajoran archaeologist, Toze Falus. Captain, we're extremely concerned about their safety. Have you had any news of them? Are you in contact? I'm asking the local constabulary to investigate."

"It's okay," said Rios.

"What do you mean? Are you in touch with them?"

Time to come clean. "I have a confession to make," he said. "We know exactly where Commander Musiker is—although we're not currently able to contact her."

Khrill's eyes narrowed. *"She hasn't—"*

"I'm afraid she has. She's gone with Elnor and Sokara into the Caanta valley to investigate whether a Romulan settlement would be viable there. The archaeologist went with them."

There was a pause while Khrill took a moment to compose herself. *"You're aware, aren't you,"* she said, *"that there's a ban on travel into that area? Perhaps you understand now why that ban is in force—"*

SECOND SELF   261

"Why have you never investigated?" said Rios. "I mean, a whole *valley*, closed off?"

"We don't have the resources to decommission an Obsidian Order base!"

"Is that what it is?" pressed Rios.

"I have no idea," said Khrill. *"That's my best guess based on available data—which seems to be borne out by what's happening now."*

"But you must have been curious?"

"Captain Rios!" Khrill's anger and exasperation were plain. *"We have had enough to do on Ordeve since the end of the Dominion War! Do you* know *our recent history? Jem'Hadar massacres, Romulan death squads! We barely had time to reestablish ourselves here when we threw open our world to thousands of Romulan refugees! Do you think any of that was conducive to sending an exploratory mission up into the mountains? The Obsidian Order barred entry into the Caanta valley. No, I am not curious to find out what they were doing there!"*

Rios held up his hands. "I apologize, unreservedly. I understand—"

"I'm not convinced you do. I'm not pleased about this. I'm going to have to approach the office of the castellan for advice."

"But what about—" She was gone. "Those Romulan ships . . ." His problem. He opened a secure channel. "Admiral Picard," he said. "You have a diplomatic incident incoming. The exarch knows where Raffi is—although not why. You might want to speak to our ambassador to the Union. In the meantime—I still have Romulans to deal with."

Not to mention those Bajorans. He didn't wait for a reply.

"Tanwar," he said into the comm, "contact the Bajorans. Ask whether they've had any success breaking those Order codes. It's time to bring people back."

They walked on into the valley. Predictably, there was little in the way of conversation. Toze handed the padd to Sokara, who periodically gave up-

262   UNA McCORMACK

dates on the status of the force field. This remained down. Every so often, Raffi tried her combadge. Futile. The comms blackout was still in place. The beacon, up ahead, was still transmitting steadily. What could possibly be there? What horrors might the Obsidian Order have perpetrated here? Would there be more evidence, of more massacres? Were they even now walking toward a site that was poisoned, the ground laid waste by weapons testing? Was there a black site here? The kind of place into which people disappeared, never to be heard from again? A prison, a torture facility. All these things were possible with the Obsidian Order. Did even Garak know what they would find? Raffi was not sure. He walked with his head bowed, revealing nothing.

After a couple of hours, Raffi called a halt. They had reached a stream, running down from the high hills to meet them, which gave an excuse to stop walking, but she was mindful, too, that Garak was not a young man. He seemed grateful for the pause, lowering himself onto a big fallen branch. He was flexing the fingers of both hands. Raffi wondered if she should check the restraints. Perhaps Toze had made them too tight. Garak would certainly not say, if that were the case.

They passed out some rations and ate. Elnor, looking around their party, said, "It's strange to see us all here, isn't it?" Nobody replied, but Elnor wasn't deterred. "Human, Bajoran, Cardassian, Romulan. I wonder what we might achieve—if we weren't always at odds."

"Oh *please*," muttered Garak. He had eaten only a little and then stopped. Raffi hoped she wasn't going to have a hunger strike on her hands.

"Don't forget the Prophets," said Toze. "They had a temple not far from here, before *he* destroyed it."

"Allegedly destroyed it," murmured Garak. "I'd ask you to remember that the charge has not yet been put before a court of law—"

"The Prophets walk with us, always," said Toze. "They are of Bajor. They have protected us, and they always will."

"Wormhole aliens," said Garak, with deliberate cruelty. "Not gods. Not prophets. They don't exist on some supernatural plane. They simply experience time differently. They can be explained without any of the superstitious nonsense that held your people back for so long. I have often thought how *lucky* it was for Bajor that we arrived. We are a sophisticated and rational people. You would have been nothing without us—"

"Toze, *no!*" cried Raffi, but he was already in motion. He reached Garak in a split second, punching him, hard, in the face. Garak gasped, and doubled over, blood spurting from his nose. But he gave Toze a look of savage triumph. He held up his cuffed hands.

"Assaulting a prisoner. Oh, you *did* learn so much from us, didn't you? You are indeed what we made you!"

Raffi had to physically restrain Toze. "Don't," she whispered in his ear. "Don't do it."

"In front of witnesses too," said Garak. "Let us make sure that this is mentioned in that court. Elnor—I shall *particularly* require your attendance."

Sokara, dragging Garak to his feet and pulling him away, said, "Can we gag him?"

"Tempting," said Raffi. She turned back to Toze, who was still shaking with rage. "Don't take the bait," she said. "Don't let him make you do something stupid. Not when you're this close to bringing him to justice."

Toze shook himself out of her grasp and strode off under the trees.

"Besides," said Raffi, lifting her voice to address each member of this woeful company, "when we finally decide we're done with this little up-country jaunt, we'll still be stuck behind this damn force field and only Garak knows the codes to lower it. We have to keep him alive."

"You could always torture the information out of me," Garak said in a helpful voice.

"If I were you," Raffi shot back, "I wouldn't make that offer in Toze's hearing."

"True," said Garak. "He's been such an *apt* pupil."

264 UNA McCORMACK

Raffi knelt down beside Sokara, who was wiping at Garak's face. "Let me see."

"I've got this," said Sokara.

"Let me *see*." Shame, perhaps, made her voice come out rougher than she intended. Sokara stood up and moved away. Raffi, conscious of Garak's sharp eyes monitoring this exchange, said, more steadily, "Could you check on Toze, please, Sokara? We shouldn't get too far away from each other."

Sokara nodded. "All right. Elnor, with me."

Elnor trotted obediently after him. Raffi turned her attention back to Garak. Sokara had cleared away some of the blood, but she carried on with the task, carefully dabbing at Garak's face until it was clean. "What a *mess* . . ."

"Those are the ridges," Garak replied. "Don't let Toze hear you say something like that. He might construe it as a racial slur. He strikes me as very touchy."

She ignored him. She was finding that this was the best way. Taking out her tricorder, she ran a quick check. "Not broken." Toze had actually held back. "Don't give him an excuse to finish the job."

"Of course, if he were a truly effective operative, I wouldn't be alive now."

Toze, Raffi thought, had shown remarkable restraint under considerable provocation. She leaned back on her heels. "Garak," she said, "do you want him to kill you?"

He shrugged. "It would be a shame, I suppose, having come this far."

"He'll do a lot more damage next time, you know."

Garak was staring straight at her. Those eyes, she thought. Like a cobra.

"Broken bones mend," he said. "The problem is everything else. Look at you, Commander."

"Oh," said Raffi, "this should be good."

"Well, there's something broken in you, isn't there? Something that can't be fixed. Even by the most potent blood poppies."

Raffi held his stare for a moment or two. Then she gave a low laugh. "You know, most of the time I'm about two seconds away from smashing up everything around me. Don't give me the excuse to get started." She got to her feet. "You need a hand standing up?"

"No," Garak said bitterly. He closed his eyes. "Whatever possessed me to come back to this appalling place?"

"I keep thinking the same thing, soldier," she said. She kept her voice light, but the truth was that Garak had struck a nerve. *Something broken.* Raffi knew that. Knew that something, somewhere, had gone terribly wrong with her life, and that the only common factor she could see was herself. Later, when Elnor and Sokara returned with Toze, she took the first chance she got to speak to Elnor.

"You keep away from him. Okay?"

She saw the first glimmer of a pout settle on the young man's face. *Damn, Elnor, not now.* "Raffi," he said, "why won't you *trust* me? I won't *tell* him anything—"

"That's not what I'm worried about, kiddo. Just stay away. He's toxic."

And I don't want you poisoned.

"This is turning into quite the diplomatic nightmare," said Picard. *"I have a number of angry Cardassians from the castellan's office regularly getting in touch to berate me."*

"Same here," said Rios. "The Romulans are kicking up a stink about Sokara's disappearance and Khrill is holding me personally to blame."

"The Bajorans have gone silent."

"Can't get a word from their inbound ships here either," said Rios. "I wonder if they know more than they're letting on."

"Our covert mission seems to be increasingly less covert by the moment."

"Nobody has mentioned Elim Garak to me," said Rios. "Not yet. But it's only a matter of time. The Romulans believe it's an Obsidian Order blackout over the Caanta valley. They're demanding full access to the area. Khrill thinks this is a move to secure entry to the area, and I'm inclined to agree."

"Have they issued any threats?"

"They're saying that unless they're allowed access to the valley, they'll bring more ships into the area to secure the safety of the refugees. That Khrill has failed to protect their liaison officer, and they'll have to do the job themselves."

"And the Cardassians are angry that Starfleet has apparently blundered into this situation. A diplomatic nightmare."

"Not sorry that's on your desk, Admiral," said Rios.

"Thank you, Cris."

"I know what I'm good at," Rios replied.

Throughout that morning, they pressed on through the forest, the beacon leading them more or less along the course of the stream and heading steadily upward. There was a steep section where Garak struggled, with his hands bound. Raffi found herself walking grimly beside him, hand ready to catch him if he fell. "Time to head back yet?" she said.

"On the contrary." His breathing was ragged, and his face looked very sore. "This is all quite bracing."

"Are you in pain?" she said quietly.

"No more than usual," he replied, and walked on.

At the top of this steep section, the trees thinned out briefly, and they found themselves looking out across a portion of the valley. Elnor pointed ahead to where thin wisps were rising up between the trees.

"Is that smoke?" he said. "Looks like wood fires . . ."

"I think it might be a settlement," said Raffi. "But who the hell can be here?"

"Cardassians?" said Sokara. His hand strayed down to the weapon at his side.

SECOND SELF   267

"Do we think that's likely?" said Raffi. "The ban on travel here was so strict that some of them wanted to stay and fight rather than come this way."

"Still," said Sokara, "Obsidian Order codes."

A good point, Raffi had to concede. Had someone come out here, years ago, before the Occupation ended? Were they about to discover some remnant of the Obsidian Order, still here all these years after their downfall? Had there been some secret project underway in the Caanta valley? There was one person here who would surely know. Raffi turned to Garak.

"All right," she said. "You've had your fun. Who are these people? What are they doing here?"

Garak gave a cold smile. "Oh," he said, "wouldn't you like to know everything that I know? Do you really think I would tell you?"

"How have you *lived* this long?" said Raffi.

"I've worked extremely hard," said Garak. "But if you want to know who's living in that valley, Commander, you should probably go and take a look."

Raffi turned back to Sokara. "Have some of your people come out here already?" she said. "Ignored the ban?"

"Not that I know," he said. "I can see the reasoning—"

"Why?" said Elnor.

"If there's a settlement here already," said Raffi, "then it's harder to relocate people."

"The Cardassian government has signed treaties that specifically ban the forced removal of populations resident in their territories," said Garak. "I should know—I negotiated the treaties when I was ambassador." He smiled at Sokara. "You should have just walked right in. The sight of Cardassian soldiers dragging civilians away from their homes really would be quite disastrous for any castellan. Although Romulans aren't very popular, are they?"

"Shut the fuck up," said Raffi.

"Really, Commander!" Garak tutted. "Such language is *most* unbecoming of a Starfleet officer! Whatever would Admiral Picard say—"

268   UNA McCORMACK

"For *fuck's* sake, Garak!" said Raffi. "Shut *up!*"

"Seconded," said Sokara.

"Thirded," said Toze.

Elnor didn't speak. When he realized everyone was looking at him, he said, "What? I'm not supposed to be saying anything either."

"Ah," said Garak. "A fellow traveler."

"Toze," Raffi said, cutting him off before anyone decided to start throwing a punch, "is there any chance that there are still Bajorans living here?"

"This long after the Occupation?" Toze shook his head. "I doubt it. It's thirty years since the Cardassian withdrawal. Why wouldn't they have come out?"

"Maybe because the force field has been in operation?" suggested Elnor. "I mean, we can't get past them."

"Could be," said Raffi, although she couldn't help thinking of those stories about soldiers who didn't believe their governments had surrendered and who held out for decades, still fighting their war. Were they about to come face-to-face with a group of militants from the Bajoran Resistance, continuing to fight the Cardassians? At least there was nobody with a Cardassian face among their group. Just a former Obsidian Order operative, disguised to look like one of them . . .

Yeah, thought Raffi, *this should go well.*

The approach to the settlement led them up a little way at first, and then the land dipped down, and they entered a small thicket. The path through this was clear, well trodden, and well maintained. As the trees began to thin, they found themselves looking down into a hollow, where about two dozen small houses stood. Raffi called a halt.

"All right," she said. "We need to approach this carefully."

"Raffi," called Elnor, from a meter away. "Come and look at this."

They joined up under the shade of a huge and ancient tree. Raffi saw a green mound. A grave. It was well kept, with plants thriving all around, and flowers too. Whoever was buried here was remembered and perhaps even loved. On a white Bajoran marker was carved:

SABA TAAN

2321–2357

FOR BAJOR

"Saba Taan," whispered Toze.

Raffi looked at Garak. "Can you shed any light on this?"

"No," said Garak.

"*No?*" said Toze, eyeing Garak with considerable distaste. "Saba Taan was the last vedek at the temple at Akantha. He was there when the Cardassians burned the town."

That, thought Raffi, was one *hell* of an alias to pick. Did Garak know? Surely it was no accident that he had chosen this name, this individual, as his cover story.

"What happened to him," she said. "To Saba Taan?"

"He disappeared," Toze said.

"Disappeared?" said Sokara. "You mean the Cardassians killed him with the rest?"

Toze shook his head. "There were a couple of survivors of the massacre at Akantha. They all say that Saba left the town before the killing began. They also say that he took the children with him."

Raffi was shivering, as if someone had walked over her grave. "Like the Pied Piper . . ." The others, she realized, were looking at her in confusion. "Forget it," she said. "It doesn't matter . . . What happened to those kids, Toze? Did they ever turn up?"

"It's one of the many unsolved mysteries of the Occupation," said Toze. "There are quite a lot of them. In general, one can assume that we've simply not found the graves yet. Bajoran Intelligence believed that the Cardassians

270   UNA McCORMACK

caught up with Vedek Saba not long after the massacre, and he and the children were killed then."

"No," said Garak firmly. "That didn't happen."

"Are you offering me an eyewitness account?" said Toze.

Garak replied, with some asperity, "I'm telling you what could be found in the Obsidian Order records. Someone should access them."

"I never read them," said Toze.

"No?" said Garak lightly. "A shame. So many page-turners—"

"Either shut up," said Raffi, "or tell us what you know about Saba Taan."

"The military here never found him," said Garak. "Neither did the Order—oh yes," he said, looking at Toze with a cruel smile dancing across his lips, "the Order was most certainly here at Akantha. Or so I read, in those records." He stared down at the grave. "Saba Taan must have been a very clever man, if the Order here never found him."

"And this was where he came," said Toze. He sounded confused and unhappy. "But why is this settlement hiding behind Obsidian Order codes? And look at the dates on the grave. They don't add up. Vedek Saba was an old man, by all accounts. Not in his *thirties* . . ."

Raffi, bending down, moved some of the flowers obscuring the lower half of the marker. "Look," she said. "Look at these."

Beneath the name, two symbols were carved into the marker, side by side. Both had been given equal weight by whoever had made this memorial. The one on the left-hand side was an elongated oval, bisected vertically with three straight lines, which were in turn joined at the bottom by a circle. There were other markings across the oval that Raffi could not decipher. She said, "This is Bajoran, isn't it?"

"Yes," said Toze, bending down beside her. "It's a religious symbol— very ancient. One of the most sacred emblems that there is." He frowned. "It's . . . not one I would expect to see at Akantha. Yes, there was a temple here, but there are many temples, and they don't typically use a sign as sacred as this . . ."

SECOND SELF   271

"Arcane knowledge," said Sokara.

"Not to a Bajoran," said Toze.

"A superstitious species," said Garak.

"Garak," said Raffi, pointing to the other symbol. "This one. It's Cardassian, isn't it?"

"Yes," said Garak.

"Go on," said Raffi. "Tell them what it is."

"I don't need to tell *him*." Garak nodded at Toze. "Do I?"

"No," said Toze. "You certainly don't. That's the symbol of the Obsidian Order. I'm not happy about this."

"Neither," said Garak, "am I."

"Come on," said Raffi, standing straight again. "It'll be getting dark soon. We should go and say hello. See if the people here can shed any light on this."

"But who will we find?" said Sokara. "Bajorans or Cardassians?"

"That," said Raffi, "is surely the billion-latinum question."

She looked ahead at the settlement, and then back at the gravestone. Both Toze and Garak were still leaning over it. Garak reached out with his bound hands, as if to touch it, and Toze pushed him away.

"Leave it," he said, his voice low and rough and angry. "Leave it alone."

"Come on," said Raffi. "It's long past time we got answers about the Caanta valley."

They left the green grave and walked down the path into the hollow. As they drew close to the first house, they saw a man sitting outside—a Bajoran. He jumped up at the sight of them and then turned and ran farther into the village.

"They're here!" he called out. "He's *back*!"

"That rules me out," said Raffi. "Any takers?"

They walked farther into the settlement. Word of their arrival was spreading around quickly. People were hurrying out of the homes—all, so far as Raffi could tell, were Bajoran.

"Toze?" she said. "Any answers?"

272   UNA McCORMACK

"I have absolutely no idea who these people are," he said.

By the time they reached the center of the village, as many as forty people had come out to greet them. There were a few children, but Raffi did not see anyone very old. A Bajoran woman was hurrying toward them, and she was perhaps the oldest person that Raffi had seen so far, perhaps in her late sixties or early seventies.

"Apra!" someone called to her. "Apra, he's *here*!"

"All right," said Raffi. "Toze, you're up front with me. Elnor, Sokara—stay back. We don't know how they'll react to Romulans. But I hope a Starfleet uniform won't be too threatening."

"Where would you like me, Commander?" said Garak.

"I won't give you my real answer to that," she said. "For now—stay behind me, and in front of Sokara. I want someone keeping an eye on you."

"You've got that," said Sokara.

The woman—Apra, presumably—came to a halt in front of Raffi and Toze. Raffi began, "My name is Lieutenant Commander—"

"Yes, yes, Raffi Musiker, I know. I'm Feji Apra. Where is he?"

"Excuse me?" said Raffi.

"Taan," she said, "where is Taan?"

"Before I tell you that, we need to make something clear," began Raffi, but Feji Apra, looking past her, caught sight of her man.

"Taan!" she cried, pushing past Raffi to get to Garak. "Oh, Taan!" she said. "We thought it would be very soon." She folded him into an embrace, like a daughter might with a father. "Oh, it is *so* good to see you again! Thank the Prophets, you're home!"

14

Cris Rios, in his next exchange with Shecol Khrill, decided to go slightly on the offensive. "Have to be honest, ma'am, I thought that your people might have got past this barrier by now. Or at least reestablished comms—"

Khrill was embarrassed. *"We can't. We can't get past the codes—"*

"They are Obsidian Order. Ancient—"

"Yes, but none that we know."

Rios couldn't resist the next jab. "Spoken to the Bajorans? They're good at this kind of thing."

"Not yet," said Khrill, and cut the comm.

Picard, who had been listening in on this exchange, said, *"It is possible, of course, that they might be Ambassador Garak's personal codes."*

"In which case," Rios replied, "we might have to tell the Cardassians our real interest in Ordeve. Find out whether they have any information."

"We must resist informing the Cardassians about this mission for as long as possible," insisted Picard. *"The diplomatic consequences would be appalling—"*

Further discussion was interrupted by an update from Tanwar. *"The Romulan scout ships are on the move, sir. And from the activity on the surface, I think the Cardassians are intending to engage them."*

"Well, she might have mentioned *that*," muttered Rios. "Gotta go, Admiral. Looks like we'll be trying to stop the Romulans and Cardassians from killing each other. Again."

274 UNA McCORMACK

There was something intensely gratifying, Raffi thought, about seeing Elim Garak so thoroughly lost for words. Gently, with considerable skill and delicacy, particularly taking into account his bound wrists, he extricated himself from Feji Apra's embrace.

"My dear lady . . ." Garak said. He was flicking anxious glances at Toze, who was in turn staring at Garak as if seeing him for the first time. Garak cleared his throat and collected himself. "My dear lady, I've never met you in my entire life. This face I am using . . . Please, don't be misled. I . . . find myself almost ashamed to say that I took it as cover—"

Feji was laughing. "Yes, yes, I know!" She took his arm. Garak stiffened, but then seemed to surrender himself to the inevitable. "Your poor face!" she said. "Oh well, if it's any consolation, I think that's the last time anyone hits you. Although some of the smaller children did tend to *bite*—"

One of the older men in the group laughed and called out, "Sorry, Taan!"

"Oh," said Garak. "Rest assured that biting children are within my range of experience."

Feji began to lead him away. "Come on. We'll go to the house first. That should help." She looked with kindness around the whole group. "All of you. Please come with me. We don't have much time, but everything will soon make sense."

Feji, still arm in arm with Garak, led them through the village. Toze hurried to walk alongside them; Elnor fell into step directly behind. But Raffi hung back—and so did Sokara.

"I have a very strange feeling about this," he said to her.

"Me too," she replied. But that was Ordeve, wasn't it? They had always known, all of them, that there was something strange about this place. Something uncanny.

There was not much more to the settlement than they had already seen. Fifteen or twenty buildings, each made from the same yellow stone that Raffi

SECOND SELF 275

knew from the old Bajoran town, and the wood of local trees. A small but sturdy replicator, of Cardassian design, stood under a wooden canopy, and seemed to be for general use. As they walked through, various people came out of their homes to greet Garak; they plainly knew the face he was wearing, and each of them named him with some variation on *Vedek,* or *Vedek Saba, dearest Taan.* One or two of the younger villagers, including several small children, stared at him, goggle-eyed, as if a legend had come to life.

At the far end of the village, they came to a small house. Garak stopped on the threshold. "You can go in," said Feji.

Garak held up his bound hands. "Circumstances prevent me from opening the door."

"Why don't I get rid of those?" said Feji.

"No," said Toze quickly.

"Besides," said Garak, "I don't want . . . I don't want to see what's in there—"

"Oh, of course you do!" said Feji. "Curiosity, you always said, was a great quality. Or a dangerous one, depending on your mood. Come inside, Taan. I'll be with you the whole time. I promised I would."

"Stop talking," said Garak, through clenched teeth, "as if we've met before."

"I'm not sure she can," said Raffi gently.

"She can *try*," said Garak.

"I'd rather she didn't call you *vedek* either," said Toze.

Feji smiled. "No, he never liked the title. That's why I always used it. Come inside."

She stepped into the house and beckoned to Garak. After a moment or two, he followed her inside. Toze went next, and Raffi came behind.

"Wait here," she said to Elnor and Sokara. "Just in case."

Raffi entered a very small house, no more than one room, really. The bed took up one end, a curtain drawn partway across. There was a small kitchen area, and the rest of the space was filled with a desk and chair. Garak sat

276 UNA McCORMACK

down on the chair, heavily, staring at the padds and papers stacked neatly on the desk. Feji turned on the lamp. The room became—Raffi had no other word for it—almost cozy.

"Welcome home, Taan," said Feji, with great warmth.

Garak put his head in his hands. Raffi could almost hear the *snick* of the cell door closing behind him. "Garak," she said softly. "Saba Taan was you, wasn't he? Or you were Saba Taan. I'm not sure which way around. But you're the same person, aren't you?"

Garak sat up and gave Raffi a brave smile. "It's beginning to look that way, isn't it?"

"Did you have any idea?" said Raffi.

"No . . ." he said.

"But?" she prompted him.

"Those codes that I used, to bring down the force field. To let us through, here."

"You said they were Obsidian Order codes," said Raffi. "Was that another lie?"

"Not a lie as such, for once," said Garak. "More a . . . simplification. They were my codes. Personal codes. Not even T—" Something seemed to catch in the back of his throat, and he swallowed, hard. "Not even Tain knew about them." He nodded at the papers on the desk. "That's a translation of *The Tempest* into Cardassian. *Shakespeare . . .*" he muttered, like a curse. "*That* seems to be a long treatise on the works of Eleta Preloc. As for *that* . . ." He pushed some papers to cover one particular document. Raffi caught a glimpse just in time: an envelope, written in Federation Standard, addressed to *Professor Julian Subatoi Bashir*. Who knew what that might contain? "It's my handwriting," said Garak. "Or a forgery so competent that I must admire the skill."

"I know," said Feji, "that this is a great deal to take in all at once."

"On the contrary," said Garak breezily. "My past self frequently lays traps for me. At least this time it isn't a bomb."

SECOND SELF   277

Feji began to laugh. "I always liked that story," she said.

Garak smiled at her. "I do too. Perhaps I'll tell you it one day."

"I'm sure you will," she said. "I know that you have."

Toze turned to Feji. "I don't understand all this. What exactly is going on here?"

Garak, slyly, said, "Haven't you worked it out yet? Keep up, *Koma Tath*, or we'll soon be leaving you behind."

"Don't make me regret not killing you, Garak," said Toze.

"Nobody will kill anyone here," said Feji firmly. "Not here. Nor after so many years." She looked at Toze with compassion. "Listen to what your heart is saying, brother. Let the Prophets speak to you!"

"Ah yes," said Garak. "The Prophets. I have to say that I never suspected them of having a sense of humor."

"They're very close now," said Feji, to Toze. "Let them speak. *Listen*."

At that moment, Elnor poked his head around the door. "Raffi," he said. "There's something weird happening out here."

"Something bad?" said Raffi.

"No," said Elnor, "just—"

"I know," said Raffi. "Weird. Can you expand on that?"

"All the people are gathering outside—"

"We should go back," said Feji. "They must be ready for you now." She turned to Garak and laid her hand gently upon his cheek. "It's nearly time."

Garak took a deep breath, nodded, and got up from the chair. He stood and took a long look around the little room. Raffi, watching, saw his eyes narrow, as if wheels had been set in motion in his mind, as if he was, already, at work on some calculations. Some scheme or other, she guessed. Was he looking for a way out of this? Or was something else happening? Garak reached out to brush his hands against the letter on the desk, as if it were some kind of anchor, and then he nodded at Feji.

"I'm ready," he said.

278   UNA McCORMACK

They went out together. Raffi and Toze followed. The whole village had congregated in the meantime. They were standing around a wooden cabinet, about the size of a home replicator, square, but tapering toward the top. There was a polished oval stone set in the front of the box: black as obsidian, but marbled white. Feji led Garak over to the box. He stood staring at the stone. He looked, Raffi thought, like a man awaiting execution.

Sokara came to stand next to her. Very quietly, he said, "What's going on, Raffi?"

Feji, hearing him, said, "If you'll listen now, please, I can give you all the answers that you want." She raised her voice, to address the whole gathering. As she spoke, many of the people, in particular the older ones, nodded along to her words, as if this was a story they told over and over.

"A long time ago, the Cardassians came to Bajor," said Feji Apra. "I don't need to tell you why. Cardassia Prime was poor, hungry, and that turned to greed and arrogance. They saw Bajor—which was rich and peaceful—and they wanted what our people had. The land, the resources, yes—but I think that the Cardassians wanted more. Something they could not take by force. They wanted to be the people that walked with the Prophets. But they were not."

Feji put her hand upon the wooden box.

"After occupying Bajor, the Cardassians moved on to her colony worlds. And so, at last, they came here to Ordeve. They did what they had done everywhere else. Took the land and drove the Bajorans away. If hunger and poverty were not enough to make the Bajorans leave, then the Cardassians used force. But there was something else here on Ordeve. Something that the Cardassians never knew about. Something they never discovered."

She turned to address Garak directly.

"You were—you will be, in time—our vedek. But you never talked about the Prophets, Saba Taan. You only ever talked about history. How each one of us must choose how to act in history. How history can, at times, seem like a never-ending cycle of violence and hate. How it falls upon us all to decide whether to participate in the continuance of that cycle, or to try to prevent it happening over and over again."

Her voice was gaining in strength.

"This," said Feji, "is the Orb of Restitution. It was brought to Ordeve centuries ago, when the monks built their temple at Akantha. Before that temple was burned—on *your* orders, Elim Garak—" (*J'accuse,* thought Raffi) "the Orb was brought here to the Caanta valley, by Vedek Saba Taan, and has remained here ever since, in the care of the children of the town, who came with him."

(Elnor, standing next to Raffi, whispered, "What's an Orb?" and Raffi whispered back, "*Not now, Elnor.*")

Feji was still speaking. "Auma's Seventh Prophecy says that the Orb of Restitution will bring peace, justice, and reconciliation after long strife."

(Elnor whispered, "I'm still not clear—" and Raffi tried her best to give a quick explanation: the Orbs were gifts of the Prophets to the people of Bajor, through which the Prophets could speak to them, sometimes even showing them the future, if they could understand the Orb vision. As she spoke, Raffi found herself thinking about the dreams that they had all had. Were these Orb experiences? Of a small and limited kind, but presentiments of the future, nonetheless? Those three figures, whom she had not known, all those years ago, were perfectly clear to her now.)

Feji turned to Garak. "Do you understand the course of history yet, Elim Garak? Do you understand your part in it?" She smiled at him. "You used to say—"

Raffi quickly intervened. "You shouldn't give him information about his future, surely?"

Garak said, "At this point, I'll take all the guidance I can. Carry on, Feji, please."

"You used to say, 'I hope by the time I get here I've learned my lesson.' What do you think, Elim Garak? Has the lesson been learned?"

"I don't know," he said, and lifted his bound hands. "Shall we find out?"

280 UNA McCORMACK

Toze moved quickly forward. "No," he said, pulling out a phaser. "No way am I going to let you put your murdering hands on an Orb of the Prophets. I'll kill you first!"

Raffi moved to intervene; Sokara, too, she saw, was ready to act. But the people of the settlement were prepared. Moving as one, they put themselves between Toze and Garak.

"Now that in particular," said Garak, "I really must remember to mention."

"Do be quiet for a moment," said Feji, with a sigh that presumably came from long experience. "Let me do the talking."

"Oh," breathed Garak, "be my guest."

Feji nodded at Toze's phaser. "Would you really shoot us? Your own people? Is that the answer here? The Orb is a gift from the Prophets! A gift from our past to our future! The sign of peace, at last, between Cardassia and Bajor. What else have you worked for, *Koma Tath*, if not for Bajor?"

"Very nicely put," murmured Garak. "Couldn't have said it better myself." His eyes were bright and sharp, darting about, watching Toze for any movement. But Toze seemed almost frozen on the spot, his hand still on the weapon.

"I don't understand," he said to Feji. "He destroyed your home. Your people—"

"Yes," said Feji, "he did."

"I've spent years tracking down the evidence," said Toze. "Half my life. Trying to bring him to justice for what he did here."

And now, when the moment came, something else was being asked of him. "Toze," said Raffi. "Don't make a terrible mistake. Don't you see what's happening here?"

"I know that he's the one who ordered the temple burned!" said Toze.

"He's right, you know," Garak said to Feji. "I was here. Undercover. I ordered the soldiers at the garrison to round up the Bajorans. I ordered them to start shooting. And I ordered them to burn down the town, starting with the temple."

"I know," she said.

"I'm very afraid, Feji," Garak said, "that given my life over again, I'd still do the same thing. I mention this, so that you are clear about the kind of man you're dealing with."

"Oh, I'm sure you would do the same again," said Feji. "Or rather, that young man would. But what about now, Elim Garak? What has that young man become?" Reaching to the wooden box, she released the clasp. A little white light emerged from the crack.

"A history of bloodshed," she said. "A chance to set things right. A chance for restitution. What will you choose, Obsidian Order? What will you choose, *Koma Tath*?"

Garak turned to Toze. He seemed, Raffi thought, to have come to a decision. "What do you say, *Koma Tath*? Do you want to make peace with the Order?"

Raffi held her breath. His tone was almost taunting. Sometimes it seemed as if Garak said what was most likely to bring down violence upon him. Had he said the wrong thing here, and now?

"I can't promise to save your temple," said Garak. "Quite the contrary. But I'll take good care of your Orb." He looked at the people gathered around and laughed. "I'll even take good care of the children."

Feji, beside him, laughed too, like that child that she once was and would—for Garak—still be. "Oh, he does!" she said. "You do!"

And that, for some reason, worked. Toze lowered, and put away, the weapon. "I hope this isn't a mistake," he said as he unlocked the restraints around Garak's wrists.

"So do I," said Garak. "But I think I prefer this prison to the other one on offer." Rubbing his wrists, he moved to stand in front of the Orb. "What happens now?"

282   UNA McCORMACK

"Wait! Nobody move!"

Raffi turned to see Sokara moving forward, a raised disruptor in his hand.

"Sokara," she said, "what are you doing?"

"This is all very touching," he said, "but I don't care about Bajor, or Cardassia, or whatever wretched history lies between you."

"What do you care about?" said Feji. She seemed to Raffi's eyes unperturbed at the interruption.

"I care about the Romulan people," said Sokara. He sounded almost close to tears. "About the people down there, beyond the river. Dispossessed and despised. Told they should be grateful by people who won't let them see their children, their spouses, their kin."

"Then we care about the same things," said Feji. "What you describe is understood by every Bajoran!"

"No!" he said. "All through the Occupation, you knew—you could hold out hope!—that one day your world would be yours again! That one day you could go *home*!" His voice caught in his throat. "That can't happen for us!"

"Sokara, please," said Raffi. "I understand how hard this is."

"How can anyone in the Federation understand this? Not you, Lieutenant! You have a home—had a family. You threw everything away. I would do anything to get my home back—and if this thing, whatever it is, can help me do that, then I'm going to use it. If I can go back, somehow, set things straight again—"

"You cannot use the Orb without the consent of the Prophets," said Feji.

"Then make them give their consent!"

"They're not mine to order!" said Feji.

"Then I'll take it. I'll use it somehow. As leverage—"

"It won't work, Sokara," said Raffi. "It'll backfire."

"I don't care what you say, Lieutenant!"

"We were friends once," she said.

"I'm Tal Shiar," he said. "You should always remember that."

"If I might say something," said Garak, sliding into the conversation. "I do rather feel as if my thunder is being somewhat stolen." He did not seem perturbed either, Raffi thought. Perhaps he was taking his cue from Feji.

"Don't worry," Feji said to Garak. "You'll get your moment to shine." Yes, thought Raffi, she was definitely not concerned about this. Something, someone, was going to intervene. *Hell,* thought Raffi, *it's not meant to be, is it?*

Sokara leveled his weapon at Feji. "You'll give me the Orb," he said.

"No," said Feji, shaking her head. "I won't."

Sokara took a step forward—and then, suddenly, came crashing to his knees, and then to the ground. Elnor was standing there, his staff in his hands. "I am sorry to have to interrupt," he said. "But I do not like Tal Shiar."

"Who does?" said Garak. "Again, Elnor, I'm impressed. And, more remarkably, I do find myself extremely very grateful."

"I would say that you're welcome," said Elnor. "But it would be a lie. Raffi," he said, almost plaintively. "I hope you don't regret bringing me along now."

"Of course not, Elnor," she said, and felt a deep rush of affection for this young man, so at odds with the world around him, so in need of someone to guide him on his way.

"Anything else you'd like to mention?" said Garak to Feji. "Any more Tal Shiar interventions on the way?"

"I don't know," she said. "That was everything you were able to tell me. But is there anything else you'd like to ask? Before you go?"

"Yes!" he said. "Where will I land? I mean, how long do I have to . . . to mount this operation?"

"A little under five months," she said.

"Five months," he said. "Practically a lifetime . . ."

Feji started to open the door of the box.

"Wait," said Garak. Now he sounded very scared. An old man, facing an uncertain future.

284   UNA McCORMACK

"Don't be afraid," said Feji.

"But I am," he said. "I am most terribly afraid."

"Tell me why," said Feji. "You can tell me anything."

"I'm afraid . . ." Garak's voice dropped to a whisper. "I'm afraid of dying alone."

"Oh, Taan," she said, her face lighting up. "Elim! You won't. I promise! And when the time comes, I'll hear *shri'tal*. Like it should be. Like family."

That word seemed to unlock something in him. Garak began to laugh. "You've heard *shri'tal* already, I think," he said. "Did I tell you *all* my secrets?"

She gave him a wicked smile. "Only you can say for sure. Reach out now, and you'll know, soon enough."

And she released the light of the Orb.

Raffi, when called upon to write about what happened next in her report, would wonder at times whether she had reached the limits of language. She remembered a bright light—of course there was a bright light—shooting out from the box. She recalled that the light seemed to surround her, and then, briefly, she saw the three figures from her dream—Gabe and Seven and Elnor—and they were no longer afraid, or telling her to go back, but instead they came to meet her. She knew, of course, that these figures were not these people, but manifestations of the Prophets, coming to her as the people who were, perhaps, most in her thoughts, but she could say now why the Prophets chose to communicate in this way.

"The cycle is broken," said Prophet-Gabe.

"Restitution has been made," said Prophet-Seven.

"Wake up from history," said Prophet-Elnor.

The vision receded, and Raffi was back in the little village. Light was still pouring from the Orb of Restitution. She saw a figure reach out for this. There was a blinding flash and, when they could all see again, Elim Garak was gone—for good.

Feji Apra closed the box. The Orb was hidden again. She knelt down beside Sokara. He was still unconscious. "I'm sorry," she said, resting her hand upon his face. "This was not your history. This is not your peace. Not yet. But perhaps this valley can be yours now. It is a good place. A blessed place. A place of peace."

There was a crackle of static, and then a voice came through Raffi's combadge.

"Raffi? Raffi!"

Raffi tapped her badge. "Cris? Cris, can you hear us?"

"What the hell is going on?"

"I guess . . ." Raffi looked around. "I guess we've just seen history made."

"Well, that sounds great," said Cris. *"But there's more history heading your way. In the form of about a dozen Tal Shiar."*

"Captain," said Tanwar. "The Cardassians are moving to intercept the Romulan scout ships . . . Wait, what's happening . . . Sir, the barriers are down!"

"What?" Rios went over to her station. She was right. The force fields had been lifted—but the beacon was still in operation, calling everyone in the area to come to the Caanta valley.

"We've detected transporter signals from the Romulan ships," said Tanwar. "Looks like . . . ten people have transported directly into the Caanta valley."

"Get that away team moving. And get me Commander Musiker—right away." With the channel open, Rios said, "Raffi? Raffi!"

"Cris? Cris, can you hear us?"

"Raffi, what the hell is going on?"

"I guess . . . I guess we've just seen history made."

"Well, that sounds great," said Rios. "But there's more history heading your way. In the form of about a dozen Tal Shiar."

Raffi's next was muffled, but sounded very much like *"Fuck . . ."*

"We've got an away team heading your way. And . . ." He read the padd that Tanwar was waving in front of him, "the exarch informs us she's moving air support toward you as quickly as she can. Can you hold out?"

286   UNA McCORMACK

"Cris," said Raffi, *"there's me, Elnor, and a Bajoran operative—"*

"A what?"

"Koma Tath."

"Have you got Garak?"

"That's complicated. Look, Cris, get those people to me as quick as you can. These people are defenseless."

The next thing Rios heard was weapons fire.

A blur of activity followed. Raffi remembered the urgency of each moment, the haste with which the Bajorans were hurried to safety, the second when the first shots were fired from the cover of the forest—and then the buzz of transporters, as her own colleagues arrived. Later, reflecting on what had happened, she would understand how from the very second that Garak left them, they were no longer being led down a fixed path. History was settled, but the future was completely up for grabs, coming into being with each choice, each action, made—here and now. She thought, *Why does it always have to be a battlefield? Why can't there be peace?*

And then, a dozen people were transporting into the area. *Oh hell,* she thought, *more Tal Shiar?* No, these were Bajoran. "Toze," Raffi said, "are they with you?"

"Of course," he said. "I don't go anywhere without support, particularly not in pursuit of Elim Garak." Toze ordered the *Koma Tath* to move out into the forest. Elnor, Raffi saw, was close behind.

Shots were fired in the distance, under the trees. Raffi saw Sokara, coming back to consciousness, as a *Koma Tath* moved to cover him. The air was disturbed by the violent throb of half a dozen Cardassian military flyers arriving.

Toze, kneeling down beside Sokara, said, "This is done now. Your people can stand down, or else we'll finish them. They were trained by the Resistance, Sokara. People who ended the Occupation. You won't get past them."

SECOND SELF 287

Sokara, listening to the distant weapons fire, nodded slowly. He took out his comm. "This is Commander Nuvu Sokara," he said, "ordering all Romulans in the area to stand down. Put down your weapons and surrender to . . . to the Bajorans."

No, thought Raffi, he would not want to surrender to Starfleet—nor to the Cardassians. After fifteen minutes, the surviving Romulans, Sokara among them, were being held in the center of the settlement under the guard of the *Koma Tath* and a watchful young Qowat Milat. A few minutes later, eight Cardassian soldiers, under the command of an achingly young officer, entered the settlement. They stood staring at the Bajorans and the Bajorans stared back. The air crackled with the violence of the past and the uncertainty of the future.

The Cardassian officer, turning to Raffi, asked, "What am I supposed to *do* here?"

"I think," said Raffi, "to start with, you should put those weapons away. You're on Bajoran soil."

The Cardassians stood down. There was some back and forth between the *Stargazer* away team and Merna. Then the exarch of Ordeve was transported into the village. Feji Apra was waiting to greet her.

"Exarch Khrill," said Feji, "welcome to the Caanta valley."

The exarch lifted her palm in greeting. "Thank you for your welcome, and for your permission to come here. I would like to acknowledge that the Caanta valley was never occupied. It has been, and will remain, Bajoran territory."

Feji smiled. She spoke quietly to some of her people, and then the box containing the Orb was brought out once again. The *Koma Tath* kneeled before it, and, after a moment's uncertainty, so did Khrill. As they knelt, a great feeling of peace stole over Raffi, and, it seemed to her, over the whole valley. Like a curse had been lifted. She wondered what JL would say to that.

When the *Koma Tath* stood, the exarch followed suit. She turned to Feji. "What assistance do you need here?"

288   UNA McCORMACK

"We would like to take the Orb home," said Feji, "to Bajor."

"Whatever you need," said Khrill. "And, with your permission, we will take the Romulans into custody." She turned to the Cardassian officer, but Feji had one more request.

"Take them, yes," said Feji, "with one proviso. We would like this valley to be made available to the Romulans who have asked to settle here. We ask that the holy sites here be protected, and that Bajorans can visit them, and we also ask that the grave of Saba Taan is maintained. And . . ." She looked at the small group of Romulans sitting nearby. "I would like Nuvu Sokara to be entrusted with this."

Khrill sighed. After a moment, she said, "I agree, of course." She turned to the Cardassian officer and began issuing quiet orders. Feji instructed that the Orb be taken back indoors, and then went over to Raffi and Toze.

"Please," she said, "will you both come with me?"

She led them inside Saba's house, where she went over to the desk and began to move the papers. "These all have their places," she said. "But there are a couple that I should pass along to you now." She took out two data rods. One she offered to Raffi, the other to Toze. "These are for you."

Toze stared down at the rod. "I . . . What more does he have to say?"

"I don't know what he put on them," said Feji. "He liked to have the last word, but perhaps some of your remaining questions will be answered."

"What are you going to say about what happened here, Toze?" said Raffi.

"I'll . . . say that he died," said Toze. "That he was killed preventing the Orb of Restitution from falling into the hands of the Tal Shiar."

"There's no body," said Raffi.

"There's a grave," said Toze. "And who will doubt my word? It was my life's work, bringing him to justice."

Feji said, "Do you think you succeeded?"

"I . . ." Toze put the crystal in his pocket. "I think this mission has been a success."

Raffi folded her hand around her rod. "Will you go back to Bajor?" she said to Feji. "You've been here, in Caanta, all your life."

"For a while," said Feji. "But I love this place. I'll miss it. And it remains a little part of Bajor. I think I'll be coming back. See it settled, again."

A little way outside the valley, Raffi said her final goodbye. "I'm sorry," she said to Sokara, "that I didn't tell you about the real mission."

"I'm sorry that I didn't tell you that the Tal Shiar were following our every move," he said.

"Yeah, well, let's call it quits, eh? Peace and reconciliation."

"I would like that, Raffi," he said.

They walked together back down into the valley. On the nearby grave, the flowers had been moved, and, beneath the two symbols, an addition had been made.

ELIM GARAK

2321–2399

FOR CARDASSIA

15

The *Stargazer* was en route to Starbase 211, where a civilian transporter would take Raffi and Elnor back to Earth. Raffi had supper with Rios, drank a little too much pisco, and went to bed, where she tossed and turned. After the mission came the letdown. Always. The dangerous moment, when Raffi might reach for chemical assistance to stop her spiraling downward. Not that it ever worked. Her thoughts became dark and dangerous, and around and around in her head went the words that Garak had said to her; words she was afraid would turn out to not be lies.

There's something broken in you, isn't there? Something that can't be fixed . . .

She should know better than to let him get under her skin. That was what he had wanted. She was sure he wouldn't want it now.

She got up and dressed, left her cabin, and wandered the decks. The ship was on its night cycle. The few members of the crew around were busy with their duties. At a quiet observation port, she found Elnor, staring out into space.

"Hey," she said, "you can't sleep either?"

"Not yet," he said. "I keep *thinking . . .*"

"Terrible idea," she said. "Particularly at bedtime. What about?"

"About the mission. About whether or not we succeeded."

"We went out there to find a solution to the refugee crisis," she said. "We did that."

"That's not the mission I was thinking about, Raffi," he said.

292 UNA McCORMACK

"We were sent to bring Elim Garak to justice," she said.

"We failed."

Raffi looked out at the speeding stars. What was that story, that old one? About an ancient spaceship pilot taking emergency medical supplies who finds a stowaway on board. There isn't enough fuel to bring him and her and the medicine to where it's needed. The stowaway agrees to jettison herself. Raffi hated that story. Hated the phoniness, the way the story was constructed to serve up its moral. Hated how the whole damn thing was set up to force the outcome. Life didn't work that way. People anticipated problems; worked things out; found solutions. Sometimes things worked out and sometimes they didn't. But you tried. You didn't just walk out of an airlock.

"I know how you like to deal in certainties," she said. "I know that you've been taught to see everything in black and white. True and false. Sometimes life is more complicated than that."

"I struggle," he said, "with these complications."

"We did good."

"But he got away!"

"I don't think so," she said.

"He will never be tried for what he did at Akantha. People were murdered—"

"No," she said. "He won't be tried. Instead, he'll watch himself make that mistake—and he knows that it was a mistake. He won't be able to stop himself, his younger self, and he'll live with the consequences. There aren't tidy solutions. Perhaps what you need to do is learn to live with complexities."

"I try," he said. "I really try."

"I know, honey," she said. She tried to think of something that might help, and, on a hunch, she said, "Elnor, what did the Orb show you? When you looked into it?"

He didn't answer right away. He was looking out again at the rush of stars, but now his expression was almost beatific.

"The galaxy," he whispered. "I saw the galaxy."

SECOND SELF   293

Raffi's spine tingled as she felt an echo of the profound joy she could see upon his face. *You're going to be okay, kiddo,* she thought. *You're going to be okay.*

A quiet, still autumn had settled on La Barre. The grapes had been harvested. The trees were in that halfway stage, the green of summer now overlaid with yellow, the leaves like gold coins. One more stormy night, and they would fall. JL's house seemed melancholy, as if saddened by the history that it contained.

Raffi had come to make her report to the admiral. "I wanted to give you my own, direct account of what happened," Raffi said. "What didn't make it into the official record."

JL, pouring the wine, halted to look at her. "There are discrepancies?"

"Yes," she said.

"I absolutely trust your judgment," he told her. "You have no need to justify your decisions to me."

"It's good to hear you say that, JL," she said. "I appreciate that."

"We can close the book on this, if you want," he said. "You don't have to tell me the whole story."

"I think I'd like someone to know," she said. "I think I'd like to know what you make of what happened." *Because for all your blind spots—you're still so very wise, JL.*

He sat, holding his glass. "Go on."

"Elim Garak didn't die on Ordeve," she said.

"That . . ." he said at last, "is a fairly significant discrepancy. Do I need to alert the authorities?"

"No," she said. "Let me be scrupulously accurate. He *did* die on Ordeve, but not when I said in my report. He was . . . He was already dead."

"Rather an important detail to omit from your report. What am I missing? Ah!" He nodded. "Does this have to do with the Orb?"

294   UNA McCORMACK

"You've got it," she said. "Elnor and I did find Elim Garak in the Caanta valley, disguised as a Bajoran vedek. His Orb encounter sent him back into the past to become Vedek Saba Taan. With his knowledge of the future, he was able to rescue the Orb of Restitution and the Bajoran children from his younger self."

JL sat back in his chair. Raffi didn't often get the chance to surprise him. She found that she was rather enjoying the experience.

"Well," said JL, eventually, "that is indeed a considerably different end to his story. The Bajorans have no idea?"

"Toze Falus knows."

"The *Koma Tath* agent?"

"Yes. He was the one who let Garak go." Raffi held up her hands. "I mean, it had to be his decision, didn't it? The rest of us—we shouldn't decide. Garak reached out, and touched the Orb . . ." She shook her head. "He was gone."

"Extraordinary . . ." murmured JL.

"I keep thinking," said Raffi, "about what his life must have been like, going back to Akantha. Watching his younger self arrive. I think he was very young—the first time. Twenty, at the very most?"

"Keen to establish himself. Not ready to admit he could be wrong," said JL. He smiled. "I've been a young man."

"Imagine seeing yourself about to make such a terrible mistake. Having to let it happen."

"Yes," said JL, "and more than that."

"What do you mean?"

"From what I have read," said JL, "my understanding is that Ambassador Garak was, above all, a patriot."

"For Cardassia," Raffi said, remembering the gravestone. "Yes, I think that everything he did was for Cardassia."

"Then think about this last century, Raffi. Think about what happened to Cardassia. Its history in that time has been one of terrible strife. The

SECOND SELF 295

most awful devastation. The Occupation, the Dominion War, the Fire. Millions upon millions of Cardassians died at the hands of the Jem'Hadar. Cities reduced to ashes. Art, architecture, music, literature—all lost. He lived through that history—played a not insignificant part in it. He knew that the Occupation would lead, in time, to the near destruction of Cardassia. Yet he committed to living through that Occupation—as a Bajoran, no less! He did not give his younger self the foreknowledge of these events. He did not attempt to change that history, in order to ensure a different outcome."

Raffi thought of that small house, the desk with the books and notes and letters. A little settlement, quiet and safe. What he must have done, in the time before his own arrival, using his Obsidian Order knowledge and training to turn the Caanta valley into a sanctuary. Moving to protect both the Orb and the children of the town from the violence of his younger self. Making the settlement in the valley viable. Protecting those children; caring for them. Feji Apra *loved* him. Raffi thought of him dying there, among Bajorans, giving *shri'tal* to people unlike him, trusting them to make sure that when the time came, he would make the right choices. Hoping that with the help of the Prophets—the gods of an alien and enemy people—he would get the chance to make amends. To set things right.

"It strikes me as quite the sacrifice," said JL. "But how else are these cycles of history broken? The Orb of Restitution. How apt." He fell silent. "I wonder," he said meditatively, "whether, given the choice, I would do the same."

The history that Jean-Luc Picard had lived through had been no less hard in its own way, Raffi thought. The supernova, the relief mission, the synth attack. His resignation had been a terrible loss for him; the years that followed barren and unhappy.

"I wonder," he said, again.

Raffi thought about her own part in this history. She was sure now, as sure as she could be, that the power surge that saved their lives all those years ago had been down to Garak. On his instructions—or maybe the direct intervention of the Prophets. The gods of the Bajorans—the wormhole aliens,

296 UNA McCORMACK

she told herself—smiling down on her. Someone looking out for her. That felt . . . Raffi didn't quite have the words for this feeling. It felt good. It felt nice. Somebody cared for her.

"Toze made the real sacrifice," she said. "All those years, pursuing Garak—almost his whole career. Finding bits and pieces of evidence. Tracking him down. And he put all that aside, trusting in the Prophets." She shook her head. "What must it be like, to be Bajoran? To know that there are beings of great power—godlike power—directly involving themselves in your lives, your history?"

"An interesting experience," he said dryly. "Remind me to tell you more about the Q, one day. Preliminary signs are that Toze's decision is paying off. The kai is beside herself with joy that an Orb has been returned. Castellan Kalis has been invited to visit Bajor to see its installation. The first visit of a Cardassian leader to Bajor since the end of the Occupation." He smiled. "I imagine you'll be invited. The honored guest of both the Cardassians and the Bajorans. Very few people have managed to achieve that, Raffi."

"Hey," she said, "I'll take the love where I can find it."

"I'll drink to that," he said, and they did. Refilling their glasses, he went on, "I know that when you took on this mission, Raffi, you were concerned that it might prove damaging for you. Going back to Ordeve. Revisiting that chapter in your history. This hasn't been the case, I hope?" He sounded anxious. "It seems to have been the opposite?"

"I'm glad I went," she said. "It wasn't easy, going back there. Stirred up more than I expected. Made me confront . . . mistakes I've made that I'm still living with. But I did the right thing back then. It didn't win me many friends at Command, at the time, but it was the right thing. It's good to be vindicated." She considered that. "It's good to be vindicated, *again*."

In the late afternoon, Picard and Laris took the dog out for a walk. The countryside was gray, hazy under thin drizzle. The trees still wore their

SECOND SELF 297

October colors, but the leaves were drooping and sad. They would soon be gone, and winter underway. They walked with space between them, the dog running to and fro, and Picard told Laris everything that happened on Ordeve.

"I'd rather he was dead," said Laris, when he was finished. "Sent into the past? Sounds like he got away with it, yet again."

"The *Koma Tath* agent seems to be content," noted Picard. "According to Raffi, he was the one that made the decision."

"Bajorans," said Laris scornfully, "that religion makes them weak. Softhearted."

"That's the kind of thing that I would expect to hear from a Cardassian," said Picard. "Not from you."

"I hate to disillusion you this late in the day, but I'm not a very good person."

"Demonstrably untrue," he said. "But he's gone now, into the past, where he can't do any more harm."

"He did enough of that over the years," she said.

Number One, who had been snuffling some way ahead, came running back, shoving his nose into his master's hand. "I mean," said Picard, "who counts as *very* good, really, when it comes down to it?"

"Oh, I don't know," she said. "How about someone who gives sanctuary to two Tal Shiar runaways? Someone who takes it upon himself to try to save an entire sentient species? Someone who resigns on a point of principle from the career that means more to him than anything? I'm just throwing these suggestions out there."

"Laris," said Picard, shaking his head, "I make mistakes, all the time. Sometimes I see people as instruments of a higher purpose. I forget who they are in themselves. I am stubborn and intransigent and often do not see what is directly in front of me . . ."

The light was fading. The leaves waited for the first storm of winter. "Daft old thing," she said fondly, putting her arm through his.

298 UNA McCORMACK

"Is this sufficient closure for you?" he said. "Will this do?"

"It'll do," she said. "Thank you, Jean-Luc. Thank you for doing this for me. For us."

For Zhaban.

"You're welcome," said Picard. "Shall we head for home?"

That night, Raffi lay on the comfortable bed in the quiet guest room, pillows piled around her, listening to the gentle rustle of the wind around the house. Number One lay curled at her side. She was looking down at a padd, pondering the conversation with JL. After a while, she said, "Play Saba Taan's message."

And there he was on-screen, Saba Taan, or Elim Garak. Still Bajoran; wearing the long earring and a vedek's robes. Inhabiting the part completely.

"Lieutenant Commander Musiker," he said. The dog, looking up at the sound of the voice, gave a quick sharp bark. *"My greetings and regards from Ordeve under the Occupation."*

The message to her from Garak had been on the data rod that Feji Apra had given her. It was oddly gratifying to think that, even among everything else that must have been happening to him, Garak had found time for this. Or perhaps, as Feji had said, he made sure he got the last word. She had watched this message several times now, trying to work out what was best to do about its contents. Even now, she had not quite come to her final decision.

"It struck me, on my arrival here in the past, that you had never seen the temple at Akantha before it met its, ah, unfortunate *end."*

When you burned it down, Raffi thought.

"And I thought that perhaps you might like to see it in all its glory, before it is no longer here. Do pass on whatever information you think is appropriate to Professor Deechi Lan at the University of Tamulna. I believe he is very well respected, whatever our mutual acquaintance Toze Falus had to say. If the

SECOND SELF 299

slandering of innocent scholars were the worst crime committed by undercover operatives, perhaps the universe would be a happier place. But I digress. Here, Commander, is the temple of Akantha, in its glory days."

Slowly, Garak walked her around the temple, pointing out features as he went. The warm glow of the candles on the yellow stone. The paintings on the walls. The prayer chambers. And, at the far end, a tall wooden cabinet.

"*I cannot show you the Orb,*" said Garak. "*Its removal to the Caanta valley was the first task that I undertook on my arrival here. The local population are very trusting of their elderly vedek and are quite content to believe that I am under instruction from the Prophets. Perhaps I am. The people here know that something bad is coming to Akantha. They are doing everything possible to help me save as much as I can.*"

In the background, there came the sound of young voices, shouting, quarreling, laughing, shrieking. Number One's ears pricked up.

"*And then there are the children . . .*" Garak, looking back over his shoulder, frowned. "*One moment, please, Commander . . .*"

This was Raffi's favorite part of the message. Watching Elim Garak, former Obsidian Order agent, now responsible for the care of a quiet rural temple, deal with an incursion into his territory from some local rascals. "*Feji Ressith!*" Raffi heard Vedek Saba bellow across his domain. "*Put down that candle immediately!*"

A heated exchange followed, which Raffi could not quite catch, and the intruders were out of the door in a matter of moments, whereupon Garak was able to return to his message. It was not simply, she thought, that this whole interruption was so amusing, providing a glimpse of his life in the Caanta valley. It was how thoroughly embedded Garak had become in this small community. How thoroughly his life was now enmeshed in theirs. Feji Ressith. Was that a relative of Apra's? A spouse-to-be? She should ask, perhaps . . .

"*Forgive the intrusion,*" said Garak. "*Bajoran children are remarkably ill-bred. They lack the discipline of a proper Cardassian education.*" He sniffed. "*I*

300   UNA McCORMACK

imagine this explains how adaptable their resistance movement is, and why it will so thoroughly trounce our too-regimented military in the forthcoming decades. But I should say a word about these children, perhaps, since I will shortly be escorting these disobedient imps to safety."

Behind him, the temple was now quiet. Garak sat back comfortably in his seat, bathed in the warm light of the candles. You might almost, Raffi thought, believe that he was at home.

"There was a period in my life—my first exile, I call it, since my time on Earth as ambassador constitutes the second and this"—he held up his hands—*"constitutes the third, when I hit rock bottom."*

His hand went up to touch his brow.

"Many years ago, still in my youth, but after my visit to Akantha, I underwent a procedure to install an implant that prevented me from experiencing pain. When I was forced to leave Cardassia Prime, I began to use the implant extensively. Continuously, in fact." He gave her a bright smile. *"I saw you, Commander, with the bud of the blood poppy. And I have read your file. I don't have to explain to you, of all people, the use of medication for the relief of mental agony. One does tend to recognize a fellow traveler—and the life of the operative is . . . how should I put this? Stressful? Yes, stressful. I do not know your route to recovery, but mine was aided by the presence of a quite remarkable young man. A doctor . . ."*

He paused. There's a story there, thought Raffi. I wonder when I'll get to find out.

"While I was recovering, I told this young man a series of stories about the reason I was exiled. None of them was what might be called a factual account."

"You mean," said Raffi, "that you told him a pack of lies."

"Not that I would call them lies," continued Garak. *"Merely, variations on a theme of guilt. One of these variations—"*

"Lies," intoned Raffi.

"Concerned my involvement in aiding some Bajoran children to escape Cardassian captivity. What can I say? Starfleet officers are so terribly sentimental

SECOND SELF 301

about children, and this seemed a sure way to earn this young doctor's goodwill. I was very short of goodwill at the time, and very eager to secure his. It is with some alarm, therefore, that I realize that this story will shortly become completely true. I do wonder, sometimes, whether the wormhole aliens . . ." He looked around the temple. *"Perhaps, here, on their own territory, I will call them Prophets, for fear of what else they might do to me. I do wonder whether they will continue to have their fun with me. I wonder what else they have planned. I have to say that I am flattered by their attention. I always believed that their interest was solely in Bajor, but perhaps the histories of our two worlds are now so tightly interwoven that we cannot help but fall within their purview . . . In which case, I should be glad, I suppose, that they are not vindictive gods. In the end, we all need some pity. Some mercy."* He sighed. *"I am sorry,"* he said, *"that I said that you were broken. Who isn't, when it comes down to it? Certainly none of us who live this kind of life. But I am sorry I said what I did. And I hope you will find whatever it is that will make you whole again."*

"So do I, you sly old bastard," said Raffi. Gently, she stroked the dog's wiry fur, and he snuggled closer beside her.

On the screen, Garak closed his eyes: a man with a great deal of history on his mind. The warm light of the temple embraced him.

"It's getting cold here," he said. *"Winter is coming. And, by my estimation, I believe, another four or five weeks before my younger self arrives. He will surely prove to be a very tiresome young man, but committed, at least, to his cause, however misguided that might be. But perhaps that dedication is what will prove to be his salvation. I never did like to lose. And while I saw Cardassia brought to the brink of destruction, I did live long enough to see her restored. Her future is in the hands of others now. I hope they take good care of her. I should hate to have to find a way to come back."*

He opened his eyes.

"Please," he said, *"pass on my respects to Laris. I will not apologize, at this late stage, for what I did, all those years ago. I doubt she would wish to hear any apology. I hope that my ultimate fate provides some relief to her. And to you,*

also, Raffi Musiker. Old spies never die, they say—but perhaps we do, in time, come to rest."

The message was coming to an end. Garak was smiling, and his bright blue eyes, behind the mask, were full of mischief, and forever irrepressible.

"Be seeing you—"

The next morning, the three of them had breakfast (coffee, croissants, and orange juice) at the kitchen table. Raffi intended to go by flyer to Paris and a transporter back to Los Angeles.

"Have you come to a decision about the future, Raffi?" asked JL.

"I have," she said. "And if that offer to join you at the Academy still stands, then I think I'm ready to give that a go."

Laris leaned back in her chair. "Well, I didn't expect that! I bet him you wouldn't—"

"Really?" said Raffi.

"I thought you'd get a taste for action again," she said. "I would've sworn you were heading back to Romulan Affairs."

"Old way of life," said Raffi. "Old habits of thinking and doing. I want to draw a line under the past. I want to try something new." She nodded at JL. "He knew I'd choose the Academy. You shouldn't have taken that bet. He never bets if he thinks he'll lose."

"I'll remember that," said Laris. "I wish you well, Raffi. And don't let *him* interfere too much."

"Me?" said JL. "Interfere?"

"Don't worry," said Raffi. "I won't."

She left an hour later. Number One stuck to her heels; seemed he wasn't pleased that she was going. Raffi bent down to scratch the spot between his ears. "My hero," she said. "Good dog." He licked her palm. "*Good* dog!" She stood up and patted her jacket pocket. "Damn," she said. "I think I've left a padd up in my room—"

SECOND SELF **303**

"I'll get it," said JL, and headed back inside.

Raffi watched him go. Once she was sure he was out of earshot, she turned to Laris. Carefully, she reached out to take the other woman's hand. Laris stiffened at her touch.

"I don't mind," said Raffi, very quietly, looking her straight in the eye, "that you went through him. But next time—you come to me directly, okay? You must *always* feel that you can come to me, directly."

Laris, pulling back her hand, looked at Raffi in alarm. "How did you—?"

"No secrets among the secret-keepers, huh? I'm not angry, Laris. I'm not upset. All I want you to know is that you don't have to protect yourself from me. Really. I'd prefer it if you just thought of me as your friend. Call it . . . absolute candor?"

And it was true, all true. Whatever Garak had done, whatever grief or regret or resentment had driven Laris to subterfuge, Raffi was prepared to forgive. She understood the workings of loss, and recovery.

JL was coming back out. "On the bed," he said, holding up Raffi's padd.

"Okay?" said Raffi, to Laris.

"Okay," said Laris, with a tilt of her head.

JL looked at the two of them. "What's this?"

"Nothing to concern you," said Raffi. "Just . . . sisterhood."

"Sisterhood," Laris agreed.

"*Mon dieu,*" murmured Jean-Luc Picard. "Is nowhere safe?"

This time, the apartment did not seem so spare. Somehow, in Raffi's absence, it had transformed into a home. Perhaps she'd done more work before leaving than she realized. There were books and padds spread out that she had forgotten she was reading, but which added to the general impression that this was a place where someone lived, rested, and was at peace. The paintings looked great. She invited Vaz Pella to dinner, her first guest here. She cooked, too, actual food from actual ingredients. Spent the whole day

304 UNA McCORMACK

inhabiting her kitchen. Filled the whole place with the rich smell of home cooking. Lit candles, dammit. Opened a bottle of Château Picard (there were usually a couple of bottles about the place). After that, they had Romulan ale, then *kanar*.

"You're not coming back, are you?" said Pella as they went on to the Bajoran spring wine.

"Nope," said Raffi, consigning a whole career—a whole way of life—to history.

"That's a really good decision," said her friend.

"I know," Raffi replied.

About a week later, Raffi was in San Francisco. She had a lunch date there, at a café near the Academy campus. Nice place, popular with young people, many of them cadets, all cheerful and happy and optimistic. Had she been like that, once upon a time? She guessed she must have been, a long time ago. The friend she was meeting was alone, though, sitting at a table on the street, reading. He looked . . . damn, he looked almost *normal*, like any of the other kids here. Maybe because he didn't have that damn staff with him. She looked under the table just in case. No, he'd left it at home. Watching him, she felt that familiar, dreadful pang of loss for another young man.

Gabe, she thought, *I'm sorry. I'm sorry I was not there.*

She pulled herself together. He wasn't Gabe. He could never be her Gabe, but perhaps, if she got to know him better, there was something she could do for him. Some support, some help, some guidance, that she could provide and that he might welcome.

Seeing her, he jumped to his feet, and gave that charming formal greeting. "*Jolan tru*, Raffi. It's very good to see you."

That was the nice thing about Elnor, she thought as she took the seat opposite him. He wouldn't say that if he didn't mean it. There were some nice things, she thought, about absolute candor. She hoped he didn't lose that completely. She suspected that he would not.

"*Jolan tru*, honey," she said. "Hey, what're you reading?"

"The admiral gave me a book," he said. "He said it might help me consider how I wanted to approach my new life." He showed her the cover. *Candide*. Jeez, poor kid. Couldn't he give him something *fun*? Comic books, or something?

"Is it helping?" said Raffi doubtfully.

"I'm not sure," Elnor confessed. "But I *have* come to a decision. I am going to see what the Academy can do for me."

"They're lucky to have you," said Raffi. "Let's hope they feel the same way about me."

He looked at her over the table, a quiet pleasure passing across his face. "You'll be there too?"

"Certainly will," she said, and was touched to see the smile turn into genuine delight.

"Good," he said. "I'm very glad. I'm glad there'll be one friendly face."

"Me too," she said. She lifted her coffee cup. "A toast," she said. "To misfits. Wherever we are."

"To misfits," he agreed. "Wherever we are. And wherever we land."

ACKNOWLEDGMENTS

My heartfelt thanks to Kirsten Beyer, who trusts me with these characters and this universe. Thank you also to Margaret Clark, Dayton Ward, Scott Pearson, and Ed Schlesinger for all your help with this book. And a huge thank-you to Max Edwards for taking such good care of me.

All my love as always to Matthew, for rewatching DS9 with me so many times, and to Verity, #TeamJadzia.

ABOUT THE AUTHOR

UNA McCORMACK is the author of ten previous *Star Trek* novels: *The Lotus Flower* (part of *The Worlds of Star Trek: Deep Space Nine*), *Hollow Men*, *The Never-Ending Sacrifice*, *Brinkmanship*, *The Missing*, the *New York Times* bestseller *The Fall: The Crimson Shadow*, *Enigma Tales*, *Discovery: The Way to the Stars*, the acclaimed *USA Today* bestseller *Picard: The Last Best Hope*, and *Discovery: Wonderlands*. She is also the author of five *Doctor Who* novels from BBC Books: *The King's Dragon*, *The Way Through the Woods*, *Royal Blood*, *Molten Heart*, and *All Flesh Is Grass*. She has written numerous short stories and audio dramas. She lives in Cambridge, England, with her partner of many years, Matthew, and their daughter, Verity.